"… a very entertaining read; Haviaras has both a fluid writing style, and a good eye for historical detail, and explores in far more detail the faith of the average Roman than do most authors."

"I can't remember the last time that a book stirred so many emotions! I laughed, cried and cheered my way through this book and can't wait to meet again this wonderful family of characters. Roll on to the next book!"

Sign-up for the Eagles and Dragons Publishing Newsletter and get a
FREE BOOK today.

Subscribers get first access to new releases, special offers, and much
more.

Go to:
www.eaglesanddragonspublishing.com

For Jean-Francois, Heather, Jessie, and Leo...
One of the bravest families I have ever known.

Για τον Ζαν-Φρανσουά, την Χέδερ, την Τζέση και τον Λίο...
Μία από τις πιο γενναίες οικογένειες που έχω γνωρίσει ποτέ.

THE HEARTS OF HEROES

A Novel of the Roman Empire

ADAM ALEXANDER HAVIARAS

PROLOGUS

There is music everywhere…in everything…

It never stops. True silence does not exist. There is always something attempting to make itself heard.

There is a resonance in the sun…in the moon…and in the stars. It is present in the wind, and in the water. It is vocal in the swaying trees, and in the grass and flowers that blanket the Earth.

Music echoes in the realms above and below, and on both sides of the veil that separates worlds.

Gods and mortals may believe that they crave silence, or even absolute peace…but they do not.

There is music in gods and mortals alike, in the fire and blood of their veins…in their laughter and their tears…in their hopes and dreams…in their miseries…and in their victories.

Though it is always present, life's music is ever changing, growing and dying in and out of hearing. Tenor and cadence shift like the waves upon an endlessly roiling sea, a sublime reflection of life's joyous peaks, and its chasms of despair.

There is music, and it is everywhere…all around us, from one world to the next…in the Gods' starry gaze, and in the loves and hates of mortals. It resonates with a powerful will, in the mind of a villain, and in the heart of a hero…

PART I

AN EMPIRE UNDER THREAT

A.D. 228

SERVUS POPULI

'Servant of the People'

I t was a crisp day in early December along the coast. The sun was high and bright, the air and sky clear as the consular liburna skipped over the sparkling waves, its eagle-headed prow stretched out to spot the way forward. The men at the oars were adept at their work. They had no need of a pausator to keep time and, now that they were out to sea, little effort was required. The winter wind snapped the main sail tightly, its crimson surface straining to display the golden aquila above 'SPQR', the initials of the Senate and People of Rome.

Senator Cassius Dio, now Consul Dio for the second time, sat in the hold of his ship at his table which was, as always, crowded with papyrus scrolls and wax tablets. It was all that he needed to continue his work on the history of Rome. For years he had been chipping away at it, like a sculptor orbiting a titanic chunk of marble, seeking to help a colossus emerge. But it seemed that he only ever had the chance to write in the cracks of his life and now, with a second consular term upon him, the task of finishing his history was further hampered.

The two-day journey to Ostia from Cumae, where he lived in a vast villa surrounded by olive and lemon groves, was an opportunity to get some work done. Admittedly, however, his mind strayed to the possible purpose for Emperor Alexander Severus' summons, though, Dio knew full well that it was Julia Mamaea, the Emperor's mother, who had summoned him. The Augusta did not easily allow anyone into her son's presence, even though the Emperor was now twenty-one years of age. The Syrian lioness remained vigilant and as protective as ever.

The Emperor had been the one to suggest Dio live in Campania instead of Rome. It was a kind gesture intended to keep Dio safe from the Praetorians who had taken a dislike to him. Of course, it made presiding over the Senate difficult, and most of his business had to be conducted through correspondence. Senators and foreign dignitaries with whom he had to meet also journeyed to Cumae to meet with him. Most did not mind. Rome had become more dangerous.

By the Gods' grace, Dio had survived the reigns of Commodus, Septimius Severus, Caracalla, Macrinus, and the 'false Antoninus', Elagabalus, but he often wondered how long he would be permitted to carry on. The world had taken a deadly turn after Severus' death, and yet Dio survived to continue his history, to carry on serving the Senate and People of Rome. It had been a precarious existence at times. He found that he could not blame Julia Mamaea for being so vigilant in protecting her son, no matter his age. After all, her mother, Julia Maesa, had urged the Praetorians to murder Elagabalus and his mother, Julia Soaemias, her own daughter, just six years before.

It was then that the Praetorians proclaimed Alexander as emperor.

What dread the Augusta must have felt when that day came? Dio wondered. Mamaea's own mother had murdered her sister and nephew and, as wretched as they had been, he felt that they deserved more than to have their bodies desecrated and then thrown into the sewers to flow out into the Tiber.

He and many others had sighed with relief when Julia Maesa finally died four years before.

Dio put his stylus down, having only written a few sentences, rubbed his weathered face, and stared at the lamps swaying gently upon their stands. He looked to where his freedman, Ampyx, slept soundly on a couch beneath his lictors' twelve fasces, the ceremonial bundles of reeds wrapped in crimson cloth with their axe heads protruding. He felt better going into the lion's den with his official bodyguard, but he did wonder if they would be as stalwart in his defence in the face of the Praetorians.

Julia Mamaea had kept the Praetorians on her and the Emperor's side by making large gifts of gold to them, gold which she had been stock-piling for years, much of which had been confiscated from others whom she had not cared for.

That was another headache for Dio, for he was the one who had to hear the complaints from those whose lands and wealth the Augusta had confiscated. There was never much he could do, try as he might to get her to stop the practice, for it antagonized the nobility and rich merchant classes to no end.

"They can also contribute to the Emperor's safety," was always Mamaea's answer.

Dio never commented on the amount of that gold which she wore about her neck and arms, and which dangled from her ears.

"What a family," he said to himself.

Ampyx stirred at that, but did not wake.

When Alexander was young, Dio had high hopes for him if he were to become emperor. His mother had protected him from the depredations of his deranged, blasphemous and cursed cousin, Elagabalus, and Alexander had remained, surprisingly, mild and civilized, inclined to benevolence and mercy. In fact, he had granted pardons to many of his would-be enemies to avoid dealing death out like so many of his predecessors who had worn the purple.

Some perceived that as weakness. However, Dio believed it to be a glimmer of hope, at least at the time. But when the Emperor did not speak up when his father-in-law was executed, and his own wife, the Empress, was exiled to Africa Proconsularis by Mamaea, he had lost hope and realized that Alexander would be as ineffective a ruler as was whispered. Try as he might, he would never come close to being Septimius Severus.

"Enough!" Dio slammed his fist on the tabletop and winced.

This time, Ampyx sat up quickly, rubbing his eyes. "Dominus?" the man asked, looking concerned. "Are you all right."

"Apologies, Ampyx. I'm ruminating again."

"You're making yourself more upset," Ampyx replied. He got up from his couch and went over to check Dio's hands which were almost as pained as his feet. "You need to stay calm."

"I know. But, the older I become, the worse my pain, the more I tend to wallow in things that have gone before. And then I am more frustrated, for it only serves to slow me down, almost as much as the excruciating pain in my ailing feet and hands."

"I'll pour you some wine for your nerves." As Ampyx set about it, Dio wondered what he would do without the younger man whom he had bought and freed after his last trip to Athenae. Not only was Ampyx a skilled healer, trained on the island of Kos at the sanctuary of Asklepios, he was also literate and an excellent note taker, something that proved eminently helpful when his hands were too sore to write. He was good with a pugio too, an added skill that he welcomed when visiting Rome.

"Consul?" came a voice from the stairs leading to the upper deck.

Dio looked up to see his head lictor, Anius, coming down. The man was Etrurian, his family having been lictors for generations. He wore his black hair short and neat, and took pride in the plain crimson tunic and cloak of his office.

"Did you call, Consul?" Anius turned and saluted at the bottom of the stairs.

"No, Anius. I was just...just frustrated with a particular turn of phrase."

Anius looked at Ampyx who raised a blonde eyebrow, but said nothing. He glimpsed the few sentences on the papyrus and nodded. "Don't worry about the visit to Rome, Consul," Anius said. "The men and I will remain near at all times. I still have friends in the Praetorian Guard."

"I'm glad to hear it," Dio responded. "I don't know the reason for this summons, especially as Saturnalia nears."

"Maybe the Emperor wants you there for the convivium publicum during the festival?"

"I think it might be more than that. Besides, he has been quite adamant about me remaining in Campania as much as possible." Dio stood uneasily, leaning on the table. "Have you had any intelligence from your contacts in Rome?"

Anius shook his head. "No, sir. None. I really don't think you're in danger. The Augusta keeps the Praetorians well-paid, so I hear."

"She does." Dio sat back down, his pained feet unable to stand the swaying of the ship.

"Can I get you anything, Consul?" Anius stepped forward.

Dio shook his head. "No. I'm fine. But you and the men can have a bit of wine in the sunshine on deck." He pointed to a grouping of small amphorae beneath the stairs. "You might as well enjoy a bit of peace while you can. If I've learned anything over the years, it's that moments must be seized when opportunity arises."

"I quite agree." Anius smiled and saluted before taking up one of the small amphorae. "Thank you, Consul."

Dio nodded and waived him off. He was glad for Anius' presence. It was a comfort to have him around, and his contacts in Rome were no doubt part of the reason he remained alive. That, and the Augusta's continued favour.

But how long will that favour last? he wondered.

He wrapped his cloak about his shoulders, settled in his chair, and leaned forward to continue writing… *Thus it is that persons, particularly if armed, when they have once accustomed themselves to feel contempt for their rulers, set no limit to their right to do what they please, but keep their arms ready to use against the very man who gave them that power…*

Dio leaned back with another sigh. "Enough writing for now. History will have to wait. The present requires my attention." He turned to his freedman. "Ampyx…we have letters to write…"

It was early the next morning, as Dio dozed upon the couch in his quarters below deck, when Ampyx nudged him gently.

"Consul…" the man whispered, not wanting to alarm him.

"Yes?" Dio said, surprised that he had slept for all the pain he had been experiencing in his feet. Winter was always worse for that. "What is it?"

"We've arrived at Ostia. They're just making berth now."

"Good. Hopefully by coming here instead of Portus, we'll be able to avoid some of the local magistrates. I can't afford to keep the Emperor waiting."

"Let me help you get ready." After pouring fresh water into a basin so that his dominus could wash, Ampyx pulled out Dio's toga praetexta with the broad purple stripe.

Above deck, they could hear Anius' voice barking commands.

"It sounds like Anius is leaning toward being a sea captain now," Ampyx chuckled.

"That's not his job. His job is to keep me alive." *I'm getting nervous,* Dio thought. "I can get myself ready. You start packing up our belongings."

"What belongings? We've barely brought anything."

"Well, we have enough in our quarters in the palace. Besides, we shouldn't be in Rome very long."

"We're not staying for Saturnalia?" Ampyx asked. "It's only a few days away."

"I'd rather not. But, as always, we must do as the Emperor commands."

Ampyx nodded, turned, and went up the stairs to see if the consular sails were being lowered and fastened before the ship entered the harbour. "We're almost there."

Dio swayed on his feet as the sailors' oars took to the water once more, manoeuvring the liburna into Ostia's ancient harbour.

Anius then appeared on the stairs. "Consul... Permission to get the fasces?"

"Granted," Dio replied, stepping back and waiting with Ampyx as each of the twelve lictors came down, saluted the consul, and returned above deck with the emblem of their office.

Gulls could be heard crying outside in the sky and upon the masts of the docked grain ships. In the distance, farther down the quayside from the dock that had been reserved for the Consul's and other imperial ships, the sounds of sailors could be heard as the day's grain shipments were unloaded. They moved like ants carrying their loads back and forth across the gang planks, piling them upon the docks where they were counted by the imperial procurators who would then see the grain safely stored in the massive horrea of Ostia.

After having eaten a few bites of bread dipped in olive oil, Dio washed his face before putting on his toga with Ampyx's help.

"You always get the folds just right," Dio said.

"There," Ampyx smiled before gathering Dio's papers, including the pages of his History which he never let out of his sight, and packed them in a satchel. "Is that everything?"

"I believe so," Dio replied, testing his feet. "The pain isn't too bad today, thankfully."

"Good. The balm is working then."

"Do you have your pugio?" Dio asked.

Ampyx pulled back his cloak to reveal the pugio hanging from his cingulum.

Dio nodded and mounted the stairs to the upper deck and winter sunshine. He made his way to the prow of the ship where the lictors were lined up and at attention, steady as the oarsmen pulled and manoeuvred into the harbour. The consul gazed out over the sprawling port city to see the shining pediments of the temples of Hercules and Rome and Augustus. The incessant, excited hum of buying and selling flowed like rushing water in the streets as the shops and tabernae on the ground floors of Ostia's tenements did a booming business with clientele from around the Empire.

Dio watched, with Ampyx standing at his side shouldering satchels of papyri and wax tablets. "There was a time, in my youth, when I would have wanted nothing more than to wade through the sweaty press of those boisterous streets, Ampyx, but now, I can't think of anything less agreeable."

"Ostia is not what it once was, Dominus. There are so many pick pockets now, the Gods would be surprised if you managed to emerge with the clothes still on your back!"

Dio laughed. "That is true."

The consular ship turned and made its way to that part of the port reserved for imperial ships, guarded by the Ostian vigiles.

"Dominus," Ampyx whispered. "Are those Praetorians?"

Dio strained to see beyond the port's vigiles and spotted a contubernium of eight Praetorians in brown and red, hardened bull's hide cuirasses and cloaks. "Anius?" Dio hissed to the lictor beside him. "Should we turn about?"

Anius stepped to the prow of the ship, the fasces gripped tightly in his hands. He searched along the eagle head of the prow to see the awaiting Praetorians and their horses. One of the soldiers waved to him. He sighed and waved back before turning to the Consul. "It is Optio Marcus Sergius, Consul. We have nothing to fear."

Dio relaxed and turned to Ampyx. "The Emperor must have sent those he trusts to escort us."

"I'm glad Anius knows him," Ampyx replied. "Still…I get uneasy when faced with Praetorian uniforms."

"Don't we all," Dio replied.

The liburna finally made berth where three wagons were waiting to take the consul and his lictors to Rome.

Once the gangplank was in place, the lictors descended first and formed up in two rows of six at the bottom. Dio and Ampyx walked down slowly after them to make their way toward the wagons.

"Ave, Consul Dio!" The vigiles saluted.

"Salve, gentlemen," Dio replied. "At ease."

"The wagons are ready for you, Consul," one of the vigiles said.

It was then that the Praetorians stepped up, led by Marcus Sergius. "Consul…" the man saluted. "The Emperor sent us to escort you directly to him at the palace."

"The Emperor has my gratitude, Optio," Dio replied.

Anius came directly to the man's side. "Is all well?" he asked, keeping his voice low.

The optio nodded, his crested helmet fluttering in the wintry breeze. "There is nothing to worry about," he whispered back. "Just an escort. The Consul is safe to enter Rome."

"Good." Anius turned and nodded to Dio who was about to get into the second wagon when a shrill voice called to him from down the quayside.

"Consul Dio! Consul Dio! I must speak with you!"

The lictors stepped forward to stand in front of Dio.

"Who is that?" Ampyx asked.

"It's Titus Flavius Rufinianus, curator of the Ostian roads. I had hoped to avoid him."

"Consul Dio! A moment of your time, Consul!" the man shouted as he made his way toward the wagons, a train of secretaries in his wake like gulls behind a small fishing vessel.

"I am sorry, Curator Rufinianus, but I have urgent business with the Emperor," Dio moved to get into the wagon.

The curator was undeterred however, and thought nothing of pushing past the lictors.

"Let him approach!" Dio said quickly before the lictors harmed him. "What is it, Curator?"

"I need more funds for repairs to the road to Rome. The early winter rains have taken a toll on them."

"Surely you could have put this in a letter to me, rather than accosting me on my way to see the Emperor?"

"I did!" Rufinianus answered, his portly face sweating from his pursuit. "You have not answered me yet!"

Dio turned to Ampyx. "Did he?"

"Yes," Ampyx replied. "But we have not yet sent a reply."

Dio nodded and turned back to the Curator. "Of course. Yes, I received your letter, and rather than write back, I thought we could discuss in person."

"I am available now, Consul. We can dine and discuss in my tablinum in the port!"

"Now is not a good time," Dio replied. "Unless you wish to explain to the Emperor why I have been delayed?"

"Oh, no, no, no. There's no need for that," he said more quietly now.

"Then how about we speak before I return to Cumae?"

"When will that be?" Rufinianus asked.

"When the Emperor no longer requires me." Dio stepped forward and put his hand upon the man's shoulder. "I will send word to you when I am coming. Is that agreeable?"

"Yes. Yes it is. Thank you, Consul. It's just that I have been getting innumerable complaints from the members of various collegia whose wagons have been damaged on the way to Rome. One wagon filled with pomegranates toppled and the entire cargo was crushed. It looked like someone had been murdered on the road, and then that caused a whole other investigation when someone thought as much and then reported to the vigiles and then-"

"Yes, yes, I understand!" Dio interrupted, knowing full well that Rufinianus was adept at exaggeration. "We'll discuss it when I return. For now, the business of the Empire and the Emperor must take precedence. You understand, of course."

"Yes. Yes, I do!" The Curator sighed and began to back away, seemingly only just then becoming aware of the lictors and their axe heads surrounding him. "I shall await your return. Please, do give my laudatory praise to the Emperor!"

"I'm sure he wishes for nothing else," Dio said.

Ampyx stifled a chuckle.

"Go then, Consul! To the Emperor!" Rufinianus saluted sloppily. "May the Gods guide you safely to Mother Rome!" And with that, the Curator and his gulls turned and flocked back to the bustling port.

"Gods…that man!" Dio muttered as he turned to get into the wagon. "Every time we make berth in Ostia!"

"In fairness," Ampyx said. "I would not want his job."

"It is, at least, safer," Dio said, his voice low.

"Try not to worry, Dominus," Ampyx said as they climbed carefully into the wagon.

Once the other lictors were settled and the baggage had been loaded onto the other wagons, Marcus Sergius' voice called out and the Praetorians mounted up. The Consul's train then began to move forward.

The crowds parted for the Praetorians who led the way toward the Porta Romana of Ostia, after which they plodded onward through the pedestrian traffic that gathered in the necropolis outside of the city gate.

The road was flanked by monuments and mausolea which were shaded by soaring umbrella pines.

The sounds of the port and city streets had faded out of earshot, giving way to the clip clopping of the Praetorian mounts and the shrill cawing of birds in the trees.

Dio's eyes began to grow heavy.

Once they were free of crowds on the road, Anius looked out of the wagon's window to see the optio leading the way. "I'm going to go and speak with Marcus Sergius," he said to Ampyx. "I'll be back."

Ampyx nodded and settled back to rest his own eyes when a gruff voice called from the side of the road.

"I must speak with the Consul at once!"

Dio jerked awake. "The Gods toy with me! What is it now?"

Ampyx looked out to see a farmer riding up from Ostia on a horse. "We are being pursued."

"Again?"

"It appears to be a farmer of some sort."

"Drive on!" Dio called out. "I can speak to him as we ride."

Ampyx waved to the rider that he should approach.

The farmer, dressed in a thick brown tunica and cloak, came alongside the consul's wagon. "Consul Dio… My name is Geminius Eutyches. I have a complaint to lodge with regard to the collegium magnum arkarum divarum Faustinarum."

"What is your complaint?" Dio asked, leaning forward to look at the man.

"I work hard for my living, Consul, and I have a large family to feed." The man looked frustrated, his face red, a mask of great displeasure. "The collegium has not paid me for five food shipments that I have made at my own expense to the puellae Faustinianae."

"What is that?" Ampyx asked his dominus.

"The collegium supports the poor families with female children. It was established by Empress Faustina."

"I see."

"I am sorry to hear of your trouble," Dio said to the farmer. "I assume you have lodged formal complaints with the head of the collegium?"

"I have, Consul. Four of them. I let the first time slide, as I thought it a simple clerical error on their part, but now they are making a habit of it."

"I shall make enquiries and order that you be paid at once… What is your name again?"

"Geminius Eutyches."

"Geminius Eutyches," Dio repeated. "You are within your rights to payment. Ampyx, make a note."

Ampyx did so, and the farmer looked into the wagon to make certain of it.

"I thank you, Consul," the farmer said, bowing his head.

"Think nothing of it," Dio waived him off.

"May the Gods smile on you, Consul!" the man called after the wagon as he turned to go back toward Ostia.

"Now, maybe I can rest my eyes and mind before we meet with the Emperor and Augusta?" Dio said as he leaned back. A moment later, however, the wagon began to rock most violently, paining Dio's feet. "Ampyx?"

"Yes, Dominus?"

"Make a note that I should not forget to meet with Titus Flavius Rufinianus when we come back to Ostia. The roads are in need of repair."

"Yes, Dominus."

Later that day, as the sun's chariot was beginning its descent westward into the sea, the walls of Rome came into view.

"Consul…" Anius leaned forward to nudge Dio where he rocked back and forth on his cushion-covered seat in the wagon. "Consul, we are in Rome."

Dio's eyes opened slowly and he took a deep breath, rubbing his sore jaw. The first half of the via Ostiensis had been abysmal, but thankfully it had smoothed out allowing him to sleep. Now, he was suddenly alert and leaned forward to look out of the wagon's window to see the Tiber running to their left, beyond the tombs lining the road, shaded by pine and cypress, and guarded by leaf-stripped plane trees whose dry, broad leaves skittered about the riverbank and among the houses of the dead.

Where the Tiber began to embrace the Aventine hill, the pyramidal tomb of the praetor, Gaius Cestius, came into view, its western face cast in the pale orange of that sleeping winter sun. *Not far now,* Dio thought as he leaned back again to gather his thoughts. *What am I in for this time?* He could not help but worry a little. Yes, he had survived the reigns of many emperors, and those of many Praetorian prefects. He had at least felt more secure when Ulpianus had been Prefect of the Praetorians, but that was no longer the case. The Guard had murdered him just a few months before. It was then that Emperor Alexander Severus had urged Dio to leave Rome for Campania. True, the new Praetorian Prefect, Julius Paulus, was also a man of sense, a jurist rather than a soldier, but it was not him that Dio, or indeed the Emperor, worried about. The Praetorian tribunes were the ones who held sway, who could extinguish a life with a nod.

That is where the Augusta's gold went.

Just to be safe, however, Dio did not tend to confide in his one-time friend, Julius Paulus, for the urge for survival was much stronger than any bond of friendship.

"Which way would you like to approach, Consul?" Anius asked. "Shall we go the hidden way?"

Dio thought for a moment, looking to Ampyx who shook his head. "No. The people should see their consul. Proceed to the Forum and the via Sacra. It is safer if the populace knows I am in Rome."

"That was going to be my suggestion also," Anius said before leaning out and shouting the instruction. At the front, Marcus Sergius waved back and pressed on through the thickening traffic to the Porta Raudusculana which was located in a dip of the Aventine where the ancient Servian wall crossed it.

"There is something about entering Rome," Ampyx muttered as they passed through the gate's arch and on down the street.

"What do you mean, Ampyx?" Dio asked, looking away from the window briefly.

"The first time I came here with you, Consul, I felt an overwhelming sense of grandeur, of awe perhaps."

"Yes, well…that is partly the intent of it," Dio said, as he gazed at the soaring domes of the baths built by Caracalla, their rooftops surrounded by a haze of smoke from the vast warren of hypocausts beneath it. "And what do you feel now as you enter?"

"Dread."

Dio was silent at that.

"The consul and you have nothing to worry about," Anius said. "His position is still sacred in Rome."

Dio nodded and looked to his freedman. "Don't worry, Ampyx. This is not our last day on this earth." *But I too feel the dread,* he thought, though he would never say it aloud, lest he should tempt the Fates.

The wagon train, led by the Praetorian contubernium cut through the crowds toward the eastern end of the Circus Maximus, many of the people hailing the Consul as he passed.

"No more wars, Consul!" one woman shouted. "Don't send our troops east again, I beg you!"

Dio looked out the window at her and saw her pleading eyes, the agreement in the faces of the people around her. He sat back.

"What was that about?" Anius asked.

"There are rumours," Dio responded with a sigh.

"Of what?"

"That Artaxerxes of Persia is plotting something."

"I do wish the Augusta would keep her mind on Rome and home instead," Ampyx blurted.

Dio turned to him quickly and hissed. "Don't ever speak such words aloud again! Do you want to get us all killed?"

Ampyx went white such that his skin matched his pale blond hair. "Forgive me, Dominus."

"Do not speak of the East," Dio added. "For Augusta's mind is always there. It *is* her home. Rome is a second thought to her," he whispered. "And so it is up to me to serve the people of Rome as best I can."

"Yes, Dominus."

"And you do so well, Consul," Anius said. "We're almost there."

The wagons drew even with the Septizodium then, the great nymphaeum built by Septimius Severus over twenty years before. The statues and columns were a little more weather-worn, but the water still danced among its arches, playing and splashing to the delight of passers-by. Beyond it, seemingly rising into the clouds, was the Severan palace complex, quiet and little used but for the occasional function.

So many memories, Dio thought as he remembered its grand unveiling banquet, and the statuary that seemed to come to life before one's eyes. Then, like a dark cloud in an otherwise blue sky, the violent memory of the downfall of the Praetorian Prefect, Gaius Fulvius Plautianus, came to mind, the image of his dead body being thrown from the high windows of the palace to be dragged through the streets. *So much violence and hate...*

They passed beneath the arches of the Aqua Claudia which fed the Palatine Hill and pressed on into the great plaza about the Colosseum to turn toward the Via Sacra which led into the Forum Romanum.

"Anius," Dio said.

"Yes, Consul?"

"We'll walk from here."

"Are you sure?" Anius and Ampyx looked worried.

"Yes. I serve the people of Rome, and so I should walk among them. Besides, the people still bear the scars of the riots between them and the Praetorians. Tell Marcus Sergius to ride ahead to the great ramp and we'll meet him there. My lictors are enough protection for now.

"As you wish, Consul." Anius jumped down out of the wagon. "Halt!" He then went to the front to speak with the Praetorian optio.

Dio and Ampyx began to gather their things.

"Are you sure you want to walk, Dominus? Your feet..."

Dio shook his head. "I can endure it. It's important."

They both got out and were enveloped by the raucous noise of Rome's streets, the echo of the people about the Colosseum flowing like a river into the Forum.

Dio looked up at the rededicated temple of Jupiter, grateful that Emperor Alexander Severus had reversed the blasphemy of his cousin, Elagabalus, who had dedicated Jupiter's temple to the Syrian sun god, Elagabal, after whom he was named. He turned to his lictors who were lined up in their usual two rows of six to flank him as he walked.

Marcus Sergius glanced back at them and Dio nodded for them to go on ahead, their horses then making their way onto the via Sacra between the temple of Jupiter and the great temple of Venus and Rome. The wagons rolled on after them to make their way directly to the great ramp leading up to the Palatine Hill.

The lictors hoisted their fasces onto their shoulders.

"Make way for the Consul of Rome!" Anius shouted, and the encroaching crowds of Romans paused in their approach as the group began their walk down the Via Sacra toward the arch of Titus.

Dio waved to people as he walked, slower than he used to, trying to ignore the re-emerging pain in his feet. He smiled and nodded to some of the magistrates he recognized.

Some people stepped forward with pieces of papyrus upon which they had hastily scrawled requests for anyone who might listen, and Ampyx took these as he walked, stuffing the scraps into one of the two satchels which he carried.

They passed the temple of Romulus where several maimed veterans sat with their hands out, and Dio instructed Ampyx to give a sesterce to each of them.

"May the Gods bless you, Consul!" one of the men shouted out.

Dio waved to the man and carried on toward the temple of Antoninus and Faustina where a group of players were preparing on the steps for an evening show. One of them mimed Dio's pained gait as he passed and nodded with a thin smile at the accuracy with which it had been performed.

The scent of incense and burning charcoal wafted from the temple of Vesta to their left, and as they passed the temple of the Divine Julius they broke into the crowded heart of the Forum Romanum with the arch of Septimius Severus directly before them, beside the Curia, the Senate house.

Crowds of people began to close in, some with well-wishes and praise, others with pressing requests that they believed should be the Consul's topmost priority. From the Curia, a group of senators began to approach.

"Consul Dio!" one of them said. "I must speak with you!"

Dio turned to the man. "I shall come to see you tomorrow!"

The senator nodded and waved, fully aware that the Emperor and Augusta must take precedence.

There will be time enough to meet the senators tomorrow, Dio told himself.

Anius and the lictors turned onto the avenue to the left that led between the temple of Castor and Pollux and the Basilica Julia, toward the Palatine. Torches were being lit for the night along the avenue, and the dark forms of Praetorians could be seen in alcoves, observing all who passed that way.

Up ahead, at the top of the great ramp, Marcus Sergius and his men had dismounted to await the Consul's arrival. From then on, they would not leave his side.

"Anius," Dio said in a low voice as he walked beside the lictor.

"You're certain, Marcus Sergius will be assigned to us for the duration of our stay here?"

"Yes, Consul. That is what he said. You needn't worry."

"And what of Julius Paulus, the new prefect? Will I be able to meet with him as well?"

Anius looked at Dio and shook his head. "I asked, Consul. Sergius said that the Prefect sends his regards, but that he cannot meet with you." His voice was low, but no more explanation was required.

Dio knew that Julius Paulus was trying to keep the good favour of the Praetorians and if he were to be seen meeting with Dio, a man the Praetorians did not much like, then it could weaken his influence over them.

"I remember days when we could all speak freely about our ideas, when Empress Julia Domna held her literary gatherings. Such optimistic days were they…"

"I wish I had been there with you," Ampyx said. "It must have been wonderful."

Dio smiled. "Yes, it was."

They arrived at the top of the ramp to meet Marcius Sergius and his Praetorians who were waiting with the wagons.

It was quieter, the hubbub of the city streets and forum far below them now, where daytime activities and the business of the city gave way to the depravities of the night.

The public entrance at the back of the Domus Augustana was crowded, the courtyard flickering with firelight that reflected off of the polished marble walls and columns.

"Consul," Marcus Sergius said as he approached. "I'm to take you directly to the Emperor and Augusta. They've been notified that you are here."

"Lead the way, Optio," Dio replied as he followed with Ampyx, Anius, and the rest of the lictors.

They climbed the stairs and made their way through the atrium to the grand peristylium where the sound of voices could be heard echoing from every direction, accented by the play of the grand octagonal fountain in the shape of a labyrinth. It had been summer the last time he had been there, and the scent of jasmine and oleander had been strong then but now, as it was winter, he smelled dried leaves and juniper berries. Great bushes of holly stood ready to be clipped for the upcoming festivities of Saturnalia, surrounded by leafless trees in earth-scented beds which had been recently raked.

Their footsteps echoed in the colonnades of multi-hued marble as they crossed the endless, alternating patterns of circles and squares which, even in the torchlight, glimmered like a jewelled carpet.

"Consul," a man greeted Dio from the middle of a group of others as he passed.

"Salve, Favorinus," Dio responded, his pace not slowing as he followed the Praetorian optio.

"I must speak with you," the man said after him.

"Yes. Tomorrow, in my offices," Dio replied over his shoulder.

They went out of the peristyle garden through a smaller room and emerged into the cavernous splendour of the Aula Regia, the great throne room of the Emperor where several groups were gathered, even though the Emperor, at a glance at the dais, was not present. A woman's laugh pierced the air up to the thirty meter high ceilings and among the columns of gold, orange, white and black marble from Aegyptus, Graecia, and Numidia.

Marcus Sergius passed the colossal, basalt statues of Hercules and Bacchus and turned to go out one of the exits beside the Emperor's dais. They emerged on the other side of the peristylium and trudged the marble length of it until they walked into the massive triclinium where state banquets were held. It was unadorned by statuary, but shone with variously-coloured marble in patterns all the way up to the ceiling, and every column of the room's three stories flashed its gilded capital as though waving a torch above their heads.

"Where are we going, Sergius?" Dio asked, tired of the long hike. He remembered it being much easier to visit Emperor Severus in the new palace, the way being much more direct without having to go through the old Domus Augustana. In fact he had asked the Augusta why she did not keep hers and the Emperor's quarters in the Severan palace where Julia Domna, her aunt, had kept lavished but functional apartments. Her own mother, Julia Maesa, had lived there as well in great comfort. However, Julia Mamaea had been adamant about not living there. She had told Dio that she wanted to make her own mark and occupy the heart of the Palatine hill the way Livia had.

"The Emperor and Augusta are in the upper rooms of the exedra, Consul," Sergius replied, his manner stiffening as he spied a group of

Praetorians eating at one of the many ensembles of couches to their far right. He nodded to the group who eyed them suspiciously.

Dio began to sweat and whispered to Ampyx who faltered in his steps. "Keep walking."

At last they exited the state triclinium and began to make their way up the grand staircase to the upper stories of the palace and the imperial apartments. At the top of the stairs, Sergius turned to Dio and the rest of his entourage. "You will all have to wait here," he said, indicating the marble benches along the corridor where food was set out. "Only the consul may enter now."

Dio looked beyond to the great double doors to the imperial apartments. They were flanked by two Praetorians.

"I'll be right here, Consul," Sergius reassured.

"Of course," Dio replied, turning to Ampyx, Anius, and the rest of his lictors. "It's been a long day. Why don't you all sit and eat. I don't know how long I'll be. We'll all spend the night in the new palace."

"Yes, Consul," Anius replied, eyeing the two Praetorians flanking the door.

Ampyx adjusted Dio's toga for him and handed him a large wax tablet and stylus. "Send for me if you require anything, Dominus."

Dio smiled. "I will." He nodded and turned to the Praetorians. "Salve, gentlemen. I'm here to see the Emperor and Augusta. They sent for me."

Without answering, each guard took a door and opened it, the breeze sucking Dio into the room and flickering the braziers and lamps that lit the corridor.

Then Ampyx, Anius and the lictors all sat down, their eyes on the doors, their ears straining to hear any commotion. When they heard nothing, they settled in to eat and to wait.

II

MANDATUM

'The Command'

Dio stood there, alone in the quiet, his eyes scanning the vast room which was cluttered with carefully placed screens and silks. Everywhere he looked there were flashes of gold on columns, in mirrors, edging furniture, and flapping in silks. The imperial apartment that led to the grand exedra overlooking the Circus Maximus far below was unrecognizable. Even since the last time Dio had been there, it had changed. He knew that Julia Mamaea had wished to emulate the power of Livia, but she fell far short of mimicking her stoicism, or her conservative frugality.

He dared to walk forward a few steps. "Erm," he cleared his throat to announce himself.

There was no answer.

He continued to walk around, observing the new statues, including one of the recently deceased Julia Maesa, the Augusta's mother. The likeness, including the style of her hair and the wrinkles in her face, was uncanny. He had never run afoul of her temper, but in that moment, he felt as though her murderous shade might jump out at him any moment. He realized that he did not like being there at night.

Suddenly, a flash of fire lit the room and Dio turned to see a slave lighting a brazier before a broad marble table covered in papyrus scrolls, styli and ink pots. The slave then lit a five-headed lamp in the shape of the Goddess Victoria, illuminating the space further.

"Is the Emperor here?" Dio asked the slave.

The young man looked up and, without speaking, bowed his head.

Dio was confused for a moment, but then realized the slave was bowing beyond him. He turned and was met by Emperor Alexander Severus who strode toward him, smiling broadly.

"Consul! Salvete!" the young man said. "It is good to see you, my friend."

Dio felt himself relax and smiled back as he bowed. "Sire. The Gods love you. I see you are well."

"As well as I can be. Yes."

Dio rose and observed the young emperor. He had recently cut his dark, curly hair short, like a soldier, such that he resembled his cousin, Caracalla. Thankfully, however, his features displayed not the simmering anger of the late emperor but were, rather, kind and keen to listen. It put Dio at ease to see him and, for a moment anyway, hope was kindled in Dio's tired heart.

"You remind me of your great uncle, Septimius," Dio could not help saying as he looked upon the Emperor.

"I take that as a compliment, Dio, though I was but a child when he passed from this world." The Emperor looked to the gilded ceiling as if straining to see to the heavens beyond it.

"He would have loved to see the man you have become, sire," Dio said kindly.

"From what I know of him, I think we would have got on well."

"I agree," Dio said, still unsure as to why he had been summoned. Nevertheless, he enjoyed it whenever he had time in the young emperor's presence, especially on his own. "May I ask, sire, why you are wearing armour in the palace?" Dio had noticed it immediately, the white bracae with brown leg wrappings adorned with golden ivy that went up his legs to a brown and gold leather skirt of pteruges which hung from a brown cuirass of hardened bull's hide with Jupiter upon the chest. He also wore a gold and ivory-handled gladius and matching pugio which were only slightly covered by his purple cloak which was pinned with an enormous golden fibula.

The Emperor looked down at his armour. "It is new. Still a bit stiff, but comfortable enough."

"It seems more fit for a triumph than for your rooms in the palace." Dio thought he might have gone too far, speaking of the Emperor's clothing thus, but it did worry him to see him so well-armed at home.

Emperor Alexander Severus was not angered, however, and simply shrugged. "It was my mother's idea. She worries for me."

"Is there a need to worry, sire?" Dio kept apace with the Emperor as he walked toward the top balcony over the exedra of the Palatine.

Far below, the torchlit outline of the great circus could be seen stretched out like a sleeping giant, the moonlight glinting off of the bronze dolphin and egg counters of the spina. The cold wind picked up as they reached the marble railing. The Emperor was silent for a moment.

Dio glanced back to see if Julia Mamaea was there yet, for he felt certain she would be listening from behind one of the many silk hangings that fluttered in the imperial apartments, or at least one of her many slaves would be. "Are you in danger, sire?"

The Emperor smiled, but there was a sadness and strain in the action. "An emperor is always in danger, is he not?"

Dio looked over the railing and around to see if any Praetorians were lingering. He leaned in closer to the Emperor. "Is the new prefect not able to control the Praetorian Guard on his own?" Dio's voice shook, for he knew all too well how much power the Praetorians wielded in Rome, but also farther abroad. "Sire…Julius Paulus… Is he keeping you safe? Perhaps you should replace him with someone stronger, a military tribune or legate we know to be loyal to you?"

"The Prefect is still…finding his feet. He tries to get respect among the Praetorians."

"Which is why he would not meet with me, I presume," Dio added.

"I suspect that is the case," the Emperor said, shaking his head.

"And the Empress? Have you written her lately? Is she well?"

The Emperor was about to answer, but then Dio noticed him stiffen, as though all the amity in him were quickly hidden, like an errant child who has been caught stealing an extra honey cake. *And so our private conversation is at an end all too soon,* Dio thought.

"And how is your History coming along, Consul?" the Emperor asked him just as a waft of clove and cedar perfume enveloped them. "Mother, you're just in time."

Dio turned to meet Julia Mamaea as she approached them. She wore a long-sleeved, crimson tunica trimmed with meander patterns embroidered with thick, golden thread. A matching palla covered her head, and a cloak kept her warm against the cold. The latter was pinned with a titanic, golden broach in the form of a sun disk. From her ears dangled golden earrings with granulated suns, and about her neck was a necklace of thick, perfect pearls alternating with golden orbs. The firelight glinted off of every part of the Augusta, but for the sockets of her brown eyes which were fully shaded until she emerged into the torchlight.

"Mater Augusti," Dio said with the reverence Julia Mamaea demanded, as he bowed as low as he possibly could while ignoring the pain in his feet.

"I trust you had a good journey, Consul Dio?"

"Yes, Augusta. Neptune was kind to us, and Helios warmed our entire journey."

"Yes. Elagabal has graced us many days of late."

She always insisted on referring to her Syrian sun god and neither Dio, nor anyone else, would ever gainsay her.

"Were you planning on joining us for Saturnalia, Consul?" the Emperor asked, seeing Dio's growing physical discomfort. "I know you like to see Rome when it is so filled with jollity."

"The Consul has much to do," Julia Mamaea said suddenly before stepping in closer. "And his safety is paramount."

The Emperor eyed his mother. He looked younger then, like a boy still on the verge of manhood, trying to decide whether the time had come to put his mother in her place. But his father was long dead, and his empress exiled, and so his mother remained the only great and constant influence in his life. In public, he ruled the world, yet in private, he could not rule his own domus.

"Emperor…" Julia Mamaea said, her hand on her son's shoulder. "There are several letters to the governors that require your attention. Why don't you see to those while Consul Dio and I sit together? I see that his feet are paining him after such a long day."

The Emperor nodded and turned to his consul. There was the glimmer of a sad smile before the younger man held Dio by the shoulders. "If you do stay for the festival, I shall see to your safety personally. You will not leave my side."

Dio returned the smile and bowed. "Thank you, sire."

The Emperor then turned and went inside to disappear among the flickering flames of braziers and glinting curtains, the busts of his predecessors watching him as he passed.

"Oh, the young," Julia Mamaea said. "They never feel the danger of the cold until it is too late. Come, let us go inside and have some spiced wine."

"I am at your command, Augusta." Dio followed her form back inside the palace apartments, noting that as she went, her servants emerged from their hiding places, like statues suddenly stepping down out of their niches.

They walked for some time until they left the exedra of the palace and entered the private apartments of the Domus Flavia where Julia Mamaea had installed herself. Servants and guards lining the shimmering corridor bowed as she passed.

Dio did his best to keep up. He was keenly aware that he was leaving Ampyx and his lictors farther and farther behind, but there was nothing to be done. *She is the true power in the Empire,* he reminded himself.

At last they arrived at a smaller, private triclinium that was painted with frescos of lush gardens with fountains and fruit trees. Birds flit in the branches, so realistic, so expertly rendered, that Dio thought he could hear birdsong. It would have been relaxing were it not for the contrast of the Augusta's red and gaudy gold form in the midst of it all, as if the sun itself had fallen out of the sky to burn in the forest.

"Please sit, Consul. Let us talk." Julia Mamaea settled herself on one of the four bronze couches that were covered in gold-trimmed pillows and furs.

Dio sat upon the couch opposite her. He eyed the low table filled with food - grapes, flat breads, sliced cheeses, bite-sized pieces of meat, and song-birds drizzled with garum. He could not help but sigh as he settled down, his body crying out. *No food, just yet,* he told himself, though he was hungry.

"I see your health has not improved in Campania," she said as she pushed back the hood of her palla. She still maintained the stiff wavy style of her dark hair, the same as her mother and aunt, except for a bit of added flair at the back. The style made her look older than her forty-eight years.

"I do my best to follow my medicus' instructions, Augusta, but I can only offer so many sacrifices to Aesculapius on behalf of my feet."

She smiled at that and motioned for one of the slaves to bring them both wine from the heated tray at one corner of the room. When they had their gilded clay cups of hot wine, they each spilled a portion onto the floor and raised them.

"To you and the Emperor," Dio said.

"And to your health, Consul," Julia Mamaea replied.

They drank and Dio welcomed the warm wine as it soothed his throat, the eastern spices alerting his senses. After a few moments, he cleared his throat. "And how have you been, Augusta? Is all well with you and the Emperor here in Rome?" It was only natural that he should ask, for if she felt the need to amass so much gold to keep the Praetorians loyal, there must have been a reason.

"I try to rule in my own way, Dio," she said, not bothering to pretend any longer that it was her son who ruled. "My aunt was too kind, and my mother too cruel. I try to find a middle ground that garners a healthy respect for the imperial throne."

"That is very wise."

Her cup paused at her unpainted lips so that her dark eyes peered at him over the golden rim of the steaming cup. "Enough of the niceties, Consul. May we speak frankly?"

"I would like nothing more, Augusta," Dio replied.

Julia Mamaea nodded her head to her servants and they departed, leaving them with their wine and the low table filled with food which neither of them touched.

When the door closed, she set her cup down, and he followed suit.

"First of all, you should not stay for Saturnalia. It is not safe for you yet."

"I am in agreement." *Thank the Gods.* "The Emperor alluded to the fact that Julius Paulus is still nurturing the loyalty of the Praetorians."

She sniffed daintily, her lips pursed. "The Prefect will never fully have their loyalty. My gold, however, does…so long as it lasts."

"That reminds me, Augusta…" Dio wondered if he should say it, but it was his duty. "I have received several complaints from some of the families whose possessions you have…acquired. It does not keep their favour toward the Emperor."

"And when it comes to the life of my son, the Emperor, whom should I fear more? A few noble families, or the Praetorian Guard?"

"I take your point, Augusta." *I must give up on that front.*

"Yes, Julius Paulus is a disappointment. Were you twenty years younger, I would appoint you as Praetorian Prefect."

Dio inclined his head. "I'm afraid that I am much more suited to the Senate than to the prefecture."

"Quite." Julia Mamaea stared across the table at Dio. "But that is not the reason I summoned you to Rome, Consul."

"I am at your command, Augusta."

"And the Emperor's?" she demanded.

"Always."

"Good. I know that you admire and care for my son. That you see his potential."

"I do. And I know that is in large part due to the risks you took, and the sacrifices you made to keep him out of the hedonistic influences of his cousin, the late emperor."

"Elagabalus was a disgrace," she said flatly. "We lived in constant danger."

"I remember all too well."

"But the danger is not yet gone. True, my mother did the world a favour by destroying my sister and her son, but is an emperor ever truly safe?"

"I suppose not."

"What do you believe the purpose of your post is, Consul?"

"To serve the Senate and People of Rome."

"Is that all?"

"No, Augusta. I also serve the Emperor and you." Dio's mind flashed back to the days of the Republic he had written about earlier in his career, the days when the initials 'SPQR' were sacrosanct. *What days those must have been,* he mused to himself. "You know that I am loyal to you both."

"You would not be Consul a second time if I did not believe that were the case," she said. "The truth is, Dio…" Here her voice softened. "I am afraid for my son. In my life, I have not truly cared for, or loved, anything or anyone but my boy. He is the only person who has ever truly mattered to me."

"You have always been a caring, stalwart mother, Augusta."

"But is that enough?" Julia Mamaea took up her cup of wine now, a slight tremor in her hand, and pressed it to her lips. She sighed. "I lay awake at night, Dio, worrying about how to keep him safe so that he might one day see the privilege of old age. If it would keep him safe, I would burn Rome to the ground without a second thought."

Dio felt a chill run down his spine, for he had never seen a mother more sincere. *She would do it, truly.*

Julia Mamaea was quiet. Her big, dark eyes looked watery in the flickering lamplight, as though she were a sad nymph, alone in that forest scene, weeping in private.

"My lady..." Dio said. "It seems to me, that Julius Paulus is not the right man for the prefecture. The Praetorians are meant to be the Emperor's protectors, as Emperor Augustus intended. Trust in them must be absolute, and for that to occur, a supremely strong, tested commander is needed as Prefect."

Julia Mamaea's eyes seemed to dry and narrow, more focussed and certain. "I knew that we would agree."

Dio inclined his head. "It is the only way to ensure the Emperor's safety. And if the Praetorian troops do not fall into line with that commander, they should be executed and replaced with loyal men of the legions. Your great uncle did as much when he won the civil war. You could do the same if it came to it. The only question is, which commander?" Dio leaned forward to take his first bite of food, a piece of cheese from a golden platter, and chewed thoughtfully.

Julia Mamaea stared at him, the beginnings of a smile at the corners of her mouth.

When Dio felt her gaze, he looked up. "You already have someone in mind?"

"I do."

"Do I know him?"

"I believe you are well acquainted."

"Really?" Dio sat up straight then, his feet on the floor, his curiosity piqued. "Who is it?"

Julia Mamaea met his eyes directly. "Lucius Metellus Anguis. The one they called 'The Dragon'."

A ringing began in Dio's ears, sharp and piercing. It was low at first, but then grew louder as the name echoed in his mind. He worried he would lose consciousness.

The Augusta continued to stare at him. "Consul? Did you not hear me?"

"I... Yes, lady. I did. But-"

"But what?" Her voice was suddenly harsh, that rare glimpse of vulnerability which she had so recently shown already a thing of memory.

"Augusta… Lucius Metellus Anguis is dead. Emperor Caracalla saw to that. You know that as well as I do."

"Do I?" Julia Mamaea's gaze was unnerving then. It was the darkness of Elagabal behind those eyes, not the wisdom of Minerva. "What I know is that the Emperor needs the strongest of commanders to lead the Praetorians. I will not allow to happen to my son what happened to Caracalla or Elagabalus! No matter how much gold I give them, the Praetorians remain a threat and now, if the rumours are true, the Persians may also pose a threat."

"I agree, that we must take swift action, Augusta. It's just that…"

"Yes?"

"My lady…we cannot raise the dead. And make no mistake, Lucius Metellus Anguis has been dead for nearly twenty years now."

"Has he?"

"Most certainly. Yes. He and his entire family were destroyed. You remember. You and I were not in Britannia when it happened, but we certainly remember when Emperor Caracalla gave the order to his men to hunt the Metelli down."

"Yes. I remember it well. I recall that Metellus and then Praetorian Prefect, Papinianus, attempted to steal the throne in Eburacum."

"It was an unfortunate decision on their part," Dio said, "and it caused their deaths."

Julia Mamaea smiled slightly, further confusing Dio. "Forgive me. I may have the wrong person in mind. It was a long time ago. The name I meant to say was 'Lucius Pen Dragon'."

"I do not know who that is."

"Let me tell you." Julia Mamaea reclined once again, her hand steady now upon her wine cup. "There was a rumour of another Praetorian involved in the slaying of Emperor Caracalla. A fourth man."

"A fourth?" The ringing in his ears persisted. "I am old, Augusta, and my mind is not as it once was. I can only recall that there were two tribunes involved, the brothers Aurelii, and an evocatus by the name of…"

"Martialis," she finished. "They slew the Emperor on the side of the road. But there was a fourth man, another evocatus."

"I did not know that."

"Now you do. And according to the records of the interrogations of other Praetorians after the murder, that fourth man was named 'Lucius Pen Dragon'."

"It must have been a different soldier then, my lady. Truly, Lucius Metellus Anguis…his wife…his children…and his men, are all dead."

"I do not believe they are," she said flatly. "And I don't believe that you are being truthful with me, Consul."

"But I am." Dio spread his hands wide. "It is true that I once admired Metellus. He was one of our greatest commanders, and blessed by the Gods. But he was a victim of his own hubris. That is why I did not intervene on his behalf when Emperor Caracalla gave the order. I knew Metellus had been in the wrong."

"You knew how to survive, Dio."

"But-"

"And I do not blame you for it. We have all had to find ways to survive, and that is what I am doing now."

"I cannot commune with the dead, Augusta. I am sorry."

Julia Mamaea breathed deeply and slowly before speaking. "Let me put it this way and appeal to your sense of survival. If you do not at least *try* to contact Lucius Metellus Anguis - or Lucius Pen Dragon, if that is the name he now goes by - you can live out your days in the Tullianum prison where the damp would no doubt wreak havoc upon your aching body."

"Augusta, please…"

"Or… You can send a letter to wherever you think Metellus may be hiding and then live out your days at your home in Bithynia once your consulship is done."

She's mad, Dio thought as he stared across the table at Julia Mamaea. "I will do as you ask then, Augusta. For you and for the Emperor. Though, I have little hope of the letter reaching him."

"All I ask is that you try, Consul. I told you of my fears for my son, and I meant what I said. I would burn everything down to keep him safe, and so I expect you to be able to write to a dead man on our behalf."

"For argument's sake, let us say that Metellus lives, though I truly believe that he is dead. What should I say? After the destruction of his family's lands across the Empire, the attempted murder of his entire family, and the hunting and slaying of his men, his friends…what could we possibly offer him that would make him return?"

"A full pardon for him, his entire family, and all of his surviving men. They could become the new Praetorian Guard."

"It would not be enough."

"I'm not finished," she said curtly. "Metellus and his family and descendants would be free to move safely about the Empire, protected from any charges in perpetuity. They would be untouchable. All of their lands would be returned to them, their homes rebuilt at our expense. We would give them new lands."

Dio was silent for several heartbeats. "I will write to whom I can, though I do not have any hope, my lady. The dead do not care for the world of the living. We may remember their deeds, but if writing my history has taught me anything, it is that the past cannot be reclaimed, only be learned from." Dio drained his cup, his tongue dry in his mouth. "And the dead are simply that: dead."

"And yet, not all is always as it seems, Dio. Even the Christians believe that their Jesus, in whose name my son allowed a temple to be built, did not truly die. Has your history not also taught you that the impossible can happen, that not everything in this world has a logical explanation?"

Dio had no words. He simply nodded his acquiescence to the Augusta's command.

Julia Mamaea then rose from her couch, smoothing out her stola and pulling the mantle of her palla back over her head.

Dio stood and bowed to her.

"Recruit the Dragon to protect the Emperor," she said. "Write it tonight, and I will have it sent by my fastest couriers tomorrow. There is no time to waste."

"I will write and report back to you, Augusta," Dio replied.

At the door, she turned back to him. "Once you have done this, return to Cumae and await our command."

"As you wish, Augusta," Dio said, remaining bowed until she left the triclinium. When the door closed and he was alone, Dio collapsed upon the couch, his hands shaking, his ears ringing.

Gods, give me strength!

It took some time for Dio to compose himself and leave the triclinium. He did not eat. He did not drink. That lush table, resplendent with food, was more like to a pile of wet ash in that moment. When he finally left, he made his way down the marble, torchlit corridors of the imperial palace to try and find Ampyx and his lictors.

He did not spy anyone as he went, and began to worry that his time had come, that in his lack of enthusiasm for the task given to him he had signed his own death warrant. He watched for the flash of a blade around every corner, in every niche.

Thankfully, none came. He reached the top of the stairs of the Domus Augustana to find Ampyx, Anius and the other lictors waiting for him.

"Consul?" Anius jumped up when he saw him and strode over to him. "Is all well?"

Dio glanced at the two Praetorians standing guard in front of the double doors he had gone through earlier. "All is perfectly well," he lied. "We can retire to our quarters in the new palace for the night."

They began to walk through the warren of halls that led from the Domus Augustana, through the stadium, and on into the Domus Severiana.

The Domus Severiana, the newer palace built by Septimius Severus on the south-eastern end of the Palatine hill, had clean lines. It was carefully planned, like a military camp, perched overlooking the eastern end of the Circus Maximus, the Septizodium, and the main thoroughfare entering Rome that led to the Colosseum.

Dio remembered when Severus had unveiled the palace, the grand banquet that had been held, and the excitement and hope for the Empire that was thick in the air then. That optimism seemed like a distant memory now. The great throne room where Gaius Fulvius Plautianus had met his end was empty and dark, and the corridors dimly lit, watched only by a few palace slaves who moved like wraiths in the shadows and had no recollection of those heady days when all seemed possible.

With Emperor Alexander Severus' accession to the throne, hope had been kindled once again, but the flame flickered weakly in the surrounding darkness.

All of it worried Dio as he ignored the pain in his feet and marched quickly to his rooms overlooking the gardens and the Septizodium.

"We'll check the rooms for you, Consul," Anius said as he directed two lictors to stand guard in the outer corridor and went with the other lictors to search every corner of the consul's apartments.

Dio's apartments in the new palace included a small atrium adorned with African marble on the floors and walls which were lined with benches for clients and senators to wait when they came to see him. Through the atrium, one came into a triclinium with four large couches around a long low table where he, only occasionally, entertained the more trustworthy senators. Both rooms were flanked by cubicula which Ampyx and his lictors occupied.

Unlike the old Augustan palace complex which was ornamented with the finest of frescos in the private apartments, the new palace was adorned with variously-coloured marble from around the Empire and assembled in geometric patterns of yellow-gold and emerald green, the deepest of blacks and the purest of whites. Dio preferred the warmth of frescoes to the cold calm of the marble, but it was much more desirable to be in the quiet isolation of the Domus Severiana to the constant interruptions of the old palace.

"All clear, Consul," Anius said when he returned to where Dio and Ampyx stood in the middle of the atrium floor.

"Thank you, Anius. No one is to disturb me for a while. I have an urgent letter to write on behalf of the Augusta."

Anius raised an eyebrow when the consul spoke so loudly, but he understood. "Understood, Consul. When you are finished, I shall take it to the Augusta for you myself."

Dio nodded and motioned for Ampyx to follow him through the triclinium where the light from two braziers glimmered on the polished surfaces of the four couches and the low table. On the other side, there were two doors, one which led to Dio's cubiculum, privy, and baths, and the other which led to his tablinum. He made straight for the latter.

While Ampyx put the satchels down on the broad marble table and set about lighting the lamps, Dio opened the cedar wood screens that led onto the broad balcony that connected the cubiculum and tablinum. He breathed deeply of the cold night air as he leaned on the balustrade, hoping to clear his head and calm himself.

"Gods give me strength," he muttered.

"Dominus?" Ampyx appeared behind him. "I've made your bed for you and set out water and wine from the sealed amphora."

Dio sighed and rubbed his head. "Thank you, Ampyx."

"Dominus, why don't you get some sleep and write your letter first thing tomorrow? It is late and you've had a trying day."

"I'm afraid that this cannot wait. I must write."

"To whom?"

Dio looked at him, surprised by his boldness.

"I've no wish to pry, Dominus, but ever since your meeting with the Augusta, you seem troubled."

Dio did not answer right away. He went back inside the tablinum to sit in his fur-covered chair at his broad table, his back to the screens which Ampyx closed behind them. "The Augusta has asked me to write to a dead man."

"I don't understand."

"Nor do I, Ampyx. Nor do I." Dio settled himself to write. "You go, and rest. I will call for you if I need anything. It's been a long day for us both."

"Yes, Dominus." Ampyx bowed, turned, and went out to join Anius and the other lictors in the triclinium, closing the tall door behind him with a thud that echoed on the marble walls.

Cassius Dio waited until his freedman was out of the tablinum before he took a long, deep breath which he tried to let out steadily, but only came out in minute convulsions. His mind was numb, his ears still ringing. He was angry that he had been played in such a way. He had been put at ease by speaking with the Emperor first, and then she had appeared to further lull him with food and wine.

Dio slammed his fist on the tabletop and winced at the excruciating pain. The Augusta had played him, and now she expected the impossible.

She's up to something else, he thought. *Why them? They have been gone so long. And Lucius? He is no more.*

In truth, Dio had not thought of the Metelli in years. It was safer that way, for all of them. But the forced recollection had brought to the surface feelings of guilt and secret, shattered hopes which he had long buried in the vault of his mind.

"This is madness…" he said as he finally managed to calm his mind and think more strategically. "I haven't survived this long by crumbling at the first sign of someone else's insanity." He stared quickly at the walls as though expecting to see blinking eyes behind the marble panelling, but long ago, he had had the room thoroughly checked for such spy holes.

Dio picked up a piece of the best Egyptian papyrus from a pile on his desk and placed it before him. He then dipped a bronze stylus into the open ink pot, and thought for a moment before writing.

To Lucius Metellus Anguis,
Former Praefectus of Ala III Britannorum Quingenaria Sarmatiana.

Hail, and greetings from Consul Cassius Dio on behalf of Emperor Alexander Severus, and Mater Augusti, Julia Mamaea,

I do not know if this letter will reach you at your home in our province of Britannia, but if you do receive it, please consider the request herein seriously, for it is made in...

Dio stopped writing for a moment, unable to put such lies to the parchment. "Keep up the charade, Cassius."

...in great sincerity.

We know that it has been many years since you left Rome's service, and we regret the actions of the past against you and your family. It was not of our doing. We also know that others in the imperial court misled you and that it was not your intent to commit treason.

But that is all in the past now.

Emperor Alexander Severus is in danger and, as a result, Rome is in danger. He needs your help. Rome needs your help.

The Emperor requests that you return to Rome in all haste with the remnants of your men to serve and protect him, you as Prefect of the Praetorian Guard, and your men as the first cohort of the Guard.

In return, you, your family, and all of your men shall receive full pardons with passes to go freely about the Empire without harassment.

In addition to this, as a show of good faith, all of the lands belonging to the Metelli and Antonini shall be returned to you and rebuilt at the Emperor's expense.

This offer is not made lightly. Your emperor needs you. We need you. And Rome needs you.

*Please accept this generous offer, Metellus, and come to Rome with
all speed.*

Cassius Dio,
   Consul of Rome
   SPQR

Dio felt sick. The letter was entirely misleading, and he felt sure it was
all a lie. He also knew that it would be read by the Augusta the moment
he handed it over.

Nevertheless, he rolled it up and tied it with a red string. Next, he
took another piece of papyrus and wrote down where, and to whom, it
should be sent.

To the ordo member, Trevor Reghan,
   Civitas Durotragum Lendiniensis, Britannia
   (Forward in all haste to the Roman supply station of the nearby hillfort)

"Anius!" Dio called out, and a moment later the lictor came into the
tablinum.

"Yes, Consul?"

"I have finished the letter the Augusta wished me to write. Please
hand it to the servant of hers who is no doubt waiting outside the doors
of my apartments."

Anius smiled. "I was about to come and tell you he was waiting."

She is predictable, Dio thought, but dared not say it aloud. "Once
you have handed it to him, please send Ampyx in to see me."

"Yes, Consul," Anius said, accepting the two items.

When he was alone again, Dio sat back, his mind racing, awhirl with
memories of Lucius Metellus Anguis. *How I failed him...* He had
thought himself reconciled to the painful guilt he had felt, but with the
utterance of Metellus' name, his own shortcomings had surfaced like a
bloated body in the wine-dark sea.

Memories of those terrifying days in Britannia flooded back now. In Eburacum, he had warned Papinianus against his thoughts of putting Metellus on the throne. He had pleaded with Lucius against any thought of taking things so far. He had pretended not to know, so that he could survive, even when it might have been in his power to rally more to their cause.

"Forgive me," Dio whispered to their shades, his eyes burning with regret. "I wasn't brave enough." For so long, he had wondered how different the world could have been with a true 'Dragon' on the imperial throne. It could have been a new, golden age of Rome. Since then, how many sacrifices had he offered to Apollo upon the altar at Cumae in an effort to incinerate his shame?

If there is a chance that any of them are yet alive, I owe it to Metellus to warn them, to keep them safe, he thought, fully aware that what he was planning was treason and would mean his death if Julia Mamaea found out. *She does not want his help. She wants to make sure he and his family are dead.*

There was only one person he could safely write to.

Dio pulled another sheet of papyrus from the pile and placed it before him. He dipped his stylus in the ink pot again, and began...

To Einion, Lord of Din Tagell
From your friend in Rome.

I write to you with an urgent warning for the Dragon's family, and for those of his men who yet live...

They are being hunted. Warn them.

The mother of Rome has asked me to recruit our mutual friend who has passed from this world to be the Emperor's protector, Praefectus of the Praetorian Guard. This, in return for a full pardon for all, and the return and rebuilding of their lands and properties.

The offer is an empty one.

I tried to relay to her that the Metelli are long dead, but she does not believe me. I have written a letter at her request to the Lindinis ordo member, Trevor Reghan, to be forwarded to the hill fort.

That letter is to be disregarded by any of the Metelli if they yet survive.

The Emperor's mother will send men to hunt down the Dragon's family and his men, and to kill them. I know not who, nor how many.

Warn them, Lord Einion. Protect them if you can.

Do not send a reply, for I feel my time is limited now.

May the Gods watch over and protect you all…

Dio, his hand shaking, folded the papyrus over and over until it was a long strip, no thicker than his index finger. He tucked it into the folds of his toga just as a knock came at the door. "Ampyx?"

The door opened. "Dominus, you wanted to see me?"

"Yes. When is the next shipment of our wine going to Britannia?"

Ampyx crossed the room and rummaged in one of the satchels he had set down. From out of the leather bag, he pulled the large wax tablet that was Dio's business ledger. His finger ran slowly down the faint, inscribed lines in the bees' wax until he found the correct entry. "Here it is…soon. One week from now, the captains Castor and Pollux are set to arrive at Cumae to take the shipment."

"That is good," Dio said, pressing the end of his stylus to his lip. He trusted few around the Empire with his secret missives when he had them, but Castor and Pollux, the sons of the late Captain Creticus, were among his most trusted. They had known the Metelli, and were in regular touch with the Lord of Din Tagell who also trusted them. It was the safest way for him to get secret messages into Britannia.

"Dominus?" Ampyx prompted. "Is all well?"

"We must get back to Cumae as soon as possible. Tell Anius to notify the crew that the ship should be ready to depart Ostia early the day after tomorrow."

"What of your meetings with the senators and all of your clients? One day won't be enough."

"It will have to be. Please prioritize them for me, and cancel with those who are not supremely important."

"So we are not staying for Saturnalia?"

Dio smiled sadly at his freedman. "I'm sorry, Ampyx. No. For I fear that if we do, I shall not survive to walk through Janus' open door into the new year."

Ampyx said nothing, but bowed and went out to discuss the plan with Anius.

Dio stood, his legs shaking a little from the numbness in his feet. He poured himself some of the newly opened wine, and went back out onto the balcony where the cold winter moon bathed the pale marble of the terrace.

He did not notice the noise of the city far below, the cries and laughter of the people whose lives his every decision impacted. Sound was muted in his ears, but for the ringing that harassed his senses.

He gazed up at the silver moon, raised his cup, and poured some of the wine over the edge of the railing into the dark void below.

"Far-Shooting Apollo… Speed my words to them… Help me to keep them safe…"

III

MATER AUGUSTI

'Mother of the Augustus'

Rome had been boisterous throughout the night, and there was a feeling of anticipation as Saturnalia approached, a prelude similar to a summer storm that washed the city clean. Except now, it was cold, the winter's chill creeping in everywhere, only held at bay by the impending fires of Saturnalia which would cleanse all of Rome of the year's filth.

There was much to do, of course, but for Julia Mamaea it was impossible to think of anything but her son's safety. There could be a dagger around any corner, waiting for him...or for her. The gold she had amassed was still keeping the Praetorians in check, but it would not last forever.

"I have to keep him safe," Julia Mamaea said as she warmed herself in front of a low brazier in her private rooms within the Domus Augustana. "My cloak," she said to the slave that stood in the shadows, shivering away from the fire.

The slave rushed to place the fur-lined cloak about her and then opened the door just as she approached to go out and then walk down the corridor. Her Syrian guards emerged from their posts to follow her as she made her way to the exedra overlooking the circus to watch the sun's rays creep over the city.

Julia Mamaea closed her eyes to feel the emergent heat from Elagabal's light, her breath showing in the cold morning air as she tried to calm the daily panic that always seemed to surface, a panic fuelled by her fear for her son. She hated the paranoia she felt, the constant worries, for it made her weak. She thought of her mother, Julia Maesa, and how she never showed such frailty. She had managed to protect those whom she wished to, but would turn on them the moment they displeased her.

Julia Mamaea believed that her sister and nephew, Soaemias and Elagabalus, had brought about their own demise, and though it had been a time of great fear for them all, Mamaea had managed to protect her son. *And I won't stop now...* she thought.

She had always looked up to her aunt Julia Domna more, but even she had not managed to protect Caracalla in the end, or Geta for that matter. "I must be stronger...more vigilant. I must be strategic," she whispered to herself as she looked down on the Circus Maximus, imagining Rome's champion charioteers thinking several moves ahead, seeing where they wanted to be in the chaos in order to secure victory.

Fear, however, had its claws sunk deep in her chest, and she rubbed at the spot where she thought she felt it lacerating her. Again and again, it showed her the image of her cousin, Caracalla, lying dead in the desert, his body savaged by those who were supposed to protect him.

No one can be trusted. She knew it, reminded herself of it. Even the Syrian countrymen at her back could be bought.

She also knew that without an heir, her son was in added danger. Both of his wives, Sallustia Orbiana, and now Sulpicia Memmia, had proved infertile. Their dynasty hung by a thread, and the Praetorians, the men of the legions, and the Senate and people of Rome knew it.

The growing financial crisis and debasement of Rome's coinage did not help the public perspective either, and the tax rebates offered to the guilds and some property owners had not had the desired effects. The wealthy of Rome would not stick their necks out, even for the Emperor.

With war looming in Mesopotamia, and rumours of the Alemanni organizing on the frontier of Germania in the north, there was menace in the very air all about them.

The Empire is teetering on a sword point, and my son could be crushed when it collapses...

It was that thought that had driven her to make her demand of Senator Dio.

It was a demand she already regretted.

Julia Mamaea set her gold-bedecked hands on the cold marble of the railing, her mind racing over her conversation with Dio who had reminded her of Metellus and Papinianus' attempted coup in Britannia. She shook her head.

The Dragon will not agree to protect my boy, she thought as she looked to the rising sun. *Matertera, you were wrong to trust in such a man. I won't make the same mistake. A mother will do anything to protect her child...anything.*

In contrast to the insanity of her nephew Elagabalus' reign, Julia Mamaea took great pride in the calm restraint which her son showed, including his tolerance and understanding when it came to his Christian and Jewish subjects. For other rulers, they had proven problematic at times, but her son had won them over.

But the world is not kind to tolerant or good men, she thought as she opened her eyes to scan the world before her. *And so, I must be brutal on his behalf.*

They had few allies, she knew, and sycophants would not stick out their necks or pick up a sword on their behalf. No. They were the last of a dynasty, and that made them vulnerable.

Julia Mamaea sighed as she stood on the precipice of the Palatine hill, a great wave of loneliness engulfing her in that moment. She pulled her cloak closer about her shoulders and watched a flock of starlings dart in the dawn-painted winter sky.

She smiled as they danced and spun on the wind, wishing for a moment that she could be one of them. But then, from out of the clouds dropped an eagle in ambush, its talons outstretched, its voice shrill and piercing. It managed to take two of the smaller birds with such speed and surprise that the others scattered, their dance at a sudden, deadly end.

Julia Mamaea watched the eagle fly away with the two flailing birds in its talons, its bold attack successful. Her eyes hardened then and she turned to look back at the palace rising up before her.

"No more weakness," she whispered to her gods. "My son and I are not starlings...we are eagles." *If the Dragon will not join with us, he and his entire family...his friends...must be destroyed. Only eagles rule in Rome.*

Her eyes widened in that moment as she happened upon a plot that might provide some assurance of her son's safety. It was the thought of Caracalla dead on the desert plain that brought it about. *Elagabal...I thank you for your guidance...* She turned quickly and went inside to the broad table where she usually wrote her official correspondence.

When she sat down, her secretary, the eunuch, Thaddeus, appeared immediately at her shoulder. He was a thin, bald man who always wore a tunica of dark silk, as if he were constantly in mourning. If she had to pick one person in her household who could be thought of as loyal, it was him, for she had saved him from the depravity of her nephew's court.

She did not turn or speak to him at first, for the scent of clove which he always wore alerted her to his presence. She wrote quickly as though worried she would lose her courage. When she finished, she read it over once, folded it, and applied the imperial seal.

"Thaddeus?" she said in a low voice.

The eunuch stepped closer and bent down so that only he could hear her. "Yes, Domina?"

"Take this order to the commander of the guard at the Tullianum prison. Do not show anyone." Her eyes locked onto his. "Not even the Emperor."

The eunuch nodded gravely and tucked the missive into the folds of his dark tunica. "It shall be done."

"Go now."

"Yes, Domina." Thaddeus bowed low, and disappeared beyond the hanging curtains into the heart of the palace.

"If I cannot recruit a dragon, I shall hire a snake…"

Julia Mamaea stood and turned to her guards. "I must make offerings to Magna Mater now," she said, and without another word, she walked down the corridor, her ladies emerging from the shadows, along with the Syrian guards, all of them falling in around her.

IV

PATIENS CAPTIVUS

'The Patient Prisoner'

The morning chorus of pain began with a special note of agony that day, for a new prisoner had been brought in. His protestations echoed down the slimy stone shafts to mingle with the scritch scratching of the rats and the constant dripping of the filthy water that crept in from the streets of Rome high above.

"No!" the newcomer shouted. "I'll pay my share! I promise, by the Gods, I promise!"

"Shut up!" one of the prison guards said before hitting him. The thud was muted within those stone walls, but the agony of the man was palpable.

Far below, in one of the danker stone cells, one of the longer term residents opened his eyes, finished listening to the show far above. He pushed back his long, filthy hair and sat up from the thin reed mat that was his bed. He grunted and stood as best he could, the back of his neck pressing against the damp stone of the low ceiling, and went to urinate in the small stone hole in the floor of the cell that served as his latrina. He listened to the rush of water far below him which, he had always presumed, led to the Cloaca Maxima, the main sewer of Rome.

Sometimes, he imagined he was one of the rats which he pushed down there when they became too numerous, swimming his way to freedom beneath the city and into the Tiber. But he had not seen the sun for over ten years, or at least that is what he presumed from the scratches he had kept up upon the walls.

He dropped to the floor and did several push-ups as he did every day, trying to keep his muscles from atrophying in the tight space.

"No no!" he shouted at himself as his mind wandered painfully in sunlit fields in the world above. The thought strangled him, made him feel as though his walls were closing in to crush him. He reached out to feel the stone of his cell, his home, and forced himself to feel the walls growing outward again.

The Tullianum could do that to you, especially if you were held there like so many men had been, men such as Caesar's nemesis, Vercingetorix, the Numidian king, Jugurtha, or Sejanus, the former Praetorian Prefect under Tiberius. Even the Christians, Peter and Paul, had been held in those cells beneath Rome, between the Capitoline hill and the Forum Romanum.

But none of them had been held or survived so long as he had in those cells of the Underworld.

The screams of the newcomer ceased as he was, no doubt, thrown unconscious into his new home, and so the prisoner lay back on his mat to stretch and begin his daily count of the stones that enveloped him. "One…two…three…four…"

He stopped his counting and cocked his ear.

"Footsteps," he said to himself. "Closer than usual…" He rolled over and got on all fours, like a stray dog in the street at night, alerted to something, or someone, coming down a dark alleyway. "Three men. That's not my breakfast" he added, a little disappointed, even though his daily ration consisted of a piece of hard bread, dirty water and, if he was lucky, a piece of moldy cheese. He counted on his fingers and then checked his markings on the walls. "Is it Saturnalia again?"

"Bah! It stinks this far down!" one of the voices said.

There was a rattle of iron keys, the sound of the voices getting closer, the glow of a torch lighting the passageway beyond the cell's bars.

The prisoner moved to the back of the cell, his muscles taut, his teeth bared. "Is it time? Has Death finally come?" he muttered, unsure now as to how he felt about that. "I'll take them down with me. They'll be my offerings." He prepared to pounce.

Three guards appeared before the cell, their heads bowed because they could not stand upright. Two of them had swords drawn while the other dangled the keys in front of him.

"What's your name, filth?" asked the guard with the keys.

The prisoner thought about it for a moment. "What do you want? You'll find I won't die so easily!" He balled his filthy fists.

"You've been down here a long time, pig. We could kill you, if that is what you desire… Or, we could take you outside to see your visitor?"

"Visitor?" His heart began to race. "I have no visitors!"

"You do today," the guard replied. "But before I take you out of here, tell me your name so that we can be sure you are the person we're looking for."

The balled fists dropped to his sides, and he felt a pounding in his head as he tried to recall. "I… I…"

"Forget it," said one of the guards with his gladius drawn. "He's lost his mind. It's no wonder. He's been down here so long."

"I'll tell the Augusta's man he's not fit," the guard with the keys said, turning away from the cell. "Your food will be along shortly," he said over his shoulder to the prisoner as they began to walk away.

Augusta? He felt panic in his chest, his senses suddenly very alert. "Wait! Wait! Come back!" He rushed to the bars and pulled at them. "Aurelius Nemesianus!" he shouted. "That is my name. I am Aurelius Nemesianus!"

The footsteps paused and the jingle of the keys returned slowly as the three guards appeared before him.

"Step back," the guard muttered.

The prisoner did as he was told and, for the first time in many years, the key wrestled with the bolt, and the rusty bars of his home screamed open.

"One wrong move, Nemesianus, and you'll be cut down in a second." The two gladii were raised to point at him and he nodded.

"Take me to my visitor."

The guard with the keys went first, and the other two urged Nemesianus to follow, the tips of the gladii a hair's breadth from his back.

It was a long walk out of the underworld of the Tullianum, and the prisoner's heart raced such that he thought he might faint. His hands clawed at the stone walls to support himself, and his lungs gulped greedily at the increasingly fresh air. When they reached the top of the hewn stairs, he saw his first glimpse of sunlight and it made his eyes water. He shielded his eyes, unable to bear the brilliance of that light, and when they reached the cold air of the prison courtyard, he collapsed upon his knees, his eyes shut tight. He felt his lungs fill with fresh air, and his breathing went from slow and hesitant, to greedy and gulping.

Then, he settled, and noted the dizzying scents of the world above his personal Hades.

This is a dream... he thought. *This is a dream. Gods...are you torturing me?*

"Is this the man?" said a new voice.

"It is," the guard with the keys replied.

"How long has he been down there?"

"Over ten years supposedly. Before any of us were posted here."

"Remarkable." The new voice stepped closer, sniffing at the air about him, and then moving back. "Are you Aurelius Nemesianus, formerly a tribune of the Praetorian Guard?"

The prisoner stopped his shaking and opened his eyes, his vision sharpening slowly until the courtyard came into view. He looked around, at the walls, the flagstones, the view of the sky above where clouds danced across its wintry blue canvas. It was the place where he had bid farewell to his freedom.

"Are you sure this is the man the Augusta wants to see?" the guard with the keys said. "He's not fit."

"I am sure," said the new voice. "And yes, he is unfit to meet with the Augusta."

The new voice approached again, a scented cloth to his face. "You are Aurelius Nemesianus?"

The prisoner pushed himself to his feet and struggled to stand to his full height for the first time. It hurt, and his bones cracked when he did so, but the luxury of the act overwhelmed his discomfort. He looked at the bald man before him from behind the curtain of his oily hair. "I am," his voice rasped. "Who are you?"

"I am Thaddeus, secretary to our Augusta, Julia Mamaea."

"Mamaea...Mamaea..." he muttered, recognizing the name, but still uncertain as to its origin.

"Augusta Julia Mamaea, Mater Augusti to Emperor Alexander Severus."

"Macrinus is no longer emperor?"

"We do not speak the traitor's name," Thaddeus replied. "He and his son were slain shortly after your imprisonment."

"That is a pity," the prisoner hissed. "I wanted to kill him myself." He looked up at the sky, remembered the smug face of the upstart Macrinus, the promises of glory and riches for their familia which he had made to Nemesianus and his brother, Apollinaris, if they helped him to slay Caracalla, only to have Macrinus blame them for the Emperor's murder.

The memories rushed back like a thousand sword cuts in the dark, and Nemesianus felt tears burning his eyes as he remembered his twin brother being slain by the Scythians. He recalled something of writing to his surviving family for help, for a defence in court, and that they had disowned him rather than defend him.

He had been alone with his brother's shade ever since.

"Are you in your right mind, or do we need to lock you up?" Thaddeus asked, trying to ascertain the prisoner's sanity.

"I'm getting there," Nemesianus said, only now noticing the Syrian guards on the other side of the courtyard. He knew then that he had a chance to die fighting and, in so doing, be free of the prison. Or, he could see what it was that the so-called 'Augusta' wanted of him.

"Do you want to go back to your cell, Nemesianus?" Thaddeus asked.

"No," came the quick reply. "I will go wherever you ask me to."

"Good." Thaddeus turned to the guards. "He can't go before the Augusta like this. Cut his hair and have him wash. Give him a clean tunica and caligae." He glanced at the prisoner again. "I'll be back in one hour to get him."

"He'll be ready," the guard with the keys said.

Nemesianus looked again to the sky, the sun, the birds flying high above Rome. *I'm free…*

They walked slowly from the Tullianum, through back alleys, and unceremonious gateways into the rich quiet of the Palatine hill. The guards had the points of the gladii and pila poised to strike Nemesianus at any moment should he bolt.

But he had no intention of doing so. He was enjoying being in the world once more, and was far too curious to see what the Gods had in store for him, whether his muttered prayers to the dark had been answered.

It felt strange to feel the wind on his scalp. He rubbed his newly-shorn hair. As he walked, his shaking hand roved over his roughly-shaved face and neck where the ragged beard had been replaced by sallow skin savaged by cuts. The tunica he wore was stiff and itchy, but it was clean. The caligae were stiff, and cut into his ankles, but he enjoyed the feel of the leather on his feet instead of cold stone. He tripped as they went up an alleyway ramp that led into the Palatine palace complex and felt a spear in the small of his back. "I just tripped!" he said to the guard who pressed him. "That is all." He stood up again. "You try living in a hole for ten years. Your body would be just as rebellious."

"I would not slay an emperor," the guard muttered. "So I would never find myself in your position."

Nemesianus turned on him, but said nothing more. He could tell they were just looking for an excuse to kill him.

"Keep moving!" Thaddeus called from up ahead. "We can't keep her waiting!"

Nemesianus continued to walk and as he did so, he looked up at the soaring walls of the Domus Augustana, the arches and gardens far above where the rich and powerful no doubt dined at that very moment. He felt his stomach tighten at the thought.

They entered a broad space surrounded by lofty brick walls and arches that were completely unadorned but for the sunlight that poured in from high above.

"Wait here," Thaddeus said as the guards formed a circle around Nemesianus. He then disappeared behind the arches and into the bowels of the palace complex.

"I should have liked to be received in the throne room," Nemesianus mused and tilted his face upward to relish the sun's kiss upon his skin. "But this is better." He breathed the light in. *Do not weep,* he told himself as the urge came upon him. *Never let them see you weep!* He sniffed suddenly at the air, like a wolf in a northern wood. *What's that?* Sniff. *Clove and cedar?* "How I've missed the world."

"Are you sure you want to do this, Domina?" Thaddeus whispered from the darkness surrounding the deep light well at the bottom of the palace. "The man is an animal," he muttered as they watched the prisoner sniffing at the air about him.

"And animals are good at hunting," Julia Mamaea replied as she observed the man from the dark.

"There is no guarantee that he will do as you command. He's been locked away by Rome for over ten long years. He's more likely to flee the second he has a chance."

Julia Mamaea smiled. "I don't think so. Not with what I am going to offer him." She turned to the eunuch and whispered so low that he had to dare to lean closer to hear. "Besides... He will have a century of Praetorians at his command, and *their* command will be to slay him if he strays."

"Ever you are wise, Augusta," Thaddeus bowed. "Is it time?"

"Not yet. I want to see if there is any trace of civility left in him."

"What do you mean, Domina?"

"Bring him the food and wine now."

Thaddeus turned to the two servants who waited behind them with a small, wooden pedestal table upon which was a silver cup of wine, and a silver plate filled with fresh bread, goat's cheese, and olives. "Take it out to him," Thaddeus ordered the servants.

The two men hoisted the table carefully and went out into the sunlight toward the prisoner.

The guards parted for the servants who went into the circle, eyeing the prisoner warily. They set the table down before him and left as suddenly as they had appeared.

"Now...watch..." Julia Mamaea said as she and Thaddeus leaned forward to watch.

Unexpectedly, the prisoner did not pounce upon the food or drink that had been placed before him. Most men in his situation would have done so. Instead, he took in the sight of what lay before him, running his finger along the edge of the silver plate before taking up a piece of bread. He raised it slowly to his face and inhaled the fresh, warm scent of it before tearing a small piece and chewing it slowly. After a couple more bites, he set the loaf down and took a piece of cheese, chewing with his mouth closed as the flavours appeared to remind him of meals long past. The olives had the same effect, and rather than spit the pits onto the ground, he removed them from his mouth with his fingers to put them back on the plate.

Lastly, he took up the silver cup and sipped the wine, slowly, carefully, allowing it to swirl around in his mouth before swallowing it. He choked on the first sip, his throat unused to such fine nectar, but then he acclimatized to the act and drank again with his eyes closed, his lips lingering on the smooth silver rim of the cup.

"What does this mean, Domina? Why watch this traitor eat?"

"It means, Thaddeus, that the breeding has not fully been drawn from him. It means that my offer will appeal to him and his aristocratic sense of entitlement." Julia Mamaea then stepped out into the sunlight and walked toward the far end of the light well where the prisoner stood.

Aurelius Nemesianus stopped chewing when the Augusta appeared, a vision of shimmering purple silk and gold coming toward him. He could smell her perfume long before she arrived, and inhaled the smell of it as she approached. She was not a beautiful woman as far as he was concerned. To him, her nose was too big, and her hair too plain. But oh, the sight of a highborn lady in that moment was as a wet oasis in the driest of deserts.

"Bow before your Augusta and liberator, slave!" one of the guards barked.

"I am no slave," Nemesianus said to the guard before turning back to the approaching Augusta and bowing as best he could for all the stiffness in his back. "I am Aurelius Nemesianus of the gens Aurelii, and my ancestors have served Rome since the first great war with Carthage."

"I know who you are, Aurelius Nemesianus," said the woman as she looked down on him. "Rise."

He stood stiffly, his hands at his sides, but his eyes met hers directly in a way that no slave ever would.

"You are a traitor to Rome. You helped to murder my cousin."

Nemesianus noticed a tremor in her voice, a sound of deep grief and anger. He knew then that he had to pick his words very carefully, or else he would never see the sun again. "I *was* guilty, Augusta," he said slowly with his head bowed. When she did not answer, he looked up at her large, dark eyes and spoke. "But I have paid for it with the loss of over ten years of my life beneath the earth...caged...like an animal."

"You are an animal," the Augusta replied. "You betrayed your oath to your emperor and attempted to set an upstart upon the imperial throne."

"I hated, Macrinus. And you are correct, Augusta. He was an upstart."

"Do not presume to tell me whether I am 'correct' or not."

If I am fast enough, I could hit her before they slay me, Nemesianus thought. *I'm not going back to that cell!* "Did you bring me up here to chide me for my past actions?"

"Mind your tongue, slave!" Thaddeus burst out.

Nemesianus turned on him, aware of the strain of a bowstring nearby. "You are the slave, eunuch, not I!" He then looked to the Augusta. "Lady… If revenge is your intent, just kill me and be done with it! I should have died long ago."

Julia Mamaea did not answer him right away, but rather stared at him for a few seconds before motioning to the servants waiting in the wings to bring him a cushioned chair.

Once more, the servants approached and set down two cedar chairs with cushions, one for the Augusta, and one for the prisoner.

Nemesianus waited for her to sit before he attempted to do so, his shaking hands upon the chair's arms as he lowered himself slowly down onto the cushion. "Is this to be my execution block?"

The Augusta smiled thinly. "No." She looked at the guards. "All of you, step back."

"Domina?" Thaddeus said.

"Now," she commanded.

The guards and Thaddeus all moved to the periphery of the light well, leaving Julia Mamaea and Nemesianus alone to converse.

"I do not want to kill you, Nemesianus," she said calmly, "though you deserve much worse."

"What is it to be then?" he asked, taking a sip of the wine he had so enjoyed, and leaning back in the divine comfort of the chair. "What possible use could I be to you other than an outlet for the vengeance you seek? After all, it is true that I did help to slay Emperor Caracalla. Why was I kept alive for so long? What possible use could I be that I was not slain?"

"You can thank the Gods for your survival for, in truth, you were forgotten for years. As to your use, Aurelius Nemesianus, you are a tool…a guarantee if you will."

"For what?"

"The Emperor's safety."

He laughed. "Me?"

She did not smile. "Yes. You." Julia Mamaea eyed him intently. "You slew one emperor, but only by protecting another can you redeem yourself."

"He has an entire legion of Praetorians to do that. What do you need me for?"

"To recruit or kill the man who could be his true protector."

"That is too cryptic," Nemesianus replied, frustrated that his dull mind was not up to the challenge she posed. "I need more information than that, Augusta."

"Lucius Pen Dragon."

Nemesianus froze as he stared into the crimson liquid of his cup. He did not look up, but felt his hand attempt to strangle the silver he held. "And who is that?"

Now, it was Julia Mamaea's turn to smile. "On the march from Edessa to Carrhae, you, your brother, and an evocatus by the name of Martialis lured my cousin into a trap and slew him. But there was one other assassin present, another evocatus by the name of Lucius Pen Dragon…also known as Lucius Metellus Anguis."

Now, Nemesianus looked up, his anger and hate written plainly upon his face. "What of him?"

"His body was never found."

"He fled like a coward before I could kill him. He betrayed us."

"Just as you betrayed my cousin."

"Why do you mention this man? He is probably dead. He was sickly and wounded when I met him, and it has been many years since." *Too many…* As the amount of time that had passed sank in, Nemesianus felt his anger boil. *I have been robbed of time and so much more!*

"I mention him because he is the man I want to recruit…or kill."

"Which is it, Augusta?"

"That depends on whether he accepts my offer or not."

"And what offer is that?" Nemesianus asked.

"That he come to Rome to protect the Emperor as Prefect of the Praetorian Guard."

Nemesianus laughed. "The man is dead."

"He may not be."

"And what is my role to be in all of this?"

Julia Mamaea was silent, choosing her words carefully before she uttered them. She sat straight and leaned forward very slightly, her dark eyes boring into his. "I want you to go to Britannia and find Lucius Pen Dragon. Persuade him to join me and the Emperor in Rome as Praetorian Prefect."

"Are you mad?" Nemesianus blurted. He heard the pull of the bowstring nearby, and the slither of drawn blades.

"You would do well to choose your path wisely at this juncture, don't you think?" Julia Mamaea folded her hands in her lap, her eyes never leaving his.

It discomfited him. *I never liked these Syrian women. They can't be trusted!* Then again, he wondered how much he would get out of such a mission, no matter how ridiculous. "Let's say that I find him. What could you possibly offer him to lure him back to Rome? Why would he trust your offer? If I recall, didn't he try to take the throne from Caracalla?"

"I will provide you with a written offer for him, but you must also tell him that there will be a full and complete pardon for him, his entire family, and all of his surviving men if he leads the Emperor's guard. They would be protected throughout the Empire. His rank and fortune will be fully restored, and all of his family's lands returned to him, the structures fully rebuilt at the Emperor's expense."

"That is a lot to offer a dead man." Nemesianus shook his head. "What if he refuses?"

"Then you are to kill Lucius Pen Dragon, his entire family, the remnants of his men, and anyone who provides aid to him."

Nemesianus was silent.

"That will be a long list, no doubt." *And much blood!* "How am I to do all this on my own?"

"You won't be alone. You will have command of a century of Praetorians."

That stopped Nemesianus. As he sat there, he tried to recall the feel of bull's hide armour on his chest and back, the sway of pteruges about his legs, and the weight of a crested helmet upon his head. Being a Praetorian tribune had been as far as he had gotten on the Cursus Honorum. *She's asking me to be an assassin, not a soldier.* His mind was still muddled from his sudden extrication from the earth, and he struggled to comprehend the situation. His mind swam with questions and he shut his eyes tightly for a moment, grasping at the mental thread of the confused labyrinth that was his mind. He remembered that he no longer had anything to live for, but the sun and air. His family had abandoned him, and his brother was long dead.

He opened his eyes then, a moment of clarity coming upon him as the sun grew more intense.

"What is in it for me, Augusta?"

"Your life."

"I stopped caring about that long ago."

"You will regain your honour."

He laughed. "Honour is overrated. I care even less about that."

He is *an animal,* she thought. "Very well. If you succeed in recruiting Lucius Pen Dragon…or killing him…your rank and status shall be fully restored. You shall receive new lands from the Emperor so that you may start anew, and a small fortune in gold."

"How much gold?"

"Three talents."

Nemesianus thought about that. Calmly, he picked up the cup of wine and drank what was left. He looked casually at his dirty finger nails before looking back to Julia Mamaea. "And if I refuse to accept your offer to take on this ridiculous mission?"

She was unmoved. Her dark eyes unflinching. "Then you will run out your days in the same rat-infested cell that has been your home for the past ten years."

He felt the fear of that prospect then, all the more terrifying that he had been reminded of the sun, the sky, and of fine food. *Apollinaris…* he thought of his brother. *Is vengeance at hand?*

Aurelius Nemesianus smiled as he looked upon Julia Mamaea. "Then I accept. On certain conditions."

"What conditions?" she asked, now looking perturbed.

"Five talents of gold."

"Agreed."

"And I want my ancestral lands, not new lands. I want you to remove my family from all their lands and transfer those lands to me. They had no loyalty to me, so I have none for them."

Julia Mamaea tried to recall how much the Aurelii had, and whether they had already made their contributions to her collectors. She smiled as it came to her. "Agreed."

"Then I accept."

Julia Mamaea rose from her chair, but Nemesianus remained seated. She motioned for Thaddeus to join her once more, and the eunuch rushed to her side.

"In addition to my five talents," Nemesianus added, "I will need horses and a generous supply of gold and silver for me and my men to use on our mission. We have a lot of ground to cover and will need to bribe a great many people as we scour Britannia for the Dragon and his friends."

"I think it important to remind you, Nemesianus, that I prefer he *accepts* the Emperor's offer and agrees to return to Rome. You understand?" She looked down on the prisoner, wondering for a moment if she was making a mistake. But she thought of her son, and of how safe he would be if Nemesianus succeeded in recruiting Lucius Pen Dragon.

"Answer your Augusta, slave," Thaddeus spat.

Nemesianus stood and faced the eunuch, his face suddenly angular and angry, his eyes burning with intensity. "I am no slave. I am Aurelius Nemesianus, and the Augusta has asked for *my* help." He turned to Julia Mamaea and bowed low. "I understand, Augusta, and I will not fail in this mission."

"Good," she answered, and turned to Thaddeus. "Give him a room in the new palace, a servant, clothing, and food."

"Domina?" Thaddeus was shocked that the man would be plucked from the Tullianum and elevated so quickly.

"Do it." She turned back to Nemesianus. "You will have access to the Palatine stadium, baths, and gymnasium, but you will not interact with the Emperor or anyone else besides your men."

"I will need time to regain my strength. I will need weapons."

"You will have access to training weapons only for now, but make no mistake. You'll be watched and guarded, and if you set one foot wrong, you'll be thrown back into the Tullianum."

"I understand, Augusta," Nemesianus bowed.

Without another word, Julia Mamaea disappeared back into the darkness of the palace, leaving Thaddeus alone with Nemesianus, the circle of guards surrounding them.

"I will go and see that your room is prepared," Thaddeus said.

Nemesianus sat back in the chair and tilted his head to the sun, his eyes closed. "You do that, eunuch. And make sure it has a big window. I want a window."

Thaddeus spat on the grass at Nemesianus' feet, but the latter did not care.

When Thaddeus was gone, Nemesianus looked at the guards surrounding him. "Why let this food go to waste? I'll finish it before I go to my room." As the guards watched, their hands hovering over the pommels of their gladii, Nemesianus continued to eat, relishing every bite, every taste, until the platter was clean. He then looked into the wine cup to see just a couple of drops remaining.

He held the cup up to the sky. "Well, Brother... Looks like I'll be hunting dragon after all."

PART II

THE BROKEN FAMILIA

BRITANNIA A.D. 229

V

SACERDOTIS SPEI

'A Priestess of Hope'

Springtime sang in a bright and beautiful way that year, for the Gods had been kind, the winds of winter brought to heel and sent back to their distant caves early. Life, colour, and light were bursting all around, and nowhere was this symphony more evident than in the blessed isle of Ynis Wytrin.

The morning mist yet shrouded the Isle from the world without, but across the rippling waters where the wind whispered in the reeds, the smoke of morning offerings swirled for the Gods. These were, as always, accompanied by the sound of the bell of the Christian chapel which had been there since St. Joseph had come with his followers to that haven beyond the reach of Rome. The gentle tolling echoed in the mist, reaching up the slope of Wearyall Hill where the Holy Thorn shivered in the cool morning breeze.

Apple blossoms from the orchard lay scattered about that deep green world. Sheep grazed alongside the priests and priestesses of Ynis Wytrin as they tended to the sowing of the spring crops. Others tended to the sick in the healing houses of the Isle which lay beside the Hill of the Chalice.

Birdsong winged its way everywhere too, on the surface of the water, about the rooftops of the dormitories, roundhouses and guest houses, among the branches of the great oak at the Isle's heart, and along the sacred avenues of yew and oak that led to the sacred hill, the Tor.

The morning chorus of Ynis Wytrin, of birdsong and sunlight, reached in through the windows of every dwelling to rouse those who were still abed, caught in that world between sleep and awake.

And so, the Isle stirred, and a new day started…

· · ·

In the guesthouse room that had, long ago, been gifted to her family, Calliope Pen Dragon lay beneath the blankets on her small bed, her eyes still closed as she enjoyed the feeling of the morning light where it angled its way in to warm her face. She smiled to herself at that, at the light of Apollo that always seemed to find her. Ever was it her comfort in the darkness of the world, and so gratitude was her first thought on the dawning of each new day.

A pained weeping invaded her thoughts, however, and she opened her eyes and turned on her side to see her aunt, Clarinda, quivering in her sleep on the other side of the room.

"Caecilius…no…no…" the older woman sobbed.

Calliope swung her long legs over the edge of the bed and went to her aunt, her lithe fingers reaching out to stroke her greying hair. "It's all right, matertera," she soothed. "He is safe…protected by the Gods now…"

The weeping stopped, and gave way to a light, convulsive breathing.

She noted the salt stains and scratches upon her aunt's cheeks then, and knew that she had had another bad night. *Gods, please give her some peace,* she prayed, for ever since Calliope's uncle's death over ten years before, at the eastern fringes of Rome's empire, her aunt had been little more than a keening shadow of her former self.

When her aunt was calm again, Calliope went through her morning ablutions, splashing her face with the cold water that she had poured into the broad wooden bowl that sat upon the table by the door. She dried her face with a linen towel and, as she finished, she caught a glimpse of herself in the bronze mirror that had been her mother's. It gave her pause to see herself, for in her reflection, she thought she spied the faces of her mother, and her other aunt, Alene, who had saved her when she was but a babe-in-arms. There were times when she did not recognize herself in her own reflection, for her mind still clung to halcyon days in Etruria and on the hillfort in Britannia when she was young and excited for a world that held much wonder and joy. Her reflection then had been one of smooth golden hair, broad smiles, and bright eyes that hung on to her parents as though beneath the boughs of a safe tree. The reflection that looked back at her was much older, the hair darker, the smile much faded.

But the Isle was safe.

Now, it was her turn to feel the sting of tears, but she refused to give in. Daring to stare at herself in the faint reflection of that old mirror, she brushed her hair with a bone comb, and then braided it back, the better to undertake her daily toils as a priestess of Ynis Wytrin.

She slid on her long, white tunica, fastened her sandals, and draped her grey cloak about her shoulders to ward off the morning chill. Before leaving the room, she started a fire in the small hearth so that her aunt would feel warmth when she awoke. When that was done, she took a handful of sunflower seeds from a bowl on the table, opened the oak door slowly, and went out into the misty morning.

Waiting for her there was the large crow whom she had healed from a wing injury three years before. He squawked when he saw her and sidled up to her where she knelt with the handful of seeds outstretched to him.

"Good morning, Corvus," she said as he ate from her hand, his black eyes gazing up at her, blinking quickly. She stroked his head and back with her other hand, and when he was finished eating, he nuzzled her. "Come. We have a lot to do today," she said, getting to her feet.

The crow made a gurgling sound and took to the air to land in a tree above her.

Calliope could see some of the younger priests and priestesses walking by, eyeing her and her black companion warily, but she made nothing of it and simply waved and smiled at them. She had grown accustomed to the wary glances of the others, and forgave them their judgements of her, their fear. To them, the crow was a messenger of death, of the Morrigan, but to her, he was Apollo's messenger, a bringer of light. Corvus was a constant comfort to her.

When the bird had first begun following her around, some of the trainees of the Isle had called Calliope the 'Priestess of Death', but Etain, the head priestess, and Weylyn, the high Druid, had quickly corrected them. They said to the others that Calliope Pen Dragon was, rather, their 'Priestess of Hope and Light', the fact that Death had harried their family for generations notwithstanding.

The peace of Ynis Wytrin could not be so easily shattered and, despite the continued sidelong looks of some priests and priestesses, Calliope Pen Dragon went about her daily duties, her crow ever perching himself in the tree nearest to her.

Everyday, Calliope busied herself with helping those who had taken her in and protected her and her family as best they could. She contributed to the community in various ways such as milking the sheep and goats, feeding the pigs with slops from the kitchens, and tending to the crops of vegetables and healing herbs. She had even begun teaching Latin and Greek to some of Etain and Weylyn's younger acolytes.

They were exhausting days, but she was safe there, at relative peace. She knew, however, that she had to stay busy, for if she stopped for any length of time, she would despair at the sundering of her family.

Her twin brother, Phoebus, had been gone for well over a year now, having set off in search of their mother who had, in her great loneliness, rejected the healing peace of Ynis Wytrin and set out into the world of Rome once more. Where, Calliope knew not, but the fear of her mother's fate was often more than she could bear. Whether Phoebus had found her, she could not tell or see in her morning meditations beneath the great oak of the Isle.

And then there was her father, Lucius Pen Dragon, 'The Dragon', as he was still referred to in fearful whispers about the Isle and abroad across Britannia. Almost ten years before, after he had returned to Ynis Wytrin from the east, healed, apotheosized, he had disappeared without a trace, without a word of farewell.

Calliope remembered how lonesome and removed he had been from all of them in the days before his disappearance. She often blamed herself for not having seen his discomfort in the world of men. The scars upon her heart and conscience were deep at that, for she felt that she could have kept him there with them, kept their family together.

Most people believed Lucius Pen Dragon to be dead and, though Calliope knew that to be a distinct possibility, a part of her still hoped, in vain it seemed, that he was somehow alive. Her memories of him haunted her, the image of his once caring face as elusive as mist blown by a sudden storm.

Calliope was grateful to Etain for their daily sessions together, how the high priestess had trained her to release her feelings of guilt, at least temporarily, and find a measure of peace in her broken heart.

The druid, Weylyn, also made a great effort to reassure Calliope of his belief in her father, of all that he had done for the island of Britannia, how he had started something which, she had to admit, she did not fully understand. "It was destined long ago," Weylyn often said, "that dragons would save this land."

She wanted to believe, and attempted to do so most fervently. But still, so many years on, not only did it seem that her father was gone forever, but that her mother and brother had also abandoned her.

And so, Calliope Pen Dragon chose to serve others, including her aunt who slept as much as she could so as to avoid the painful thoughts of waking life.

There was another source of comfort for Calliope, however, and that was in the company of the Christian priest, Father Gilmore, and his two charges Aaron and Rachel.

Gilmore, though a Christian, had developed a great respect for Calliope's father, a respect that had taken a long time to emerge from his initial fear of the 'Roman Dragon'. "But men are not defined by where they come from, but rather by the deeds they have performed, the sacrifices they have made..." Gilmore said. "The Dragon protected Ynis Wytrin, and for that, I am grateful to him."

Calliope would often sit and talk with Gilmore in the small chapel dedicated to the Christian, Mary. He had a way of calming her, of giving her a different perspective of the world, of her own sad thoughts. In return, she had taken it upon herself to help clean the chapel and make the candles which Gilmore was so fond of and which he used in all of his Christian rituals.

Some of the other priests and priestesses of Ynis Wytrin questioned Calliope's sincerity in worshipping both the Gods of her ancestors and the Christus. "They peacefully co-exist in Ynis Wytrin, just as they do within my own heart," she would reply.

Etain, Weylyn, and Gilmore all praised her for the ease with which Calliope's belief in both faiths surrounded her like sunlight. It was a reconcilement that they had all struggled with in the past, and one which they encouraged their followers to understand.

But the shadow of Lucius Pen Dragon followed Calliope wherever she went. It came up with whomever she spoke. The fear some felt at the mention of Calliope's family, at the mere sight of her, was something she had to accept and which was extremely isolating.

You are never alone... She often remembered her father's voice uttering those very words, as if out of a dream. *You are never alone...*

She maintained the hope that that was true.

The fact was, however, that even though she was surrounded by people and had three very caring mentors, Calliope felt very alone at times. That is, she felt alone except for when she was with Aaron and Rachel.

Ever since the first time she and her brother had met the two Christian youths, friendship and trust had come easily between them. Whether it was because they were two sets of brother and sister, or because they were all twins, she did not think so. It was something more, a familiarity, a sense of calm and trust. For where others distrusted or feared the Dragon's family, Aaron and Rachel saw inherent good in them, just as Etain and Weylyn did.

Later, on that particular spring morning, as the sun rose higher in the sky to burn away the mist that chilled the air throughout Ynis Wytrin, Calliope made her way to the great oak where Etain and Weylyn sat in calm converse.

Etain, the high priestess of the Isle, sat upon the smoothed log, her white robes draped over it. Her hair, which had been a fiery red when Calliope had first met her, was now greying a little, but not enough to betray her age. Her green eyes, however, sparkled with a youthful curiosity that put one at ease in her presence, even though she had considerable powers.

On the log beside her, Weylyn, the old druid, leaned upon his oak staff, his long white hair and beard dancing in the gentle breeze, his pale eyes tired, but no less curious about the world about them.

Previously, Calliope had often wondered how they, and Father Gilmore, could be so worldly when they never left the safety of Ynis Wytrin. But she eventually came to the realization that not only did they possess an understanding of human nature few did, but they also moved in worlds beyond the present one. It was something she wished for them to teach her, but they had been reticent, claiming it was not yet possible.

"Good morning, Calliope," Etain said without turning to look at her.

Weylyn smiled to himself, and so did Calliope.

"Lady," Calliope said as she approached them. "You are more alert than a doe in a wood."

Etain turned and smiled brightly at her. "I could hear Corvus following you."

Calliope looked up to where the crow had just landed in the branches of the oak tree, rubbing the sides of his beak on his perch and then cawing.

Weylyn observed the bird, his face serious at first but then yielding to a smile. "You are very fortunate to have such a friend, Calliope Pen Dragon. Please, sit with us before Etain and I go to see to our newest learners."

The druid had always looked much older than Etain, but his curiosity about the world was such that his mind was undefeated by time. What had slowed him down was his grief at the loss of his companion and helper, Morvran. Two years previously, when Weylyn had ventured out into the world of men, he and Morvran had been attacked by bandits on the road to the great henge on the plains near Sorviodunum. Morvran was killed defending Weylyn, who but barely survived himself for his wounds. The grief had almost overwhelmed Weylyn, but Etain and Gilmore had come to his aid and helped him to weather it.

At Calliope's suggestion, Weylyn had found solace in his curiosity and read all of the scrolls in the chest which her family had left in Ynis Wytrin, including Socrates, Caesar, Arrian, and Longus who had been an acquaintance of her parents long ago.

"How many new pupils have come?"

Etain looked from Corvus to Calliope. "Three boys and three girls. There is always a large intake prior to Beltane." The high priestess took Calliope's hand. "How are you today, my dear?"

Calliope did not answer right away, but thought about it a moment, and this brought a deep sigh.

"Your aunt?" Etain asked.

Calliope nodded. "She had a bad night. She cried in her sleep again, more than usual."

"I'm sorry, dear." Etain sighed then too.

"Her grief has its claws deep in her heart and soul," Weylyn added. "Have you not been able to reach her, Etain?"

"I have helped her as much as I can, but her soul clings desperately to her grief over her brother. Until she decides she wants to leave grief behind, there is little I can do."

"I'll make her a stronger mixture of the herbs you taught me," Calliope said.

"That will but make her more comfortable. It will not help her to heal." Etain squeezed Calliope's hand. "But yes, you must do what you can for her."

The high priestess and druid looked upon the young woman, trying to mask their pity for her and not succeeding, for Calliope was one of the most astute priestesses they had ever trained.

"I know you bear a great burden for your family, Calliope," Etain finally said. "There is your aunt, and the worries you carry for your mother and brother."

Calliope looked out to the distant waters of the lake and marshes. *I need to let go of my own grief,* she thought, and as she did so, Etain nodded and smiled most kindly at her. That is, until the next question was posed in Calliope's mind. *And my father? Have you seen anything?*

Etain then shook her head, almost unable to look upon the girl before her. "He is gone, Calliope, hidden from us all."

"If even Etain cannot see him," Weylyn said, "then he dwells in worlds far beyond our knowing."

"If you cannot see him, or reach him," Calliope said to Etain, "then perhaps what everyone says is true? He is dead."

They did not reply, but the piteous look returned in both of their faces.

Calliope shook her head and fought back her tears.

In that moment, Corvus winged his way down to land upon her shoulder and stared directly at the priestess and druid.

"May I please help with the new pupils?" Calliope asked. "The distraction will be good for me." *I need to stay busy.*

"I'm afraid not. I've already asked Olwyn to help, Calliope. But I will let you know if there is something you can do later."

Calliope nodded, clearly disappointed.

Weylyn looked at Etain, unable to hide the surprise on his face, but she shot him a look.

"You have already done so much today," Etain said to Calliope. "Perhaps you should see Gilmore? He is touching on something new with Aaron and Rachel today."

At the mention of Aaron and Rachel, Calliope's features softened and she nodded. "I'll do that." She made to leave.

"Come and see me later," Etain said.

"I will," Calliope replied.

When she was gone, Weylyn turned to Etain. "Why don't you want her to help with the new pupils? She has gifts unlike anyone else."

Etain turned to him, her face suddenly creased with worry. "Because soon, she will have to go out into the world again."

"What? Why?" Weylyn asked.

"Because… Rome is coming."

Calliope walked slowly among the clusters of narcissus and blossoming clover toward the chapel that lay between the great oak and the slope of Wearyall Hill. She paused at the side of the wattle chapel, beside the well of Joseph, and there, she dispersed the faint hint of anger she had begun to feel toward Etain.

She closed her eyes and felt the wind upon her cheek, listened to the dripping of the water in the well. She allowed her breath to go in and out, slowly, calmly. She opened her eyes again to see the young priests in the nearby gardens, by the Christian dormitory, staring at her and at the crow she had brought which now perched itself on the roof of their sacred chapel.

Calliope waved at the priests who returned the gesture, though hesitantly. Beyond them, she spied the hunched form of her aunt, Clarinda, where she sat alone on the windswept heights of Wearyall Hill, looking out at the distant world for hope that would never come.

It was too much, and so Calliope tore her eyes away from her aunt, and went into the candlelit dark of the chapel.

She made the sign of the cross, as was the custom which Gilmore had taught her, and walked down the aisle to sit apart from the priests and listen to Father Gilmore's lesson.

At the front, she saw Aaron and Rachel.

Aaron turned to see her, and he smiled, his eyes alight with joy at her coming.

Gilmore cleared his throat, and Aaron turned back to the priest.

Rachel elbowed her brother and glanced back at Calliope with a wink.

Gilmore's face reddened, but he looked to Calliope and indicated the stool to his left, beside Rachel and Aaron.

Calliope stood and made her way down to the seat, the few other priests there watching her, fighting the sting of jealousy with which, no doubt, Father Gilmore had intended to test them.

Gilmore smiled kindly at Calliope, and continued.

"The mother of our Christus, the Holy Virgin, Mary, had five great joys, each symbolized by the points upon the pentangle. These joys represent what is good in the world, what is pleasing to God."

One of the priests raised his hand to speak.

"Yes, Kevyn?"

"Are you speaking of the five joyful mysteries of the Virgin?"

"Which are?" Gilmore asked, indulging the youth.

"The Annunciation, the Visitation, the Nativity of the Christus, the Presentation of the Christus in the Temple, and the Finding of the Holy Child in the Temple."

"Very good, Kevyn. Those are indeed the five joyful mysteries, but they are not what I was referring to. I am speaking of the five great *joys* of the Holy Mother." Gilmore looked down at Rachel, Aaron, and Calliope. "They are... Friendship... Fraternity... Purity... Politeness... and Pity."

At this last, Calliope shook her head very slightly, but Gilmore noticed.

"Yes, Calliope? Do you have something you would like to say?"

"Forgive me, Father Gilmore, but does 'Pity' not seem out of place in this list of joys?"

"How so?"

"Well," Calliope began, "pity, while well-intentioned, or even sometimes unintended, can make the recipient of it feel weak and ashamed. Surely, a joyful thing must be uplifting."

"That is an interesting point of view, Calliope." Gilmore paced in front of the stone altar, his hand slowly rubbing his grey and brown beard. "Let us try replacing 'pity' with 'compassion'. They are essentially the same, are they not? In their essence, pity and compassion are the understanding of another's suffering. Their intention is the desire to alleviate that suffering. This is a reflection of God's love and a way to serve others."

"I do not think they are the same, Father," Aaron said.

Gilmore turned to him. "How so?"

"Well," Aaron ran his hands through his black, curly hair, his blue eyes focussed on his guardian. "It seems to me that pity carries with it a sense of superiority, though with it a desire to end someone's suffering. While it could be well-intentioned, pity can create distance and resentment. On the other hand, compassion can bring hope. It carries the possibility of fostering a connection. It is a relationship between equals."

"I agree with Aaron," Rachel said beside her brother. "It does seem more logical to replace the fifth joy of the Blessed Virgin with 'Compassion'. Is that not what the Christus exemplified?"

Father Gilmore tried not to smile, and he would have were not the other young priests behind them, listening so intently. "One cannot simply 'change' the Blessed Virgin's Joys."

As Calliope listened, she wondered why Father Gilmore was holding back in all that he had to say and teach. Was it not a disservice to his acolytes? "Father Gilmore?"

"Yes, Calliope?"

"Did the other Mary, the Magdalene, have any joys to speak of?"

Gilmore froze and turned to the altar, his back to all of them. *Rachel and Aaron are not ready for the knowledge. Not yet.* He collected himself before turning back, and eyed Rachel and Aaron most intently.

What is he afraid of? Calliope suddenly wondered, a feeling of regret at the question coming upon her for all the discomfort it appeared to cause him.

"The Magdalene, who was indeed a favourite of our Christus, did not have joys or mysteries attached to her name. She was a sinful person who found redemption in the love and forgiveness which the Christus offered her."

"Surely, there must be more to it?" Calliope pressed, intrigued by the way Gilmore always avoided questions about her. "Did the Christus not favour her for a reason, other than seeing her as someone in need of forgiveness?"

Gilmore was silent again, and some of the priests began to whisper. "Silence."

They quieted and listened.

"I will end today's lesson on this." Gilmore walked forward to be among them, turning on the spot and meeting their eyes. "The Magdalene was indeed a sinner, and also of great import to the Christus. If 'Joys' were to be assigned to her, they would entail Transformation, Devotion, Courage and Love."

Calliope smiled.

"And these," Gilmore continued, "were only possible through the forgiveness which the Christus bestowed upon her."

Calliope's smile faded. *More holding back.*

"That is all for today," Gilmore said to the group.

The young priests all stood, crossed themselves, and then filed out of the chapel.

Rachel, Aaron, and Calliope stood too and were about to leave when Gilmore stopped them.

"You three. Wait," he said, watching until the last of the priests were gone. He looked to them, his face stern, a mask for his worries. "Calliope… How did you come to know of the Magdalene?"

"We told her," Rachel said, her chin up, her brown eyes gazing unafraid into Gilmore's.

Gilmore looked to Calliope. "And how much do you know of her?"

"Only what Rachel and Aaron have told me… That she was a favourite companion of Jesus, and that she went everywhere with him, though few acknowledge it."

"What else?" he demanded.

"That…that…" She did not want to say, to betray their trust.

But Aaron spoke. "We told her that we believe we are linked to her in some way. That you have never told us how, nor why you refuse to speak of her or how important she was to the Christus."

"That is because it is not safe to speak of such things, Aaron," Gilmore said.

"I don't understand," Aaron replied.

"If she was so important, why not give voice to her deeds?" Rachel demanded. "Why not speak of who she was? Don't you tell us that all men and women are sinners? If that is the case, then surely much could be learned from the Magdalene?"

"It is not that simple!" Gilmore's calm began to crack, his voice echoing in the chapel. But he calmed himself.

"Father Gilmore…" Calliope began. "What are you not telling us about her? I have watched and listened to you and all you have to teach. I have come to admire many aspects of your faith in the Christus, and of the Christian God. But is not truthfulness and honesty also a part of that faith? What are you not saying?"

To their surprise, Father Gilmore knelt on the floor before them, his hands reaching out, shaking slightly, to hold Rachel and Aaron's hands.

"I will say this once, and once only, for you are not ready for the entirety of the knowledge."

"Go on," Aaron said.

Gilmore swallowed hard. "The Magdalene is more important than you know. You were brought here, in part, because of that importance."

"That makes no sense," Rachel said.

Gilmore shook his head. "I can say no more, except that you both, Rachel and Aaron, would be in the gravest of danger if anyone, other than myself, Etain, or Weylyn, knew the truth of her story. It is why you cannot ever leave this place."

"So Ynis Wytrin is our prison?" Rachel said.

"No," Gilmore replied. "It is your sanctuary."

"More secrets!" Aaron said, standing quickly and running from the chapel gasping for fresh air.

"Aaron, wait!" Rachel said, glancing at Calliope and running after her brother.

"God, protect them…" Gilmore said to himself.

When he opened his eyes, he saw Calliope Pen Dragon standing before him with great compassion in her eyes. She had felt his fear. A part of her had felt guilty for trying to wring it from him. But she also felt for her dearest friends and how much pain it caused them not to know about so much.

"My only purpose is the safety of those two children." His voice shuddered as he spoke. "I cannot fail."

Calliope looked upon the man before her, and it seemed to her that the burden he carried far exceeded the weight of worry she felt for her family. She reached out and laid her hands gently upon his head. "All will be well, Father. I will speak to them…" Suddenly, Gilmore ceased his shaking and in that calm, Calliope perceived the truth of the secret which he guarded so vigilantly. At first, it was confusing, almost scary. But then a great thought of light burst in her mind, and it struck her to her core.

He removed her hands from his head and grasped them, his aged eyes pleading with hers.

Calliope knelt in front of him. "I know all too well the pain that can be caused by a family's secrets, and how impossible it might be for others to understand. Knowledge is always a blessing, and a curse."

"It is also a great danger to those the knowledge relates to," he said.

Calliope nodded. "You are not alone, Father," Calliope said softly. "I will help as best I can."

He looked up at her. *Perhaps she is an angel?*

"I'll speak on your behalf with Aaron and Rachel." She helped Gilmore to his feet. "All will be well."

Calliope Pen Dragon turned and left the chapel then, leaving Father Gilmore staring in wonder after her.

"God," he said as he turned to the altar. "What is your purpose in bringing her into our lives?"

Outside again, Calliope looked for Aaron and Rachel, and spotted their silhouettes against the sky as they sat beneath the Holy Thorn on Wearyall Hill.

Clarinda was nowhere to be seen, and Calliope supposed that she had gone back to sleep.

She set off up the path that led past the priests toiling in the field about the Christian dormitory, making for the summit of the hill.

High above her, Corvus soared on the wind, the gusts tossing him about like a leaf on a raging river, though he kept his course to stay with her.

She hummed as she walked, a habit which she had developed as a child. It was a tune which, her mother had once said, her aunt Alene would hum when holding her and her brother. It was a gentle, lilting melody that calmed her every time.

Calliope looked at Aaron and Rachel where they sat and felt for them. *How have they been able to remain here the whole of their lives and never know?* She also wondered at the burden which consumed Gilmore's life, and she admired his selflessness. *It is no easy thing to be hunted by Rome.*

She knew it all too well.

When Calliope reached the summit of the hill, she approached her friends who were leaning against the bole of the Holy Thorn.

They often went there to stare out at the wide world before them, knowing only that they would never be permitted to explore it. If they did, and if something unthinkable should happen to them, then the consequences would be disastrous for all. According to Father Gilmore, that is.

Seeing them there, beneath those blossoming hawthorn limbs, she felt something which she could not explain. They were at home beneath the limbs of the tree which Joseph had planted with his staff, they seemed to get relief from it, the same way the water from the Well of the Chalice cooled and calmed a fiery mind and wounded body.

"Are you both all right?" she asked as she approached, Corvus coming to land upon the ground beside her. "I've never seen you challenge Father Gilmore in that way." She smiled, and Aaron returned the smile a little sadly, indicated his sister.

Rachel had been weeping, and wiped her eyes to dry her tears.

Calliope went to sit on her other side so that Rachel was between her and Aaron. She took her friend's hand.

Rachel was calm again, a smile curling at the corners of her mouth. She swept away the strands of her dark hair which stuck to her tear-wetted cheeks. "I find Father Gilmore so frustrating sometimes. He is supposed to be our guardian - from where and how, and appointed by whom, we do not know!"

"Some days he's more like a jailer than a guardian," Aaron said, shaking his head.

"He is stern with you, true," Calliope said. "But in his heart, he cares only for your safety." She thought about what she had sensed in Gilmore. It was not just a deep-rooted fear for their safety. It was something more powerful than that. *It is Hope,* she realized. *A faith in something great.* She had felt something similar when her father had returned whole and healed from the east, and she had felt his strong embrace once again. *Before he left this world...*

She pushed the thought away and continued. "I am familiar with the pain of secrets, the frustration of not knowing. For a long time, there was much I did not know about my own father, how he came to be...well..."

Rachel and Aaron looked at her, and they could see the pain which she yet dealt with.

"But you eventually found out," Rachel said, intending it to be a comfort.

"Yes, I did," Calliope replied, "and with that knowledge came new pain and uncertainty." She stared out at the world, felt the breeze that whipped around them, and enjoyed the fall of hawthorn petals upon them. "Perhaps it is not a good thing to rush to knowledge, but to let God give it to us when we are ready to receive it."

"Perhaps it is like that story Phoebus told me once?" Rachel said. "About the woman, Pandora, whose curiosity unleashed a world of pain."

"Yes," Calliope said. "My brother likes to tell that story."

"I miss him," Rachel said, her voice low.

"As do I," Calliope said.

"I pray to God that he is safe," Rachel added.

"Phoebus is strong," Aaron said, setting aside his frustration with Calliope's brother. They had been close, he and Phoebus, but since the disappearance of Lucius Pen Dragon, he had changed, grown harder, more sullen.

"He is also very angry," Calliope said, trying to fight back her tears, frustrated that she had veered from her purpose to speak on behalf of Gilmore. "But while my brother is angry and selfish for having gone off without a word, Father Gilmore is being as honest as he possibly can with you. One day, I feel certain that he will tell you the truth before the end…when he is ready…when you are."

"I suppose we must be content with the knowledge we do have for the moment," Rachel sighed.

"Which is?" Aaron asked.

"That there is something about the Magdalene which we cannot know, and that it somehow relates to us." Rachel pushed herself to her feet and stood before them. "That it is a dangerous knowledge we are not ready to learn."

"That's not really satisfying," Aaron said.

"No, it is not." Rachel closed her eyes and felt the wind upon her face, her long dark hair swirling about her head.

"Also, that there is someone who cares so much about you that he is willing to dedicate his life to your safety." Calliope stood too, her arm around Rachel.

"But why would he do that?" Aaron asked.

"Because it is his purpose, given to him by God," Calliope said.

"But why?" Rachel asked.

"The 'why' of it is a knowledge for later, I suppose."

"Calliope, you are more cryptic at times than Etain!" Aaron laughed.

Calliope blushed.

Rachel observed the two of them. "I need to go and finish with the flower beds, or Father Gilmore will lecture me on timeliness."

"I'll come with you," Aaron offered.

"No. You stay for a bit with Calliope." She smiled mischievously. "How often do you two get to be alone?" With that parting comment,

Rachel turned and strolled down the spine of the hill back toward the chapel.

When Rachel was gone, Aaron turned to Calliope. He stood close, but not too close, waiting for her to reciprocate. They clasped hands beneath the branches of the Holy Thorn, searching each other's eyes.

"And how are you, Calliope?" It felt nice to say her name so close to the source of his inspiration. He knew it was supposed to be wrong, to feel so much, to be inspired by her more than any lesson Gilmore taught them. *But did not the Christus exemplify Love?*

Calliope felt her heart pounding beneath the layers of her clothing. Her stomach felt strange, and her head light. And it was wonderful. She and Aaron had little time alone, such as it was, but when they did, the feelings that emerged were inexplicable. *Oh, Lady Venus, is this what it is to love?*

Without another word, Calliope and Aaron leaned in at the same time to press their lips together, so soft, so innocent, so life-affirming.

The sun broke from the clouds then to shine upon the hillside, warming their heads.

When their lips parted, their arms hugged each other close so that they could feel the other's breathing. They lingered in that closeness for several moments.

"You are a wonder to me, Calliope," Aaron said. "How can you help so many when you have been through so much?"

She did not answer him, but enjoyed the feel of holding him close.

"You give me hope for this world," he said, pulling back to look into her eyes.

His smile was broad and radiant to her, and filled her with joy. "And you are the sun that burns away my clouds, Aaron."

He kissed her again.

"Aaron!" the voice of one of the younger priests shouted from downhill. "Aaron! Father Gilmore is looking for you! Come now!"

Corvus took to the air from where he had been pecking at worms upon the grass, and swept down the hill toward the priest.

The man saw the winged shadow coming toward him, crossed himself, and turned to flee back to the chapel.

"Did you train Corvus to do that?" Aaron laughed.

Calliope smiled. "No. But he is a very smart bird!" She laughed too.

"I have to go," he said. "But I'll see you later."

"Yes," Calliope replied, her hand stroking his cheek before he tore himself away and went back down the hill.

She watched him go, amazed at how much she felt for him, grateful for the calm that affection gave to her.

Aaron was no warrior, and his body was tall and lanky. But he was beautiful to her, his eyes the kindest she had ever known.

Father Gilmore disapproved, and whenever they had a chance to be alone, he called Aaron away from her to do some task or other.

So many secrets…

Her mind went back to her own family, and she felt the clouds of her sadness and worry returning. She stood tall, however, beside that ancient, sacred tree on the top of the hill. She closed her eyes, stuck her chest out defiantly, and spread her arms. The wind pulled at her cloak and hair, and threatened to push her down the steep slope. But she stood rooted to the green ground.

Then the wind fell back, and the sun burned through once more to warm her face.

Calliope opened her eyes again, and for the briefest of moments, she saw Venus and Apollo standing before her. Their eyes whirled with stars as they smiled upon her. She blinked, however, and they were gone.

The clouds had returned.

Calliope turned then, and made her way back down the hill to where the long dock jut out into the lake. She made her way to the end of the dock, her mind awash with memories of mingled pain and joy.

Corvus came to land on one of the posts beside her, his shiny black eyes observing the droplets of tears rimming her eyes as she stared out over the reedy waters.

"Mama… Phoebus… Where are you?" she whispered. *Why did you leave?* "Baba?" she called to her lost father. "Where are you? Are you in Elysium, or the halls of Olympus, never to return? I miss you so much…"

Calliope Pen Dragon then let her tears fall and her body shudder with the grief she kept to herself.

She remembered that day, ten years before when her father had appeared on that very dock healed and whole, fully renewed…a god… That return had filled her shattered world with joy and hope for the future, only to have them vanish with him.

"It would have been less painful if you had not returned." She hated herself the moment she said it, but there was a seed of truth in the words. "I'm sorry I did not see your struggle in the world of men."

Calliope reached down to cup a handful of the dark water below, raised it up, and let it fall in the breeze. "Oh divine Gods... Please protect my brother and mother...lead them back to me..." She took another handful and did the same. "Give me the strength to do what I must for my family..." One last time, she cupped her hand and raised it high. "Oh Apollo...divine grandfather... Show me the Dragon, my father, so that I can stop wondering..."

For so many years, Calliope had lived in hope, held it close to her heart, nurtured it like a Vestal keeping her flame. It had been no easy task to keep hope, and the hole of loss seemed ever to be widening, threatening to engulf her.

And yet, she had a feeling...

Her worries, however, were more acute when it came to her mother and brother. Phoebus, she had not seen in over a year. It had been much longer since her mother had left.

She closed her eyes and reached out with her mind, her heart.

Phoebus... Mama...?

She envisioned them, tried to hear their heartbeats, observe the blink of their familiar eyes, remember the lilt of their voices.

Hear me... she urged. *Come back to me.*

But there was nothing, save for the wind on the water and the scratch of Corvus' talons on the wooden dock beside her.

"What trials do they undergo, Corvus, that they are not open to me... that they do not hear me?"

After a while, as the evening mists began to engulf the marshes, Calliope stood and set off for her room to check on her aunt, Clarinda, whose grief had long ago overwhelmed her and chewed her up.

"Come, Corvus. Matertera needs us..."

VI

NAVIS NIGRA

'A Black Ship'

The night was dark, deeper than was natural, and the stars in the heavens struggled to send their light. In that black canvas of the cosmos, Draco…ille Anguis…the Dragon, writhed in pain and rage as the hunter, Orion, set upon him again and again with fiery arrows that cut into him. But the Dragon whirled and darted, jaws agape, roaring so that the other constellations shuddered in their fixed homes, their lights near extinction. He would never give in to the hunter, would see the world burn in his fiery jaws before that happened.

Far below, beneath this clash of Titans, a young woman stared up at the sky with tears in her eyes, wanting to scream but unable to make a sound. Barefoot, she clambered over the jagged rocks of a promontory that jut into the raging sea. Waves crashed against the rocks, wetting her path. But she carried on, her feet cut and bleeding as she made for the edge of the headland, her eyes on the heavens, on the Dragon who now spun in an ouroboros of fire that lit the world.

The hunter fired his bow over and over. He cut and slashed with sword and spear, but every attempt failed, sending flames to earth, even as the Dragon's fire grew brighter and hotter.

It was then that the girl saw it, a ship that was darker than the night, cutting through the roiling sea. Every wave it touched turned to foaming blood, and in those violent breakers the bodies of men, of women, and of children were felled beneath the harsh gaze of the crimson eyes upon the prow.

The girl watched, horrified, as the myriad faces of innocents were ploughed under the ship's beak, cut down like soft wheat beneath a reaper's scythe, their eyes gazing their last upon the world before disappearing into the merciless depths.

She tried to scream again, and this time, her voice rang out across the water to slam into that black ship. *NOOOOOO!*

Upon the deck, beneath the flapping sail bearing a bloody eagle, a hundred faceless warriors unsheathed their blades and turned their heads to her screaming visage. The ship turned toward her, approaching more quickly now, the warriors slamming their spears on the dark deck.

In the sky, the hunter retreated, blinded by the Dragon's light, so bright that it looked to cut a hole in the heavens. The fire of that sight came closer, unbearably burning.

With steam rising off of the rocks about her bleeding feet, the girl gazed over the cliff's edge to see the bodies of the fallen slamming against the land's rocky teeth, piling higher and higher as the ship pressed upon them.

She made to turn, to run, but the blood was slick upon her wounded feet, and she slipped over the edge. Her hands grabbed at the rocks. Blinded by her tears, she held on, her white robe flapping in the dark over that abyss.

The ring of light from above came closer, unbearably hot, unimaginably bright. The menace about her was everywhere, above and below, seeking to dash her upon the rocks so very far below among the faceless dead.

She could not hold on much longer, and looked over her shoulder to see the warriors climbing, slashing at her feet and legs as her blood dripped into the sea.

Climb! she commanded herself. She strained to reach for the lip of the world above, for safety, and pulled with all of her might only to find herself facing luminous, otherworldly eyes filled with anger and vengeance, and the swing of a moon-bright blade.

She cried out then, lost her grip upon the rock, and fell into the darkness below, speeding toward the outstretched swords and spears of the faceless warriors...

Death did not come.

The girl awoke in a sunlit wood, upon a bed of soft green grass instead of black and blood-soaked rock.

The roar of the sea, and the clash of battle were gone, replaced by the trickle of water and of the song of white birds in the gnarled boughs of the ancient oaks about her. A white horse grazed nearby and, laying in the long grass, three white hounds with red-tipped ears slept fitfully.

The girl wanted to weep, but found the urge leave her as quickly as it came in that place of peace. Then, she felt a soft hand stroke her brow and she looked up to see the goddess.

Her eyes were filled with compassion and calm. *Be still...Calliope Pen Dragon... Be calm...* She smiled, her pale face framed by her fiery hair which hung down like ivy at the edge of a clear waterfall.

Epona? the girl said. Is it really you? So full of relief, she reached up to hug the goddess as though she were her missing mother.

Shhh, the goddess urged. *No tears can be shed here in this sacred place. There will be tears enough in the world of men.*

The girl sat back upon her knees, and looked at her intact feet, her flawlessly white gown. *I am dreaming.*

If that is what you wish to call it... She looked beyond the girl to the branches of a tree, and a moment later a white crow swept down to land beside her. The hounds opened their eyes and looked upon them, and the horse approached to nuzzle his divine mistress. *You must remember that you are never alone.*

I feel alone, the girl said. *My family has abandoned me to face the Black Ship...* Steel and blood, and faceless death flashed in her mind, only to be replaced by blinding light a moment later. When her vision returned, she saw the goddess looking at her.

A trial approaches.

I know, the girl responded. *What will happen? What must I do?* she pleaded.

But the goddess shook her head, her smile a memory. *I cannot tell you all that I know. It is forbidden.* She reached out to place her hand upon the girl's cheek. *You must prepare yourself.*

For what? What is coming?

You will be leaving Ynis Wytrin soon...

The girl felt the well of her sadness overflow. She did not want to leave those who remained dear to her. *Aaron...*

The goddess smiled again, and there was hope there. *You must purify yourself in the spring fires of Beltane.*

Why? the girl asked.

To keep hope, to remember you are never alone... The goddess reached out to run her lithesome fingers down her face. *Now, your tears may fall…*

Calliope wailed in her bed, in the darkness lit by a single lamp.

"It's all right, niece," a frail voice said. "I'm here. I am with you."

A cold, wet cloth was pressed to Calliope's forehead, the water mingling with the tears that ran in torrents down her cheeks and onto her neck. She opened her eyes to see her aunt looking down upon her.

"I know, dear…" Clarinda said. "It will soon be time to leave."

"What do you mean?"

"The Far-Shooter appeared to me last night. He told me."

"Apollo?" Calliope asked. She knew her aunt had been a priestess at Delphi, but had thought that in all of her deep, drowning grief she had lost her ability to speak with the Gods. She had been wrong, it seemed.

Clarinda nodded.

"What about you, matertera?"

Clarinda's face was sad, resigned. "I will never leave this place, dear."

The nightmare still clawed at Calliope, lacerating her will, her hope. She reached out to the world as she sat up, staring at the flame of the clay lamp upon the table. There was a definite shift in the air. She felt the hope that she had nurtured now tainted with a familiar dread she had all but forgotten.

Calliope wiped her eyes and shook her head. She felt dizzy in that moment, nauseous as the room about her spun. She pulled away from her aunt and rushed out into the misty morning.

"Calliope, wait!" Clarinda called. "Come back!"

But Calliope did not stop and Clarinda watched her form disappear into the whiteness of the morning mist.

"Lord Apollo… I pray that they survive the storm…" She then fell to her knees and raised her thin arms to the sky. "I offer my life to save theirs…"

Calliope ran barefoot around the base of the Hill of the Chalice, the dew-wet grass clinging to her feet as she made her way past the Healing House to the valley beside the Tor. She rushed along the avenue of ancient yew trees, her hands bracing against their warm brown trunks, and darted beneath ivy-clad arches until she reached the waterfall where the red waters of the Well of the Chalice tumbled to fill the healing pool.

Her breathing ragged, she knelt beside the red pool, the song of the waterfall loud in her ears, but not loud enough to drown out the sound of a storm and clash of battle. She splashed her face and the cold water revived her, awakened her.

For several heartbeats she stayed there, her tunic wet and cold, her body shivering. She found her strength however, her calm, and stood slowly to make her way up the path, beneath the ivy and gnarled wisteria across a grassy carpet to the stone with a lion's head spouting the sacred water. There she took up one of three clay cups, filled it, and drank slowly.

She had spent many a moment over the years at that well, drinking of that water held to be holy by all the inhabitants of Ynis Wytrin. For a moment, her vision blurred, and she thought the cup in her hand morphed into the shape of a chalice before her eyes. She shook her head and saw the plain cup once again.

"Gods... What are you trying to tell me?"

A loud cawing came from the uppermost branches of the nearest yew tree, and Calliope looked up to see Corvus looking down at her. She held out her hand and the crow immediately glided down to land upon it. She lowered him to the ground where he bounded across the grass to drink from the tumbling water.

"I've had such terrifying visions," she said to the bird before looking at the cup in her hand and setting it back beside the fountain.

Calliope stood and walked farther along the path until she came to the secluded green haven about the sacred wellhead which was orbited by offerings to the goddess and the Christus both. She gazed into the depths to see the water dripping and dancing about strands of green that were as the wet hair of a forest nymph.

She liked it there, for the world could be shut out in the deep silence, thought about in a more objective way, or not thought about at all.

She whimpered unintentionally as she sat upon a rock bench beneath an overhang of ivy, and realized that she was afraid, terrified of the prospect of a return to days of blood and violence, of days when Rome stopped at nothing to harm her family. She could see the eyes of a thousand wicked men and women who had, in the past, sought to use her mother and father for their own ends, and though she had been too young to fully comprehend, she did understand evil intent.

A part of her mind thought that since her father was no longer among the living, they would leave the rest of her family alone.

But the nightmare image of that bloody eagle upon that black ship, driving it forward unrelentingly, clawed at her heart.

Calliope forced herself to close her eyes and breathe slowly, ignoring the shivering of her body. She set aside the image of that black ship and focussed on the comfort the Goddess Epona had given her. *I'm not alone… I'm never alone…* she reassured herself.

In her meditation, she heard the soft approach of footsteps and opened her eyes to see Olwyn Conn Coran, a priestess a few years older than Calliope, and one whom her father had saved many years before. It was she who had first led the Dragon's family to Ynis Wytrin.

"Calliope, are you unwell?" Olwyn approached to sit with her. Her eyes were kind and concerned, but not worried, for she knew the strength of Calliope Pen Dragon more than most. She brushed aside the long braid of her auburn hair and turned to her. "Did something happen?"

"A vision," Calliope replied. "A nightmare."

Olwyn looked from Calliope to Corvus who stood upon the stone wall above them, watching over his mistress. She stood and went to pat the crow who leaned into her hand. She was one of the few others who could approach the bird. "Etain thought something had happened," she said without looking at Calliope. "She sent me to check on you."

"I'm fine, really." Calliope stood and went to the wellhead again to look into its depths. "I just need some time."

"It seems time has caught up with you," Olwyn said, her hand reaching out to take Calliope's.

The latter turned. "What do you mean?" The worry returned to her eyes.

Olwyn looked at the ground for a moment. "Etain also sent me to bring you to her."

"Why? Has something happened?" That familiar dread returned, and the sight of that black ship appeared on the horizon of her mind. She felt the fear and uncertainty, and felt her fingers grasping at the cliff's edge. "Tell me, Olwyn!"

"There is a letter from Lord Einion of Din Tagell."

Calliope ran as quickly as she could, Corvus winging after her.

IGNIS ET FERTILITAS

'Fire and Fertility'

When Calliope arrived at Etain's small stone domus beside the Healing House, she did not wait to knock, but opened the door immediately, bursting in, breathless and sweaty. She came to a sudden stop upon the threshold when she saw Weylyn and Etain sitting before the hearth, along with Clarinda who was grasping a rolled missive.

Olwyn Conn Coran arrived shortly after and closed the door behind her.

"Both of you, come in," Etain said, no trace of a smile upon her face.

"What is happening, Etain?" Calliope asked. "Weylyn?" She looked from one to the other of them, but they both looked at the missive in her aunt's hand.

"This just arrived from the Lord Einion in Din Tagell. He sent one of his fastest riders." Etain looked at Calliope's shivering form. "Olwyn… Please put my cloak about her shoulders so that she may be warm and clear headed."

Olwyn went to the door and removed Etain's long, pale cloak.

Calliope felt warmer already, more calm as she sat upon the stool beside her aunt, with Etain and Weylyn across from them.

"Oh, Calliope…" Clarinda whispered.

"Let her read it for herself," Etain said to Clarinda, her voice taking on a tone of import and severity.

It worried Calliope. She took the letter from her aunt with some reluctance and began to read…

Calliope and Clarinda,

This letter is very important, and I pray to the Gods that it arrives quickly and safely, for your lives may depend upon it.

I have received word from a friend in Rome that your family is in imminent danger. The Emperor and Augusta are sending men to Britannia to seek you out, all of you, in an attempt to get at our departed friend and brother, Lucius.

The Emperor's men may already be in Britannia. We do not know how many they are.

I urge you to come to safety in Din Tagell as soon as possible. I'm sending warriors to get you and escort you safely to my court.

If either of you is in contact with Adara or Phoebus, you should also let them know. I have sent riders to look for them - discreetly - but have received no word of their whereabouts.

Come as soon as you can, and may the Gods watch over you.

Einion

When she finished reading, Calliope was silent, staring into the flames of the hearth as Etain and Weylyn watched her closely.

Beside her, Clarinda was rocking, holding her hands to her face. "I can't leave here...I can't..."

"Calm, child," Etain said. "I don't believe you need to. But Calliope does."

Calliope looked surprised. "What do you mean? The Lord Einion said we both need to come."

Weylyn cleared his throat gently, his hand upon his beard. "It is the Dragon they are after...his wife and children. Rome does not even know of Clarinda's presence in Britannia."

"How can you be sure of that?" Calliope asked. "How can we be sure of anything?"

"Nothing is certain," Weylyn replied.

"Including whether we will be safer in Din Tagell than we already are in Ynis Wytrin!" Clarinda said. "I'm not leaving here. This is my home now."

"Matertera," Calliope pleaded. "You read the letter. We *must* go, if not to keep ourselves safe, then to protect Ynis Wytrin from the eyes of Rome."

Etain did smile at that. *Such courage in this young woman.* "Clarinda is right, Calliope."

"What?" Calliope rolled up the letter and tossed it into the fire where it bent and crackled into ash. "She needs to get to Din Tagell too!"

Etain looked to Olwyn and Clarinda. "Leave us, please. We need to speak with Calliope alone."

"Yes, lady," Olwyn said as she helped Clarinda to her feet.

"Don't worry, niece," Clarinda said, her hand upon Calliope's shoulder. "It is Apollo's wish."

Calliope felt her eyes burn as she looked up at her aunt and caught a rare glimpse of courage returning to her face, the certainty in her eyes.

When Olwyn and Clarinda were gone, Weylyn rose and poured a cup of water for Calliope which he handed to her. His old, gnarled hands shook a little, but they were still possessed of strength, both physical and ethereal.

The silence was deep as Calliope sat there with Etain and Weylyn, and she wondered whether that would be the last time she was alone in their presence. The thought made her sad.

"Tell us of your vision."

Calliope bowed her head with the weight of the memory of the sea… the storm…the black ship.

"I stood upon a promontory over the sea, my feet bleeding from the jagged rocks I had climbed over. It was dark, but in the sky there was a thunderous battle between the Dragon and the Hunter."

"Draco and Orion?" Weylyn asked.

"Yes. They fought, and the Dragon was wounded many times, but continued to fight." She closed her eyes, reaching back to see once more the dreaded sight that had invaded her sleep. "Then, the Dragon took hold of his own tail and spun with such speed and ferocity. The circle grew as bright as the sun in that night sky…"

She could see it again, blinding and brilliant and terrifying.

In Calliope's eyes, Etain and Weylyn could see the memory of it in the reflected fire, and they felt a creeping worry.

"Go on," Etain said. "Courage, Calliope."

"When the Dragon lit the sky, upon the thrashing sea was revealed a black ship with a bleeding eagle upon the sail. Upon the deck were faceless warriors in black, armed with sword and spear. The ship turned to sail at me, a bloody seafoam at the prow where countless bodies of the dead bumped against the hull to be pushed onto the rocks far below." Calliope wiped her brow, now sweaty as she recounted her vision. "The fire in the sky bore down upon me, as did the ship… I slipped and held onto the cliff's edge with all my strength. That's when I saw him."

"Whom did you see?" Etain pressed.

"A face with luminous green eyes filled with anger and vengeance, and a deadly, swinging sword. He reached for me and I lost my grip upon the rocks." She drank the water and swallowed. "I awoke in a green glade with the Goddess Epona holding me."

"What did the goddess say?" Etain leaned forward. She had always admired the Dragon's family for their ability to commune directly with the Gods. It was not until Calliope's father's apotheosis that she had truly understood. "Try to remember, dear."

Calliope sat tall then, her courage reinforced by the memory of Epona's kindness. "The goddess told me that a great trial approaches and that I must leave Ynis Wytrin."

"She made no mention of your aunt?" Weylyn asked.

Calliope shook her head. "She said that I must purify myself in the fires of Beltane…to keep hope…to remember that I am not alone…" The memory of that heavenly voice was a tonic to Calliope in that moment, more than any herb or tincture. It calmed her, and gave her strength.

Weylyn and Etain looked at each other, their eyes speaking, their minds conversing in silence.

Calliope could have tried to listen to what they thought, but she was too exhausted to make the attempt and did not want to intrude. Morning sunlight filtered in through the window to touch and warm her feet.

"I need to go outside," Weylyn said. "The sun is up, and I must sit in it while you two talk."

"But I need your advice, Weylyn," Calliope said.

The old druid smiled as he took up his walking stick and went to the door. "Etain and I are of one mind, dear girl." He observed her with his kind, squinting eyes. "You are so like your mother and father." He shut the door behind him and sat upon a nearby bench in the herb garden outside the small domus.

When Weylyn was gone, Etain sat beside Calliope and took her hands in hers. She breathed in and out for several moments and then her far-seeing, green eyes stared into Calliope's. "Your vision confirms Einion's letter. Rome is coming for you, your mother, and your brother."

"Do you know where Mama and Phoebus are? Have you seen anything?"

Etain shook her head. "No. They are beyond my sight. If they do not reach out to me, I cannot see them. They are upon their own paths." *And they are paths devoid of innocence...* "You must get to the safety of Din Tagell, for yourself and your family."

"And for Ynis Wytrin," Calliope added. "And for Aaron and Rachel too."

Etain nodded slowly. "Yes." *She knows.* "Father Gilmore told me of your conversation."

Calliope laughed. "He always does." There was no animosity in her laughter. She had always thought it amusing that if she told one of the triad of wise ones something, the other two would know soon after. *Oh to have such friends!* Then it dawned on her that she did have such friends, that she and Phoebus, Aaron and Rachel, had a very strong bond.

"Much depends upon Aaron and Rachel," Etain stated. "This sanctuary must be protected at all costs and they..." Etain paused, trying to find the words. "They *are* hope."

Calliope fell to her knees and set her head in Etain's lap. The older woman stroked her hair and soothed her with her humming, extricating the fear from her like a surgeon does a tumour, and reinforcing her with calm strength. "That is why Father Gilmore is so vigilant."

"Yes," Etain answered. "And much also depends upon you and your kin."

Calliope looked up at her. "I don't understand."

"You will." Etain held her face in her hands as she spoke. "You must adhere to the Goddess Epona's command, and attend the Beltane celebrations three days hence, and then you must leave Ynis Wytrin with the warriors Einion sends."

"I will," Calliope replied, tears rimming her eyes. "I know that I must leave, and I will... But I don't want to."

"I know. And I do not want for you to go." Etain's voice shuddered.

Calliope heard something different in the high priestess' voice, and before she could say anything else, Etain spoke again.

"Calliope Pen Dragon, you have been, and always will be, a blessing upon this isle."

"And it has been my joy to serve here, lady. I am forever grateful to you all."

They were silent for a time, still as the fire crackled and their tears dried, their emotions of gratitude and sadness taking their course.

"Go now. See to your aunt, and then you can help the others with the Beltane preparations."

Calliope got to her feet. "You will take care of my aunt after I am gone?"

"Of course, dear. Her place is here. She will be safe and invisible to the eyes of Rome."

"Thank you." Calliope then turned, put Etain's cloak back upon the peg, and went out into the morning sunlight. She found Weylyn sitting in the herb garden and went over to him. "I understand what I must do, Weylyn. I have to go soon."

The old druid stood, set his stick against the bench, and turned to where she stood among the waving stalks of rosemarinus. "I know you do. The path ahead will be difficult, but you, above all others, have your father's courage."

Calliope hugged him, and the affectionate action surprised Weylyn. *Why do I feel like I am bidding my own child farewell all over again?* He felt his lip quiver beneath his beard. "Go now. Be calm in the peace of this place before you set out."

Calliope released him and turned to walk barefoot down the path, back to the guest house and her aunt.

Etain them emerged from the small domus, her eyes dry once again, to come to Weylyn's side.

"Are you sure this is the way?" Weylyn asked her. "Gilmore will never allow him to participate in the rites."

"I will speak with him. Even our dear priest cannot counter the will of the Gods, *or* of the Christus…"

"And what of our hopes for Britannia?" Weylyn asked. "What of the Dragon's family, Etain?"

Etain clasped his hand and tilted her head to the sky. She felt the wind and sun upon her face, listened to the whispers of the future given to her in strands of song and melody.

"Hope will survive. It always does. But I see an abrupt end at the fading of the sun…and a new beginning."

Together, they looked out over the green hills of Ynis Wytrin, across the avenue of yews, toward the great oak, and the flowering apple orchards beyond. There was nothing more to be said.

. . .

The morning of Beltane arrived, and Ynis Wytrin awoke to a riotous chorus of birdsong about the Isle. It had been a calm night, that last spring evening before summer and the grazing and growing season.

There was much excitement, especially among the younger priests and priestesses, for the day would bring with it much celebration, feasting, and dancing long into the night. That is, all of that would take place after the requisite offerings to the Gods and spirits of the land to ensure the fertility, purity, and prosperity of the land and its people.

Calliope awoke early and, much to her relief, peacefully. She had always enjoyed the celebrations of Beltane, the joy and optimism they brought.

When she was young, the festival of Floralia had always been a time of joy on the family's latifundium in Etruria. It was a time of colour and bursting life with multi-hued flowers everywhere one looked. She remembered her father wearing a corona of spring flowers as he danced with her, a rare carefree moment in time. She also recalled her mother filling her room and the rest of the domus with fresh flowers that scented their home with a heady perfume. The memory made her smile, but briefly, for those had been fleeting days of joy in a life that seemed to have been harried by the hate of others. That home, and those Etrurian crops, had long been burned, destroyed by Rome.

She often wondered how the Gods could allow such beautiful memories to be the source of so much anguish but, upon reflection, she knew the doing of that was her own. Nostalgia could be a bitter friend.

Calliope had much preferred to celebrate Beltane since she had come to Ynis Wytrin, for it was fresh and new to her as the spring, and therein, she could also make her offerings to the Goddess Flora.

That Beltane, however, she awoke with a sadness in her heart, for she knew that when the sacred fires were extinguished, the dancing done, and the flowers fallen, she would have to leave Ynis Wytrin. *Will I ever return?* she wondered as she sat on the edge of her bed to get dressed.

Across from her, Clarinda slept soundly, a gift from the Gods at the dawning of summer.

Calliope washed and spent a bit longer tidying her hair in front of the bronze mirror. She wanted to look her best for the day and, if she was honest with herself, for Aaron. She insisted on setting aside sadness. *There will be time enough for that later.*

She hoped that Aaron and Rachel would be permitted to attend the festivities.

Father Gilmore was at times a little reluctant to allow it, but Etain always seemed to prevail upon him in the name of the great harmony of Ynis Wytrin. When the prayers in honour of the Blessed Virgin were completed, and the communion of the Christus finished, then he would allow Aaron, Rachel, and the other priests who wished to do so to join the celebrations.

At the thought, Calliope felt her heart skip a beat that made her smile. *That is the face I would present to Aaron,* she thought as she observed her bronze reflection.

There was a gentle knock at the door.

Calliope set the mirror down upon the table and opened it slowly so as not to wake her aunt.

Etain stood there in the mist, sunlight cutting into the whiteness to light the high priestess. "Good morning, Calliope," Etain said, her visage radiant in the morning light. "Bendithion ar Galan Mai – boed haul, ffyniant, a chariad i'th daith."

Calliope twisted up her face a little as she tried to remember the wish of the Britons at Beltane.

"Do you remember the words from our lessons?" Etain asked.

"I think so… 'Blessings on Beltane… May there be sun…prosperity…and love…'" She thought a moment about the final part. "'On your journey.'"

"Very good," Etain said as she stepped forward to hug her.

There was warmth there, and joy, but also that painful hint of nostalgia before a farewell. They had spent many a Beltane together in Ynis Wytrin, each one bringing more healing. Calliope lingered in that surrogate, motherly embrace and felt herself calmer for it.

When Etain let go, she smiled at Calliope.

"What is it, lady?" The younger woman tilted her head in question, curious about the somewhat mischievous look upon Etain's face.

"You must come with me to greet the warriors sent by Lord Einion. They have arrived."

"Oh. Yes. Of course," Calliope said, her disappointment inexpertly hidden. She glanced back at Clarinda one more time to see she was still sleeping, and then went out, closing the oak door behind her. "It is odd that they should arrive on the day of the sacred festival," Calliope said as they walked across the grass.

"Yes, but such is the will of the Gods, I suppose," Etain added.

They walked slowly past the great oak, the young priestesses nearby bent over the dew-heavy grass with small phials to collect the precious liquid.

Calliope bent down to wet her hand in the grass and rubbed the dew on her face and into her skin. The first time she had seen the priestesses do that, she had thought it odd, but then Etain had explained that dew collected on Beltane morning had magical properties that brought youth and beauty. It made sense to Calliope when she looked upon Etain's timelessly youthful face, despite her age. She thought of Aaron again as they approached the chapel, and bent once more to gather more dew.

Etain watched with amusement. "Good morning, Gilmore," she said as the priest emerged from the chapel. "The blessings of the Gods, of the Christus, and the Blessed Mary upon you on this joyous day!"

Father Gilmore watched them pass with a smile upon his face.

"And to you, my friend!" he called back to Etain just as Aaron and Rachel emerged from the chapel behind him.

Calliope caught Aaron's eye and they both smiled.

"I trust that our Christian brethren will join us for the festivities later today?" Etain asked Gilmore with a twinkle in her eye and an amused look on her face.

"Yes, yes, Etain. We will be there also with our blessings. God's bounty is universal, is it not?"

"So it is," she replied. "We must go now. The warriors have arrived." Etain led Calliope on in the direction of the docks.

"What warriors?" Aaron asked.

Gilmore looked sheepish and busied himself with the flowers he had picked for the altar. "Do not concern yourself with it for now, Aaron. We have much to do if you wish to join the celebrations later."

"Yes, Father," Aaron replied, watching as Calliope and Etain rounded the priests' dormitory and made their way along the shoreline to the docks at the base of Wearyall Hill. He and Rachel looked at each other and knew that something was amiss.

. . .

The water was still along the shore, reflecting a bright morning sky where bulging white clouds roamed lazily like sheep upon the hillside of the Tor.

Calliope and Etain followed the path along the reedy shoreline until they came to the dock.

"There's no one here," Calliope said.

"They are coming," Etain replied as she stared out into the mist and pointed. "They told me."

"They told you?" Calliope squinted beyond the tip of the priestess' long finger. "What do you mean? How did they-" She spotted them as the barge cleared the mist and pulled toward them. "It can't be?"

Etain smiled and nodded. "It is."

They walked to the very end of the dock together to meet the warriors sent by Lord Einion of Din Tagell.

Calliope felt her heart filled with joy and relief in that moment as she watched the barge come closer and closer, for at the prow stood a woman in brown leather riding clothes, and a long sword and dagger belted at her side. Her braided blonde hair hung about her shoulders, framing a smile as she waved to them. "Briana!" Calliope called out.

Beyond the Briton's shoulder, his arms crossed and a wide grin on his bearded face, the Sarmatian lord of his people, Dagon, also waved and called out. "We're told you need an escort, lady Pen Dragon!"

Etain felt Calliope grip her hand and she leaned closer to the girl, feeling the welling of emotion at the appearance of two of her parents' closest friends.

"Is that Antiope?" Calliope asked.

"Yes," Etain replied as they gazed at the tall, young woman behind Dagon and Briana, standing with the three nervous horses in the aft of the long barge, between the oarsmen. "She has grown much since we last saw them."

As the barge came in alongside the dock, making for the shore, Calliope noted that Antiope appeared to be even taller than her mother, and just as beautiful with long, braided blonde hair and bright grey-green eyes that took in every aspect of the world. Just from looking at her, one could tell she had the physical strength of her father, and the speed of her mother. There was a quiet kindness about her, but also a determination and alertness not found in many her age. It was obvious that Dagon and

Briana had trained Antiope well and intensely, as befitted a Sarmatian princess of royal blood, and a noble Dumnonian.

Briana leapt onto the dock from the prow of the barge as it still moved and embraced Calliope tightly. "You're safe!" she said, holding the girl who had always been like a daughter to her. "Don't worry. All will be well."

Calliope held her tightly, breathing in the mingled scent of horses, sea air, and woodsmoke.

Briana had always been like a mother to her, there for her, training her to be strong, to understand the plight which Calliope's parents had endured continuously. "I'm here now." She held Calliope back to look at her. "You're a woman now. Fully grown."

"It's been so long," Calliope said.

"I know," Briana replied. "Your mother and Phoebus?"

Calliope shook her head. "Have you seen or heard from them?"

"No, love. But I know in my heart that they are still with us. We'll find them…we'll find them…" She stroked Calliope's face and then turned to Etain and bowed to her. "Mother," she said, for the priestess had also been as a mother to her and her brother, Einion, ever since they had taken refuge in Ynis Wytrin after the murder of their father.

"It fills my soul to see you, Briana." Etain stepped forward, embraced Briana, and kissed her cheek. "Ynis Wytrin has missed your presence."

Briana raised an eyebrow. "And you?"

"You are ever in my heart. You know that," Etain replied. "I am pleased that you can still reach out to me."

"I practice as you taught me, and I am teaching Antiope to do the same." Briana watched as her daughter helped Dagon get the horses out of the barge and onto the grassy slope of the shore.

"The way of the warrior, and of the priestess then," Etain said.

"Yes, though she prefers the former, I think," Briana said proudly. "She takes after her father in that." Together they watched Calliope run to the end of the dock to greet Dagon. "Still no sign of Adara or Phoebus?" Briana asked.

"No. I cannot reach them."

"And Calliope?"

"She is strong, and very powerful," Etain said.

"She always has been."

"And she has seen Rome coming."

Briana turned to her. "So it's true?"

"I'm afraid it is as Einion was warned. Rome is hunting the Dragon's family once more."

Briana's face darkened. "Then the sooner we get her out of Ynis Wytrin, the better for her and the Isle."

Etain nodded. "The better for us all."

"Dagon!" Calliope cried out as he lifted her up.

"Little Anguis!" the Sarmatian laughed as he twirled her around the same way he did when she was a child. "My heart sings to see you!"

"And mine," she said, her face flushed as he set her down upon the planks. "I had no idea that Einion was sending you to fetch me."

"We insisted," Dagon said.

"*I* insisted," Antiope said as she left the horses cropping at the grass and strode toward them.

Dagon rolled his eyes at his daughter. "All right, yes. Antiope insisted and we agreed wholeheartedly. We were too eager to see you and this blessed isle again."

"Father, we really should set out for Din Tagell right away," Antiope said, her eyes constantly scanning the far shoreline across the water.

Dagon looked at Calliope. "We've made her hypervigilant."

Calliope turned to Antiope and smiled. "I've missed you too, Antiope." She hugged her warmly and the younger girl raised her arms to return the embrace of the girl who had always been like a distant, older sister.

"Still no sign of Phoebus?" Antiope asked.

The worry washed over Calliope's face. "He's still searching for our mother."

At this, Dagon looked to Briana who was approaching them with Etain.

Briana shook her head.

"Your mother and brother are strong, and cunning warriors in their own rights. I'm sure they're safe, wherever they are." Dagon placed his hand on Calliope's shoulder.

"Uncle Einion has sent men across Britannia in search of them," Antiope reassured. "They'll find them."

Calliope did not answer, but took Antiope's hand and squeezed.

"Come," Etain said. "You must be tired after your long journey. I've had the roundhouse readied for you. You can clean up and rest before the celebrations."

Dagon and Briana followed Etain, and Calliope and Antiope followed.

Antiope clicked and whistled and the horses immediately fell into line behind her.

"I see you have the Sarmatian way with horses," Calliope said.

"My father taught me well," the girl replied with a smile. "He also told me of the bond your father, Anguis, had with all his horses."

Calliope said nothing as they walked and the barge pulled away again to disappear into the morning mist.

Later that afternoon, as Calliope, Antiope, Rachel, and Aaron helped the priests and priestesses of Ynis Wytrin prepare for the feast, the dances, and the sacred fires, Briana and Dagon sat beneath the great oak in conference with Etain, Weylyn, and Father Gilmore.

A cool breeze rustled the branches above them, the new-green leaves fluttering stiffly.

Weylyn stared up at the leaves, eyeing their movements, heeding the warnings they offered. He remembered a story Adara Pen Dragon had told him once, of a great oak in the mountains of Graecia through which the king of the Hellenes' gods, Zeus, spoke to their priests. He liked that. *The great oak knows all...tells all,* he thought as his mind returned to the voices about him.

"We are on the precipice of a great threat," Etain said. "Calliope saw it in her vision, and the letter which Einion received from Rome confirms it."

"What exactly did the letter say? Who wrote it?" Gilmore asked Briana.

Briana stood, adjusting the sword at her waist. "It was sent to Einion through an agreed upon, secret way by a senator who was always friendly to Lucius and his family."

Dagon closed his eyes for a moment, sending up a prayer to his friend's shade. It pained him every time he heard mention of Lucius. *How I miss him.*

Briana continued. "The missives are usually sent in the wax seals about the neck of the wine amphorae that Einion imports from the senator's vineyards. The one with the message is specially marked with a small dragon in the wax."

"Ingenious," Weylyn commented.

"Essential," Dagon added. "The Emperor's mother has spies everywhere."

"Yes, that's all fine, but what did the letter from this senator of Rome say?" Gilmore rubbed his beard roughly as he stared up at Briana.

She could see he was nervous for his charges. *He is right to be.* "The senator said that the Augusta is offering full clemency throughout the Empire to Lucius, his entire family, and all of his friends and warriors if he would come to Rome to protect the Emperor as Praefectus of the Praetorian Guard."

"That is quite an offer," Weylyn said, his disbelief etched upon his face.

"And clearly a lie," Briana added, "as the senator warns."

"The Augusta is also offering the return of all of Lucius' family lands and the rebuilding of everything at imperial expense." Dagon stood and turned to look out at the water. "Rome's lies know no end."

"I don't understand," Gilmore said, his hands splayed wide. "I know we don't like to speak of it, but Lucius Pen Dragon is dead. Much as we avoid saying it. He left his wife and children over ten years ago. He is not returning."

They were all silent, but for the wind in the oak's leaves above their heads.

Weylyn stood and reached up to touch a branch, his staff taking his weight. "It seems more likely to be a trap to ensnare the Dragon's family, and his warriors."

"And to find Aaron and Rachel." Gilmore balled his hands into fists.

"I doubt that Rome knows of their existence, my friend," Weylyn added.

"And it is crucial that it stays that way, for all our sakes." Gilmore crossed his arms and looked to Etain. "That is why it is imperative that all of the Dragon's family leave Ynis Wytrin and never come back."

The high priestess looked into her friend's eyes and she felt sadness at the fear with which he wrestled in that moment. "Calliope is leaving, but Clarinda will stay. She is a lost soul and no threat to Rome. It is my duty to care for her now, until..." Etain did not finish.

Briana spied the look in Etain's eyes, heard the thought. *She is not long for this world.*

"Aaron and Rachel are safe for now, as they always have been, thanks to you, Gilmore." Weylyn put his old hand upon the priest's shoulder. "To Rome, it is the Dragon's family and friends who pose a constant threat, and tyrants such as the Emperor and his mother never rest easy when they perceive a threat. There is a paranoia that comes with such power."

"Weylyn is right," Dagon said, turning to look at them all as he stood beside Briana. "They, and my countrymen, according to the senator's letter, are being hunted. The Augusta is sending a letter to Trevor Reghan of the Lindinis Ordo to be taken to the hillfort, the place where Lucius' family last lived." Dagon paused for the memory of fire and death that had engulfed that once-beautiful home and wiped out myriad joyous memories for them all. He felt Briana's hand upon his arm, giving him strength. He cleared his throat. "The letter is a ruse and the senator urged Einion to ignore it completely. He said that men are coming to hunt the Dragon's family and friends. We need to get them all to safety, and to be ready."

"But how can you prepare against an unknown number?" Gilmore asked.

"In Calliope's vision, she saw an army," Etain said. "And so, an army we should expect."

"Have you so much faith in her visions?" Gilmore stood.

Etain met his gaze unwaveringly. "Yes. The Gods speak to her. They sent her to us."

Weylyn, who was now holding a low branch of the great oak spoke. "She is a key to the safety of this land," he said.

"And what of her brother and mother?" Gilmore asked. "How do you propose to protect them when they have willingly quit the embrace of the Isle?" He shook his head. "Some people are beyond even your protection, Etain and Weylyn."

Etain stepped toward Gilmore, her hands upon his shoulders. "We are not the only ones protecting them."

"Even the Dragon fell victim to Rome's fire and hate," Gilmore muttered.

"I'll thank you to stop speaking, priest," Dagon growled. "I for one will stop at nothing to protect Lucius' family and the men who served him. Who still serve his memory!" Dagon's white fist gripped the hilt of his long sword, the blade that had been his uncle's and which had seen endless battles. A king's sword. A sword that served the Dragon. "Tonight, we honour the Gods. Tomorrow, we ride for Din Tagell to prepare for Rome's attack." He stormed off to find Calliope and Antiope, to reassure himself that they were well.

Briana watched her husband go. "Please forgive him," she said to the elders. "It has not been easy, especially since the letter arrived. It has brought up…much."

"Should we forgive the feelings of a fervent friend and ally of the Dragon's family? Someone who cares so very deeply and has always set the welfare of others ahead of his own?" Etain shook her head and smiled at Briana. "No. There is nothing to forgive, dear. Your husband is right."

"I worry that the end is near," Gilmore said. "Can it be so, Etain? Weylyn? After we have fought so long to protect all we hold dear?" *Aaron… Rachel… This isle which has been a refuge to them and to Joseph and his followers long before?* Gilmore crossed himself and pressed his clasped hands to his head.

"Do you remember the last words you spoke to Lucius Pen Dragon before he disappeared?" Etain asked the priest.

He looked up and sighed. "I said 'the more men who hold good in their hearts and deeds, the better a place the world will be.'"

"And?"

"That there is *always* hope."

"And that is what we shall hold to, Gilmore," Etain said. "Goodness and Hope."

Briana watched as Gilmore clasped hands with Weylyn and Etain beneath the boughs of that broad and ancient oak. In the near distance, she could see Calliope and Aaron close beside each other as they leaned upon the wicker fence of one of the animal pens, watching Antiope and Rachel help prepare three cows for the purification rites. Briana watched Calliope and Aaron slowly lean against each other then, and looked to see if Gilmore spotted them.

The priest did not as he clasped hands with Weylyn and Etain.

The high priestess, however, looked at Briana and smiled. *It is so.*

. . .

As evening fell and the sky began to darken, the whole of Ynis Wytrin gathered together in the large field between the crops at the southwest precinct of the Isle. Two great bonfires had been prepared to form a wide passageway and the druid priests and priestesses of Ynis Wytrin gathered at the far end near to where the Isle ended and the vast marshes began.

Etain and Weylyn stood at the front of the gathering to begin the rites.

The high priestess wore her pure white robes, and walked barefoot. About her neck the crescent moon of gold glimmered, and her hair was loose, illuminated by the increasingly brilliant flames behind her.

Beside her, Weylyn stood grey and silent, his white beard fluttering in the wind. His head was adorned with fresh ivy and looked as though it had sprouted from his crown. He leaned upon his staff, his ancient eyes observing with pride the young acolytes before him. His warlike days were far behind him now, and he reminded himself of that as he clung to the Hope and Goodness which Etain had so wisely reminded them of.

Etain had not tried to convince Gilmore that the Christians should also join them for the purification rite. She knew that that was too much to ask. The Christians saw fire as a thing of evil in some ways and so, while she and Weylyn led the Beltane rites, Gilmore, Aaron, Rachel, and the priests saw to the preparation of the feast and the blessing of the food.

Together, Etain and Weylyn looked on all of the young faces before them, smiling and rosy-cheeked. There was assuredly hope and goodness there. The three cattle at the front lowed, their heads adorned with strands of hawthorn, primrose and lilac blossoms. Behind, three sheep and three goats were similarly adorned. The surrounding crops seemed to look on, releasing bursts of apple and pear blossom on the wind so that each petal burst into brilliant silver and white before giving itself to the flames.

Etain looked at Calliope with her aunt, Clarinda, and smiled. They were flanked by Briana, Dagon, and Antiope whom, the high priestess admitted to herself, she was so very relieved to have welcomed back to Ynis Wytrin that day. *Hope indeed.*

Etain stepped forward first to speak the words of blessing to all of them, her arms raised to the sky.

·   ·   ·

"Bless, O threefold true and bountiful,
    All of us, our loved ones, our children.
    Bless everything within this blessed isle, and in our hearts.
    Bless the kine and crops, the flocks and corn.
    From Samhain Eve to Imbolc, from Beltane Eve to Lughnasadh,
    With goodly progress and gentle blessing,
    From sea to sacred lake, and every river mouth.
    From wave to wave, and base of waterfall.

Be the Maiden, Mother, and Crone,
    Taking possession of all that belongs to us.
    Be the Horned God, the Wild Spirit of the Forest,
    Protecting us in truth and honour.
    Satisfy our souls and shield those whom we love,
    Blessing every thing and every one,
    All our land and our surroundings.
    Great Gods who create and bring life to all,
    We ask for your blessings on this day of fire."

When she was finished, Etain lowered her arms and looked upon them again. *Bless and protect them, the Dragon's family and our friends...* She turned to Weylyn who then stepped forward, his grey robes dragging upon the ground, his staff thumping on the hollow earth.

   With his arms wide, his staff in his left hand, and his eyes intent upon the world about them, Weylyn spoke, mustering a strength of voice that had long departed him.

"We light the fires of Beltane,
    sending smoke up to the sky.
    The flames purify and protect,
    marking the turn of the Wheel of the Year.
    Keep our animals safe and strong.
    Keep our land safe and strong.
    Keep those who would protect them
    safe and strong.

May the light and heat of this fire
bestow life upon us and our herd."

He lowered his arms and stared directly at Calliope, Briana, Dagon, and Antiope. "Blessings on Beltane. May there be sunlight, prosperity, and love on your journey."

Calliope met Weylyn's gaze and, for a moment, she felt a chill, for in that look she saw his own uncertainty of the time to come, the great and weighty import of the choices they all had to make. Then, beyond the Druid, at the end of the fiery gateway, she thought she could see the shimmering forms of Apollo, Venus, and Epona waiting for her.

Etain noted the look in Calliope's eyes and felt a tingle at the back of her neck. "We must proceed through the sacred fires of purification!" she called out suddenly to all of them.

Dagon, Briana and Antiope began to walk, following Etain and Weylyn on their path through the fire which was now high and bright, casting an orange glow upon the dark canopy of the sky.

Then Olwyn Conn Coran and other priestesses and novices followed with the cows, sheep and goats in tow. The animals pulled, but were urged forward between the flames, their spirits purified in so doing, even as the flowers upon their heads threatened to wilt, but remained intact once on the other side of the passageway.

People flowed about Calliope and Clarinda who remained rooted to the spot.

On the other side all turned to watch and wait for the Dragon's daughter and sister.

"Something is wrong," Briana said to Etain as she observed the faraway look upon Calliope's face.

"The Gods are here," Etain whispered, feeling her skin shiver, even in the face of the rising flames.

"I'll help them," Dagon said, stepping forward, but Weylyn grabbed his arm tightly.

"You cannot," the Druid said. "To go backward through the fire brings misfortune."

Just then, Aaron and Rachel came running up to join them.

"What is wrong?" Aaron asked Antiope, the fire illuminating his dark hair and face as he shielded his eyes.

"I don't know," Antiope replied, her eyes on the two women on the other side of the fire.

"Someone should help them!" Rachel said.

"No!" Etain replied. "The journey through the fire is their own."

On the far side, Clarinda gripped her niece's hand. "The Gods are with us, Calliope. Do you see them?"

"I do," Calliope replied. "Are you ready?"

Clarinda nodded. "Let us walk together."

Calliope and Clarinda began to walk slowly across the grass toward the flames, the walls of which seemed to rise higher and higher on either side. A deafening roar filled their ears that was almost like the crashing of the sea upon a rocky cliff. They stopped suddenly, and Clarinda screamed, her arms up above her head to shield herself.

"Stop this!" Aaron shouted, but Calliope neither saw nor heard him.

She held her aunt close, and looked up to see a flaming eagle, its talons outstretched, coming down to maul them as it screamed shrilly above the roar of the flames.

Calliope Pen Dragon pushed her aunt forward toward the safety of the Gods' arms on the other side, but then she was forced back into the fire as the eagle attacked her, talons raking at her head and face.

Above, a black shadow swept in like a fury, to circle and squawk at the eagle and all looked to see Corvus flapping his wings wildly above the fires.

"Why are she and the crow acting like that?" one of the younger priestesses asked, earning her a deadly look from Antiope who stepped forward to her father's side.

"What's happening?" she asked Dagon.

He shook his head. "I don't know."

"Just wait!" Etain urged, trying to see with all of her strength what Calliope saw, but she could not do so, for all her power.

Calliope felt her skin burning, her cloak now aflame as she crumpled in the centre of the passageway.

The eagle bore down for a final attack, and it was then that she held out her hands as though in offering.

You are not alone, she heard a voice in the distance, as though spoken from the stars themselves. She looked to Apollo, Venus, and Epona who nodded to her. Calliope pressed upward to the sky to repel the eagle, and in so doing, a fiery dragon burst forth from her palms to shield her and clash with the eagle. She screamed, her robes now burning brightly.

"I will not burn like my father!" she cried, the tears streaming from her eyes. "I will not burn!"

As the dragon coiled around her, the flames fell back and the eagle faded into the black with a screeching cry, while Corvus circled the fires, his black eyes never leaving his mistress' form.

Calliope collapsed then, and now all could see that the flames had actually caught on her.

"NO!" Aaron shouted and ran into the fires to her side.

Rachel went to go after him, but Briana caught her. "No, Rachel. He's got her!"

Aaron ripped the fiery cloak away from Calliope and swept her up in his arms, making for the other side where Dagon caught them.

The flames of the bonfires settled then, whatever had possessed them now departed, and all gathered in a circle about Calliope and Aaron.

Etain and Weylyn pressed in, just in time to see the bloody scars on Calliope's face disappear as Aaron held her to his heaving chest.

"Calliope?" Dagon said as he knelt beside them, holding her hand. "Calliope, are you all right?"

Briana held Clarinda close, for as she looked down upon her niece she shivered and wept.

Clarinda looked for the Gods who had been there, who had beckoned them into the fire, but could no longer observe them.

"All is well, matertera," Calliope said hoarsely to Clarinda. "I am safe." She looked up at Aaron then, and wrapped her arms about his neck. *How can I leave him?*

"Give them space!" Etain said aloud to all. "The Gods have spoken to her. Her trial is at an end for now, and she lives and is purified!"

"As are we all!" Olwyn shouted to the gathering.

"As are we all," the others repeated.

Dagon pat Aaron on the back. "Good lad. I'll take it from here." He picked Calliope up and turned to Weylyn. "She's fine, but we'll take her back to her dormitory to make sure." Dagon walked off, breaking from the gathering of priests and priestesses. Briana, Antiope, Clarinda, Aaron, and Rachel followed close behind them. Corvus followed from above, his black wings hidden in the night shadows.

"All is well!" Etain said to the confused acolytes. "It is now time for the feast, dancing, and celebration!" She turned to Olwyn. "See that things continue as normal. Distribute the flowers and set the May pole to spinning. All must be as normal as possible."

"Is it, lady?" Olwyn asked.

Etain shook her head.

When they were alone, Weylyn turned to Etain. "Did you note how the flames retreated when Aaron joined with her?"

"Yes," she replied. "And it both encourages and terrifies me."

Back in the room of the guest house at the foot of the Hill of the Chalice, Calliope sat up in bed, surrounded by the others, an array of worried, firelit faces.

"I'm fine, everyone. Really. Just a little singed." She tried to laugh, but it convinced no one.

"There," Antiope said as she finished dressing the burn on her wrist. "That won't take long to heal."

"Thank you," Calliope said.

Briana looked to where Aaron and Rachel stood stunned beside the bed. She wanted to ask Calliope what she had seen, but did not want to frighten the two of them. It would have to wait.

"We should go and enjoy the feast which our Christian brothers and sisters have prepared for us, no?" Calliope said.

"Should you not rest?" Aaron moved to her side to take her hand.

"I've been through much worse before, Aaron. What I need is to celebrate this wondrous night with all of you." She held his hand.

Briana smiled sideways at Dagon whose frown seemed now to be permanently etched on his face. She elbowed her husband and he snapped out of his fretful state.

"Come," Antiope said, wanting to help Calliope. "Let's get to the feast before all the food is gone." She pulled Rachel by the arm and went out.

"Come on, Aaron!" Rachel called back.

Aaron hesitated a moment at Calliope's side.

"Please go. Save me a spot. I'll be along in a moment. Briana will help me dress."

Aaron nodded, stood from his kneeling position beside her, and went to the door.

"Aaron?" Calliope said.

He turned quickly. "Yes?"

"Thank you for helping me."

"Always," he said, his voice low, before he closed the door and went out.

"You sure you're fine?" Dagon asked when they were alone with her.

"Yes. The Gods showed me something within the fire," Calliope stated, her voice now in earnest.

"What was it?" Briana asked, sitting on the bedside.

"I was attacked by a flaming eagle. It...it was terrifying and powerful..."

"We saw nothing of the sort," Dagon said. "All we saw was you moving around, waving your hands and..." He stopped, and stared at her face which had been, so briefly, raked with scars. He kissed her head. "I'm just glad you came through."

"What else did you see?" Briana pressed. "How did it stop?"

Calliope looked down at her hands which were as still as they could be. "The Gods...they... They encouraged me to try...to..."

"To what?" Briana said.

"A dragon shot from my hands to meet the eagle."

"What?" Dagon said. "A dragon?"

"I've never felt such power," Calliope said, the memory of the flames flickering in her mind, but no longer a thing of fear.

"My brother, Lucius, used to feel things like that," a voice said from the shadows on the other side. "It used to scare me and Caecilius. It definitely scared our father... It seems you have something of it too." Clarinda looked at her niece, something strange in her gaze now, more of a distance. She sat up.

"Matertera?" Calliope turned to her aunt. "Are you hurt?"

Clarinda shook her head. "No. You helped me...again...as you always do." There was guilt in her voice, regret. She continued. "Apollo has shown you something, Calliope. Do not ignore it."

"But what did the vision mean?" Dagon asked.

"I think you already know what it was, Calliope. Don't you?" Briana looked at her.

"It means that Rome's hunters are already here in Britannia to hunt the Dragon's family and friends." She looked at Dagon and Briana. "We must leave here tomorrow."

. . .

Ynis Wytrin glowed that night as groups of priests and priestesses gathered around the sacred fires that were lit in the fields, beside the crops, among the flowering orchards, and along the marshes. Atop the Tor, a great beacon had been lit where some had already begun to dance and chant in a great, seething circle.

Everyone made offerings of food, drink, and of flowers to the Gods and spirits of the land upon altars, in the hidden glades, before the ancient trees, and beside wells and streams. All this to ensure the peace, prosperity, and fertility of the land which they all honoured and loved.

The scent of the foods of the sacred feast wafted around like mist in the morning. The comforting smell of fresh oatcakes and flat breads cooked over hearth stones reached out, and the smokey note of roasting meat from the offerings made by the young Druids tantalized everyone. Bowls of cream and curds mixed with fresh thyme and honey from the hives delighted. Salads of young spring greens of dandelion, nettle, sorrel and chickweed mixed with goat's cheese and the olive oil sent by Lord Einion of Din Tagell were a pleasant treat to mark the occasion. And there was honeyed mead and ale, which the monks brewed regularly, both of which added to the easy atmosphere.

Etain, Weylyn, and Father Gilmore sat together about one of the fires near the great oak, observing the smiles upon their followers' faces, the joy that the sacred start of summer always brought with it. However, they could also hear the gossip among the young priests and priestesses, of how Calliope Pen Dragon had brought danger into the sacred fire, how she was a danger to them all.

Gilmore had listened to Etain and Weylyn as they explained what had happened, and the old priest shook his head in dismay. "The sooner she leaves, the better."

"It was a warning from the Gods, my friend," Weylyn reassured him. "That should be a comfort. We are prepared."

"Are we?" Gilmore turned to him. "If Rome were to lay siege to Ynis Wytrin, all would be lost. We are not equipped to defend ourselves."

"Rome cannot find us here," Weylyn replied.

Gilmore looked to the fiery beacon on the Tor. "You think not? Romans have eyes as much as we do."

"Rome sees only what it knows," Etain said. "It does not know of the sacred isle, nor can it distinguish between the beacon on the Tor and the thousands of other sacred fires that burn throughout the land this night."

"Still. I want the girl gone from this place," Gilmore insisted, setting his mead down, no longer enjoying the taste.

Etain reached out to him. "Did not your Christus say 'As I have loved you, so you must love one another.'?"

"I know very well what is written and what is said."

Weylyn finished chewing a piece of goat meat and set his wooden plate down. "The Christus also advised that you should not resist the evil person, but rather offer them a different path."

"And I have done so!" Gilmore protested.

"Exactly," Etain said softly, ever the peacemaker between her two friends. "Calliope Pen Dragon has taken to both our ways and yours with ease and true faith. She is the perfect expression of the peaceful co-existence of this isle. That should be pleasing to us all."

Gilmore was silent as he watched Dagon, Briana, and Calliope walk from the guesthouse to join the others at the feast.

Etain noted the dark look in his eyes. "She is goodness itself. She is born of the Light."

"Then why do I feel so afraid?" Gilmore turned to Etain and in his eyes she saw the pain that his deep worries caused him. "I cannot fail Aaron and Rachel, nor all those who have come before them, all that they too sacrificed..."

"You have not failed, my friend," Weylyn said. "All is as God wills it, no?"

"Calliope is leaving for Din Tagell tomorrow," Etain said. Her voice was low, laced with a sadness that she could not dispel. "For now, let us all enjoy this evening of peace and of love, for 'greater love has no one than this: to lay down one's life for one's friends.'"

"You quote the Apostle John to me?" Gilmore shook his head.

"I do but tell you what Calliope Pen Dragon is doing for us all in leaving Ynis Wytrin. For in doing so, in going out into the world of Rome, she may be laying down her life to keep us all safe."

Gilmore noted the glimmer of a tear that ran down Etain's cheek as she spoke and gazed out over the dark water to the world beyond.

. . .

The young night that marked the dawning of brilliant summer wore on as the flower-crowned celebrants of Ynis Wytrin finished their feasting and continued to dance about the sacred fires, their faces flushed with broad smiles. They danced about the Summer Rod, a great pole erected between the ancient oak and avenue of yews which was decorated with ivy and spring flowers.

All about the Isle, the air tingled with the mingled scents of fire and flowers, of sweat and joyfully-inebriated celebration.

At the roundhouse near the apple orchards, there was one fire where the joy seemed to be dampened. The incident at the sacred fire at the outset of the rituals had cast a pall over the evening as Calliope's friends worried about her and agonized over the time to come.

They did not speak about the threat of Rome before Aaron and Rachel, not wanting to alarm them unduly, but the glances cast across the fire told of hardship ahead.

"There is something you are not telling us," Aaron insisted as he looked about the fire. "I know what I saw when I went into the fire. I just don't know what it all means."

"It is not so easy to explain, Aaron," Briana said to the young man she had seen grow up ever since she had come to the Isle many years before.

"Besides," Dagon said, "I think Father Gilmore would prefer to explain it to you himself."

"We love our protector, Dagon," Rachel said, "but he will provide us with only one perspective." The girl leaned forward, her dark eyes lit like amber in the glow of the fire. "We are not so sheltered as you would believe. We know there are many ways to the world."

Aaron half-listened, more intent upon Calliope and her bandaged wrist. She turned to him and smiled. He then took her hand in both of his and closed his eyes.

Calliope felt a welling of affection that made her feel utterly safe, and completely hopeful. She looked upon Aaron with silent shock.

"It is Beltane," Antiope said suddenly, "and I want to dance!"

"Yes!" Calliope said, determined to enjoy her last night in Ynis Wytrin instead of dwelling in the darkness of her worries. "Come!" She pulled Aaron to his feet and Rachel joined them.

"Mother? Father? You coming?" Antiope called back.

Dagon shook his head.

"You go ahead!" Briana called to her daughter, watching as the four of them danced off to one of the fires, their laughter echoing about the nearby orchard. "You're of a dark disposition this night, my love," she said as she curled up beside Dagon.

"Can you blame me?"

"No. It is upon my mind too," she sighed. "I remember when I came here…the celebrations of Beltane were able to outweigh my worries, but now that I am older, it seems more difficult to set them aside. Even for an evening."

"I wish Lucius were here. And Barta. And so many…"

"I know."

"I worry that the Gods are toying with us all…with Calliope… And that breaks my heart. She is so good, so hopeful… I have trouble understanding how she can be so."

"She is of her mother and father's love. And that is no small thing."

They were both silent.

"I worry for Adara," Dagon said.

"As do I."

"She was so vibrant, beautiful, and strong." Dagon laughed, remembering seeing Briana train Adara years before, and how the Dragon's wife had taken to the use of a sword with ease. "I never thought so much anger would fill her." He put his hands to his face, praying that she was safe.

"Grief and loss will do that to even the strongest person," Briana said, her voice cracking.

"I pray that Phoebus or Einion's men find her before Rome does. If not, I will not rest until…"

"Stop, my love. You are angry for things that have not yet come to pass. The Gods have a plan and purpose in mind, and we will play our part."

"Which is to get Calliope safely to Din Tagell."

"Exactly." Briana wiped her eyes and watched the others dancing wildly about the fires. She listened to their laughter, their singing, and envied them all of it. She knelt in front of her husband and stroked his faded hair, her hands resting upon his bearded cheek. "For now, the Gods have given us this night of hope and love. Let's honour it." She kissed him.

"Would you have me lay you down in a wooded glade to make love?"

"I'm older now. I'll settle for the comfort of our bed beside a warm hearth." Briana smiled and pulled him to his feet to lead him inside the roundhouse.

Dagon stopped at the threshold to look back to where Calliope danced with the others.

"Let her enjoy this night. She is safe," Briana said as she pulled him inside and closed the wooden door behind them.

About the orchard fire, Calliope, Antiope, Aaron, and Rachel danced beneath the star-pocked sky of what would otherwise have been a perfect Beltane night. They did not care if the other priests and priestesses had skittered off at their coming, to disappear like frightened satyrs and nymphs in the fiery night. They spun and sweat, and sang and howled with a release of joy that succeeded, if only for a short time, in eclipsing the worries on the horizon.

Calliope spun and stomped her bare feet upon the grass, while Aaron and Rachel skipped and clapped their hands. Antiope jumped and leaped and flipped like a doe darting across a loamy field.

"How do you do that?" Rachel asked, unable to control her laughter as she watched her. "You're like a rabbit!"

"This night, I am!" Antiope yelled. "I am a rabbit! I am a deer! I am a horse flying upon a grassy plain!"

"And I'm exhausted just watching you!" Rachel laughed as Antiope grabbed her hands and spun her round and round until they tumbled head over heels, giggling.

"I don't ever remember such a fun Beltane as this!" Aaron said to Calliope as they paused to catch their breath beneath the bough of an apple tree. *She is so beautiful, kind, and brave,* he thought, even as Gilmore's story of Adam and Eve popped fleetingly into his mind. *Dragons are different than serpents.*

"Floralia was *never* this much fun!" Calliope wiped her brow where her blonde hair stuck to her forehead. She felt the sweat soaking her bandage, which had begun to unravel. She unwound the bandage to start it over anew, but when she removed it, she saw that her burned wrist was completely healed. "I don't understand. How did this-" She looked at Aaron who met her gaze.

"I could not bear to see you hurt," he said.

Calliope felt her heart tighten and set her hand upon the side of his cheek.

His eyes closed and he placed his hand over hers, pressing it harder to his face.

It was then that Calliope felt a cool breeze upon the back of her neck, and a voice that she recognized from times before, a voice that had always given her comfort.

He is good and kind... As are you... the voice said.

Then Calliope saw her.

Venus stood behind Aaron, her moon-bright eyes filled with compassion for the young woman and man before her. *It is your time, Calliope... yours and his...*

Calliope watched as Antiope tried to show Rachel how she jumped and flipped.

Rachel shook her head and opted to spin and wave her arms joyously.

"Come with me," Calliope whispered to Aaron as she pulled him away from the orchard and the fire.

"Where are we going?" he asked as they ran together, the sweat cool on their brows.

They ran among the shadows, weaving around the various fires where priests and priestesses gathered, dancing, singing, and laughing in joyful camaraderie. Some of the young men with antlers upon their heads darted off toward the Tor where the fiery beacon at its peak beckoned them. They pursued flower-clad priestesses who flitted like nymphs in the moonlight to tempt them onward into the hidden pathways and sacred avenues of oak and yew where mossy beds awaited them for the sacred rites.

Calliope and Aaron, however, ran in the opposite direction, hands clasped, each the centre of the other's world in that moment. They ran past the Christian chapel where a light glowed from within, and then past the Christian dormitory, careful not to be spotted by the priests and initiates who sat outside partaking of the mead which they had so skillfully brewed.

As they passed, Father Gilmore emerged from the chapel to observe the night, the jollity and frivolity of that ancient festival which, if he was honest, he used to enjoy much more. *Things are different now*, he thought. A niggling sense made him look to the northeast, up the hill. He sighed, and then went back into the chapel, to the prayers which he felt compelled to utter that night.

Calliope and Aaron made their way along the path that hugged the slope of Wearyall Hill, the moon their only torch in the darkness. The higher they climbed, the more brilliant the night became, fires dotting the land like thousands of fireflies in a forest.

There was playful howling on the wind in the distance as they went up, laughter, and ecstatic cries, and upon the Tor nearby, they could make out the dancing, twirling forms of the others about the great fire lit there.

Soon, the outline of the Holy Thorn came into view, quiet and comforting in the dark.

Corvus alighted upon its delicate, flowering branches, awaiting the pair, his eyes observant and blinking in the dark. He squawked when he spied Calliope approaching.

Aaron paused in his steps at that, but Calliope held onto him.

"Corvus," Calliope said to the bird as they approached the tree. "Go now. See to the others."

The crow waited a moment, as if contemplating the command, and then swept down past them and into the fiery night.

"You know, some of the priests are afraid of Corvus," Aaron said.

"People are afraid of what they do not understand. To some, he represents Death, but to me he is friendship and loyalty. He is the eyes of Apollo."

"And yet, you bring me to Joseph's sacred tree," he said as he reached out to touch one of the hawthorn's delicate, white blooms. "How do you move with such ease between worlds, Calliope?"

She noted that there was no judgement in his voice, only an openness and a respect. "I am a willing part of both worlds," Calliope replied. "Ynis Wytrin has made me so. Yes, I honour the Gods of my ancestors… *my family*. I do so with a willing heart, for they have always protected us, even at the most horrific moments of my life." She stopped herself, not wanting her thoughts, or her speech, to turn dark. "I also love and admire the Christus and his teachings of love and forgiveness, and service to others." She sat down beneath the Holy Thorn, and Aaron sat beside her, their bodies close.

"Do you not feel disloyal to one by worshipping the other?" he asked.

Calliope looked confused by the question, but she smiled and held his hand. "How can one feel anything but gratitude, joy, and hope when both faiths honour wisdom, kindness, understanding, strength, and courage? When all that is beautiful in this world is created by those deities we worship? Must it be one or the other?"

"Father Gilmore would say so."

"And yet, he too sits beneath the great oak with Etain and Weylyn, not to convert them, but to converse with them, to understand their perspectives of the world and the Gods."

"And what of...love?" Aaron said, hesitancy and hope in his voice, in the moonlit reflection of his eyes.

Calliope smiled, her eyes fixed on his. "Yes. Love, above all else, is to be honoured by us all, for what is a world without it?"

"Gilmore says the Christus taught that love for God, and love for one another are fundamental to a meaningful life."

"I agree." Calliope squeezed his hand. "What is life without love, either for one's fellow man, or a love of Venus' making. There is no life without it."

"No, there is not," Aaron said as he took her other hand.

"And this sacred night is about the love that created this world we inhabit, a love that binds us together, and which flows through all things..." Her words faded out, and just as the silence between them was about to get uncomfortable, Aaron leaned in to press his lips to hers.

Calliope felt the softness of his touch, the sweetness of his breath.

Aaron in turn felt his heart pounding rapidly, as though life pulsed in and around them both, protecting them, giving them strength and warmth. It did not feel wrong in the least what they were doing, but rather more like a welcome homecoming after forty nights in the desert.

Aaron...

A gentle voice spoke in his head, though he did not open his eyes, for in that moment, he saw himself and Calliope standing before the Christus who smiled at them with such kindness in his eyes. And beside him, clasping his hand, was a dark-haired woman of great beauty and strength, her red robes blending harmoniously with his brilliant white ones.

All is well... the woman said, her voice like a song. *Love is everything...*

Calliope felt Aaron hesitate, and opened her eyes to look upon him. She too had heard the words that spoke to his mind and heart, though she had not seen the holy couple. To her, the words had been spoken by Venus and Apollo who stood in the darkness beyond, beautiful and iridescent as they smiled upon her where she sat beneath that sacred hawthorn.

Aaron's eyes opened and met hers.

"I love you, Aaron," Calliope said.

"I love you too, Calliope Pen Dragon," he replied. "And I shall only ever love you."

In that tender moment, they kissed again and lay down together beneath that silver moon, the sound of the crackling fires of the world, the laughter and joy of all others fading into silence. Their eyes and ears, the touch and sense of their bodies revolved only about each other.

As they explored each other with a pent-up, innocent longing, all fear and worry burned away, and the world, at least for a time, was solely a place of goodness and purest joy. They felt the warmth and safety of that sacred union in those sweet moments beneath the starry sky, as petals from the sacred thorn fell upon them like blessings from above.

Calliope felt her eyes well with the happiness that engulfed them both, and as Aaron looked down at her, he kissed her tears, her cheek, her forehead and neck. Her hands clasped him close, never wanting to let go and as the intensity of their union soared, so too did the feeling of life and love within their hearts.

Gods bless us... Calliope thought to herself as Aaron kissed her again and lay down to hold her close beneath his cloak.

Together they looked up at the moon and stars, feeling that all was as it should be, that the world was indeed a place of hope and beauty, that light could overcome anything.

How can I tell him I have to go? she thought as her eyes grew heavy and she struggled to linger in the remnants of the intense sensations they had created together.

For the moment, at least, as the fires across the land faded, Calliope and Aaron's breathing rose and fell as one where they lay upon the petal-strewn grass, protected by those divinities who watched over them all.

It had been a night without dreaming for Calliope, only feeling. She had felt the rise and fall of Aaron's breathing where her head lay upon his chest. She had locked in her mind the warm feeling of his body beside hers, and the gentle touch of his fingers and lips upon her skin. There was a lingering warmth within her that she wished to hold onto.

Is this what Eden was like? she wondered, even as the morning sun's rays streaked across the living green land as though to alight solely upon them where they lay.

As Aaron began to rouse, slowly, groggily beside her, the harsh reality which the Gods had shielded her from for a night, came rushing back.

"I don't want to leave," she whispered, the sadness welling up. "But I have to keep you safe...my love..."

Aaron's eyes opened slowly, two illuminated, amber orbs that sought only her, that were filled with love for her. He sat up and kissed her, once, twice, three times. "What did you say?" he asked, his smile innocent and open.

"I said 'my love'."

"Good morning." Aaron put his arm about her and looked out over the land to see the sunlight reflecting on the mirror of the marshes, illuminating the trees, and setting all the world alight. "I feel..." he shook his head as he smiled at her. "I feel... Oh, I don't know how to explain it. All seems right. Colour and light are brighter about us, aren't they?"

She smiled. "Yes."

"And the birds are singing beautifully!"

"They are."

"We are united now, Calliope," Aaron said. "I feel it in my heart and soul."

"Yes, my love," she said, her lip trembling.

His smile faded and concern passed into his features like a cloud before the sun. "What is wrong? Do you regret what we did?"

She shook her head. "Never."

He looked relieved at that, and reached to clasp her hands. "I will marry you, Calliope. I will see to it that Father Gilmore accepts it. I had a vision…of the Christus and…and of her…" He stopped suddenly, a realization coming upon him as intensely as that morning sunrise. He smiled. "It was her! It is as it should be. It is right!"

"What is right?" Calliope asked.

"Our union." He got on his knees before her and held her face gently in his hands. "Father Gilmore will understand. He knows it is right, that the Christus would see it as right."

"You are very excited," she said, unable to keep from smiling, even as she wiped the tears away.

"Don't cry, Calliope. I will speak with him and make him see."

At his touch, she felt lighter, but there was an opposing force at work, actively seeking to take away the hope he filled her with. "It's not as simple as that, Aaron."

"What is not simple about it?" He spread his arms wide as though to embrace the world. "I love you, and you love me!" He jumped up and spun before pulling Calliope to her feet and hugging her close, covering her face with kisses. "I never thought such feelings were possible!"

Calliope looked upon him and wished with all her heart that she did not have to tell him, for she knew the pain would be too much. "There is something I have to tell you, my love. Aaron?"

He stopped spinning and came to her. "What? What is it? Anything you say to me is a joy, Calliope. Anything!"

Gods, give me strength and wisdom… "I don't know how to tell you what I must, but…"

He grew serious and stopped to listen. "What is it? You can tell me anything, you know that, don't you?"

She nodded, uncertain. She did not want to tell him. She wanted to go back to the previous night. "Aaron…"

"Yes?"

"I'm so sorry…but…I have to leave Ynis Wytrin."

The sight of his downfallen face was as a lance to her heart. His eyes faded, and his brow creased as his head shook back and forth, unbelieving of the words he was hearing. "When? Why?" he demanded, the hurt acute in the timbre of his voice.

"Today," she managed to say, her voice quavering.

"I don't understand!" He pulled away as she tried to hold his hand. "Why? Why do you have to leave Ynis Wytrin? It's not safe!"

"Rome is coming."

"Then let them come. I'm not afraid of Rome!" There was defiance in his eyes, strength in the air around him.

"You should be," Calliope said. "Rome has taken everything from me."

That hurt look. "Not everything."

"And I would keep it so," she said.

"Where you go, I too will go. I'll not leave your side!"

She could feel her eyes burning, but she knew she had to get through it, to say what she had to say. "Aaron, you cannot come with me. It is not safe for you beyond the shores of this isle."

"So Father Gilmore says!"

"And he is right." She stood there looking at him beneath the Holy Thorn, the Tor lit by the morning sun behind her. "Word was sent from a friend of my father's in Rome to Lord Einion that the Emperor's mother has sent hunters to kill my father and the rest of my family."

"Calliope… Your father died over ten years ago!"

"Please don't say that," she turned to look over the Isle.

Aaron ran around to face her. "It's true! You have to accept that! And your mother and brother have abandoned you! Just like me and Rachel, your family has been torn apart. But God has given us a chance at happiness now, in each other!" He held her fast, the glimmer of the hope they had kindled the night before reflected in his dark eyes. "Marry me, and stay here where you will be safe."

She shook her head. "If I remain here, none of us will be safe. Rome will come, and Rome will burn Ynis Wytrin to ashes. Trust me, I have seen it happen."

"Do you give in to fear and lose hope so easily?"

"No, my love," she said, wiping her eyes. "I must leave to keep hope alive for us all."

"Do not speak of hope now," he said, crossing his arms. "I have lost all of it in a matter of moments."

"You and Rachel are too important to risk being taken by Rome. You know this." She remembered Father Gilmore kneeling before her, weighed down by the burden of keeping them safe, unable to tell them the great secrets he held locked within his heart and soul. "And how can you say you have lost hope so easily? Do you mean it? Is what we shared so easily forgotten?"

"Of course not!" Aaron looked out over the land, unable to comprehend what was happening, trying unsuccessfully to reconcile the contrasting emotions that clashed so violently within him. "What if I never see you again?"

Calliope had the same worry, but she would not voice it. *I must give him strength.* "You will see me again. Somehow, when the danger is over and the threat from Rome is no more, we will be together."

He took hold of her hands then and stared into her eyes. "Swear to me, before God, that you will love me as I love you, wherever you go, whatever you do."

Calliope hugged him and spoke with such fervent emotion into his ear that he froze on the spot to listen. "Wherever I go, you will go with me…ever in my heart. I will only ever love you, Aaron. You and no one else."

He had no more words or protestations to offer, only his warmth, his embrace, and the beating of his heart which sped beneath the folds of his tunica. *God… Protect her always…* he prayed.

Gods… Calliope shut her eyes among the curls of Aaron's dark hair, inhaling the scent of him. *Keep my love safe…always…*

When Calliope and Aaron descended Wearyall Hill, the bell from the chapel was chiming, and the work of the day was already underway, the animals being fed, the crops tended, prayers being sung, and offerings being made. Smoke and incense wafted about the Isle, and herons strode slowly among the reeds at the edges of the marshes where chickadees alighted on wavering rushes.

"There you two are!" Antiope called out to them as she and Rachel walked with Briana from the oak tree toward the roundhouse. "We lost you last night!"

Rachel eyed her brother and Calliope, and in that moment she felt the weight of their mingled joy and anguish. Without a word, she went to them and held them both in her arms at once. "All will be well," she whispered. "I know it."

"Father Gilmore was looking for you, Aaron," Antiope said when she joined them.

Aaron looked at her and then to Briana.

"You'd better go and see him," Briana said. "Just to reassure him."

Aaron nodded, and turned to Calliope. "I don't want to leave you yet."

"We're not leaving until evening. It is safer to travel at night," Briana said. "Hidden from the eyes of Rome."

"Go to Father Gilmore," Calliope said to Aaron, kissing his cheek. "I'll wait for you."

He nodded and went away with his sister to find the priest.

"So?" Antiope said, elbowing Calliope. "Good night?"

Calliope looked at the younger woman. "Blessed," she said, and meant it, despite the conflicting thoughts racing through her mind, of the pain of love, and of leaving.

"I thought so!"

"Are you all right, Calliope?" Briana asked, giving her a hug.

"Yes. And no. I wish we didn't have to leave."

Briana could feel her shudder, and her heart broke for her. "You may yet see each other again."

"I don't think so," Calliope whispered before pulling away and heading for the guesthouse. "I just need to be alone... I'll see you shortly."

Antiope looked at her mother. "Do you think she didn't enjoy herself? Maybe Aaron was unkind?"

Briana shook her head. "Quite the opposite, I think." She turned to walk. "Come. Let's help your father gather the supplies. We have a long journey ahead of us. The celebrations are over."

Calliope entered the guesthouse and allowed her eyes to adjust to the darkness inside. She looked to see her aunt sleeping upon her bed in the shadows cast by the small fire in the hearth.

She stood in the middle of the room, looking at its stone walls, and remembered the last time she had had to leave that place. The memories came rushing back like assassins of her happiness.

She and Phoebus had been much younger then, scared in the face of so much uncertainty. Her father had been healing of his terrible wounds in those long ago days in that small domus, when her mother and Etain had done their best to help him. But the Dragon's anger had been great, and that had been the beginning of the splintering of their family.

Calliope wiped away the tears that fled from her eyes as she looked into the fire. *Gods…is there a world without pain anywhere?* She shook her head at the naivety of the question. She knew better.

She looked about the room to see what she should bring with her to Din Tagell, especially as she felt, somewhere deep within, that it was unlikely she would return. Apart from some clothes, and the burden of a legion of painful memories, she had little; her mother's mirror and the comb she used to brush Calliope's hair with, but nothing more.

Then, she spotted the strong box beneath the table along the wall, and went to pull it out. She gripped it and pulled so that it grated on the flagstones. Calliope turned to look at her aunt.

Clarinda stirred and sat up in her bed. She groaned and felt her head with her hand. "What are you doing, niece?"

"Packing," Calliope replied. "We leave for Din Tagell later today." She undid the box's latches and flipped the lid up, the iron hinges creaking as she did so.

"I don't want you to leave," Clarinda said, her voice deeply sad.

"I know. I don't want to go either." Calliope turned away from her to stare at the table, leaning on the edges of the box.

"Did you and Aaron spend the night together?" Clarinda asked. "It was Beltane after all."

Calliope nodded her head, but said nothing, simply stared down into the dark contents of the box.

"The pain of love is a trial that I have not had to endure," Clarinda said, coming to stand beside her.

Calliope felt her aunt's hand on her shoulder and pressed her cheek to it. "Will you be all right here?"

"No. But I'll survive, just as I have these many years. Apollo will be my light in this dark world of mine. I have that…and the memory of your uncle, Caecilius, to keep me company."

"You might be happy at Din Tagell, you know."

Clarinda shook her head. "No. It is not the place for me. I do not fit in, and the cliffs are far too tempting…" her voice faded out.

Calliope stood to look at her. "Promise me you will not harm yourself. Please, matertera! I couldn't bear to think of you being hurt."

"Oh, dear… My wounds were inflicted a long time ago, and I have learned to live with them. As to my person? Don't worry. The Gods will take me when it is my time."

Calliope wept and hugged her. "Will I ever see you again?"

"If Apollo deems it." Clarinda held her face and kissed her forehead. "You are strong, Calliope. Whatever lies ahead, you can overcome. I...I resented your father his strength, and I was envious of the love he and your mother had. I was weak, and let my jealousy get the better of me for a long time. But...that strength and love created you and your brother. You are both so very special and, truly, I know the Gods love you and watch over you. When you are feeling lost, remember the strength and love of which you are a glorious creation."

"Mama and Baba... Their faces begin to fade in my memory at times..." Calliope pulled up a stool and sat before the box.

"It is your way of avoiding the pain of memory. There are times I forget Caecilius, and our youth together in Rome feels like another lifetime. Even our days in Delphi... They are lost in a deep mist."

Calliope said nothing more, but peered into the box to pull out the scrolls of Arrian, Caesar, and Longus. So few of the scrolls from their library had survived the fires, such that to look at them only caused her sadness. She set them on the table and reached into the box again to pull out the deeds to the hillfort and estates in Etruria. "These are now useless," she muttered, setting them aside.

Then she extracted several wrapped items that were the armillae and torcs that had been her father's awards for his service in Rome's legions. She looked at each one of them briefly, ready to wrap them back up and put them back when a bronze dragon head caught her eye. She pulled at it and from out of the folds of the linen came a twisted torc, the ends of which were dragon heads.

Calliope looked up at her aunt who nodded.

"You should have it," Clarinda said, taking it from Calliope and spreading the ends enough to get it around Calliope's neck. "The Dragon's daughter." Her face grew worried. "Perhaps you should hide it? If someone sees it-"

"I'll not hide it," Calliope said quickly. The bronze felt warm against her skin, the dragon heads a comfort resting loosely against her collarbone. She then removed a larger, more delicate wrapping that revealed a brilliant corona aurea, the award her father had received when he had saved his legate's life in Numidia. She had heard the story a few times when she and Phoebus were children, her brother pressing their father for tales of battle and war. Now, however, that spoke only of a man who no longer existed. "You keep the rest, matertera," she said. "I don't want anything else."

"What of the remaining aurea and denarii?" Clarinda said, reaching in to remove two leather pouches of gold and silver coin. "You might need to bribe guards, or purchase more supplies."

"Dagon and Briana have enough. Keep these for Phoebus if… when…he returns to Ynis Wytrin. He'll need them more."

The box appeared to be empty then, and Calliope looked at the few things on the table. "So much of a life reduced to a few baubles and scraps of papyrus… It makes me sad."

Clarinda leaned forward then. "Is that something else at the bottom?"

Calliope leaned forward and reached down to feel about the base of the box, her hands grasping onto a piece of dark linen. As soon as she touched it, she remembered what it was. "It's still here…" Hesitantly, she lifted the heavy bundle and set it flat upon the table to unfold it.

The image of the dragon with outspread wings lay before them, its otherworldly metal casting a strange blue glow upon their faces.

"The Dragon," Clarinda said. "Given by the Pythia of Delphi to our ancestor ages ago at Apollo's command."

"I had forgotten about this," Calliope said, remembering the image flashing upon her father's cuirass every time he rode to battle. It was the only thing to survive the fire unscathed, unmarked. She reached out to touch it and it felt scorching. In touching it, the dragons of the past flashed in her mind, their destinies, their burdens, their loves, joys, and losses. So much pain and glory, it was too much to think on in that moment. "I cannot take this," she said quickly. "It must be kept safe here in Ynis Wytrin." She turned to look at Clarinda. "Will you see to it? You and Etain?"

"We will." Clarinda then reached down past Calliope and folded the dragon's image back up in the linen.

Calliope watched as the glow dimmed and the dragon was set back at the bottom of the strong box. *It is as a tomb,* she thought. *The Dragon is no more.*

With everything but the torc about her neck set safely back into the box, Calliope closed the lid and pushed it back under the table. She then took her large leather satchel and began to fold and pack her three tunicae in it, and her spare cloak of black wool, the white one having burned. On top of them, she placed her mother's mirror and comb, each wrapped in scraps of linen to keep them safe as they travelled.

"I should go. The day is young, but there are many to whom I would bid farewell."

Clarinda nodded. "Of course, dear. You go. Leave your satchel here for now. I'll see you before you leave."

Calliope saw that her aunt was on the verge of tears again, only these were not the usual ones for her lost brother, for her nightmares… They were of love, for her, the niece who had helped her to weather grief. "I'll be back soon," she said to Clarinda as she went out the door, her throat burning. When she was outside, Calliope heard her aunt begin to weep, and it tore at her heart. She rushed from the small domus and made for the oak tree across the green where Corvus waited in the branches for her.

"I can't do this," she said. "How can I leave?"

The crow alighted from its high perch to land on the log at her side with a squawk. He then took flight and circled her, drawing her eyes about the sacred Isle where the sun lit the blossoming orchards, and deep green avenues, the budding crops and the smokey altars.

Calliope followed Corvus who led her on a circuit of that blessed place from the Well of the Chalice to the foot of the Tor. She greeted many who had been kind to her over the years, most of whom were not aware of her imminent departure. Some avoided her and Corvus as they approached, but she did not take it as anything but a simple lack of knowing. She did not want to leave the Isle with anger in her heart.

After a while, Calliope came to the roundhouse where Aaron and Rachel sat with Dagon, Briana, and Antiope. The three horses were saddled, their saddle bags packed and waiting upon the ground to be hung over the animals' sides.

At her approach, Aaron ran to meet her. He was hesitant to speak at first, but he found his words, his hands clasping hers. "Dagon and Briana have explained what is happening."

"Then you know why I must leave," she replied, "even though it pains me so much to go. I would stay with you, but in doing so, I would be endangering you."

"And Father Gilmore explained that to me." Aaron rubbed his jaw roughly. "He underestimates me. He always has."

Calliope's face softened and she put her hand on the side of his cheek. "Father Gilmore loves you and has dedicated his life to keeping you and Rachel safe. And Dagon and Briana have done as much for me. Should we honour their sacrifices by giving ourselves over to Rome and undoing all their work?" She hugged him tightly in an attempt to ingrain the feeling in her memory. "I will not give up hope of seeing you again, my love," she whispered, and she felt him squeeze her more tightly. "Let us sit together, all of us, and break bread before we leave."

That afternoon, they sat together about the fire, eating and drinking of what was left of the previous night's feast, lingering in the feeling of togetherness for as long as it lasted.

Calliope and Aaron no longer hid their feelings for each other from everyone about them, but sat together, arm in arm, whispering sad expressions of their love and hopes, no matter how unlikely. It made them feel better to do so.

In truth, none of them could really know what future lay beyond the immediate danger posed by Rome.

After a while, with the approach of evening, Etain, Weylyn, Father Gilmore, and Olwyn arrived to join them.

Clarinda was there too, having brought Calliope's satchel from the guesthouse for her.

"The time has come for you to set out," Etain declared as she stepped up to Briana and Dagon.

"We'll leave by the marsh pathways," Dagon said. "There is less chance of us being seen."

"Very wise," Weylyn said. "Which way will you travel?"

"We'll head over the Cantaco hills and then along the coast to Din Tagell. That way, we can better avoid the fortlets along the Dumnonian border."

"You don't want to go anywhere near Isca Dumnoniorum," Weylyn warned. "Chances are the Augusta's men have landed there."

"We'll be ready if we meet them!" Antiope said, slapping the sword at her waist and crossing her arms.

Weylyn looked at the girl and imagined her an Amazon warrior of old. "You have your mother and father's fighting spirit, Antiope," Weylyn said. "May it always serve you well." Weylyn turned to Calliope then, beginning the process of farewells when no one else wished to. "And you, Calliope Pen Dragon... You are you father's daughter. Never forget that. You have been a blessing here, as you shall be wherever the Gods lead you."

"Thank you," Calliope said, "for everything."

The old Druid smiled and pat her hand. He then stepped aside for Gilmore.

The priest approached Calliope, his eyes spying the dragon finials of her torc. "I know that we have not always seen eye to eye," he chuckled briefly. "Your father and I rarely did, but it did happen."

"I know," Calliope said with a smile. "Thank you for sharing your knowledge with me. And..." Her voice dropped. "Please know that I truly love Aaron, with all my heart."

Her boldness surprised Gilmore, but rather than give in to the retort that first came to his mind, he paused and smiled. *There is love there, to be sure.* "I know," he said. "And you show that love by leaving to keep him safe." He then reached into the folds of his brown tunica and pulled out a newly carved crucifix upon a twine string. "This is for you, such that the blessings of God and all of Ynis Wytrin go with you. It was made of a piece of the Holy Thorn planted by Joseph."

"Thank you," Calliope said as she accepted the gift. "I shall keep it close."

Olwyn came to hug her then too. "Farewell. May the Gods smile on you always, and may your road lead you back to us one day." The priestess' eyes glistened in the evening sun as she stood before Calliope. "Be well."

"And you, Olwyn," Calliope said. She then turned to Rachel and hugged her close.

"You are like a sister to me," the girl said, her dark hair falling over Calliope's shoulders as they embraced.

"And you to me. I'll miss you more than I can say." Calliope felt her friend shudder. "Take care of each other," she said, turning to look at Aaron who was beside them.

"Always," Rachel replied, standing aside for her brother.

Dagon and Antiope began to fasten the saddle bags on the horses, unintentionally adding urgency to the moment with the noise.

Aaron glanced at them and back to Calliope. "I love you," he whispered to her.

"I love you too," she said, holding him close. "'Psyche mou', as my mother used to say."

"'My soul'," Aaron replied.

She nodded. "You are my light, Aaron. Stay here. Shine and be safe for me."

Gilmore turned to give them more space, his fears of her wanting Aaron to go with her now fully allayed.

"I will never love another," she said.

"Nor I." Aaron kissed her then, uncaring of all the eyes upon them.

Calliope felt her tears about to fall, and pulled gently away, her hand upon his chest, his heart. "Some day…I promise, I will see you again."

"I pray to God that that day comes," Aaron said.

Calliope then turned to Clarinda who held out the satchel to her. "I love you, matertera."

"And I love you," Clarinda said. "Go. Live and be safe. I'll be fine here. This is my place." She looked up at the darkening sky which had shifted from a pale blue to a pink and purple expanse. "Apollo willing, we shall see each other again. In this life, or the next."

Calliope hugged her aunt then, and in so doing, it was as if she were also holding her uncle, Caecilius, and her long-departed aunt, Alene. Without another word, she turned to Etain.

The high priestess' green eyes were filled with a measure of sadness, for she had cherished her time with the Dragon's daughter. She led Calliope aside a few paces, away from the others. "Ynis Wytrin will miss you, Calliope Pen Dragon. I will miss you."

"And I you, lady. You have given so much to me, to our family."

"And I will continue to do so, so long as there is breath in this body of mine." She smiled. "Continue the work I have taught you. And reach out to me once in a while, as I've trained you to."

"I will. I promise."

"If your mother and brother come to Ynis Wytrin, we will tell them where to join you so that you are together again." Etain stroked Calliope's hair.

"Is it possible that we should be together again…after everything that has happened?"

"There is always hope where there is goodness, Calliope. You are the epitome of that. You are strong, and the Gods love you." She looked down at the young woman and smiled as she held her hands and closed her eyes. "You take more than your past memories with you on the road ahead. So much more…so much hope."

Calliope looked at her and wondered of what she was speaking. She could feel the warmth radiating from the priestess, the silent blessing of protection which Etain attempted to weave about her. At that moment, she thought she could also sense Weylyn and Gilmore doing the same, each in their own ways.

"Thank you all," Calliope said at last when Etain released her hands. "May the Gods watch over you always, and protect this place."

No one replied. There was nothing more to say as each of them dealt with the rush of their own emotions.

"I would have married her, Father," Aaron said at Gilmore's side.

The old priest felt deeply for his charge then, and put a tender hand on his shoulder. "My son…in your hearts, you already are. Even I can see that." He sniffed. "God has indeed blessed you."

"Then why do I feel so much pain?"

"Because great joys are never without great sorrows. And though that may be, experiencing those joys is worth the sacrifice."

"Ready?" Dagon asked Calliope as he took her satchel and strapped it to his horse.

"No. But I will go."

"You can ride with Antiope," Briana said as she mounted up onto her brown mare. She looked to Etain and Weylyn and bowed her head.

Etain nodded, her hand on her heart. "The Gods watch over you on your journey. Send word when you arrive at Din Tagell."

"We will," Briana said.

Dagon and Antiope then mounted their own horses, and Calliope turned to look one last time about Ynis Wytrin before climbing up to sit on the fleece behind Antiope.

Dagon waved and then led the way from the roundhouse, past the nearby crop toward the path into the marshes. Briana followed, and then Antiope and Calliope in the rear, the latter craning her neck to look back at the forms of her friends.

"Goodbye," Calliope whispered hoarsely as the horse approached the path.

"Calliope, wait!" Aaron shouted as he ran across the field toward her, ignoring the protestations of Father Gilmore and his sister.

"Stop!" Calliope said to Antiope as she jumped off of the horse's back and ran toward him, tears streaming down her cheeks.

They met in the middle of the field for a final embrace, a last teary kiss, the memory of which would be their comfort in the lonely moments of their separate lives.

"I love you, Calliope!" Aaron said desperately into her hair as he held her.

"I love you too," she wept. "I always will!" She shook her head. "I would have stayed beneath the thorn with you for all time, my love."

"May God grant that we may yet again, one day," he said, kissing her hands, her cheeks, her forehead as he observed the tears upon her face. He closed his eyes and wished for her to feel happiness and strength.

And in that moment, she did.

They kissed one last time before she pulled herself away and went back to Antiope.

"We have to go now," Briana said, however reluctantly.

Calliope nodded and mounted up behind Antiope one more time. "Go, please," she begged the younger woman. "Go!" As the tears began to fall, she looked back one last time to see Aaron standing alone in the middle of the field, his arms open to the sky in prayer for her safety.

At the same time, Corvus soared high above, cawing loudly on the wind as he followed them into the marshes.

"Ride, Antiope! Ride!" Calliope cried, and the horse darted forward to leave Ynis Wytrin behind, swallowed by the evening mist.

VIII

VIRI AQUILAE SANGUINARIAE

'Men of the Blood Eagle'

The wind was blowing fiercely along the Tava estuary, its icy claws digging deep through the layers of wool and iron into the bones of the men on guard duty along the walls of Horea Classis. It was springtime in Caledonia, but it might as well have been the darkest days of winter in Etruria.

Legionary Sextus Paganus had only been in the legions for about a year, and it was not at all what he had hoped it would be. Others had told him he would travel across the Empire to exotic locations, fight primitive barbarians, and enjoy their women and riches. But nothing of the sort had happened. After his training, he had been assigned to the II Augustan legion on the far arse side of the Empire and, even then, he was not in the south where the legion was based in Isca. No. He had been sent with a detachment of new recruits from that legion to man the fortress of Horea Classis to freeze his balls off every day while watching for any possible sign of attack out of the highlands to the northeast. No fighting. No clean women. No booty, and no warmth. He could not help but think what spring was like in Etruria at that moment, with sunlight and gentle rains that did not fall sideways and stinging. Poppies and irises would be blooming everywhere on the soft hills and among the vineyards, and spring lambs would be ambling about the fields while boar darted in the forests.

Such thoughts, however, only heightened the boredom at Horea Classis.

Just two more years to go in this place until I get to visit home, Sextus Paganus told himself. But it never helped.

The fortress, at least, was large and it seemed like there had once been big plans for it to be a capital in the north. But those plans had long ago been abandoned. The eleven hectare base had everything that was required - masonry walls, a principia, a praetorium, barrack blocks, storehouses, and granaries along the Tava where supplies arrived regularly for the outlying forts and fortlets of the Gask frontier. The only saving grace was that Horea Classis had a bathhouse where the troops stationed there could thaw their frozen bones on occasion.

Sextus Paganus looked down the length of the walls to either side of him to see his fellow troopers talking with one another or even sleeping in that dim greyness of the Caledonian morning. The good thing about morning guard duty was that he could watch the porpoises diving in the estuary. Seeing them there, Neptune's children, he felt comfort in the knowledge that they brought him good luck, that the Gods had not forgotten him in that lonely northern outpost. That morning, there were several of the creatures jumping and diving in the cold and rushing water, and so Sextus passed his time watching them.

He watched one of the larger ones perform a flip the likes of which he had not yet seen. "Did you see that?" he shouted to the soldiers nearby.

None of the others answered him.

The porpoise performed another flip, and then attempted a third, but in that moment, as it hung in mid-air, a spear on the end of a long rope pounded into the creature's smooth body with an explosion of blood.

Sextus Paganus felt his heart scream first, and then his mouth. "NO!"

The other guards took notice at last and all of them turned to see the lumbering form of a black-hulled oneraria. On the deck, several men roared with laughter as they took bets on who could skewer the swift porpoises as they rushed before the prow. Above the men, the square sails at the front and on the main mast were also black. Upon the main sail was what appeared to be a crimson aquila and nothing else.

Sextus squinted, trying to ascertain who was on the ship, suspecting that it was someone important. No mere merchant ship bore the aquila of Rome, and yet, it looked nothing like a vessel of the navy. He had seen a lot of ships come and go from Horea Classis, but never one such as that.

Down the wall, someone sounded a cornu, and the men stood at attention.

"Bastards!" he shouted at the ship as the sails dropped and the oars were thrust out to guide it to the docks of the fortress. He looked sadly at the blood in the water where the porpoise's corpse was dragged behind the ship by the spear attached to a rope. Gazing down on the body was the figurehead of a black snake with painted red eyes that appeared ready to devour the poor creature.

Sextus felt rage build inside him, and wished he could spear the whoresons who had perpetrated the blasphemy. Unable to stopper the anger boiling inside him, he left his post and descended the stone stairs from the top of the walls to go out the Porta Decumana that faced the estuary. He looked around for the commander or one of the tribunes, but they were nowhere to be seen. "Probably still sleeping," he muttered to himself.

He spotted his centurion, Rutilius, marching out to meet the ship with a contubernium of men who had been manning the east gate of the Via Principalis. "State your business!" the centurion shouted at the ship in his loudest parade ground voice as it approached a berth.

The men on the ship did not answer. They stood there looking down on the centurion and his men, arms crossed, no uniform to speak of but all black tunicae, bracae, caligae, and cloaks. Their weapons were new, however, the hilts and pommels of the gladii glinting in the grey light.

"Tell me who's in charge, or no one is setting foot on that quayside!" the centurion shouted, his vinerod pointing at the group.

"I am in command!" came a steady voice from the stern of the ship.

"And who are you?" the centurion asked as he noted the black bull's hide cuirass, adorned with a bronze eagle that was so dark, it was almost invisible. "What's your business in Horea Classis?"

Sextus Paganus arrived just then to join the others, his breathing rapid as he got closer to the men from whose ship the mutilated porpoise hung.

The leader of the men on the ship stepped onto the railing and jumped onto the dock to stand in front of the centurion.

"I asked you a question," Centurion Rutilius growled. "Why are you here?"

"I'm here on imperial business that you do not need to know, Centurion," the man said. He then produced a leather tube and pulled out a papyrus scroll with the Emperor's seal upon it. "Can you read?" The man stared at him. "This states that you are to give me whatever I ask for. No questions."

The centurion grabbed the scroll and read. When he finished, he looked into the man's eyes and felt a cold brutality in that icy stare. "It says here you are a Praetorian detachment."

"Yes."

"What are Praetorians doing so far north without the Emperor?"

"I said no questions."

"May I at least know who you are so that I may tell Tribune Valera? He's in command of Horea Classis at the moment."

"I will answer only that," the man said, brushing back his black cloak to reveal the crimson eagle upon his chest, and the gladius and pugio at his sides. "I am Aurelius Nemesianus, commander of the 'Blood Eagle' century of the Praetorian Guard, and I'm not in the mood to be waylaid. We have urgent business to carry out. Now…from the state of this place, you seem not to be very strict in your duties, so now is not the time to be stringent."

The centurion looked back as his men, his face reddening by the second beneath his horizontal crest. "You mind your mouth, Praetorian," he growled.

"I think not," Nemesianus replied with disdain. "I've given you my name, and as you can see by my imperial orders which you have read, I report only to the Emperor and Augusta. You are to provide me with all that I require for my mission. No questions. No problems." Without waiting for a response, Nemesianus turned to look up at his men on the ship. "Optio Evander!"

"Yes, sir?" a bulky Praetorian with shorn blond hair replied from the deck.

"Start unloading the weapons and supplies! Take the men to the southern gate."

"And what is at the southern gate?" Centurion Rutilius demanded.

Nemesianus huffed. "That is where we will be waiting for the supplies you shall bring us."

"What supplies do you need?" The centurion's voice was less defiant than it had been.

"Why did you kill that porpoise?" Sextus Paganus shouted from several paces away, behind the waiting contubernium of men.

Nemesianus glanced at him, but ignored him and turned back to the centurion. "We require forty-one horses and two covered wagons drawn by strong mules. Nothing more, as we are moving quickly."

"Forty-one horses?" the centurion laughed. "That's almost our entire herd! The fortress will have none left if you take that many!"

"That will be your problem to remedy, Centurion, not mine. I should have thought Horea Classis would have been better equipped."

"I...I will need to speak to Tribune Valera."

"You do that." Nemesianus waved his hand toward the fortress walls. "Just be quick about it."

"I should cut you down for your arrogance, Praetorian," Centurion Rutilius said.

"That would be a mistake," Nemesianus said casually as his men assembled behind him, a great black shadow covering the quay. "You see, whereas you are armed with beardless boys from the backwaters of Rome's empire, my men have seen action many times over. They've been to war, and to prison, and have enjoyed both. Why, even my optio here, Evander..." he indicated the bulky blonde one behind him, "...he's even been a gladiator for a spell. He was too violent for the Praetorians, so he enlisted at the Ludus Magnus in Rome to keep his fighting skills sharp."

"And to pay off some gambling debts, sir!" Evander blurted out.

Nemesianus smiled over his shoulder. "Yes, well... Boys will be boys." He turned back to the centurion. "All that to say, you wouldn't have a chance, Centurion. The forty of us could no doubt take this fortress ourselves, and this piece of papyrus with the Emperor's seal upon it means there would be nothing you could do about it." Nemesianus eyed the young men behind Rutilius. "Any more stupid questions?"

"I'll go speak with the tribune while you assemble your men outside the southern gate."

"Good dog," Nemesianus said.

Rutilius made to draw his blade, but the slither of forty more behind Nemesianus stopped him in his tracks.

"Don't," Nemesianus hissed.

"Back to your posts!" Rutilius barked at his men as he turned and marched back toward the fortress to find his tribune.

When they were gone, Nemesianus turned to the rest of his men. "Well, that was fun!"

They all laughed and began to hoist their satchels and several chests which they proceeded to carry toward the southern gate in a long line of march like a black serpent slithering out of the sea.

Nemesianus turned back to the ship where the captain and crew waited for orders. "Captain Glaucus!"

"Yes, sir?" a leathery old greybeard appeared at the prow.

"You can head back south to join Captain Amphion at the port of Isca Dumnoniorum. Wait for word from us there."

"How long will we have to wait, sir?"

"The hunt shouldn't take long, but if it does, you'll be paid for your time, never fear."

"As long as there's gold and silver in it, we'll be waiting!" The captain rubbed his beard and laughed, his white teeth contrasting with his tanned skin.

"Oh, there will be," Nemesianus said. "Speaking of which, I've left you and the crew a little coin to tide you over. It's in a chest in the hold."

"Your servant, sir!" Captain Glaucus bowed. "Happy hunting!"

Nemesianus laughed and turned to go join his men when he was stopped by a young legionary who stood in his way. "Out of my way."

Sextus Paganus did not move, but stood there facing the Praetorian, his eyes glancing at the rope dangling at the stern of the black oneraria.

"You're cute, but you're not my type. Go bugger your friends in the barracks." Nemesianus went to go around the trooper, but the lad moved to block his way.

"Why did you allow your men to kill that porpoise?" Sextus demanded.

"Excuse me?" Nemesianus' face darkened.

"The creature did nothing to you and you killed it! Even after Neptune brought you here safely! You've brought ill omen upon all of us by doing that."

"You like to watch the porpoises play, do you?" Nemesianus growled.

"The Gods will damn you to Hades for what you've done, you Praetorian bastard!" Sextus, possessed of a fierce need to strike the man who had allowed the murder of the one thing that gave him joy in that place, swung hard at the Praetorian's head.

Nemesianus caught the young man's wrist and without a thought, drove his pugio down into his neck. "I've been to Hades already. And I don't care for it." He then pulled the gasping, choking legionary to the ship's stern. "You like porpoises? Join him!"

Nemesianus withdrew his blade and shoved the trooper's body over the side of the quay into the bloody water with the dead porpoise. "He can lead you to the Underworld."

"Hey!" one of the soldiers atop the walls shouted. "You killed him!" He pointed at Nemesianus whose only answer was to lift the papyrus scroll with the imperial seal for him to see. The soldier disappeared back inside the fortress.

"Time to hunt dragons," Nemesianus muttered as he wiped and sheathed his pugio and set off to join his men.

Rain set in as Nemesianus and his forty men rode west to join the Gask Ridge frontier road. It was cold and dreary, and matched the mood and dark purpose of their mission.

Nemesianus rode in silence, his hard eyes raking over the landscape as if he expected to find his quarry around any rock, or tree. He had little hope that he would find those he was looking for, but was happy to go through the motions if it meant he was free and outside in the world instead of locked up in the Tullianum in Rome. And now, he could do what he wished, and no one could touch him for it. He patted the leather tube with the pass which hung beneath his cloak.

Nemesianus remembered the splash the soldier had made when he dropped his body into the water. "Porpoise boy," he mused.

"What's that, sir?" Evander asked.

"Nothing."

He remembered too the look on the tribune's face when one of the troopers rushed to tell him about the killing. The tribune and the centurion had been helpless to do anything as Nemesianus waved the papyrus with his orders in their face.

It had been with great reluctance that the tribune at Horea Classis had handed over so many horses, as well as the wagons and mules.

Nemesianus had demanded extra food rations too, for good measure. Before leaving Rome and the port of Ostia in their two black onerariae, they had been well equipped with coin, weapons, food and wine. The rest, they had commandeered from Horea Classis and the truculent garrison.

The main disappointment, though not unexpected, was that the tribune, centurion and others had no idea of the whereabouts of the Dragon or his men, even though they had apparently been highly active in the campaigns against the Caledonii. There had been, however, a reverence among the men when they spoke of the Dragon Praefectus who had once fought for Rome, something which Nemesianus found difficult to reconcile with the frail and wounded evocatus, Lucius Pen Dragon, whom he had once known. Most assumed that the Dragon and his men were long dead.

What Nemesianus did discover was the location of the fort which the Dragon had occupied along the ridge, a place called 'Bertha', known among the older troops as 'The Dragon's Lair'.

"What is the plan, sir?" Evander asked as they rode at the head of the column. "Do you think the Dragon, his family, or what's left of his men are here in Caledonia? I could think of nicer places to hide across the Empire than here!"

"Quite," Nemesianus answered, scanning the mist that blanketed the distant hills. "I doubt they would be welcome here, even among the Venicones. From what we've heard, the Dragon and his men thoroughly trounced these tribes. I should think they would want blood more than we do!"

Evander laughed. "Do you really think so?"

"Not really." Nemesianus turned in his saddle to look back at the men. "These Praetorians are the worst sort of men… That is, exactly the sort of men we want. They've all been in trouble because they seek violence. The problem is that guard duty on the Palatine Hill provided little occasion to indulge those needs."

"That's why I became a gladiator!" Evander said proudly, patting the gladius at his side.

"Well, maybe you are the most hungry…after me, that is." Nemesianus shook his head. "No. I don't think the Dragon - if he is alive, which I doubt - is in Caledonia. Nor would his family or his men be here. Yes, the older troops along the Gask Ridge might have given him aid, but you've seen them, yes?"

"There's not much to see," Evander said. "This is the armpit of the Empire. Rome seems to have given up here in Caledonia, and so have the troops stationed here."

"Exactly. If they harboured the Dragon, the tribes would have broken the peace and slaughtered them all to get at him by now. No, we need to go where the Dragon once had allies."

"To the south, you mean?"

"Yes, but first we need to check the forts and signal towers along the Gask frontier."

"That will take some time. Precious time we don't have."

Nemesianus looked sidelong at Evander. *The man is not intelligent, but he is brutal. That's good at least,* he thought. They came to a road where the river Tava narrowed and a bridge spanned it to head north. Nemesianus reined in. "Time to split up," he said to Evander before holding up his hand to halt the column.

"You going to tell me the plan yet, Nemesianus?" Evander asked, wiping the rain from his face.

"Yes," Nemesianus replied as he looked along the line of riders. "Men of the 'Blood Eagle' century!"

They cheered, if not with enthusiasm, then with grim determination and a longing for the promised rewards Nemesianus had spoken of on the ship.

"It's time to get to work!" he shouted. "We have a lot of ground to cover in looking for Lucius Pen Dragon, or Lucius Metellus Anguis, as he was known in these parts, Praefectus of the Ala III Britannorum Quingenaria Sarmatiana..." he paused and leaned over to Evander. "What a mouthful!"

The other man laughed.

Nemesianus looked around the muddy area of that crossroads to ensure no one else was around, and then turned back to continue addressing the men. "While Centurion Carcer and Tarchon are beginning their search in the south from Isca Dumnoniorum northward, we will begin here in the north and sweep southward."

"It'll take forever!" one of the men grunted.

"Yes," Nemesianus said. "That's why we're going to split up into smaller groups. That way we can cover more ground. We are in enemy territory here, so be on the lookout. You've all seen the map of the frontier here. There are many forts and signal towers, some still in use, most likely not. We're going to split up into ten groups of four. I'll make for The Dragon's Lair with Rhesus and two others. Evander will make for the fortress of Inchtuthil with Cavillor and two others, and then the rest of you will head south along the frontier to Fendoch, Alauna etcetera. I don't care who goes with whom or to which forts. Just move quickly and quietly. If anyone gets in your way, kill them discreetly. If you see an opportunity for easy booty, or even fun with a Caledonian whore, then you're welcome to it."

There were some scattered cheers and nods of approval among the men.

"If you see or hear about anything or anyone related to the Dragon, his family, or his men, you are to send one rider with word to me while the rest pursue the lead. Whomever it is, tell them that the Emperor is looking for the Dragon, and that he is needed urgently in Rome. We don't want them to know what we are really up to."

"And what is that, sir?" Segundo, one of the decana, asked.

"Officially? To proffer the Emperor's offer."

"And unofficially?" Rhesus, another decana, asked.

"To send them all to Hades."

More nods from the men.

The rain began to abate then, and though the clouds did not cease to press down upon them, Nemesianus took it as a sign. "You see? Some god favours our hunt!" He looked the men over. He could see they were ready, eager to get going. Whether they followed his orders or not remained to be seen, but he was not necessarily looking for an orderly march across the whole of Britannia. *No. It's more like unleashing rabid hounds on the hunt in a forest,* he thought. "Choose your groups and pick your destinations!" Nemesianus commanded. "And when you've checked them out, we'll meet at the fort of Camelon near the crossing of the Bodotria and head south from there."

The men formed themselves into groups of four as commanded and then, after referring one more time to the maps, they set off in various directions.

"Wagons!" Nemesianus called to the drivers. "You stay with me!"

"Yes, sir!" the drivers replied.

"Evander," Nemesianus said. "You and Cavillor will travel to Bertha with me and Rhesus, and then go on to Inchtuthil from there."

"Whatever you say, sir."

Nemesianus watched as the groups of riders disappeared into the distance in the direction of the glens and the wall of highlands where the lands of the Caledonii lay. "Survival will be their first test, I suppose," he muttered before kicking his horse toward the crossing of the Tava estuary and the fort of Bertha.

The ride was slow going, for the roads had long ago fallen into disrepair, and the bogs and burns dotting the lowlands were more numerous than expected, made worse by the days of rain they had experienced since arriving in Caledonia.

No reports came back to Nemesianus of any word or sightings of Lucius Pen Dragon, his family members, or his men. The forts and signal stations of the Gask Frontier were run down and dilapidated, the few men still stationed there more interested in gambling and mingling with the locals who, in some instances, had formed small vici outside of the timber and stone walls.

In every place, any discreet mention of the Roman Dragon or his men was met with either silence, awe, or ignorance on the part of Rome's remaining troops, or disdain and spittle from the local tribesmen.

The common theme everywhere was that no one had seen or heard tell of the Dragon, his family, or his men in years. It was widely rumoured that the Dragon was dead, and that his tortured soul still haunted the bloody glens where he had laid waste the forces of the Caledonii, Selgovae, Maeatae and other tribes that he had defeated on behalf of Rome.

Hate and fear, it seemed, outlived the man himself, even though the blood, gore, and bones of battle had long ago been swallowed by the hills and bogs of that miserable land.

When they arrived at the place called Bertha, the fort known as 'The Dragon's Lair', they found that that too was abandoned. The remains of the fort, which lay at the confluence of two rivers, were crumbling and over-grown with bracken and moss. At the bottom of what had been the gates, the white caps of skulls could be seen among the sprouting ferns, the spikes that jut from the walls above having lost their grisly ornaments to time.

Evander shivered on his horse which he struggled to settle. "I don't like it here, sir."

"Are you afraid of a few shades, Evander? A man as big as you?" Nemesianus laughed.

Evander looked back at the other men with them.

Rhesus and Cavillor appeared just as uncomfortable, as did the men driving the wagons.

"Perhaps we should make offerings to the Gods while we're here?" Evander whispered. "Janus can guide us and Mars can protect us."

"You can if you wish," Nemesianus said with disdain, "but I exhausted all conversation with the Gods in the Tullianum a long time ago." He then kneed his horse forward toward the gate. The oak doors had fallen off their hinges and the wood now rotted in the incessant damp that engulfed everything. "No one's been here for years." Nemesianus turned to look back at the men when a loud scream burst from the gateway.

A boar exploded from the undergrowth and charged Nemesianus' horse which reared violently, throwing the rider down.

As the beast turned on Nemesianus and was about to charge, his enormous head swinging his tusks, the Roman drew his blade to meet it.

The spear from Rhesus took the animal in the rear, making it pause long enough to allow Nemesianus to rush in and slash its thick throat.

The animal wailed and was soon silenced, the tang of the blood seeping from its neck and permeating the air as it ran into the rivulets of water filling the ditches.

Nemesianus gathered himself quickly and got to his feet. "Looks like we'll be dining on boar tonight!"

Rhesus and Cavillor laughed nervously, but Evander shook his head.

"Bad omen, sir. We shouldn't be disturbing this place."

"Do I need to get someone else to be my second?" Nemesianus suddenly shouted at the former gladiator. "Next you'll tell me you're afraid of the rain!"

Evander looked down from his horse at Nemesianus. *I could just kill him and say the Caledonii did it,* he thought. But somehow, he knew that Nemesianus would not be that easy to kill. *He couldn't have survived in the Tullianum for over ten years without some dark god protecting him.* "Apologies, sir," Evander said. "It won't happen again. You can count on me." The words tasted foul in his mouth, weak, but he knew that if they were successful in their mission, he would never need to worry about coin again.

"Rhesus!" Nemesianus barked.

"Yes, sir?"

"Gut that thing as quickly as you can and hang it from the wagon."

"Yes, sir," the man said before sliding off of his horse and drawing his pugio.

"Well, Evander?"

"What, sir?"

"You and Cavillor better get going if you're to make Inchtuthil before dark."

Evander and Cavillor looked at each other and then back to Nemesianus. "But it will be dark long before we reach the fort!"

"Yes. I suggest you take turns on watch so that the Caledonii don't cut your throats in the night."

They made no response at first. The only sound was the rippling of the rivers and the slurping cuts Rhesus made as he went to work on the boar.

"That's an order!" Nemesianus shouted, startling the horses.

"Yes, sir," Evander grumbled as he and Cavillor turned their horses and continued on the broken road that led north from Bertha to the once-great legionary fortress of Inchtuthil.

Nemesianus watched their backs as they rode. *I wonder if they'll live out the night?* he asked himself.

It was the same story as Nemesianus, Rhesus and the wagons travelled south again from Bertha to the fort at Camelon - the locals and remaining garrison troops whom they questioned along the frontier had not seen or even heard of the Dragon or his men in years.

Nemesianus was frustrated, but not surprised. "I knew this would be the case," he said to Rhesus and the others who had joined him at Camelon on the third night. "These lands are not friendly to the Dragon. He was their persecutor, not their friend." He looked at the men who stood around him in the run-down principia of the old fort. Water dripped from the ceiling, and black mold had formed about the walls. It stank, but it was better than bivouacking out in the open.

None of the men had reported engaging with the enemy, and when they had helped themselves to the locals' food and women, there had been no resistance. Neither had there been any gold.

"This land is dead, sir," a black-haired man named Dis said. "It's like they've given up."

"I wouldn't say that!" a big voice said at the open doorway of the principia.

Nemesianus looked beyond the men to see Evander and Cavillor come in, their cloaks dripping with rain water. "So, you're not dead!" he said.

The men laughed.

Evander shook his head. "No, sir, but the few men who were stationed at Inchtuthil were. We found their bodies nailed to the walls and beams inside the fort."

"How many?" Rhesus asked.

"Forty or so," Evander shrugged. "We didn't linger long enough to count them all. But there were definitely no survivors."

There were some worried grumblings, but Nemesianus put up his hands.

"That's enough!" he said. "Are you surprised? Rome has given up on Caledonia."

"Should we engage the Caledonii?" Segundo asked. "Show them some Praetorian steel?"

Some of the others growled their agreement at this.

"No!" Nemesianus roared. "Have you forgotten why we're here? We're here to hunt down Lucius Pen Dragon - *the* Dragon - his family, and his friends."

"But no one knows anything about him, his family, or his men's whereabouts!" Evander said.

"That is true...north of Antoninus' wall. But to the south, it may well be different."

"Carcer and his men are probably having more luck," Dis said.

"And we will meet up with him soon enough," Nemesianus added, "but not if we sit around here debating."

"What do you propose?" Evander asked.

Nemesianus walked into the middle of the men and looked down at the broad map of Britannia which lay spread out on a rotten wooden table. He pointed to Camelon, their current location. "Tomorrow, we head south to Antoninus' wall, cross it at the last fort of Veluniate, and then continue east to here." He pointed to a spot on the map.

"What's there?" Rhesus asked.

Nemesianus crossed his arms. "If we've only found enemies of the

Dragon in Caledonia, or peasants or troops too green to remember anything useful, we'll go to where we know he has, or *had* friends."

"And where is that?" Evander bent over the map, his hair dripping onto the surface.

"What's there?" Dis asked, looking at where Nemesianus finger had pointed to.

"The hillfort known as 'Curia'."

"Who is there and how can they help us?" Evander crossed his arms and stared at Nemesianus.

He's holding a grudge, Nemesianus thought. *We'll see about that.* "That is the main fortress of Rome's allies in the north: the Votadini."

"Our allies?" Rhesus scoffed. "You mean the ones we brought the silver for?"

"Some of the silver," Nemesianus corrected. "But yes."

"Why waste time there?" Evander asked. "We should ride south to meet up with Carcer and the others."

"Because, Optio, apart from being a supposed ally of Rome, Afallach, Lord of the Votadini, was also a good friend of Lucius Pen Dragon."

The men were silent at that.

"We may well find some of the Dragon's men in his court." He walked around the table to face Evander. "But by all means, we can skip it and ride south if that is what *you* prefer, Optio."

"I was just saying-"

"Too much!" Nemesianus drew his pugio faster than anyone could have imagined, and set it against the pulsing vein in Evander's neck. "Either you ride with us without complaint, and follow my orders, or we can nail *your* body to the gates of Camelon as a decoration for the Caledonii to admire!"

Evander met Nemesianus' gaze evenly, but the others could tell that he was afraid. They all were. Their leader was capable of anything and attached to nothing. He was dangerous. "Of course I'll ride with you, sir. Wherever you say."

The blade withdrew a little, leaving a thin, bleeding line on Evander's neck.

"Don't make me regret recruiting you," Nemesianus hissed into his ear before standing back, his pugio sheathed once more. "Dis and Cavillor, you and your men are on first watch. The rest of you, get some rest. Tomorrow we pay a visit to the Votadini."

The next day, Nemesianus and his men of the Blood Eagle century rode south to the line of the Antonine Wall. The morning was crisp and clear with sharp clouds cutting across the sky above the vastness of the Bodotria estuary. The remnants of the wall undulated with the land, its ten foot high earthen ramparts rising and falling between the abandoned forts and fortlets that were connected by the military road on the southern side of the wall.

"There's no one here," Dis commented to Segundo as they rode two by two. "It's deserted."

"After Severus' campaign, they pulled back to the wall built by Hadrianus," Nemesianus said over his shoulder. "These lands are now held by the Votadini."

"Then where are they?" Segundo asked. "There's not a peasant in sight!"

"Oh, they're here," Nemesianus said more quietly. "You can see how they've scavenged the stone and timber from the forts."

They continued to ride along the road flanked by thick green grass and bursts of yellow gorse. Several hours later, as day gave way to evening and the sky swirled in shades of grey and purple, the terrain flattened as it fell away to the shores of the estuary and the final fort of Veluniate.

The fort that formed the eastern terminus of the wall was abandoned like the others, though the remains of the principia and barracks provided decent enough shelter for the night.

"We'll camp here, and then set out for Curia tomorrow," Nemesianus said as he dismounted in the crumbling courtyard of the principia. He kicked an old bucket against the wall where its rotten wood crumbled. "We're moving too slowly."

"The terrain looks more level from here to the east," Evander said as he approached him a little hesitantly, his hand on the hilt of his pugio beneath his cloak.

"If you're thinking of killing me when my back is turned, you'd better not miss."

Evander removed his hand. "Don't worry, Nemesianus. It didn't even cross my mind."

Nemesianus turned to face him. "Good. It would be a waste for us both when the rewards for carrying out this mission are more than we can fathom."

"So you say. Do you even trust the Augusta to keep her word?"

Nemesianus shrugged. "Maybe. The fact that she pulled me out of that cell gives me hope. She just wants the job done. If we can bring proof of the Dragon's death, or indeed drag his family back to Rome in chains, then I think we'll get our rewards."

Indeed, every night as he lay down to sleep, since his conversation with the Emperor's mother, Nemesianus had been dreaming about the reclamation of his lands, his wealth, and the power he would wield over the family who had abandoned him. It was what kept him warm during those cold Caledonian nights. That, and the thought of killing anyone close to the Dragon, the same as his brother had been cut down.

"Come with me," Nemesianus said as he led Evander out of the principia to a staircase that led to top of the eastern wall. "Look." He pointed along the shoreline to a dark patch in the distance. "According to the map, the Votadini fortress of Din Eidyn lies there. We'll ride past it tomorrow and make for Curia from there."

"You want to ride in the open?"

"Yes. Why not? They are Rome's allies, and we're here on behalf of Rome's emperor. Better they see us."

"I wonder what kind of welcome we'll get."

"A cold one, I'm sure." Nemesianus turned to face west along the wall, taking in the cracked remains and tiled rooftops of the fort, the empty granaries, the cold bathhouse, and the silent workshops. "All for nothing," he muttered.

That night, camped inside the broken walls of Veluniate, Nemesianus and his men listened to the howling of a gale on the wind outside along the shores of the Bodotria. It whistled as it tore through every bush and rounded every squat tree and remnant of Rome's walls.

At one point in the night, Nemesianus thought he heard the sound of thunder come and go, but the lack of lighting told him otherwise, as did the men on watch who reported seeing shadows speed across the fields to the east.

"This land is riddled with shades!" one of the men from the watch reported to Nemesianus and Evander the next morning as the horses were saddled. "They prowled around us all night!" The man, a hardened criminal, shook as he spoke.

"I've no need for cowards in this century," Nemesianus said as he got in the man's face. "If you're not up to the task of facing what's to come, you can fuck off back to Rome with nothing!"

"No, sir. I...I'm fine. It's just that-"

"Just what? Those?" Nemesianus pointed to the track that led east. There in the mud were the prints of horses' hooves. "Shades you say?"

"But, sir. I didn't hear anything but-"

Nemesianus' fist connected with the man's jaw, sending him to the ground. "You didn't hear ten or more horses riding past our position?" Nemesianus' face was red, a vein pulsing on the side of his right temple. *I can't allow this incompetence!* he thought. *We won't make it south at all if they keep this up!* "Help him up!" he ordered Evander.

The gladiator dragged the trooper to his feet, steadying him until his head stopped spinning. "Just tell him it won't happen again," he whispered to the man.

The man nodded. "Sir...sir...I made a mistake. It's this strange land! I promise, it won't happen again, sir!" The man stood on his own now, his chin up, regret in his eyes as he looked upon his Praetorian commander.

Nemesianus looked back at the man and smiled with pursed lips. "I know it won't." He then drove his pugio into the man's chest, the blade finding its way expertly between the ribs to puncture his heart.

Evander gasped as the body fell backwards into his arms, the blood seeping rapidly out of the wound in its chest.

"May the Goddess Nemesis accept our offering this day," Nemesianus said as he looked down on the body which his optio held. He looked up at the men who surrounded him, some their eyes wide with shock, others curious, and others unsurprised, for the man's incompetence could have gotten them all killed. "Morning sacrifices are done now!" Nemesianus shouted. "Let's go!" He turned to Rhesus. "Raise the vexillum for the journey. We want the Votadini to see that Rome is here!"

. . .

Again, it was a grey morning as they rode in silence eastward, watchful for the horsemen who had tracked them in the night. Every man wondered how long it would be before the Votadini showed themselves, and whether they would be received as friends, or attacked as foes, for in that faraway land at the edge of the Empire, anything was possible.

It did not take long. As the men of the Blood Eagle century passed by the smoke-crowned fortress rock of Din Eidyn, a sound like thunder came down from on high as though descending the heights of Olympus. Soon, two turmae of riders were making their way toward them, a forest of hastae lance shafts surrounding a high vexillum bearing a white horse on a red background.

The men drew their gladii and spathi, but Nemesianus put up his hand. "Hold!" he ordered.

"Are you joking?" Dis said, his panicked eyes looking all around as they were surrounded. "I'll not be cut down like a dog!"

"I said HOLD!" Nemesianus burst out. "These are Rome's allies!" he shouted, loud enough for the approaching horsemen in front to hear him.

The men lowered their blades and waited as a path opened up and a rider and horse, both in bronze scale armour, approached beneath the fluttering vexillum of the white horse held by another rider behind him.

"Salve!" Nemesianus said to the leader.

The rider, whose horse was larger than those of Nemesianus and his men, reined in a few paces from the Romans. A spatha hung from his side, and a gladius was strapped to his saddle horn. The bronze scales that covered him jingled like a bag of coins as they shifted, and the cavalry helmet atop his head was ornamented with bronze laurels about the crown, and horses on the cheek guards. He held his long hasta lance easily in his right hand, its tip glinting in the morning sun.

Nemesianus looked around at the riders who outnumbered them and then back at the leader, an older man he observed, but not one to be underestimated. "I said, salve!"

"I heard you," the leader replied. "Who are you and what are you doing in the lands of the Votadini?"

"You mean Rome's lands?" Nemesianus said.

The man was silent a moment and shook his head, a slight smile on his lips. "I mean the lands of the Votadini. Rome has withdrawn behind the wall of Hadrianus. We keep the Empire safe on this side of the wall."

"So you are loyal to Rome?"

"We are Rome's allies."

"Is that the same thing?" Nemesianus pressed.

The leader did not answer as he observed the vexillum with the bloody eagle upon it. "We were told to expect you, but I've never seen your century's banner. What is your unit?"

"We are a special detachment of Praetorians on a mission for the Emperor and Augusta."

That gave the leader pause. "Praetorians this far north?"

"Yes," Nemesianus replied casually. "Now, tell me who you are and how you came to expect us?"

"I am Pendaran, praefectus of the cavalry forces of Lord Afallach of the Votadini," the warrior said proudly. "The tribune from Horea Classis sent word to us about your imminent arrival in these lands."

"So he could warn you?" Evander put in, making Nemesianus smile.

"So we wouldn't kill you," Pendaran replied.

Nemesianus and his men observed the forest of spears and lances that surrounded them.

"What is your mission?" Pendaran asked.

But Nemesianus shook his head. "I would speak directly with Lord Afallach about our mission. It is…sensitive. Is he in residence at Curia at the moment?"

Pendaran stiffened at the name. "Curia? I don't know of a place by that name other than the one in Rome. The Lord Afallach is currently at the fortress of Dunpendyrlaw."

"Ah, then we are speaking of the same place!" Nemesianus clapped his hands. "Will you lead us there?"

Pendaran thought for a moment, observed the faces of the men with Nemesianus and felt a great distrust come over him. *These are not honourable men.* "I will lead you there, but only you and two of your men may enter the fortress. We are at full capacity and cannot accommodate all of your men and horses. The rest may camp on the lower slopes of the fortress, in the field."

"I thought Curia was massive?" Nemesianus stated with a chuckle.

"It is." Without another word, Pendaran turned his mount eastward, followed by his vexillarius so that half of the Votadini went in front, and half brought up the rear.

Nemesianus and his men rode in the middle.

"I don't like this," Evander said as he rode beside Nemesianus.

"Neither do I!" hissed Rhesus. "We shouldn't go!"

"It will be fine. They are Rome's allies and we have our orders directly from the Emperor. We bring good news, remember?" Nemesianus winked at Evander and Rhesus and continued on after the Votadini across fields of spring green with the rushing waters of the Bodotria to their left.

The distance was not long, and by the afternoon the great fortress of Dunpendyrlaw came into view, rising over seven hundred feet above plains of wheat, barley, and grazing pastures for cattle and hundreds of horses.

"I suppose it is massive," Nemesianus muttered to himself as they rode down the last slope across fields where peasants tilled the soil about scattered roundhouses. "They don't seem worried at all about attack."

"Pax Romana?" Evander ventured.

"More like the power of Lord Afallach," Nemesianus said as he turned to see the Votadini horsemen behind them. "We need to be careful."

As the column of riders approached the fortress, it rose higher and higher into the sky, looming above them such that it looked like a sleeping giant ready to roll over onto them if some god but pushed from the other side.

Dunpendyrlaw had been the ancestral fortress of the Votadini for longer than any living could remember, and it had been the Lord Afallach, and his father Coilus before him, who had strengthened and reinforced the triple ramparts that encircled it. The top was crowned with a masonry wall six feet in height, the stone of which was quarried from a massive gash in the eastern end of the fortress that made it appear as though the Gods had once attacked it.

There were fortified gates on both the eastern and western sides, each of them reached by sloping tracks that were deliberately vulnerable to the defenders on the ramparts above. The wall of the uppermost ramparts was ringed with guards whose spear points glinted in the sun and gave the fortress the appearance of being crowned with steel.

"No wonder the peasants seem so relaxed here!" Evander said. "No one would dare attack this!"

"And yet, we are simply going to walk in," Nemesianus quipped as he looked up the steep slopes. "Quite a hiding place, is it not?"

"Quite," Rhesus said.

They rode on after Pendaran and the Votadini toward the western side of the fortress and as they drew close, a cornu sounded from the top of the gatehouse.

"Halt!" Pendaran called out and turned his mount to ride back to Nemesianus. "Have your men rest in the field to the southwest. I'll take you in to see the Lord Afallach."

"Very well," Nemesianus answered casually before turning to Dis behind him. "You and Cavillor take the men to that field over there." He pointed. "Keep them out of trouble, but stay alert. Leave the peasants alone for now."

"Yes, sir," Dis said, the disappointment in his voice a little too evident.

"I mean it." The look in Nemesianus' eyes told him all he needed to know.

Dis wheeled his horse, spoke to Cavillor, and they took their men to the field to wait.

"Now," Nemesianus said to Evander and Rhesus. "Let's meet this Votadini lord."

They kneed their mounts up the steep approach, the smell of dung, steel, and fire filling their nostrils as the eyes of every Votadini warrior raked over them and their every movement.

"I don't like being this vulnerable, Nemesianus!" Evander hissed. "This is worse than being in the arena!"

"Shut up!" Nemesianus turned to look at him, the brazier fire at the gate glinting in his eyes.

Once through the gates, Pendaran led them between a collection of thatched roundhouses.

"You see?" Rhesus whispered to Evander beside him as Nemesianus rode in front. "They're really peasants!"

"Look again, you idiot!" Evander said.

In the doorway of every roundhouse, armed warriors were gathered, sharpening longswords and axe heads, watching the Romans as they passed. All of them had scars, battle wounds from their years of fighting the Selgovae, Maeatae and the other tribes on Rome's behalf.

"Just stop talking, both of you!" Nemesianus said over his shoulder.

The sound and smell of horses exploded into their senses then as they came to a series of four stone-built stable blocks with tiled rooftops in the southern quadrant of the hillfort. To the north of these was a large stone building used for the food stores. Overlooking the northern rampart was a small square temple with two columns flanking the entrance above which the pediment was adorned with a carved image of a goddess upon a horse with sheafs of wheat draped across her lap.

"Do you wish to make offerings to Epona before you meet with Lord Afallach?" Pendaran asked Nemesianus as the rest of the riders went to the stable blocks to tend to their mounts.

Nemesianus noticed that half of the Votadini horsemen had remained outside the western gate to watch over his men.

"No need," he replied. "We'll just meet with Lord Afallach right away."

"I will go and see if he wishes to meet you. You may wait outside the armoury." Pendaran pointed to a long stone building that overlooked the deep crevice of the quarry far below. He then kneed his horse past an 'L' shaped domus that looked more Roman than any of the other structures.

Nemesianus led the other two to a spot just above the abyss. "I'd dismount if I were you," he said.

They did so and tied their horses to hitching posts beside the armoury.

Immediately, Votadini stable boys arrived with water and straw for the horses.

"Do we get nothing?" Nemesianus asked them with a smirk.

The boys said nothing, but went back to the stables to care for the mounts of the recently returned warriors.

"Not big on hospitality, the Votadini," Rhesus said.

"No," Nemesianus replied as he eyed the warriors watching them from every perch, around every corner. "Not at all."

"Where did Pendaran go?" Evander asked.

Nemesianus looked to their right and pointed at the largest structure on the summit. "In there."

They turned to see a sprawling hall with thick stone walls, high windows on the second storey, and a sloping thatched roof.

"So that's where the Lord of the Votadini sits," Nemesianus mused, "*friend* of the Dragon..." He tried to remain fixed on his mission, not to let anger or hate blind him in that moment, for he knew that even though Lord Afallach had been close to and trusted by the Dragon in war, it was a time of peace now and most believed the Dragon to be dead. "We'll see how loyal this *friend of Rome* really is."

IX

DOMINUS EQUORUM ET ARGENTI

'The Lord of Horses and Silver'

"Lord Afallach?" Pendaran spoke as he approached his lord who stood behind the southern stable block looking out over the cliff at his ancestral lands.

Afallach, Lord of the Votadini, stood still, his regal form outlined against the blessed blue of the sky and racing clouds. The wind rushed up the sides of the hillfort to flutter his crimson cloak that was bordered with a silver interlace wherein were hidden horses and dragons. Beneath his cloak, he wore a brown cuirass bearing the Goddess Epona and two rearing horses, and a skirt of matching pteruges with horse head strap ends that swayed in the wind. He wore his longsword and pugio at his side, particularly as the Tribune Valera at Horea Classis had warned him of the arrival of the Praetorians whose leader had murdered one of their men.

"My lord, are you well?" Pendaran asked.

Lord Afallach turned to face his praefectus. "Do you believe me to be a good leader, Pendaran?" he asked, the thin braids of his long greying hair whipping about his shoulders.

Pendaran was confused at first, and wondered where this sudden chink in the armour of his lord's confidence had come from. He remembered the young force of nature he had once been when he had borne the banner of their people for his father, Coilus, the confidence, the resolve. He was yet possessed of those qualities, but as happens to men of war, life had worn on him. His eyes had lost their fire and were ringed with worry. His bodily injuries inflicted more pain, especially his left leg which caused him to walk with a pronounced limp. But Pendaran and all of the men were proud to serve their lord, the slayer of the Boar of the

Selgovae. "Epona has blessed us in your leadership, lord," Pendaran replied.

"Am I a good friend?" Afallach asked.

Pendaran took a step closer. "There is no better friend to any of us."

Afallach nodded and managed a thin smile. "Are they here?"

"Yes. Three of them. The rest of their century are down in the south-western field, as you commanded."

"Your impressions?"

Pendaran breathed deeply and let out a long, worried breath. "Arrogant and dangerous. What happened at Horea Classis does not surprise me now. They are killers, the lot of them."

Afallach sighed and shook his head. "We've had peace for years now and, though it has been uneasy at times, the Gods have blessed us with it. Our lands have thrived." He turned to look out over the plains where he used to ride as a child. "But I fear our peace is about to be shoved over the cliff's edge."

"If that is to be, then we are ready, lord." Pendaran stood beside Afallach as he turned to look at the great hall where his sister, Lucretia, waited in the king's doorway at the back of the hall. "Your sister has some thoughts before you meet with the Praetorians."

"Then I shall take counsel with her first," Afallach said as they walked toward the hall. "Have all of the braziers in the hall lit, and a full complement of guards. We need to project strength."

"You always do, lord," Pendaran said before bowing and going to carry out his orders.

"And Pendaran?"

"Yes, lord?" he turned back.

"Tell Brencis and the others to stay in the barracks until the Romans are gone."

"Yes, lord."

Afallach turned to his sister where she stood in the doorway flanked by two guards.

Lucretia, the daughter of Coilus, preferred to dress in the Roman fashion, as had been encouraged by their father. That day, she wore a red stola and matching himation with silver wave borders that complemented the silver torc about her neck. She was tall and, though thin, projected a great strength and an iron will born of the suffering she had endured as a prisoner of the Selgovae and the men of Ulster. Her long, raven-black hair was streaked with grey, and her green eyes had a permanent blackness about them. She never spoke of her ordeals.

When she and Afallach had been young, she had been endlessly jealous of their father's favour of her brother, but ever since Afallach had risked his life to rescue her from Argentocoxus' men, she had been his staunchest ally and advisor. Together they ruled the Votadini as their people's sacred protectors.

"All you all right?" Lucretia asked as her brother limped toward her.

Afallach glanced at the guards and nodded. "I'm fine. Father was always better at flattering Romans in such a way that he got what he wanted."

"But we don't need anything from these Romans."

"We need peace, for as long as the Gods grant it to us." Afallach followed her inside and the guard shut the door behind them.

Inside, they stood in the private rooms at the back of the great hall. It was the only place where they could speak without being overheard. The walls of the private rooms, just like the interior of the Roman domus Coilus had built, were painted in white and crimson with lamp-lit scenes of Roman gardens that seemed utterly foreign in that windswept land of the north. Three couches sat about a low table where fruit and cheese was laid out on silver platters. Their father had loved Rome, and had wanted to replicate some of what he had seen in the vast villas of the south.

Lucretia poured her brother some wine in a silver cup and handed it to him. "Here. It will calm you and help you to focus."

Afallach took the cup and sipped.

"I've been watching these Praetorians from the upper window," she said. "Do not trust them. They are arrogant yes, but their leader seems… cunning…brutal."

"How do you know from watching them from the window?"

"After so long in captivity…watching so many wicked men…" she paused. "I just know."

"Maybe I should just kill them now? We could easily ride out and slaughter all of them."

"And then what? Are we to force the Emperor to send his legions to crush us? What then would happen to the Votadini?" Lucretia shook her head. "No. For the moment, we are the power in these lands, and the other tribes don't dare supplant us. If we lose Rome's favour, however, that would change quickly."

"Then what do you suggest? You read what the tribune said they are looking for? Or *who*, rather."

"And you cannot let on. You must hide your feelings." She gripped his shoulder.

"I cannot betray Lucius' family, Lucretia."

"And you won't." Lucretia knew how much that family meant to her brother, how much it weighed on him that they be protected. When word had come of the death of Lucius Pen Dragon, her brother had lost himself in a darkness she had never seen before. She had never met the man who had inspired such loyalty in her brother. She wished she had. And she felt for the son of the Dragon who had come to them not two months past, unwilling to accept the death of his father. But she could not allow her brother to squander their kingdom's position out of senti-mentality.

"Brother, listen to me…" Lucretia continued. "Meet these men as a friend of Rome, an ally. Listen to what they have to say, and promise whatever you need to get them to leave. Ask for the usual payment of silver. Feign being the greedy horse-lord they think you to be. You must harden your heart and not react to any mention of the Dragon or his family."

"I will."

There was a knock on the oak door that led into the throne room.

"Enter!" Lucretia called.

Pendaran opened the door and stepped in. "The men are in position, lord, and the braziers are lit in the hall."

"Very good, Pendaran. We're coming."

Afallach and Lucretia left the warmth of the private chambers and entered the hall by way of the hidden corridor behind the screen where two wooden thrones sat upon a dais overlooking the hall.

To either side of the dais guards stood beneath red vexilla bearing the white horse of the Votadini. Twenty guards in full scale armour and helmets stood between each of the columns lining the wings of the long hall, as well as on the upper gallery overlooking the hall. Their spears and swords were polished to brilliance, their blades sharpened to deadly edges.

Along the walls of the hall, behind the guards, there were long tables filled with all manner of polished silver plates and cups, goblets and spoons, censers, and bowls with silver granulation and golden inlay about the rims. The room was lined with a lord's treasure, decades of payment from Rome to the Votadini as surety for their loyalty and aid on the northern frontier.

Afallach sat himself on his throne, adjusting his longsword and the thick silver torc about his neck as he did so.

Lucretia spoke to the servants about having a tray of wine to offer to their guests and then seated herself beside her brother. "Ready?" she asked him as they looked out over the hall which was speckled with light from the reflected fire on the silver treasure.

Afallach gazed at the burning hearth in the middle of the hall and beyond it to the guarded double-doors at the far end. "Bring them in!" he ordered.

Pendaran bowed and went out to get the awaiting Romans.

Epona, give me strength and wisdom, Afallach prayed.

A few minutes later, Pendaran entered the hall with the three Praetorians, all of them dressed in black armour and cloaks, their leader in a black cuirass bearing a dark, bronze eagle that appeared to bleed.

"Hail, Afallach, Lord of the Votadini!" the man in front said as he followed the Votadini praefectus to the other side of the round hearth where they faced the dais. "The Emperor and Augusta send greetings to their greatest ally in the north."

"And they have my gratitude and greetings in return…"

"Aurelius Nemesianus."

"Nemesianus," Afallach repeated. "And?"

Nemesianus looked at the two men behind him. "My optio, Evander, and one of my decana, Rhesus."

"Welcome to Dunpendyrlaw."

Nemesianus smiled and inclined his head.

"What would Rome have of us?" Afallach asked.

"I see you are a man who gets right to the point. I like that." Nemesianus said, eyeing the woman beside Afallach. "And who is this lovely lady? Your wife? It is indeed refreshing to see Roman beauty in so remote a place as this."

Afallach eyed him directly. "Lady Lucretia is my sister. Together we rule these lands."

"Ah. A woman in power is something that we have also grown accustomed to in Rome, what with the Augusta and her family. It is a new world indeed."

Lucretia made no sign of a smile, but instead looked to the servant with the tray of silver goblets.

The girl, who was dressed in a simple grey tunica with a meander border, stepped forward with the tray.

"May we offer you some wine after your long ride from Horea Classis?" Lucretia said.

Nemesianus smiled. "Why yes, that would be most welcome!" he said, accepting the silver cup and sipping the wine while Evander and Rhesus downed theirs. "Delicious. Thank you," he said. "Is it Etrurian, or Campanian? I can't tell."

Lucretia did not answer, but left the question hanging as Nemesianus shrugged and finished his wine before handing the cup back to the servant.

"What can we do for you, Aurelius Nemesianus?" Afallach asked. "Why have you brought a century of Praetorians to Dunpendyrlaw?"

"I'm glad you asked, Lord Afallach. We are actually a special detachment of the Praetorian Guard on a unique mission for the Emperor." Nemesianus produced his imperial pass from the Augusta and held it out to Afallach.

Pendaran took the scroll and handed it to Afallach who read it over.

When Afallach finished reading it, he handed it to Lucretia. "I see you have the Emperor and Augusta's permission to obtain whatever you need, and to do whatever is required to carry out your mission." Afallach leaned forward, his hand on the pommel of his sword. "But you haven't told me the nature of your mission yet, have you?"

Nemesianus crossed his arms casually. "That is next."

"I hope you do not require more horses for your mission," Lucretia said, handing the scroll back to Pendaran who returned it to Nemesianus.

Nemesianus shook his head. "No, lady. We have obtained all the mounts we require from the garrison at Horea Classis."

"I'm guessing they were not happy about that," Afallach ventured.

"They were somewhat reluctant, but complied in the end."

"If you do not need horses from us," Afallach said, "what *do* you need?"

"Information," Nemesianus replied.

"Information?" Afallach repeated. "That is all?"

"Yes."

"Pertaining to what?"

"To *whom*, actually," Nemesianus said. He began to walk casually about the enormous hearth fire, observing the stock still guards about the hall, and the silver that lined the walls which cast fiery orbs all about. He stopped and gazed into the fire where great logs burned, pulsing with flames of red, orange, and blue. "Fire can indeed change a man, can it not?"

"That is a strange thing to say, Praetorian," Afallach said. "You still have not said whom you would have information about."

Nemesianus looked directly at the Lord of the Votadini then, his gaze dark and unflinching. "Lucius Pen Dragon."

Afallach stared back, forcing himself not to show any sign of emotion.

"I'm sorry," Nemesianus added. "I should have said Lucius Metellus Anguis."

Afallach stared back, his face stoney and still.

"You fought alongside him and his Sarmatian cavalry in Emperor Severus' war against the Caledonii years ago?"

"Yes," Afallach said. "The Dragon Praefectus. He was Rome's greatest warrior. The best I've ever seen."

"He was also a traitor who tried to usurp the imperial throne!" Evander burst out.

Nemesianus shot him a look.

It was Afallach's turn to smile. "Which, I believe, was at the insistence of your own Praetorian Prefect, Papinianus. Is that not true?"

"I believe so," Nemesianus answered. "Politics has never been to my liking." He came back around the fire to step closer to the dais where Afallach and Lucretia sat.

The guards to either side of them took two steps out, but Afallach put up his hand.

"It's all right," he said to his guards. "He is our ally."

"I appreciate that, Lord Afallach," Nemesianus said, his eyes looking over Lucretia. "Much has happened in the past...war...politics...

betrayal…fire…" He rubbed his chin. "The Dragon, his family, and his men have found themselves in the middle of it all, haven't they?"

"The great among us are necessarily forced to the front to raise the rest of us up," Afallach said. "Lucius Metellus Anguis was both a scholar and a warrior."

"And the society that separates its scholars from its warriors will have its thinking done by cowards, and its fighting by fools," Nemesianus replied.

"Thucydides was correct in that," Afallach said. "Elagabalus proved the theory."

"You know your histories?" There was surprise in Nemesianus' arrogant voice.

"The Dragon taught me many things," Afallach stated. *Lucius…my friend…*

"I'm sure he did."

"And there are no fools here in Dunpendyrlaw," Lucretia added, her voice cold, her eyes more so.

"That is evident, lady Lucretia." Nemesianus smiled, then turned back to Afallach. "The Dragon is a dear friend to you. I can see that."

"He was. Yes." Afallach leaned back, his leg beginning to ache.

"Was?" Nemesianus said.

"He is dead."

"Are you quite sure?"

Afallach looked down on the Roman. "You should know, should you not? Rome burned him and hunted his family."

"Yes. I did hear something of that. But are you certain it happened?"

"Quite."

"His family, and his friends - saving yourself, of course - are all dead? All the men of his cavalry ala…the Sarmatians? They are dead as well?"

"Like I said. Rome saw to it."

"That's odd," Nemesianus said, sounding confused.

"What is?"

"It's just that, I heard a rumour that Metellus…or Pen Dragon… whatever name he's going by… I heard that he had returned to Britannia after the slaying of Emperor Caracalla." *And my brother!*

"Emperor Caracalla died over ten years ago, didn't he?" Afallach said. "Besides… How much time he gains who does not look to see what his neighbour says or does or thinks, but only at what he does himself, to make it just and holy."

Nemesianus stared at Afallach a moment, then shrugged. "Marcus Aurelius never held much sway for me. Nor stoicism for that matter. But I have found rumour and gossip to be useful at times."

"You will have an endless search if you're looking for the dead," Afallach said. "There have not been dragons in this land since the end of the war with the Caledonii. My concern has been solely the protection of the Empire's northern border. And my people and I have succeeded in that."

"Yes. You have. I can see that. But perhaps there are yet dragons in the south?"

"I doubt it."

"How can you tell if you are concerning yourself solely with what you do here in the north?"

"I will tell you something, Aurelius Nemesianus." Afallach stood up then, and limped toward the Praetorian so that he faced him, looked down on him. "Lucius Metellus Anguis was indeed my friend. His family was my family. And I wish they were still alive, for the world is indeed a better place with such people in it. But they are all dead. Every last one of them. As much as it grieves me to say it."

"But do you know it for certain?" Nemesianus' nostrils flared as he stared back at the Lord of the Votadini.

"I do."

"That is a shame, because the Augusta's offer is unlike anything I've seen or heard of." Nemesianus produced another scroll, one wrapped with a red ribbon and the imperial seal upon it.

"What is that?" Afallach asked.

Nemesianus pursed his lips and handed it to him. "Read it for yourself. It is the offer the Emperor and Augusta are making to the Dragon and his family, as well as all of his surviving men…if there were any surviving, that is."

Afallach unrolled the papyrus and read it. When he finished, he looked up at Nemesianus. There was anger in his eyes, his jaw set and flexing. "I would that Rome had offered this to Lucius long ago, for then he, his family, and his men might still be alive, and the Empire more secure than ever."

"Prefect of the Praetorian Guard, the restoration and rebuilding of all his lands at imperial expense, a full pardon, and freedom for them all across the whole of the Empire…" Nemesianus shook his head. "Even the dead would rise again for such an offer."

"Except they can't," Afallach handed the scroll back to Nemesianus. "I'm afraid you've wasted a journey to our remote corner of the Empire, Aurelius Nemesianus."

"It seems that way. But, perhaps Fortuna will favour the other half of my forces in the south?"

That caught Afallach off guard. "There are more of you?"

Nemesianus smiled. "Oh, yes. Many more. We are sweeping the entirety of Britannia. It is the Augusta's wish, after all, that the Emperor have the very best and bravest protector. A scholar *and* a warrior, if you will."

Afallach looked at his sister who had come to stand beside him. He turned back to the Praetorian before them. "There is nothing but heartache in searching for the dead, especially the dead of one's familia. I did search for them, and found nothing."

"And yet, is it not true you believed your own sister to be dead, until you found her?" Nemesianus turned to Lucretia. "Your captivity must have been tortuous." He reached out to touch her hand, but she recoiled. "I myself was imprisoned in a hole in Rome for over ten years." He laughed. "People thought I was dead, and yet, here I am!"

Afallach and Lucretia said nothing for a few uncomfortable moments, as if awaiting a sentencing in a court. "Did you not come for anything else, other than asking about the dead, Aurelius Nemesianus?" Afallach broke the silence.

"No, I don't believe so."

"What about my payment from Rome for securing this northern border?"

"Payment?"

"The silver that is owed to me," Afallach stated flatly.

Nemesianus' eyes narrowed as he looked at the silver treasure about the hall. "I think you have enough silver, Lord Afallach."

"There is never enough. Give me the silver Rome owes me. The silver my praefectus tells me is hidden in coffers inside one of your wagons."

Nemesianus looked at Pendaran who stared back at him, hand on his sword.

"You may send one of your men here to get it while you wait with us," Lucretia said. "Rome must make good on its promises."

Nemesianus reddened, but he controlled himself, all too aware of the spears that surrounded him. "Rhesus… Go and get the wagon."

"Yes, sir," Rhesus said, turning to go out of the hall, accompanied by the two guards at the doors.

"He won't be long," Nemesianus said. "Do you have any food?"

"We do not." Afallach said.

"All this silver, and no food. It is strange, is it not?" When Afallach did not answer, Nemesianus went for another stroll, his finger reaching out to glide along the smooth surfaces of glowing silver along the walls. As he walked, he spoke aloud to Afallach and Lucretia who stood beside the hearth fire. "You are correct in that Rome must make good on its promises. It has made promises to me also."

Evander stood still, eyeing the guards and the serving girl who waited to the right of the dais.

"Is that so?" Lucretia said, her disdain no longer hidden.

"Yes. But I too believe in making good on my own promises."

"Do you, Aurelius Nemesianus?" Afallach said, his eyes following the man along the hall.

"I do." Nemesianus walked back into the middle of the hall to face Afallach. "And I promise you this, Afallach, Lord of the Votadini… If in our sweep of the island of Britannia, we find any trace of the Dragon's family, his men, or indeed the Dragon himself, we will return here with a full legion of men and burn Dunpendyrlaw to the ground."

"You threaten me in my own hall?" Afallach demanded.

"No. I make you a promise in the hall you inhabit by Rome's good graces." Without taking his eyes off Afallach, he spoke again. "Evander?"

"Yes, sir?"

"Rhesus should be back with the wagon now. Go and help him to unload the Lord Afallach's silver payment."

"Yes, sir." Evander turned and went to leave the hall, accompanied by another two guards, looking back over his thick shoulder as he left Nemesianus behind.

They waited in silence, Afallach and Lucretia returning to their thrones while Nemesianus walked casually about the hall, observing the silver, and the faces of the guards.

"I should kill him now," Afallach whispered to his sister when Nemesianus was at the far end of the hall, looking out the huge double doors for the wagon.

"If you do, it will be the end of us all," she whispered back. "This man is evil. He means to do what he says. Don't give him an excuse!"

"Ah!" Nemesianus said suddenly from the other end of the vast hall. "Your silver has arrived!"

A few moments later, Evander and Rhesus began unloading strong boxes which they placed around the hearth fire.

"The Emperor and Augusta are most generous!" Nemesianus went around each of the boxes and opened them to reveal silver coin, jewelry, and an array of polished silver platters, bowls, and cups. He laughed. "Some of these may even come from the burned out ruins of the Metellus villa in Etruria! Who knows?"

"Is that all you have brought as payment?" Afallach demanded, trying to distract him by acting the greedy client king.

"You are a mercenary among mercenaries, Lord Afallach. But, I suppose that that is to be expected among the barbarians of the north."

"You and your men should leave our lands now," Lucretia added before her brother could respond to the taunt.

"Perhaps we should, lady. Though, it would have been a pleasure to spend more time in your company, with food of course."

"You will find plenty of food on your way to Hadrianus' wall," she replied.

Nemesianus bowed. "I'm sure we will." He began to walk away. "If, for some reason, it turns out that you do find that the dead have returned to the world of the living, Lord Afallach, do be sure to convey the Emperor and Augusta's message for me. Send word to me in Isca Dumnoniorum where my ships will take the Dragon and his family and men back to Rome so that the Augusta may reward them."

"The dead do not return, Praetorian." Afallach stood once more as Nemesianus and his two men turned to leave.

"We shall see," Nemesianus answered before following the others out into the sunlight.

"Pendaran, make sure they leave the borders of our lands."

"Yes, lord." The praefectus went after the Romans then, leaving Afallach and Lucretia alone in the hall with the rest of the guards.

Outside, as Nemesianus, Evander, and Rhesus reclaimed the wagon and the two remaining horses, Nemesianus whispered to Evander.

"Have three of the men hide themselves somewhere nearby. I want them to watch this fortress closely."

"Why? What are they looking for?"

Nemesianus smiled. "I have a suspicion that this lord of horses and silver will be sending messages imminently."

"Yes, sir," Evander answered with a smile of his own.

A couple of hours later, as the sun began to fall past its zenith into the west, Afallach stood with Lucretia looking out over the southwestern ramparts. They watched the long file of the Praetorians set out to join the main Roman road that would take them south, past Trimontium, and on toward the wall of Hadrianus.

"This isn't over, is it?" Lucretia asked her brother.

Afallach shook his head. "All the world knows Lucius is dead, and yet Rome, the very force that sought his death, refuses to accept it."

Lucretia placed her hand on her brother's shoulder.

"I understand that Phoebus refuses to accept his father's death. It's normal, especially as he did not see it happen the way you saw our own father's. But it has been over ten years that Rome has not shown an interest in the Dragons."

"We have to warn Phoebus and the others," came a voice behind them.

Afallach turned to see Brencis standing there with Dima, Magar, Boas and Deva.

The Sarmatian warriors looked out with determination at the departing Praetorians.

"We need to ride out to warn the others," Boas said. "They need to know they're being hunted.

"How do you know what was said?" Lucretia asked.

"We were in the upper gallery," Dima replied.

"That was reckless." Afallach looked at them and his eyes rested on Brencis. "Phoebus and all the others are in danger. You're right. We need to warn them. I'll send riders to Ynis Wytrin and Einion at Din Tagell. Did Phoebus say where he was headed?"

"All he said was that he was headed into the lands of the Brigantes to search for his mother." Brencis looked at Afallach and shook his head. "He's too angry. I'm afraid he'll make a mistake. Even in the mountains of those lands, Rome has eyes."

"And he certainly stands out with that wolf of his following him around!" Dima added. "One of us should have gone with him."

"He wouldn't have had it," Afallach said. "Nevertheless, we have to find him and warn him about the Praetorians."

"You don't think the offer is genuine?" Magar asked.

Brencis looked at him, his eyes wide. "You think they would actually do that, cousin? We've known Romans long enough to know that that offer is nothing but a trap, a lie. None of us are safe, and certainly not Phoebus, Calliope, and Adara, wherever she may be."

"That settles it!" Afallach said as the Praetorians disappeared into the distance. "First thing in the morning, I want you all to ride out. Warn the other dragons who are hidden across the lands of the Votadini. Tell them to travel in twos to the south searching for Lucius' family. If they find them, they are to escort them safely and secretly into Dumnonia to Einion's court."

"And if we don't find them?" Brencis asked.

"Then they should still go to Einion. I'll send word if I have news to report. Lucius helped us all in the past, saved each of our lives at one point or another. It's our turn to repay the debt and help his family."

"And if we can't?" Magar asked.

"Then Rome will devour us all." Afallach turned to look out over the fortress of Dunpendyrlaw and tried not to imagine the flames with which Nemesianus had threatened him. *I'll not let my father's fortress burn!* "Go now. Make your offerings to Epona. Take whatever provisions and weapons you need from the stores, and trust that the Gods will help us to protect our friends."

"May Epona speed us to their sides," Brencis said as he and the other Sarmatians bowed to Afallach, the Lord of the Votadini who had given them shelter and security for the last decade and more.

When they were gone, Lucretia turned to Afallach. "Come. Let's go inside."

"You go. I want to be alone for a moment," he said.

She kissed his cheek and went back to the hall with Pendaran to see to the payment of silver which the Praetorians had reluctantly handed over.

Alone now, Afallach watched the darkening sky from the high ramparts of Dunpendyrlaw. He remembered battles and blood, and the joy and sense of belonging he had felt with Lucius and his warriors. That feeling of invincibility had long ago faded from memory, and now every attempt to display strength to the world outside of his fortress required a titanic effort.

"So many battles…" he mused. "So much glory… For what? Remembrances of loved ones long dead?" A sadness flowed through him then, unwanted, uncalled for, but acute in every way. "Oh, Epona…" he prayed. "Protect my people, and my friends… May we ride to glory still for yet hundreds of years…"

He looked up at the indigo sky and saw the first stars alight on night's canvas.

The Lord of the Votadini then turned and went back to his hall to drink wine with his riders before they set out.

It was early, the sun only just peeking out from behind the clouds when a loud galloping on the damp road above them woke Segundo and the other two Praetorians. They roused slowly, having slept in the ditch all night.

"Get the horses!" Segundo ordered, looking to where they had tied them behind a great cluster of gorse-covered rocks. He shook the other two and jumped into the road to watch as three riders sped southward. Standing in the middle of the road, he looked to the north but no others were coming. "Nemesianus was right. That's them! It's got to be!"

"What did Evander order us to do?" one of the men asked.

"We're to follow from a distance and see where they go. If they split up, so do we. If that happens, one of us is to report to Nemesianus at Coria where he'll be waiting along the wall, while Evander heads southwest toward the isle they call Mona. Let's go! They're travelling quickly!" Segundo swung himself up into his saddle and the other two followed.

The three of them thundered down the road after their quarry.

.   .   .

"You see them?" Brencis said to Deva as they watched the Praetorian riders set off in pursuit of Dima, Magar, and Boas, whom they had followed at a distance as planned, in case anyone had been lying in wait.

"I see them. Stupid Romans."

"Now, it's our turn to hunt," Brencis said as he adjusted his spatha and the mail beneath his cloak.

They kicked their horses and flew after them.

X

GLADIUS FRACTUS

'The Broken Sword'

The Gods had blessed the people of Viroconium Cornoviorum that market day in late spring, for the sun had shone brightly from its rising until its inevitable sleep. It had been as though the prayers of every merchant and trader from miles around had been heard. The journeying had been fair, the business excellent. The customers in the vast forum and along the porticoes of the main thoroughfare were hungry and eager to spend on everything from cattle, hogs, and sheep fleeces, to pottery, copper, clothing, and horse tack. There was wine in variously sized amphorae from Gaul and Italy, olives and oil from Graecia and Iberia, and garum from the seaside rot vats of Numidia. The shouts of excited sellers were met with a chorus of back and forth until the cacophony ended with a joyous jingle of coin.

Viroconium, one of the largest cities of Britannia, was situated on a major crossing of the River Sabrina, at the western terminus of Wattling Street. Along this route, an army of traders from Gaul travelled from the ports of Regulbium, Retupiae, Dubrae, and Portus Lemanis in the southeast, alongside merchants from Londinium and Verulamium. Every roadside mansio along the way was at capacity, and every taberna drunk dry on a daily basis.

Added to this mania of mercantilism were troops on leave from the fortress of Deva to the north who made straight for the lupanaria of Viroconium to play among big-breasted she-wolves. Then there were the many retired veterans of the legions and their families from the colonia of Glevum to the south who sought items for their own, carefully-tended domus, and adornments for their stola-clad wives.

The smoke from the hypocausts of the great bathhouse crowned the city only to dissipate in the sunshine over the embankments of the former fortress of the Twentieth Legion that surrounded the walls. The old fortifications gave way to the fields and forests that flanked the river where insects buzzed and waterfowl honked in the rippling shallows.

As evening fell over Viroconium that day, thank offerings filled the altars of the temples of Jupiter, Vesta, and Mithras about the city. The setting sun cast a glow of orange and gold over the countryside as braziers, torches, and lamps were lit about the city, numbering almost as greatly as the stars in the clear sky. The brothels and tabernae filled up, as did the theatre, and laughter exploded out of the doors and vomitoria of all of them to play long into the night.

As the mansiones in and around the city were completely full, many were left to camp out of doors on the final night of the market before heading home.

Gaius Favonius, a retired legionary who now traded in quality fleeces from his small farm near Salinae, was one of the many who had been forced to camp beneath the stars that night. This was not a problem however, for the night was clear and dry, and he was in a good mood. The day had been highly successful with the sale of all his fleeces, as well as all of the woollen clothing which his wife, Nola, and his daughter Fenella had spent the year making.

"What a day!" Favonius exclaimed as he looked out over the river valley of the Sabrina and the flight of birds skimming low over the water. He had decided to camp outside the city walls, to the southwest along the river. That way, they would be able to make for home easily the next morning. The copse of trees they had found was located away from the other traders who camped without the walls. This allowed them to enjoy their family's success away from strangers.

"Gaius," his wife called over to him. "Come and sit with us! Let us toast our success today!" She brushed her black hair aside and held up his old legionary's cup filled with wine that they had purchased at the market.

Favonius turned to look at his wife, daughter, and two young sons. *How the Gods have blessed me!* he marvelled as he looked upon them.

"It's getting cold, dearest," Nola said. "Come, sit by the fire."

"I'll just check on the horses first," he said as he went around to the other side of their large wagon where the horses cropped at the grass beneath the trees to which they had been tied. He gazed into the woods to the faint outline of Wattling Street where, on the other side, beyond the roadside monuments, an army of raucous merchants camped.

"We do know how to pick a spot!" he said as he returned to his family. "Much quieter here above the river."

"And more mosquitoes, Pater!" his twelve-year-old son, Lew said as he smacked his arm.

Favonius laughed. "Sit closer to the fire, my boy. They hate the smoke." He sat down beside his wife against the wagon and accepted the cup she still held for him. "Did I ever tell you children about how bad the mosquitoes were the time I had to march across the Pontine Marshes outside of Rome?"

"Yeesss," the children moaned in unison.

"Well...they were so big, they would have carried you off like a bloody great eagle!"

His daughter laughed at that and ruffled her younger brothers' hair.

Favonius raised his cup. "Here's to us and the blessings the Gods have given us!" he said. "It's been a wonderful day!"

"The Gods' blessings!" his wife replied, cuddling next to him before the fire, smiling at their daughter, Fenella, who sat across from them with the boys, Lon and Lew.

"I never thought that our endeavour would prove so successful," Favonius mused as he sipped. "I was worried when I left the legions."

"I remember," Nola said, tracing a scar on his forearm with her finger, admiring the silver bangle about her wrist which he had bought her.

"With the profits from today, we can finally build that addition onto our domus, *and* grow our herd!" He shook his head. "I still can't believe it!"

"You've worked hard, Pater," Fenella said.

"We all have, love," he replied. "The clothes you and your mother have worked on are a big part of our profits."

"I think people were very happy with my stitch work," the girl said with a smile.

"Happy?" her mother said. "They were ecstatic! There wasn't anything else like it in the whole forum!"

"And your stolae and tunicae were the talk of the market stalls, Mater," Fenella returned.

"What about us?" Lon, the elder of the two boys said. "We're the ones who shouted loud enough to bring in customers!"

"Quite right!" their father agreed.

"Yes," Fenella added. "Even the donkeys were jealous!"

Lon elbowed his older sister and she in turn laughed and pulled at his ear.

"We all excelled today!" Favonius said. "And when we get back to Salinae, we get back to work."

"Can we host a convivium to celebrate?" Fenella asked.

"Of course we can!" her mother replied. "We need to show our appreciation to our farm hands and neighbours."

"Especially Tribulus," Favonius muttered. "Ever since the sheep ate his asparagus, he's been angry with me."

"He should get a more trustworthy cat!" Lew said.

"Cats are for moles, you dummy!" his brother retorted.

"All right, all right," their father said as he tossed another log onto the fire in their midst. "You boys should get some sleep now. We leave early in the morning for home."

"Can I drive the wagon?" Lon asked as he lay down beside his sister and brother.

"Of course, you can," Favonius said as he held Nola close.

They sat quietly then, Gaius and his wife, both watching their boys quickly doze off into a deep slumber, safe in their sister's arms.

Nola smiled at Fenella, proud as ever. She had always been determined not to torture and belittle the girl the way her own mother had done to her, and she had succeeded. She watched as her daughter's big glossy eyes stared into the fire and were lulled to sleep by the flames' dancing.

"A good day," Favonius repeated to her.

"Thank you for taking care of us, love," Nola said, kissing his rough hand and holding it to her breast.

Favonius kissed her soft hair and adjusted the blanket over her. He then checked for his gladius, close at hand beneath the edge of the pelt on which they lay. He felt his wife drift off in his arms and smiled. *Thank you, oh Fortuna, for blessing us...*

. . .

It was the sound of wood grating on wood that roused Gaius Favonius' senses. And then the metallic note of coins sliding around.

"Shh!" a voice hissed somewhere in the blackness behind them.

Favonius looked around without moving. It was dark, but the moon was high and bright. The sound of crickets was loud, but not enough to drown out the sound of the intruders. His hand slid beneath the pelt to grip the pommel of his gladius. His heart began to race as it always had done before a fight.

"Get the box!" someone hissed from the end of the wagon to his right.

"Hurry up!" came a harsh whisper in the dark to Favonius' left.

He felt the wagon shake and knew that there was someone inside it. *Three men,* he told himself. *Bastards!*

He knew he didn't have long, that he could not allow them to rally. He also knew that if one of them ran with the box of coin, all of his family's hard work would be lost. He disentangled his right arm from his wife who suddenly grew stiff, aware of the added voices. He put his finger to his lips and slowly shifted, ready to get up.

He stood quickly, his gladius sliding free of its sheath. "Get out of here, whoresons!"

Immediately, to his left, a great big brute of a man slashed upward with a rusty blade, narrowly missing Favonius' chin as his training kicked in and he rolled backward, stopping just short of the cliff above the river valley.

Favonius scrambled to his feet and made to rush to his wife and children, only to find his way blocked by the brute and another man while the man with the box dragged it out of the wagon with a loud thump as it fell onto the grass.

"Pater? What's happening?" Lew said.

"What have we here?" said the brute as he looked down at Fenella and the boys.

"Get away from them!" Nola roared, holding out a small pugio.

"Don't worry, mother!" the brute said. "You'll have your turn after your daughter!"

Favonius charged in, and the clang of steel rang out as he engaged the brute once more, cutting and thrusting, parrying and dodging.

"Pater!" Fenella shouted, as the other man dragged her away from her screaming brothers, even as her mother fought the third man who had left the box to set upon her.

"I'll kill you!" Favonius shouted, his dormant rage returning as he plunged the point of his gladius into the brute's chest. The blade stuck in the man's ribs and his body fell backwards with a loud thud. He left the body and turned to face the others, each of whom had a blade to Nola and Fenella's necks.

"If you're smart, you'll let us leave with the box," one of the men said.

"You're not going anywhere!" Favonius growled.

"Pater, please!" Fenella pleaded.

"Maybe we'll just take your daughter as surety…" the man holding her said as he licked her cheek. "And for a bit of fun as we spend your coin!"

The two men laughed.

Favonius searched the darkness for a weapon, a way to get at them without endangering his wife and daughter, further. "Boys, get behind me!"

Lon and Lew scrambled away from the fire.

Lon made for the brute's body and tried to dislodge his father's gladius, only to have the brute cry out suddenly, his arm whipping out to slap the boy so that he flew into the grass with a scream.

"By the Gods, you'll pay!" Favonius shouted at the men.

"No! You'll pay!" the one holding Nola shouted back as he felt her chest and she screamed.

At that moment, a great battle cry rent the air and darkness from behind the men who held the two women.

Nola cried out as she pushed away from her attacker, his blade grazing her jaw, making her scream as she tumbled toward her husband on the other side of the dying fire.

From out of the darkness, the jaws of an enormous black wolf leapt up to take the man in the throat. He dropped his blade instantly and clawed at his gurgling neck as the beast tore into his flailing body.

The man holding Fenella screamed then, one hand grasping at his kidney where a sword had slashed him. He released the girl and spun to parry another slash.

A man in a ragged black cloak lunged for him and they faced off as Favonius rushed to pull his daughter to safety, only to be grabbed from behind by the brute who still held his gladius in his ribs.

"Gaius!" Nola cried, blood seeping from her wounded face.

"Remus, kill!" shouted the black-cloaked newcomer, pointing at the brute, even as he retreated under the third man's attack.

The wolf, his jaws bloody from the first victim, turned on the brute, leapt over the fire, and lunged.

Favonius ducked just in time to get out of the animal's path of attack and watched in horror as it tore out the man's face.

Fenella and the boys screamed and rallied to their mother who kept them safe between the wagon and the fire.

Toward the cliff's edge, their rescuer continued to fight the third man and they thought he would slay him.

Their blades met fiercely, and with an ear-shattering clangour, the cloaked man's sword suddenly broke in half as he parried a vicious slash.

The attacker laughed, and pulled back for a killing blow, but not before the man caught his arm and drove his forehead hard into his face.

There was an audible crack of the attacker's nose.

Their rescuer spun, dislodging the blade from the attacker's hand as he spun and slashed across his belly. The rusty blade tore roughly at the ragged clothing and skin, and a moment later, his guts came pouring out.

The body fell against the man in black whose feet slipped on the offal and caused him to stumble over the cliff's edge.

"No!" Favonius cried out as he ran for the cliff and caught the man's forearm, the body of the attacker crashing down the steep, rocky slope to the river far below. "I've got you!" he said as he strained, struggling to grip the man's blood-covered arm.

"Gaius, look out!" Nola cried as the enormous wolf appeared behind Favonius, a deep, menacing growl rising from deep within its enormous body.

Favonius looked back over his shoulder, his eyes wide in fear as the wolf appeared ready to lunge, its fangs bared, white in the moonlight.

"Remus, stop!" the man hanging over the cliff's edge said. "Help!" he commanded, reaching out with his left arm.

The wolf leaned over and the man grabbed hold of its leather collar. The beast then pulled back, and Favonius did the same so that together they pulled the man away from the cliff and onto the bloody grass.

As Favonius let go, he saw what looked like dragons coiled about the man's forearms. He wondered if some dark god had waded into their midst, drawn by the blood and violence, and immediately ran to his family to see that they were all right. "Nola, you're bleeding!" he said as he looked over his wife, panicked.

"I'm fine," she said, still breathless. "Just a surface cut."

"Fenella…boys? You all right?" Favonius said, looking over each of them.

They nodded absently, the shock setting in.

"It's all right…" he reassured them. "We're safe now."

They all watched then as the man in the black cloak got to his feet and picked up his broken gladius from the grass. "Not again," he muttered to himself, and before the others could say anything, or thank him, he screamed and threw the useless blade over the cliff. He then turned and knelt before the great wolf.

To the surprise of the family watching him, the beast nuzzled and sniffed him as if to reassure itself that he was unharmed.

"I'm fine, boy," the man said as he rubbed the beast and pressed his head to its thick neck.

"Stay calm," Favonius whispered to his family before going slowly to the mauled body of the fallen brute, and pulling his own gladius free. He rushed back to his family's side, even as the man stood and began to walk toward them, the wolf at his heels.

"Please," Nola said. "Don't hurt us."

The man sighed and shook his head. "You're no longer in danger, lady." Though hoarse, his voice was unexpectedly kind and sounded much younger than his rough appearance allowed. Now that he neared the fire, they could see that he was no more than twenty-five or so. His hair was dark, the stubble of his beard likewise, and beneath the caked blood upon his face and body, he was handsome, despite the scar across his left cheek.

But there was no sign of joy in his eyes which, to Favonius and his wife at least, seemed to hold a world of sorrows.

Favonius looked at the dragon tattoos upon his forearms as he stood before the fire.

The man looked at each of them. "Are you all right?"

"Yes. Thanks to you," Favonius replied, eyeing the wolf who sat beside his master. "How…how did you come to find us?"

"I was encamped just below the cliff nearer the city. I heard the screams."

"Is that your pet wolf?" Lon asked, the fear beginning to ebb out of his system.

The man nodded and stroked the animal's head. "Remus is my friend. I saved him from a baiting arena near Trimontium."

"Trimontium?" Favonius' eyes widened. "You've travelled far!"

The man looked at Fenella. "May I trouble you for a bucket of water for him? He is thirsty."

Fenella looked at her father and Favonius nodded. She went away to get the water and returned with a bucket which she placed hesitantly beside the man, not daring to get near the wolf, unnerved by the beast's bright yellow eyes.

The animal went around to his master's other side and began to lap at the water.

"Thank you," the man said, spying the wine skin that lay by the fire. "May I?"

Favonius looked down at the skin. "Of course!" he bent quickly to pick it up and tossed it to him. "I thank the Gods they sent you... Who are you?"

The man looked back across the fire, not answering immediately, but then there was a sudden faraway look in his eyes. "Phoebus... Phoebus Pen Dragon."

"Well, Phoebus Pen Dragon," Favonius said. "Whoever you are, we thank you for helping us and welcome you to share our fire and food this night. It's the least we can do. I am Gaius Favonius." He turned to his family. "This is my wife, Nola. My daughter, Fenella. And my boys, Lon and Lew."

The family stared back at him, the faces betraying varying looks of fear, reticence, curiosity, and gratitude.

"Where are you from?" Fenella asked suddenly.

He looked at her. "Nowhere...and everywhere..."

"Where's that?" Lew asked.

There was the first glimmer of a smile upon the man's face. "I have no home. I travel a lot."

"Doing what?" Lew persisted.

"Helping people as best I can." He reached out to pat the wolf, sparing a quick thought for all those whom he had helped, and those whom he had not been able to save. They haunted him, those shades of the innocent dead, reminded him of his failures every time he closed his eyes. "I've been searching for my mother."

The words were said suddenly, as though it was a thought that followed him constantly.

"Is she missing?" Nola asked, compassion in her voice.

"Yes. For several years now."

Favonius and Nola exchanged looks.

"You fight well," Favonius said, not wanting to press. "Where did you learn?"

After a moment of silence, he answered. "My father taught me."

"Was he a man of the legions?" Favonius asked.

He nodded. "Yes. He was." He wanted to say more, to tell them about his own family, who they were, who his father had been. He wanted to talk about how lonely he had been since his disappearance, and how many families he had tried to help over the years since. But he said nothing more. He held up his arms before the fire to look at the blood-caked dragons about his forearms.

"I saw you in the market today," Lon said. "I remember your dragons."

The man looked at the boy. "I was buying a sword."

"The one you just broke?" Favonius asked.

"Unfortunately, yes."

"Well, as you saved us, Phoebus Pen Dragon, I will give you my own gladius."

The man shook his head. "No. If that blade survived your time in the legions with you, you should not part with it."

"But you need a good blade, lad," Favonius insisted. "If you're to help others as you have helped us, you must have one."

"There is only one sword for me," he said, his voice almost a whisper. "All others seem to break in my hands."

Favonius watched the younger man and wondered what he was not telling them. *This lad has been through more than most,* he thought. "Well, at least you can rest with us, and share our food before we leave tomorrow."

"Thank you," he said. "That is kind of you."

"Think nothing of it," Favonius said. "You can all sleep, and I'll keep watch." He looked beneath the wagon to make sure the box with their coin was still there.

It was.

"Remus. Guard," the man said to the wolf, pointing to a spot a few paces from the fire and wagon.

The wolf went and sat quietly in the moonlight, its eyes searching the darkness, its ears alert.

"Good boy," the man said before laying down on the other side of the fire, across from the family.

"If you like, you can travel with-"

"He's asleep, Gaius," Nola said.

And they watched as their rescuer slept, his wolf keeping a watch in the darkness.

Favonius went to his family and huddled them close about him, his mind and heart filled with gratitude for what the Gods had done that night.

None of them managed to sleep for some time.

It was late morning when the man opened his eyes, rose, and went to where his wolf still stood sentry over the camp. He pat the animal.

The animal licked his face, attempting to clean the dried blood.

"Stop it, Remus. No." He stood up and looked around.

The sky was grey that day, the sun in hiding far beyond the low hanging clouds that brought with them the threat of rain.

In an iron pot over the fire, the daughter stirred some porridge, while her mother made a poultice of dandelion and rosemarinus for her cut jaw.

The boys were also up, seeing to the horses while their father dragged the bodies of the brute and first attacker away from their camp to the edge of the cliff.

Favonius gazed over the precipice to see the body of the third attacker far below on the rocks, a bloody mess about it. "Bastards!" he said, spitting on them. He brushed off his hands and returned to the fire. "Before we set out, we should go back into town to notify the magistrate of what happened." He turned to the man who now sat beside the wolf at his family's fire. "Would you watch over our camp while we are gone? It will be much faster without the wagon and horses."

The man thought about it. "I suppose. Perhaps I can use a cloth and more water to wash up. Travelling with so much blood on me can draw…unwanted attention."

"Does that happen a lot?" Fenella asked, eyeing him.

"Say no more," Favonius said, his hand up to stop his daughter's enquiry.

"I'll get the cloth and water," Nola said.

As she did so, Favonius sat himself beside the man. "I am grateful to you, Phoebus Pen Dragon. Today would be a very different day had you not arrived."

"Please, I-"

"Let me finish," Favonius said quickly. "I can see you have been living in the wilds for some time, and I'm sure you've helped a great many people in your travels."

"Not all of them," the man said absently.

"Nevertheless, you helped us, and the Gods demand that I return the favour."

"You don't want to get involved with me, Gaius Favonius."

"But we already are," Favonius replied, smiling at the younger man. "I know you have places to go, but we would welcome you to stay with us for a time at our farm in Salinae. It is safe and quiet there, and perhaps we can help find your mother. I still have contacts in the legion at Isca, and a few in the Roman administration in Londinium. I could ask them to-"

"Rome cannot help."

They could see a darkness spread over his features, and the scar on his cheek seemed to grow redder, angrier.

"But I can," Favonius insisted with a smile, patting the man on the shoulder. He stood and went to the wagon for his satchel, his cingulum, and gladius. "We're going into the city now." He glanced at the strong box which he had placed back inside the wagon. *I trust him.* "Think about it while we're gone, and help yourself to more food. We'll be back soon."

Favonius and his family then left Phoebus Pen Dragon alone by their fire with his wolf, and set off for the city to report the attack. As they left, Fenella turned to look back at the lonely young man staring into the fire.

. . .

The sun was getting higher in the morning sky and the clouds began to burn away, the threat of rain paused for the moment.

Phoebus would have liked to enjoy the calm of that secluded spot, but the blood-stained grass nearby reminded him that no place was truly safe except for Ynis Wytrin. He missed the Isle of the Blessed, the peace, the calmness that filled him so easily there, that is, when he allowed it to, and he had not done so for a very long time. When he had been there, at the heart of the Isle, he had been filled with a world of hurt and a sense of abandonment that harried him at all times.

Except when he was with her. *Rachel...* he thought, missing her touch, her voice, and the sense of peace he only enjoyed in her presence. He wondered how she was, if she was angry with him for leaving.

His worry for his mother, who had also disappeared into the wilds beyond the blessed borders of Ynis Wytrin had, however, become stronger than anything else. He had lost his father, twice over, and so he refused to accept that his mother was also lost to the anger which had filled her.

"Dragons are blessed and cursed by the Gods..." he said to the flickering fire.

Then he remembered the rumour he had heard in Viroconium the day before as he had snuck through the market stalls, while Remus hunted in the forests outside of the city.

"There are Praetorians in Britannia," he heard a group of veterans say, "and they're hunting dragons."

At least, that is what he thought they said, but even if it was not true, the thought had been planted in his mind and the worry for his mother had grown more urgent and acute afterward. *Could it be that they are still, after so long, hunting us? Why won't they leave us alone?*

He was relieved Calliope and their aunt, Clarinda, were safe in Ynis Wytrin, but he worried also for his grandparents in Lindinis, exposed as they were to anyone with ill intent.

He tossed the wolf a piece of dried meat which Nola had set out, and then served himself more porridge. He thought about Favonius' offer to join them at their farm. It was tempting, the thought of a bed instead of rough camping in forests and on windswept moors. The last time he had slept in a bed had been months before when he had visited with the Lord Afallach and the hidden dragons.

Lord Afallach had urged him to stay for a while, but as no one in the north had had word of, nor seen, Adara Pen Dragon, Phoebus decided to continue his search. He stuck to rough goat tracks and moved cross country during the days, and joined the Roman arteries by night if he could not sleep.

All the while, Remus, whom he had rescued, had remained by his side and saved him many a time from bandits along the road.

Phoebus stroked the wolf's head as the beast lay down beside him, sleeping while his master kept watch this time.

"Favonius and his family are good and kind, and Salinae is on the way south," he said to himself and the sleeping wolf. "Perhaps we should stay with them for a while?"

He thought about it as he waited for the family to return.

Viroconium was disorganized and dirty the day after the great market, like a badly hungover legionary on furlough after a heavy night of drinking. The streets were littered with vomit and detritus and several unconscious men who had fallen out of the tabernae doors in the early hours.

The smoke from the hypocausts of the great bathhouse began to billow up into the sky above the tiled rooftops, and the forum was already full of the usual stalls, though they numbered far fewer than the day before as many merchants had already begun to travel back to their homes.

Gaius Favonius and his family walked beneath the colonnade along Wattling Street, between the baths and the forum.

Favonius clutched the long bundle of linen which contained the gladius he had just purchased for the man who had helped them.

"Are you sure he'll accept it?" Nola asked her husband.

"He needs one," Favonius replied. "I'm happy to provide him with one. It's the least we can do for him…unless he takes us up on our offer to come to the farm."

"What if he takes all of our things, Pater?" Lew asked. "Aren't you worried?"

Favonius put his hand on Lew's shoulder. "He won't. A man doesn't risk his life to help people he only intends to steal from. I can tell he's a good one."

"I'm hungry!" Lon said suddenly to his mother. "Can we go to the baker and get a pork pie?"

Nola looked to her husband. "We could use some more provisions for the journey home."

Favonius thought about it a moment. "Good idea. How about you take the children to get supplies while I go to find the magistrate?"

"I don't want to go shopping," Lew protested. "I want to stay with you, Pater!"

"Fine then," Favonius said, ruffling his younger son's dark hair. "You come with me, but you have to stay quiet."

"Of course I will, Pater. I'm not a baby." The boy rolled his eyes.

Favonius smiled at his wife, daughter, and older boy. "I'll see you soon."

They went their separate ways in the forum, Nola, Fenella and Lon heading for the bakers' stalls, while Favonius and Lew made for the administrative offices of the local magistrate on the western side of the vast forum.

"The magistrate is in an important meeting right now," a secretary in the aula just outside the magistrate's tablinum said to Favonius. "I can't disturb him right now."

"But it's important!" Favonius explained. "My family and I were set upon by three men last night."

"Did they steal your possessions?" the secretary asked.

"They tried."

"Did they harm you or your family?"

"My wife was wounded."

"Did they run away?"

Favonius looked at the other men waiting on the benches. "The men are dead. That's why I'm here. To report the bodies."

"Well if they are dead, then they aren't going anywhere quickly, are they?" the secretary said, tapping his stylus on his wax tablet. "You'll have to sit and wait with the others." He pointed to the benches and went to speak with another group.

Favonius looked at Lew. "Be glad that we're farmers, my boy. It's much safer. Bureaucracy will kill a man." He went to sit with his son and wait. He scanned the benches to see a couple local landholders and merchants, as well as a couple of soldiers in strange black uniforms. The latter gave him pause, but he was too annoyed with the secretary to care.

"Do you think Phoebus Pen Dragon will like the gladius you got him?" Lew asked, eyeing the bundle his father had across his knees.

"He'll be reluctant to accept it, I think. But we should repay the man's kindness for helping us."

"You say you were attacked?" asked one of the older landholders, a man with a grey beard and deep blue tunica trimmed with gold.

"Aye," Favonius said. "They came upon us in the night. Three of them." Others were listening now, for they were all concerned when it came to local raiders and thugs. It was always a risk around the time of Viroconium's great market days with so many coming from all around.

"But the man with the wolf came to help us and slew them all!" Lew explained excitedly. "It was a great battle!"

"Sounds like you were very brave," the landholder said, smiling at the boy.

"He was," Favonius replied with a smile, his thick arm about his boy. *Gods, may we never have to deal with such a thing ever again,* he prayed, his eyes upon the altar in the middle of the forum before him.

"I want to be a dragon warrior like him," Lew said. "I'll get the same tattoos on my arms and everything!"

"You'll work the farm and herd the sheep like me and your brother. It's peace time now. No need for fighting." Favonius was proud of his boy, despite his romantic notions of battle. He hoped he would not be harried by nightmares after the previous night's events. "What is taking so long?" he said aloud. "Have you been waiting long?" he asked one of the merchants.

The plump man sighed. "Over an hour already!" he sucked his fingers which were covered with honey from a pastry he had been eating. "And all I want to do is pay a fine."

Some of the others laughed at that.

"I don't want to wait that long. Come one, son," Favonius stood. "We'll come back later. Let's go find your mother."

They were only a few steps into the courtyard of the forum when two men in black armour stepped out from the aula where they had been sitting.

"Excuse me, citizen!" one of them called out as he walked toward Favonius and Lew.

Favonius stopped and turned. He eyed the man up and down and did not like the look of him, his eyes. He did not recognize the uniform with a bleeding aquila upon it, though he noted that his weapons were of the highest quality. "Yes, what is it?"

"I couldn't help but overhear your conversation back there," the man asked. "You say you were attacked last night?"

"That's right. But it's taken care of. I just wanted to report the bodies to the magistrate." Favonius looked at the big man behind the one who addressed him. "I'm sorry, but I have to get going. I'll be back to report it to the magistrate."

The soldier smiled and knelt before Lew. "You say a 'dragon' helped you fight the men?"

"Yes!" Lew answered quickly. "Him and his black wolf!"

"Why do you call him a 'dragon', this man?" the soldier asked.

"The tattoos, of course!" Lew responded, pulling up his sleeves.

"Come on, son," Favonius said, pulling at the boy. "Don't make up stories." He looked at the two men before him. *There's something not right about these men!* His soldier's senses screamed. "Boys and their imaginations. I'm sorry, we really must get going." Favonius pulled Lew away and began to cross the forum hurriedly, making for Wattling Street.

"But Mama's over there!" Lew said, pointing to the market stalls on the far side.

"We need to go now!" Favonius said.

"What do you think, sir?" the second soldier said to the first.

"I think we have our first lead. Follow him, Victor. See where he leads you."

"Yes, sir!" the man said before his black form darted across the forum after the man and his boy.

The soldier then turned to go back to the aula. "That's enough waiting," he said as he marched straight to the magistrate's tablinum door and kicked it in. "I'm here on behalf of the Emperor, and I'm through with waiting!"

"Come on, Lew!" Favonius said as they hurried down the street and through the southern gate of the city.

"What's wrong, Pater?"

"Something about those men I didn't like."

They hurried among the monuments flanking the roadside and then turned right down the track that led through the trees to their campsite.

Favonius broke into a run, his son following after him.

When they arrived at the camp, they found Phoebus Pen Dragon looking out over the ravine, praying with his palms upward. "You have to leave, quickly!"

The man turned, the wolf at his side, suddenly very alert.

Favonius arrived panting. "You have to leave now. Disappear!"

"What happened?" Phoebus asked.

"There are soldiers in black armour with a bloody eagle upon the chest. I don't recognize them, but they were asking what happened here, asked about a 'dragon'." He looked at Phoebus' forearms. "I think they're looking for *you*."

Remus looked to the trees and began to growl.

"Go now. These aren't mere robbers. They're trained. I can tell."

"We can fight them, Pater!" Lew protested.

Favonius shook his head. "If you can find your way to Salinae to join us later, that is good, but for now you need to go."

"I'm sorry if I've put you in danger," Phoebus said as he picked up his satchel and cloak. "May the Gods grant you a safe journey home."

"And you, wherever you go," Favonius replied, looking over his shoulder to the woods. "Now go. And thank you for helping us."

"I can stay and help," Phoebus said.

"No. Just go. I can delay them if they come."

"Farewell," Phoebus said before running south along the cliffs with Remus following. They then turned down a steep path to the river far below.

Favonius watched them disappear and sighed with relief when they were out of sight. He then turned to his son. "Lew, let's pack up camp and then take the wagon back to the city to get your mother, brother, and sister."

"Pater!" Lew said. "You forgot to give him his present!"

Favonius looked at the bundle still clutched in his hand and sighed. "I guess the Gods have other plans. Let's get to work." He leaned the bundle against the wagon and they set about rolling the fleeces they had slept on about the fire, and packing the iron pots in which they had cooked their breakfast.

When that was done, Favonius began hitching the horses to the wagon, and it was then that the sound of footsteps came into his hearing. "Lew, hide!" he hissed. "Who's there?" he called out, moving to the open ground away from the wagon on the other side of the fire. When no one answered, he drew the gladius that hung from his cingulum.

One of the men in black armour from the forum appeared around the back of the wagon.

"Salve, citizen," the man said.

"What do you want?" Favonius demanded.

"Why are you in such a hurry to leave?" The man's eyes were cold and hard, and he looked as though he was someone always on the verge of violence. "I have some questions for you."

"Well, maybe you can sheathe your gladius first," Favonius nodded at the sword which he held so casually.

"Where's your son? Maybe he'll be more apt to answer my questions if you won't."

"Here's an idea," Favonius said, seeing Lew hiding beneath the wagon behind the man, trying to reach for the bundled gladius he had left there. "How about you and I walk back to discuss it with the magistrate."

"I don't think so," the man said, levelling his blade at Favonius. "Tell me about this 'dragon' who helped you last night."

Favonius smiled and shook his head as he stared back at the man. "I don't think so." He readied himself, in a fighting stance, but not before Lew came rushing at the soldier's back with the new gladius in hand. "Lew, NO!"

But the boy was already moving. He slashed at the soldier's hamstring, but it was not enough to stop him as he spun and thrust, pinning the boy's body to the side of the wagon with his blade.

"AAAH!" Favonius shouted. He reached the attacker in three bounds, swung and took him deep in the side of the neck.

The body fell to the ground, blood spurting in every direction, but Favonius paid it no heed as he pulled the blade from his son and took him into his arms.

"Lew...Lew... It's all right. I'm here, I'm here!" His hands shook and his eyes blurred with tears.

"Pa... Pater... Help me..."

"It's going to be all right, Lew... I'm here..." Favonius held his son, and looked down at the wound through his chest where his lifeblood flowed as freely as a mountain spring.

"Pater... I'm... I'm cold..." He smiled briefly, coughing blood. "Did I...did I fight well?"

"You did, son," Favonius said, his tears falling onto his son's forehead. "I'm so proud of you."

Lew smiled, and then took his last breath.

Gaius Favonius held his son tightly to his chest then, and roared his anguish over the river valley, sending birds scattering in every direction from the trees.

Phoebus and Remus travelled south the whole of that day, following the winding flow of the Sabrina, staying as hidden as possible in the trees and shrubs that reinforced the river's banks. As they went, he felt a deep dread in the pit of his stomach, for what might have been a welcome respite with a kind family on their farm had been replaced by a sudden menace.

He worried the whole of the day, and whether that worry was more weighted toward the safety of the family he had dared to help, or the thought of Roman soldiers looking for a 'dragon', he was not sure. What he did know was that he had to get away, get into the wilds quickly.

By nightfall, he was ready to collapse, and so he laid himself down in the middle of a remote field beneath an expansive sky to watch the stars emerge, and the moon cast its cold glow over the land.

Wrapped in his black cloak, a pugio his only remaining weapon, Phoebus lay there beside Remus, his only friend, and began to torture himself with the list of his failures.

The wolf's yellow-gold eyes scanned the darkness around them, alert to every mouse and mole that might be a feast, searching for any threat that may come upon them in that lonely openness.

Remus' breathing calmed Phoebus whose hand reached out to touch his back as though the animal were a talisman of some sort. "I've failed to find her, Remus," he said. "What if Mama is dead and no one knows it?" The thought of that burned his eyes and a shot of pain stabbed at his gut, not of hunger, but of such guilt that it made his head spin.

He had hoped that Brencis or Lord Afallach would have had word of his mother in the north, that their ranging riders would have had some sort of news, no matter how small, that might have given him hope of tracking her, of finding her. But they knew no more than he.

Thankfully, Lord Afallach had secretly given his most trusted men instruction to make quiet enquiries of their allies.

The loneliness of the task he had set himself in leaving Ynis Wytrin began to settle upon him like a heavy boulder fallen from a crumbling cliff. That loneliness had been temporarily held at bay whenever he had helped others on his journey - a lame veteran trying to plow a field on his own, a girl who had been set upon by Romans while picking wild garlic along a river and, more recently, the family of Gaius Favonius when they were attacked. There were many others too, people whose faces faded in his memory, whose cries when he failed them haunted him, and whose gratitude echoed for too short a time. The Gods, it seemed, did have a plan for him, but he wondered when they would help him achieve what he so desperately sought: his mother and the safety of what family he had left to him.

His mind raced among all these thoughts and he sat up to search in his satchel for his last chunk of incense. On a flat bit of shale which he also carried, Phoebus lit the wood shavings from his small tinder box, and set the incense alight, his hands pleading to the night sky.

"Apollo… Avus… Guide me on my path. I don't know where to go, or what to do anymore." He paused, his mind too much of a tangle to clearly form his prayer. He hoped the Gods would be able to hear his feelings instead. But then, as the smoke wafted about him and swirled up into the night, he prayed to the one person who had remained silent those many years.

"Baba… Why did you leave us? Why did you have to pass into Elysium without so much as a word? I miss you…" He began to weep, and pounded the ground. "You're the reason Mama left!" The moment he said it, he exhaled painfully, shaking his head. "I know you used to say we were never alone, but I've never felt more alone than I do in this moment."

Remus sat up and looked up at the moon then. The wolf's eyes softened and looked from that silver sliver above to Phoebus.

"I'm not totally alone," Phoebus smiled and ran his hand through Remus' thick coat. "We'd better rest. We have to keep moving tomorrow." Phoebus then laid himself back on the ground, his eyes focussing on the moon as his lids grew heavier and heavier…

.   .   .

The sound of screaming woke him, and the shaking of the earth threw him to the ground when he tried to get to his feet.

Phoebus Pen Dragon looked for his wolf, but Remus was gone. The stars effused a strange light and suddenly, a thousand of them burst into flames only to have those flames fall from the heavens to set the surrounding field alight.

The screaming was suddenly very near, and Phoebus turned around to see his sister calling to him, pleading... *Brother! Come home! Help us! Help us!* She wept tears of blood as she looked upon him, and grasped painfully at her gut as if she had been stabbed.

"Calliope!" Phoebus made to run to her, but then was stopped when more screams cracked the earthly plane behind him.

He spun to see an Amazon warrior, a bloody blade in her hand, dripping so much that it flooded the ground around her. Her hair was soaked with gore, her skin stained crimson. She let loose a great battle cry and turned to her right, sword raised high above her head.

"Mama?" Phoebus shouted, making to run to her only to find that his feet were rooted to the earth. "Mama, I'm coming!"

His sister and mother's keening tore at his heart as he tried to move to either one of them, unable to do so. They did not look upon him, however, for they gazed upon something that filled them with such dread that they had no eyes for him.

Phoebus stared into the darkness with them where, cutting through the fields of fire that surrounded them, black and bleeding ships sailed toward them, their hulls grating the land like a rush of grinding rocks.

The ships towered above them, not slowing, but speeding, even as their hulls splintered upon the earth and blood and bodies poured out of every crack. Upon the decks, a thousand swords pointed at them, matched by a thousand eyes, and a thousand curses.

Phoebus grasped desperately at his side for the sword that was not there, fumbling and scratching until his fingernails were ripped away and his hands bled freely.

The flames rose to the heavens about Phoebus, his sister, and their mother, and as they prepared to die, an even greater terror shattered the air behind them as a thousand black riders screamed and crashed into them such that the world became one of fire and death.

The last thing Phoebus saw was the great ouroboros of flame encircling them, closing in, blinding them and binding them.

Suddenly, the flames disappeared, and there was a fleeting moment of quiet. Phoebus was alone.

Then he heard the deafening clang of sword on sword, and the feeling of a blade breaking in his hand returned like a memory of a thousand cuts. There was no song in the clang, but flat notes of fell breaking and helplessness.

"GODS!" he screamed, feeling as though he would never again be able to fight with a blade unless it was that which he had longed for, that which had belonged to his father.

Water suddenly engulfed him, drowning him and dragging him to the bottom of a dark pool where he grasped at a watery altar for succour and sanctuary, only to be swept away in a violent current, the air in his lungs but a thing of memory…

Phoebus gasped and screamed and sat up suddenly. Sweat poured from his brow and he shook uncontrollably.

Remus sat staring at him, calm, his eyes gazing into him as if he had been watching the horrors unfold in his master's mind.

Phoebus wept then, his hand rubbing roughly at his eyes as if he tried to claw out the visions that had harried him in his sleep. "I can't go on like this!" he screamed up at the moon.

That silvery light suddenly held his eyes, and he was calmed, soothed by it, the stillness about him and the animal beside him.

You must go on…

Phoebus froze. His eyes looked down from the moon and stars to see the Lord of the Silver Bow standing before him.

"Apollo?" Phoebus said, his voice but a hush. He fell to his knees before his grandfather and wept.

Apollo stood before him in the stillness, his blue cloak whipped by a wind Phoebus could not feel, his divine form lit by a sun Phoebus could not see. In his eyes were the whirling stars in duplicate, shining and shooting across the heavens as they gazed upon the young man. *You must go on, Phoebus…you must fight on.*

"I can't… I'm so tired…" He felt his body want to collapse upon the ground. "What did I just see in my dreams? What did you show me?" Phoebus asked, unafraid to pour out his questions and demands at Apollo's feet. "Are my sister and mother dead?"

They live.

Phoebus felt relief fill him, give him strength.

But the Black Ships have come, Apollo said, the last note of his voice echoing like those grating hulls upon the earth.

"But why? Why are they here?"

Because Rome hunts...for Death...and the Dragon.

"And what am I supposed to do? I don't understand!" Phoebus shouted.

You are the son of the Dragon... Apollo said, taking a step closer to him. *You* are *a Dragon...*

Phoebus shook his head. "Then why do I feel so weak?" he demanded. "Why did father abandon us to this world of hate and pain?" Suddenly, Phoebus stood up and faced the god before him. "Where is he? Why did you take him away from us?"

I did not. He is Everywhere. He is Everything.

"That's not an answer!" Phoebus shouted.

It is Truth.

Apollo then stepped right up to Phoebus, his star-whirling eyes looking down at him with love and compassion. He reached out with strong and ethereal hands to touch his crown.

Phoebus suddenly felt the lack of pain and deep hurt with which he had been living. He felt alive. He felt the memory of purpose and strength return to his mind, and to his body. He felt truly calm for the first time in a long while. "Thank you."

The time is near, Phoebus, and Death's beginning is always difficult. You must be ready...

Phoebus closed his eyes, his breath steady, his mind clear at last.

When he opened his eyes again, Apollo was gone, and Remus, who had been silent as he stared at the god the entire time, began to howl at the moon as if wailing for the emptiness of his departure.

The night at an end, the sun rose to cast shadows behind every blade of grass and flower about Phoebus. Sunlight spread, its warmth reviving the ground at his feet, its light filling his eyes again with new determination and hope.

"Rome is coming," Phoebus said, Apollo's words ringing in his mind and memory. He remembered the nightmare visions he had seen, of his mother and sister, of the black and bleeding ships. "We are the Dragons," he said as he held his arms up to the light to see the images upon his skin. He remembered his father's smile as he trained him in the sunlight upon the grassy mound of their hillfort home so many years ago.

Remus growled and nudged his leg.

Phoebus then picked up his satchel, rolled the fleece he had slept upon, and tied it. "We're going south, Remus. After we check on our friends, I'm going to get the sword that will help me to stop Rome once and for all."

With the morning sun rising higher in a vast blue and white sky, Phoebus and Remus set off across the field, now a little less fearful of the Death which the Gods had warned him of.

XI

VITA INANIS

'An Empty Life'

The ways of the past do not easily die in our hearts and minds, especially if one is not the arbiter of the change that has influenced the life one loves so very much. We are addicted to nostalgia, and that addiction, more often than not, keeps us from joy in the present.

The moment Delphina Antonina read those words on the latest scroll from her favourite Etrurian playwright, she had to stop. They struck too acute a chord in her mind as she sat alone in the tiny garden at the heart of their domus in the town of Lindinis.

She thought of her husband, Publius Leander Antoninus, and how he had once been a joyful, life-loving man, a caring husband and father. They had had many wonderful years together, but the powers that be in Rome intended something else for their family.

And Publius blamed it all on their association with the Metellus family, or the 'Pen Dragon' family as they were now called.

"Lucius turned our world to ash in the wind!" Publius often said, and had done for years.

"Addicted to nostalgia," Delphina repeated the words she had read and reached down from her chair to touch the fresh rosemarinus border near her couch. She smelled her hand and closed her eyes as she did so, letting the scent of the herb soothe her. She understood her husband's addiction. Truly. For she too sometimes found herself longing for the past, for those long ago days on the sun-drenched slopes of Mount Hymettos outside of Athenae when she would watch their daughters play in the olive grove and swipe some honey from the hives. She often remembered seeing their daughter, Adara, ride her favourite horse along the mountain pathways, her black hair trailing in the wind behind her, a broad smile spanning her face. She remembered bringing the walls of their villa to life with paint, brush, and pigment, and the happy convivia they hosted when guests always left feeling inspired.

As a magistrate of the city, Publius had enjoyed much respect and had been able to do much good for both the Hellenes and Romans of Athenae, all of whom looked to him. Those had been heady days indeed, when Publius had marched in the great Panathenaea of the city alongside the populace.

But whereas Delphina remembered those days and expressed her gratitude to the Gods for having granted them that time, Publius lingered constantly in those memories and saw them as having been wrenched out of his helpless, aged hands by others, by Rome, and by his daughter's husband. A part of Publius had been happy Lucius was dead, and he hoped that his death would now ensure their safety, and that of their daughter, and their two grandchildren.

Delphina knew her husband's mind, his resentments, very well. In his mind, violent change had been forced upon them the way a rough wastrel forces himself upon a young and beautiful girl picking flowers in a field. Publius had lost all the standing and respect he had once enjoyed, as well as his ability to do good. Their two younger daughters had gotten as far away from them as possible. Their beautiful home on Hymettos had been burned to the ground, and several attempts on their lives had been made as they had been hunted across the Empire. Now they were stuck in isolation in Britannia where Helios rarely deigned to shine, in a tiny domus barely big enough for the two of them. They had no friends, and they no longer saw their daughters or their grandchildren.

And Publius blamed it all on Lucius and his hubris which, he believed, the Gods were punishing them all for.

Delphina, however, yearned to see things differently. She remembered the great joy upon her daughter's face when she had met and married Lucius, the blessings that their children were upon all of their lives. She thanked the Gods for having protected them against the intentions of evil men. They had survived great trials and violence which would have seen the demise of most others long ago, and that survival had also been largely due to Lucius and the men he surrounded himself with.

Lucius Pen Dragon, however, was gone, and Delphina now struggled with the emptiness she felt at no longer seeing her beloved daughter or grandchildren, or even knowing that they were safe.

For a time, after they had escaped from Delphi to Britannia, they had dwelled together in the windswept fortress of Din Tagell. But that had not lasted. Publius had hated the isolation of that rocky, barbarian fortress, harried constantly by the sound of wind and the cacophony of gulls. He had refused the sanctuary of Ynis Wytrin also, not wishing to live in hiding among Druids and Christians. In Delphina's mind, it was her husband's absolute refusal to live in either place that left them lonely, sad and isolated in Lindinis, encased in a tiny home and choked by the smoke from the local fabricae.

Publius longed for a measure of public life and service, and so, shortly after their arrival from Din Tagell, he made approaches to the Ordo of Lindinis as a simple, retired landowner by the name of Publius Leander. He had decided to choose public life over family and safety and, despite Delphina's protestations and fears, he had succeeded.

The Ordo welcomed him into their midst, into what Delphina believed to be their dark and dishonest world of schemes, all in the pursuit of provincial wealth.

Delphina did not like the Ordo members or their wives, except for a Briton, a man named Trevor Reghan, who was one of the longest standing members, and who had been friendly to her daughter's family years before.

She thought of all of this daily while Publius was out on Ordo business, even as she tended meticulously to the small garden of lavender, wild marjoram, thyme, mugwort, and rosemarinus which orbited her small couch.

With a painful sigh, she sat up and set her bare feet upon the cold pebble ground. She ran her hands through her white hair and tied it back with a small leather thong from one of the letters her granddaughter had sent her many years before.

She stepped into the small atrium of their domus and turned to observe her world of confinement, breathing in and out calmly, as was her habit when the nostalgia threatened to strangle her.

From a small side street, their domus was accessed by way of a plain black door which gave onto an atrium with a lararium on the left and a small kitchen to the right. The garden lay directly ahead with a cubiculum and a triclinium to the right, and another cubiculum and a small room for her art to the left. The largest room, her husband's tablinum, lay at the back of the domus.

It had pained her when Publius suggested that they sleep in separate cubicula, but as his anger often emerged in his sleep, she acquiesced to his wish so that she could manage at least a modicum of slumber.

Delphina turned to the lararium and there, in the flame she kept burning, she lit a chunk of incense and set it upon the small stone altar before the images of Vesta, Jupiter, Diana, Venus and Apollo.

"Oh Gods... I thank you for my blessings, large and small, and I pray to you, as ever, for the safety of my children and grandchildren, wherever they are, whatever they are doing. Please continue to watch over them and protect them."

Her heart beat painfully, the sound an echo in the ears as she gazed upon the fluttering flame of the clay lamp and the swirling smoke of her offering. No matter how much she tried to nurture optimism and gratitude, she found that she could not fight her sadness, and the deep loneliness which her husband had forced upon her.

Lindinis was not home, and never would be for her, no matter how many times she strolled the stalls of its sad market or listened to the gossip of the local women.

As long as my family is safe, she thought.

Later that evening, as darkness filled the streets of Lindinis, Delphina stood in her small studio, staring at yet another blank expanse of white plaster upon her easel. Painting had required much more effort for many years, mainly since the death of Antonia Metella in Delphi.

Antonia had become a dear friend, along with the sculptor, Emrys, and in their Delphic exile, they had developed a shared appreciation of the peace that art gave them in the midst of their world of chaos. But with Antonia's death, the inspiration Delphina and Emrys felt had drowned in their grief.

She often thought of Emrys and his apprentice, Carissa, and hoped that they were thriving in Gaul where they sought to escape the pain of the past and start a new life.

For Delphina, the death of a grandchild and the departure of her daughter's husband on a road of vengeance and blood had also ensured the death of her artistic will. Her inspiration was now like a man who had given up and laid himself down upon the cracked earth of a desert plain to die.

Everyday, however, Delphina stood before her easel and plaster, a brush or a piece of charcoal poised in her hand, trying to create something, every effort like a desperate breath to stay alive, to keep going, to create anything.

"Oh Divine Muses…" she prayed, inhaling the scent of the pigments that surrounded her. "Help me to feel alive again…to honour you as I once did…" She closed her eyes, her hand hovering over the plaster square, and envisioned a bright river at the bottom of a tunnel of green trees, willow and oak, their limbs covered in ivy, strangled by mistletoe. She had no idea how the vision had come to her, for she had never seen such a thing.

Her hand began to move, tracing thin black lines along the river's edge, the pebbles of the shore, and the roots of the trees which gave way to their soaring arches.

Delphina smiled as she worked, relished the feelings that began to emerge.

But a loud and hurried pounding upon their domus door burst in on her creative flow like an unwanted and drunken guest at a family cena. She tried to ignore the pounding, hoped the person would go away.

The pounding, however, continued.

Delphina set the charcoal down and walked to the atrium to lean close to the door. "Who is it?" she demanded.

"Lady Delphina," a voice said, not wanting to yell.

"Yes?" she replied, quickly picking up a small pairing knife from the kitchen behind her.

"I have a message from Lord Einion," the man said, his words barely above a whisper.

Delphina thought for a moment and then opened the small hatch in the top of the door to peer out into the street.

She recognized the man from Din Tagell, one of Lord Einion's riders, but could not recall his name. She made to unbolt the door.

"No. Do not open. It is safer locked," he said, leaning closer to the door.

"But why?" she asked.

He did not answer, but looked to either side down the dark street. "I bring a message for you and your husband from Lord Einion." He reached beneath his cloak and produced a small, rolled piece of papyrus which he handed her through the latticed iron of the opening.

Delphina accepted the scroll and looked at him. "Please. Come in for water and food."

The man shook his head, the braids of his long hair twisting as he turned to look both ways again. "Thank you, but I cannot. I must get back to Din Tagell in all haste."

"Is something wrong?" she asked.

"It is in the message," he said. "Forgive me, but I most go. It is safer to travel at night."

"But what about…"

He was gone, his footsteps echoing hurriedly down the street.

Delphina closed the hatch and went to the lararium, cut the string with her pairing knife, and began to read the message by the light of the lamp.

Publius and Delphina,

It has come to our attention that men from Rome are searching for your family. We know not how many, nor who they are, but they are coming.

For everyone's safety, I suggest you come to Din Tagell until they give up their search, or until the threat is eliminated.

"Eliminated?" she repeated.

Your family is joining us at Din Tagell. I regret to say that I do not have additional men to escort you here, for they are all engaged in the search.

If you can get yourselves to Din Tagell safely, I urge you to do so.

May the Gods bless you.

Einion, Lord of Din Tagell

Delphina felt her hands begin to shake, and she gripped the edge of the lararium to steady herself. *Not again,* she thought. *Gods protect us.* "Publius, where are you?"

She went back through the domus to set the letter upon her husband's desk in the tablinum, and returned to the studio to try and assuage her fears by continuing her sketch.

She took up the charcoal once more, her hand hovering over the whiteness, trying to rejoin the lines she had been drawing. But it was no use. Her mind was awash with Einion's words.

Men from Rome are searching for your family.

She set the charcoal back down, feeling her momentary defeat acutely, and sat herself upon the wooden stool to stare blankly at the plaster.

"Delphina!" Publius Leander Antoninus called into the domus when he arrived sometime later. He turned to slide home the bolt on the door and hung his cloak on one of the pegs beside it. "I'm sorry I'm late. I was going over some things with a few of the Ordo members." He went to the lararium, took a small branch of cedar from the dish, and set it alight in the flame before placing it upon the altar. "They want to pursue my idea of a proper colonnade in the square!" He smiled as he spoke, excited by the prospect. "We're going to use all the local fabricae too, so that will keep the work and profits here."

When Delphina did not answer, he turned to the interior of the domus.

"Where are you? Is everything all right?" He looked into the garden to see if she was sleeping there, but she was not. The kitchen was dark. Neither was she in her cubiculum as he passed on his way to the studio. "There you are!" he said, leaning in the doorway. "Why didn't you answer me?"

Delphina turned to look at her husband. There were times she did not recognize him, his white hair and matching beard betraying her memories of how he used to look. *I suppose I am also a victim of nostalgia,* she thought before standing up and going to hug him. She lingered in his embrace.

Publius' smile faded. "What is it, love?" He glanced at the plaster. "I see that you have started a new piece. That's wonderful!" He let go of her and looked at it. "A river in the forest? Is that it? I see the British terrain is having an effect upon you."

"I started it but could not continue because I started to worry," she said.

"I'm sorry. Truly. I…oh, Gods. You finally started to work again and I stoppered the process." He grasped her hands.

Delphina shook her head. "It's not you, Publius." Her eyes locked onto his. *He is happy right now, but he needs to know.* "We received a letter from Lord Einion. I set it upon your table."

His face darkened and he went directly to his tablinum, lit the bronze, three-spouted lamp which hung from its stand, and took up the scroll which Delphina had laid open for him to see.

She appeared at the door, watching him as he read the short but urgent missive. She waited for him to look at her, but he did not.

Publius rounded the table and sat in the large chair which was covered in sheep's fleece. He stared at the letter, not wanting to touch it again as if it were a dirty thing. "Gods damn it," he growled. "I can't do this again."

"I know." Delphina stepped into the room and sat in one of the two chairs before the desk. "I was thinking we could leave in a couple of days, after the next market. I want to get something nice for Adara and the children."

He looked up at her, the warring anger and confusion clear upon his face. He shook his head. "Whatever do you mean? This is not good news, Delphina."

"I know. I was quite upset at first, but then I thought that once we are all in Din Tagell, at least we'll be together again!" She smiled wistfully. "We haven't seen our daughter in so long…and Phoebus and Calliope must be so grown up now."

"Delphina…" He tried to keep his voice calm, but could not manage it. He breathed slowly through his nose and he looked from the letter to his wife. "We're not going to Din Tagell."

"Whatever do you mean? Of course we're going. We have to!" She pointed at the letter. "You read what Lord Einion wrote. Men from Rome are looking for our daughter and grandchildren. That has never been a good thing, Publius!" Her voice approached a shout, and he sat back to look at her.

"You are distraught, and you are not thinking clearly."

"I'm thinking very clearly, husband," she replied. "Our family is in danger once again. We must get to safety. We must be with our daughter and grandchildren."

Publius shook his head. "Delphina... They want nothing to do with us. They are grown, and have lives of their own."

"They are in danger."

"And they will deal with it. They always have, and without us."

"I want to go to Din Tagell," she insisted.

His face hardened then. *I'll not be moved,* he resolved. "I am only just beginning to gain respect here, to make headway with my public life once more. Granted, it's not Athenae, but it is something and I don't want to throw it all away."

"Damn your 'public life'!" she shouted.

"It's all I have!" he rebutted.

She shrunk in her chair as though he had slapped her. "You have *me*, Publius."

"I know." He tried to soften his voice, but it did not calm her.

"And you have a duty to your daughter and her family."

"The daughter who left us alone in Athenae? The daughter who married the man who was the cause of all our misery...the reason we find ourselves in this provincial dung heap?"

"The man you encouraged our daughter to marry."

"That was before I knew who he truly was."

"And I thought I knew who *you* truly were," she bit back, shaking her head. "What happened to you?" she demanded.

He was silent for a moment. "I grew wiser."

"Is that what you call it?"

"And I'm tired of running, Delphina." His shoulders slumped. "I can't do it anymore. I just can't!"

He looked pitiful to her, and though her disappointment in him was severe, she knew in her heart that he was in earnest. He was someone who had always felt a deep need to be of public service. And that was indeed the man she had willingly married so many years ago, the man with whom she had raised three beautiful daughters. *I should be easier on him. We're all afraid, and my place is with him,* she thought, and was about to tell him as much when he slammed his hand upon the table.

The lamp swung upon its stand, casting wild shadows about the walls and pigeon hole shelves behind him.

"We're not going to Din Tagell, and that's final!" he shouted.

Delphina stood from the chair without a word, and walked out.

"Where are you going?" he demanded.

"To sleep," she replied, closing the door to her cubiculum a few feet away.

Publius put his head in his hands, leaning upon the table's edge, staring at the letter before him. He pounded the tabletop again and pushed himself up. He remembered his togate days of glory and public service when his wife beamed to look at him and he had marvelled at her creations. Now, her inspiration and her paints had dried up, and the hems of his plain, blue tunica were worn and faded. He turned to his small library and looked for the map of Dumnonia he had. Having found it, he spread it out upon the table, weighing the corners down with four polished rocks he had taken from the banks of the river.

He traced the Roman road southwest to Isca Dumnoniorum and then westward into the barbarian wilds where Lord Einion held sway. He had seen that land once, and he had hated it. It was barren and windswept and uncivilized.

"So far...so isolated..." he said to himself, shaking his head. He thought about going to Delphina's cubiculum, about apologizing for his stubbornness, but he decided against it. "Perhaps she'll see reason after a night's rest?" He then blew out the lamp and went to the kitchen to seek out a crust of bread and a piece of cheese for his lonely cena.

Delphina did not emerge from her cubiculum the next morning before Publius left to take care of some Ordo business, including quotes from the various fabricae for the construction of the proposed colonnade.

He could hear her in her in her room, and stood by the door for a few moments, contemplating knocking and trying to speak with her.

In the end, however, he could not. The conversation they needed to have would be a long one, and he had business to take care of.

After making his daily offering of oil and incense at the small lararium in the atrium, Publius took his grey cloak from the peg, put it on, and went out.

Antonia heard the door lock from her cubiculum and, only then, did she emerge.

. . .

A grey, early morning light had settled over Lindinis to dull the roof tiles and cobbled streets as Publius set about his task of getting quotes for the proposed colonnade.

It was already late morning, but he had accomplished much, having received his quotes from two local masons for the granite columns that would be required, and then quotes from two local fabricae where they produced the imbrices and tegulae required to roof the colonnade so that it would last for years to come.

Grasping his leather folder with the papers inside, Publius stopped in front of the small bathhouse at the centre of the town and looked across the square to where he envisioned the colonnade being built, along the western side of the Fosse Way where it ran through the town from north to south. This would give merchants who rented stalls beneath the colonnade easy access to unload their wares before getting their wagons out of the way, and it would greatly improve the look of the town rather than having the usual ramshackle array of tents and awnings.

The sound of harsh laughter reached his ears and he looked to see a group of what appeared to be soldiers gathered beneath the broad limbs of the oak tree at the centre of the square.

"What are you looking at, white hair?" one of them shouted.

Publius was about to go over and demand to know what their business was, but upon seeing their black weapons he thought better of it and began to set off for home in the opposite direction, northward out of town. He had only got a few steps when he recognized a familiar voice calling to him from the doorway to the bathhouse.

"Publius!" the man called. "May I speak with you?"

Publius turned to see Trevor Reghan coming toward him. As always, he was dressed in the finery of his tribe with rich brown bracae and leather boots, and a dark green tunica and cloak bordered with an interlace of eagles, dragons, and hounds. "Salve, Trevor!" Publius called back, only just spotting the man behind him in black armour with a strange-looking aquila upon his cuirass. His smile faded, for as Trevor walked toward him, he seemed ill at ease. There was something in his eyes Publius could not quite make out.

Trevor was not his usual friendly self, his normally broad smile distinctly absent from his features. "Salve," Trevor replied, his eyes meeting Publius' directly for a moment before speaking. "Publius, may I introduce you to-"

The man quickly stepped around Trevor to face Publius himself. "Aurelius Nemesianus," he said, extending his hand to take Publius'.

Publius reluctantly took the man's hand and immediately wished to pull away for how hard he squeezed.

"Erm…" Trevor began again. "Nemesianus is a special Praetorian envoy from Rome."

"Praetorian?" Publius asked.

"Yes. A special unit, sent directly by the Emperor and Augusta," he cut in again. "I'm here on imperial business to speak with members of the local community about important matters."

Trevor stood aside a little. *Be wary, Publius,* he thought as he watched the old man light up at hearing that.

"From Emperor Alexander Severus?" Publius said, his voice bordering on excitement, for the young emperor was rumoured to be a decent fellow, more like Septimius Severus than the late and detestable Elagabalus, at least from what Publius had heard.

"And the Augusta, Julia Mamaea," Nemesianus added.

"Of course!" Publius replied. "But why come all the way to Britannia? What could possibly concern them in our little corner of the Empire?"

"Well, rumour has it that your town of Lindinis was being considered for civitas status, but it was never approved."

"That was long before Publius joined the Ordo," Trevor said.

"Even so," Nemesianus said, not taking his eyes away from Publius. "The Emperor and Augusta do not like loose ends, or broken promises."

"Of course not." Publius looked to Trevor and then back to Nemesianus. He tried not to look upon the strange, bloody eagle upon the man's armour, or his weapons. "We do try our best in Lindinis to make what improvements we can. Don't we, Trevor?"

"Yes, Publius. We do."

"I can see that." Nemesianus looked at the edge of the plans sticking out of Publius' folder. "You have a new building project in mind?"

Publius looked at his folder and smiled, opening it to show the imperial emissary. "Why yes. See?" He showed him the plans. "A great colonnade to improve the look of the town, but also to provide shelter from this abysmal British weather so that market business can be conducted in comfort."

"An excellent notion!" Nemesianus lit up and smiled at Publius.

"You know… With civitas status finalized, the project could be paid for from the imperial coffers."

"Really?" Publius asked, his voice doubtful. "I've never heard of such a thing in my time in public service."

"It's a new program. The Emperor wishes to help those communities in the most remote parts of his empire."

"Well!" Publius shut his folder and stood a little taller. "That *is* good news! The funding will certainly help to speed things along here with our project."

"But there will be some administrative time to process the necessary forms etcetera," Nemesianus leaned in. "You understand."

"Yes. Of course. I know how things work," Publius said with a nod. He looked at where the colonnade would go and could envision it, the unveiling, the praise for what he will have done for Lindinis. *And official civitas status!* he thought.

"I will need to gather all of the details, of course," Nemesianus added, "costs, types of materials, plans… The Emperor would like to see what he is paying for." Nemesianus looked around. "Is there somewhere private we could speak about this and where you can gather the information for me? I've been instructed to be discreet so as not to raise expectations."

"Of course," Publius replied, looking around. "Trevor, is the basilica in use today?"

"Yes. The road worker's guild is meeting there at this moment."

"I really must be going soon. Anywhere is fine," Nemesianus said, placing a friendly hand on Publius' shoulder.

Publius thought for a moment. "Most of my plans and numbers are in my tablinum at home. I was just on my way there now. Do you mind meeting in my small domus?"

Nemesianus smiled. "Not at all."

Publius turned to Trevor. "Would you like to join us, Trevor? You are head of the Ordo after all."

"Yes. I think I should," Trevor said quickly.

"Excellent," Publius said. "This way."

Nemesianus began to follow Publius with Trevor Reghan beside him. He glanced back to the men in the centre of the square. "Dis! Accompany us!"

One of the men then broke away and ran to catch up with them. "We are always supposed to go in twos," Nemesianus said to Publius as they walked.

"The rules for Praetorians must have changed in the last decade," Publius said. "I've never heard that."

"Many changes have been made," Nemesianus said as Dis came up beside him. "You'd be amazed at the sort of men they're recruiting now!"

They walked for a short time until they arrived at the black door of Publius' domus. He opened the door with his iron key, and before he could go in, Nemesianus turned quickly to Trevor Reghan. "I see that the domus is much smaller than I expected. I shall meet with Publius Leander on my own." He turned to his man. "Dis. You also. Wait out here with Trevor Reghan whilst Publius and I discuss these exciting plans of his."

"I'm sure it's fine," Trevor said. "I can stand. I should be a part of the conversation."

"I insist," Nemesianus said, his voice low as he stepped closer to the Briton.

Trevor Reghan met his gaze eye to eye, and he did not like what he saw, a cold, calculating man who was only slowly letting his mask slip. *I see you, Praetorian,* he thought, and he knew that Nemesianus had guessed his own suspicions. That is why he did not want him in the so-called meeting.

"Dis will keep you company," Nemesianus repeated, going in after Publius and shutting the door.

Trevor stood in the narrow street staring at the black face of the door that had just closed.

"I'm sure they won't be very long," the trooper named Dis said.

Trevor crossed his arms and waited while Dis took out his pugio and began to clean his fingernails with the razor sharp edge.

And they call me a 'barbarian', Trevor thought as he stood there, worried for what was being said within.

"Delphina!" Publius called from the atrium once the door was closed. "We have a visitor!"

As Publius went to look for his wife, Nemesianus quickly scanned the small domus and chuckled to himself. *It's almost as small as my prison cell.* "Good." He almost laughed aloud. "This will make things easier."

"What's that you say?" Publius said as he emerged with Delphina from her studio.

"I said it's good of you to see me," Nemesianus replied, eyeing Delphina as she approached with her husband.

"Delphina," Publius said as he led her into the atrium. "This is Aurelius Nemesianus. He's a special Praetorian envoy from Rome."

"Praetorian?" Delphina said, her eyes widening. She felt a sudden stab of fear but tried to hide it.

"Yes," Publius confirmed, a little confused by his wife's response. "He's here about a new building program and wishes to help confirm the status of Lindinis at long last."

"That seems like a strange task for a member of the Praetorian Guard, no?" Delphina said, rallying herself.

"I'm leading a special unit," Nemesianus said with a smile that did not convince her.

She eyed the man, his weapons, his armour, but said nothing more.

"Well…" Publius looked behind him into the domus. "Let's discuss things in my tablinum. There is more space there." He turned to his wife. "Dear, can you bring us some water?"

Delphina looked at her husband, a sudden urge to shake him becoming quite overwhelming. But she remained calm, nodded, and went into the kitchen.

"Come," Publius said, leading the way to his tablinum.

"How long have you lived in this place?" Nemesianus asked.

"Oh…a few years," Publius said as he entered his tablinum and indicated one of the chairs in front of the broad desk covered in papers.

Nemesianus adjusted his gladius and pugio and sat himself down as Publius turned to look at him, a large papyrus sheet spread out before them.

"These are the more detailed plans for the colonnade," he said as he weighed down the edges.

It was then that Delphina brought in a pitcher of water with two clay cups, and a small bowl with a few olives.

Publius looked at her. "Is that all we have?" he asked.

"I haven't been to the market in days," she answered, looking to the Praetorian in their midst. "I'm sorry, Aurelius Nemesianus."

The man put up his hand. "Not at all. You were not expecting company. I understand."

"No, we were not," Delphina replied cooly.

Nemesianus smiled thinly, and then looked at Publius. "Perhaps we can discuss the details of the new program, as well as the status of the town?" He looked from Publius to Delphina.

"Oh, ah, yes. Of course," Publius said. "Dear, would you mind leaving us to our discussions?"

Delphina stared back at her husband. "Perhaps I should remain? After all, I did draw up these more detailed plans?" She looked down to see that the map of Dumnonia was still spread out upon the tabletop.

"Not at all, lady," Nemesianus said. "I wouldn't bother you with such frivolous things. I won't take up much of your husband's time. I know he is a busy man."

Delphina inclined her head. "Then I shall leave you to it." She went out of the tablinum then and into her studio. Once inside, she stood in the middle of her room, her hand upon her chest to try and calm her racing heart. She looked up to the ventilation hole in the wall that led into the tablinum. She then settled herself upon a stool beneath the vent, and sat to listen.

"Now," Publius began. "As you can see, the plans for the colonnade will greatly improve the practical aspect of the square, but also the aesthetics, making it more Roman in design."

The Praetorian then stood up. "I'm afraid that I am here under false pretences, Publius Leander Antoninus."

Publius froze. "Publius Leander," he corrected.

"Publius Leander Antoninus," Nemesianus insisted. "Former magistrate of Athenae."

"How…how… I'm sorry, but you are mistaken, sir."

Nemesianus smiled and shook his head. "I am not."

Publius tried to talk, but his throat was suddenly dry. He took up his cup of water and drank it. "I'm sure I don't know what you mean."

"It's all right. I understand why you panic. But let me assure you that I am here with good news."

"So you are not here about the confirmation of Lindinis' status and the building of the new colonnade?" *Gods, what have I done?* Publius thought.

On the other side of the wall, Delphina listened intently, almost able to hear her husband swallow loudly.

"I am here at the request of Emperor Alexander Severus and our Augusta, Julia Mamaea, with an offer that affects your entire family."

"I'm…I'm afraid you've made a long journey for nothing, Aurelius Nemesianus. My wife and I are the only ones here…and…"

"I understand. But let us say that you are not…hypothetically speaking. Let us say that you have a daughter, and two grandchildren."

Publius shrugged, trying to look confused, but unable to stop the sweat that was forming on his brow.

"Let us say that your son-in-law is the famed praefectus, Lucius Pen Dragon."

Publius gulped. "I don't know who that is."

"Lucius Metellus Anguis, then."

The silence was painfully drawn out, and Nemesianus used it like a torturer's implement to make Publius squirm.

"Have I said something wrong?" Nemesianus suddenly asked. "You know the man of whom I speak."

It was not a question.

On the other side of the wall, Delphina prayed that her husband would not reveal anything, that he would keep his mouth shut.

"The man of whom you speak died many years ago," Publius said.

"I have heard this," the Praetorian replied. "But the Emperor and Augusta do not believe it to be true."

"With respect to their imperial majesties, that is false. Lucius Metellus Anguis died over ten years ago when he took my family away."

"So you *do* know him?"

"I did." Publius stuck out his jaw and shook his head. "To my family's disgrace and destruction, yes. I knew him. And I hate him for what he has done to us."

"Where might I find him?"

"I told you. He is long dead."

"Where might I find his grave then?" Nemesianus pressed. "Surely the 'Dragon' would have a proper burial somewhere, especially in these lands."

"There is none. He disappeared."

"So it is possible he is not dead?"

Publius shook his head. "He is dead. Of that you may be certain."

"Then where might I find your daughter and grandchildren?"

Publius could not hide the panic in his face. "I have not seen them in years. Why do you ask?"

"Now that we have let fall the charade that you do not know of whom I am speaking, I may tell you." Nemesianus walked about the room, behind Publius, casually gazing at the scrolls upon the shelves. "Emperor Alexander Severus, and our Augusta, Julia Mamaea, have instructed me to find the family of Lucius Pen Dragon, as well as his surviving men - his 'dragons' - so that I may offer them a full imperial pardon."

"A pardon?" That took Publius unawares.

"Yes. For Lucius Pen Dragon, his wife, his children, you, and *all* of his men. This, of course, includes the return of all your lands, and the rebuilding of your homes at imperial expense."

Publius sat down. *This cannot be!* he thought. *Gods, would you bless us so?* His mind raced as he went over the implications of what Nemesianus had just said. *We could stop hiding. Stop running. We could rebuild our lives and go back to the way it was!* He realized that all that would not be gift. Something would be required in return. "And what would the Emperor and Augusta wish in return for their great generosity?"

"The Augusta is greatly fearful for the Emperor's life. There is unrest among Rome's enemies, but also among the troops. The Emperor requires the protection of the greatest warrior in Rome's legions, one believed to have the protection of the Gods... The Augusta believes that your son-in-law is that man. She wants him to return to Rome to take up the mantle of Praefectus of the Praetorian Guard."

Publius said nothing.

Nemesianus came back around the front of the table to look down at Publius who was slumped in his chair as though he had been winded by a blow to the gut.

"It is a most generous offer, Aurelius Nemesianus," Publius said after a few moments. He rolled up the plans for the colonnade, which now seemed pointless, and set them aside.

Nemesianus' eyes fell upon the map of Dumnonia then and he leaned forward quickly as Publius put the plans back on his shelf, his back to the Praetorian.

"I'm afraid that the Emperor and Augusta's offer is in vain," Publius said finally. "My son-in-law is truly dead. He abandoned my daughter and grandchildren and disappeared over ten years ago. I would that that were not the case, that we could all return to our properties and lands in Rome and Athenae, but it is impossible."

"If Lucius Pen Dragon is truly dead and gone-"

"He is."

"I have been instructed to make the offer of pardon to your daughter and to those men of Lucius Pen Dragon's who yet survive. It may be that one of them is strong enough to protect the Emperor."

"They are all dead, as far as I know, Aurelius Nemesianus."

"Are you certain? Your son-in-law commanded the loyalty of a great many men. Surely some of them survive?"

"Not that I am aware of," Publius said. He saw Nemesianus looking over the map on the table.

"What is there of interest in Dumnonia?" Nemesianus suddenly asked.

"Oh...ah... I have been looking to invest in some mining operations. Tin, mainly."

"I see. It looks like a wild and remote land."

"It is," Publius replied with disdain, catching himself too late. "I mean, I've heard it is. My interest is merely financial, of course."

Nemesianus looked around the room and out the door into the tiny garden. "Of course," he said, smiling.

"I'm sorry to disappoint you, and more so, to disappoint the Emperor and Augusta."

"I'm sure you are," Nemesianus said, his voice even, low. "But I have travelled a long way to make this important offer and carry out the Emperor and Augusta's request. I would not feel I had discharged my duty properly if I did not at least speak with your daughter, Adara, and your grandchildren...Phoebus and Calliope, is it? When do you expect to see them next?"

"I do not see them," Publius growled. "Nor do I know where they are. As I told you, it is only my wife and I here."

"Yes, you did say that."

"I do wish that we could accept the Emperor and Augusta's offer," Publius added. "But it is quite impossible. I am sorry."

"As am I, Publius Leander Antoninus," Nemesianus said. "My men and I shall, however, be in Britannia for a while on other business. So, if you hear anything, or if you happen to speak to your daughter or grandchildren, do let them know we are looking for them."

"I will indeed," Publius said. "Now, if you'll excuse me..."

"Of course." Nemesianus turned and went out of the tablinum, turning to look into the studio where he saw Delphina standing in the middle of the room, straightening the folds of her stola. "Lady, I thank you for your hospitality."

Delphina inclined her head and watched as Publius led the man into the atrium and showed him out the door. When the door was barred again, she approached her husband to stand before him. Her hands and head shook with fear, with anger, and with disappointment. "How could you?"

"I thought he wanted to help us."

"He doesn't want to help us, or you, or this town! And he certainly doesn't want to help Adara and the children!" Tears formed around her eyes, making the slight amount of makeup she wore run down her cheeks in rivulets the same grey colour as when she rinsed her brushes. "They have been hunting our family for years, and now you've all but approved and signed the death warrant on all of us!"

"I've done no such thing!" Publius bit back, his eyes full of fear.

"And you blame poor Lucius... If anything happens to our daughter and grandchildren, it will be because of you, not the dead of this family!"

Delphina stormed off into her cubiculum then and fell to her knees beside her bed to pray to the Gods for their protection of her daughter, Phoebus and Calliope, wherever they were.

Publius stood quite alone then in the atrium of their tiny domus, staring at the flickering flame of the lamp in the lararium. "Gods... forgive me..."

Outside in the street, Nemesianus found Dis leaning against the wall of another domus a short distance down the street.

"Where is that other Ordo member?" he asked.

"He left a short time ago. Said he had to take care of some business, but that he would meet you at the centre of town beneath the oak tree if you have any more questions."

"He did, did he?"

"You don't trust him?" Dis asked.

Nemesianus shook his head. "I don't trust any of them, but one thing is certain…" He nodded to the black door behind him. "They're the ones we've been looking for. It's the Dragon's wife's parents."

"Did you…" Dis looked around to see they were alone. "Did you dispatch them?"

"No. But they might help us lure out the wife."

"How can you be sure?"

"Fear, and desperation."

"What's next then?" Dis asked.

Nemesianus began to walk and the other followed. "I want you to remain here. Watch their domus. Wait to see if anyone comes."

"How long?"

"I'll let you know. What I do know is that we have to catch these bastards and bring the Augusta some heads if we're to get our own pardons and payments. The incident in Viroconium was no coincidence."

"You think it was the Dragon?"

"Or his son. Or one of his men. Either way, Victor is dead. He was no deserter." Nemesianus stopped walking, and rubbed his chin. "I think I may know where most of them are hiding."

"You do?"

"He had a map of Dumnonia on his desk. Rome's reach does not extend far into that land, at least not anymore."

"You think they are in hiding in the wilds?" Dis smiled.

"Possibly." Nemesianus gripped the handle of his gladius tightly, drumming the handle of his pugio with the fingers of his other hand as he thought. "Pen Dragon and his men may be hiding in Dumnonia… While you wait here and watch them - and only watch them! - I'm going to get a message to Carcer, Tarchon and the others to muster at Isca Dumnoniorum."

"It'll take months," Dis said. "The men are spread out across Britannia."

"They're on the alert now. A little time will lull them, make them think we've given up looking. By the time the men gather, we'll be ready."

"And until then? Are we to just sit and wait?"

"Of course not, Dis. The hunt will continue." Nemesianus laughed. "And something tells me it's going to be most interesting!"

The two of them carried on to meet the others, completely unaware that Trevor Reghan had entered a domus on the other side of the street from a back entrance, that he had been listening to their conversation. When they were gone, out of earshot, he went out of the domus and rushed by back ways to get to the centre of town before they did.

XII

VIA DOLORIS ET SPEI

'A Path of Hurt and Hope'

The journey had been long and difficult, and had taken Phoebus Pen Dragon farther than he had wished to travel on his way south. But it had been necessary, for the Fosse Way from Corinium to Aquae Sulis had been far too busy, riddled with the soldiers in black armour whom Gaius Favonius had warned him about.

Phoebus and Remus travelled southeast, over the dales and across the plains, almost as far as Sorviodunum, before turning westward. All the while, he wondered who those soldiers were, why they had come and why, of all people, they might be looking for him.

They travelled by night, mostly, easily when the moon was high and bright, and with more difficulty when the summer rains poured down, turning the fields to mud beneath his feet. It felt as though the lands of the southern downs fell away more quickly, as if rushing toward something beneath a big sky.

Phoebus was searching for something as he turned west, stealing himself and Remus along small cattle tracks, hidden from sight by high hedges and rows of oak and rowan. The sky began to look familiar somehow, and as he walked, his mind went back to happier, less lonesome days beneath the sun. He remembered the clang of swords as he trained with his father and his men during the day, and the crackle of the big, round hearth fire at night, surrounded by smiling faces and laughter. Life had never been completely free of worries, but it had been accented by moments of great joy and optimism.

But there had also been black days of terror, of hatred and fire that had turned that past joy and optimism to cinders. The memory of those end-days exploded into his mind as the path thinned and the sky opened up in a great leap from the clifftop. There, spread out before him, silent and asleep as the sun began to rise, was the hillfort, the 'Dragon's Domus'.

"Home," Phoebus said, as Remus sat beside him, sniffing the air of that place. He looked around and suddenly realized where he was. *The cliff...* His heart began to race and he took a step toward the edge to peer over the jagged rock to where his father had fallen over the edge after saving his mother. Or so he had been told.

For a brief, painful moment, Phoebus could see his father's burned body at the bottom of the cliff, his glazed eyes staring up at him, trying to mouth something incoherent.

"Ah!" he fell backward, away from the edge and onto the grass. "Why did I bring us here, boy?" he said to Remus.

The wolf nuzzled him and licked his cheek.

He already knew the answer though, and shook his head at his own sentimentality. Terrible things had happened in that place, but it had also been one of the places where he had been happiest. By returning there, he knew a part of him had hoped to reconnect with long lost joys. *But it doesn't work that way,* he told himself. *The land remembers.*

Phoebus pushed himself to his feet and looked toward the grassy mound of the hillfort, the overgrown terraces of the battlements, and the summit plateau where their home had once been. It now appeared to be a grassy, green tumulus. All of it.

He searched for any sign of smoke, movement, or sound that might indicate that the Roman supply station was manned, but it was impossible to tell from that vantage point.

"Let's go," he said, patting Remus' head and following the path down the hill.

The approach to the northeastern gateway was overgrown on both sides. An emerald and moss-green tunnel had been formed by an alliance of the fern and sapling undergrowth with the oak, sycamore, and chestnut trees that had taken over the embankments. The dappled path stretched away from Phoebus as he stood there with Remus, straining to hear or see anything.

Phoebus drew his pugio and began to walk. "With me," he commanded.

Remus fell in beside him, his ears perked up, alert to every bird, rabbit, and forest mole.

They went slowly, Phoebus picking his way carefully so as not to snap a twig or cause a tumble of rock on the broken pathway that might alert anyone to their presence. When they were halfway up the path, Phoebus stopped to look to his left along one of the defensive levels to the ruins of what had been the bathhouse his father had built near the well there.

The foundations were somewhat visible beneath the tangle of vines and bracken, and grass had claimed the piles of crumbled walls and broken roof tiles that had not been taken by local scavengers.

Remus began to growl, a low, deep rumble starting in his chest.

"What is it, boy?" Phoebus whispered, his pugio poised in front, directed at the point among the undergrowth where the wolf stared.

A boar suddenly burst from a crush of fern, darting across the path before them, past the ruins of the bathhouse and onward along the old defences.

Remus lunged after it.

"Remus, no!" he ordered, and the wolf skidded to a halt and looked back at him. "That thing will gore you," he said. "With me."

Remus returned to his side, his yellow eyes peering into the green dark.

They continued up the path more carefully now, for if someone was on the summit, they would surely have heard them or the boar.

Toward the top, in the mud, Phoebus noticed the faint impression of horses' hooves. He crouched low to the ground beside Remus, searching the grassy slope toward the summit plateau for any signs of movement.

The Roman supply station, which stood a little to his right, was the only structure in usable condition, though the ivy climbing parts of its walls indicated that it was out of use for at least a year. Far to the left, the sad ruins of the temple stood a few feet tall with the roof collapsed to one side, and the columns that had stood at the front laying broken upon the ground.

As for the rest of the structures - the stables, the barracks, and the storage pits where they had kept food - all of it was gone, claimed by the earth and grass, buried by time.

Phoebus felt his eyes burn as he walked forward along the grass where he had played with his sister, ridden his pony, and trained with his father. He looked to where the great hall had been, their home, and saw only emptiness, as if it had never existed. "Remus...search," he said.

The wolf set off to range about the hillfort, first sniffing at the broken doorway of the supply station, and then moving on to roam the perimeter of the battlements at a run.

Phoebus made for the supply station and, with his pugio poised, entered. It was dark inside, and a strong stink of mold emanated from where an abandoned saddle lay rotting on a shelf. He searched for any sign of food, but found none. The rows of shelves were broken and completely empty. The floor was scattered with dirt and blackened straw, and the beams in the ceiling reverberated with the sounds of swallows in a nest. That made him smile.

Upon a weapons rack at the far end of the structure, there was nothing but a single, broken pilum, the tip of which had broken away, leaving only the wooden shaft and iron spear butt.

Phoebus took it off the rack and wiped the cobwebs away. He tested it on his knee to see if it would break, and it did not. "That's something, anyway," he muttered as he made his way back outside into the morning light.

He climbed to the top of the summit plateau where the hall had stood. He felt empty as he turned on the spot, trying to recall exactly what it had been like, the round hearth fire of the hall, the upper gallery where his and Calliope's room had been, and from where they would watch the gatherings below when they were supposed to be sleeping. The exact images eluded his mind, though, all of it having taken place too long ago. He wanted to remember the laughter, the pride, the light and song, but every time he tried to grasp one of those memories, it was replaced with fire and the sound of screaming.

He remembered when his father returned there, long after the Praetorian attack on their home, and how he had wanted desperately to go with him. Now, however, he understood why his father had refused to take him along. It would have been too overwhelming for a child. Even then, in that moment, with the hearth fire cold and buried beneath his feet, the pain was excruciating.

Standing where the great double doors of the hall had been, Phoebus looked to the collapsed main gate at the southwest entrance. His teary eyes roamed eastward along the battlements to see Remus sniffing around the interior of the ruins of the shattered temple of Apollo. He started down the slope toward the temple, using the broken pilum as a walking stick and testing the ground where the storage pits had lain, so that he should not fall into any of them.

"Remus? What have you found?" Phoebus gasped when he saw the interior of the temple for there, upon the broken altar, lay offerings of bread, the remnants of oil which had dripped over the edges, as well as sheaves of wheat which lay limp across the stone, lichen covered surface. "They're still making offerings," he said to himself. For a moment, he considered seeing if any of the nuts or dried fruit were edible, but decided against it. "This place is still sacred."

He shivered when he spotted something behind the broken pieces of the statues of the Gods which had been laid there. Above them all there was what appeared to be a carved, wooden image of a dragon with offerings about its base. It was roughly made, and with little skill, but it was there, and it was honoured.

Phoebus fell to his knees, grasping the rough edge of the altar. "Baba… They still remember you…" He began to weep then, as if he were that young boy who had run and played about that great grassy mound. "I miss you so much. Why did you leave us?" His fist pounded the top of the altar. "Why…why…"

He turned and sat, leaning against the altar, allowing the years of grief to wash over him, to at last flood him with the memories beyond the fires.

Remus came to him then, suddenly alert, and pulled at his leg.

"What is it?" Phoebus asked, wiping his tears away.

The wolf sniffed frantically at the dirt in the middle of the temple.

"Those are just the footprints of the villagers still leaving offerings," Phoebus said.

But Remus persisted around one particular set of prints.

Phoebus stood to look closer and knelt to run his fingers over the prints. "Hobnails." He looked at the broken walls of the temple and around the plateau. "Romans."

The memories he had been holding onto faded quickly out of his mind then, and he stood, alert now. He was about to rush from the temple when he stopped himself and turned back to the altar, the pieces of the Gods, and the image of the dragon. He approached and, reaching into his scrip, pulled out his last piece of dried rabbit meat. "This is all I have, at the moment," he said as he placed it upon the altar. "Guide me…"

Phoebus exited the ruins and searched around on the ground. He found the faint print of hobnails heading toward the southwestern gate, the print of horses's hooves following after them, the shoes similar to those at the northeastern gate. "They're recent." He ran to the top of the grassy battlements and stopped suddenly, having forgotten how steep it was, what had happened just beneath where he stood.

"I killed my first man down there," Phoebus said to Remus, as if the wolf fully understood.

In a way, the beast did, for it was highly attuned to the man who had saved it, with unflinching loyalty.

Phoebus knelt so as not to draw attention to himself from a distance. He remembered driving his gladius into Crescens' son's chest as he was about to kill Calliope, and then fleeing with Paulus, Ula and Aina to the village.

It seemed that the bad memories were always easier to recall, and in terrible detail.

"The village!" Phoebus suddenly remembered, his eyes following the hobnailed prints to the gate and the road that led to the village in the valley below. "Remus! Let's go!"

Without another thought, Phoebus began to run, his mind once more going to the darkest of thoughts and fears for those who had always helped his family.

The Praetorian's smirking face came into view again, dark and blurry, wickedly lit by the hearth fire behind.

Culhwch tried to scan the room but his eye was already swelling, and the blood which poured from the wound on his head blinded him. He could see Paulus' form on the floor on the other side of the table. *Paulus...my son!* He wanted to scream, but tried to preserve his strength. He could try and yell for help from the other villagers, but they would only be cut down. The ropes about his legs and wrists were tight and cut into his skin.

"Have fun, but don't kill her!" the Praetorian before him called out. "I want a turn!"

Culhwch struggled at his bonds at that, for Alma's voice roared defiance as she fought with the other two men. "I'm going to kill you," he growled at the Praetorian before him.

The man turned back, his smile fading as he grabbled the long, bloody strands of Culhwch's hair and pounded his jaw yet again. "Now… Maybe if you tell me where the Dragon and his family and men are, we'll only have her the one time each!" He laughed.

Culhwch watched the door of his and Alma's cubiculum and heard the struggling within. *Gods…keep her safe…* he prayed. *If ever we have honoured you, keep her safe. Free us!*

The attack had happened very quickly while they were eating their evening meal.

Paulus had come with his wife, Morna, and their children, Aife and Devyn, to share a meal with them. One moment, the evening had been joyful, the next, dark and chaotic.

When the men had knocked at the door, Paulus had thought quickly and sent his wife and children out the domus' back door to flee across the field to the home of the sisters, Ula and Aina. The men, however, had rushed in quickly when Culhwch had opened the door, knocking him unconscious and rushing Paulus with a club to his head that sent him to the floor.

When Culhwch awoke, he saw his son lying still upon the floor, and his wife being dragged off by two men in black to the small cubiculum.

Alma's screams were loud now, but the sound of a series of punches knocked the wind out of her.

Culhwch's muscles were near to bursting with the effort he made to try and break the ropes, or at least the wooden chair, but he had built it with his own hands and knew it would not yield. "ALMA!" he yelled.

Phoebus heard the cry as he approached the main street of the village, but he went cautiously, nonetheless, Remus at his heels. When he reached Culhwch and Alma's small stone domus at the end of the street, he pressed himself against the corner and peered around.

At the opening of the small window of the cubiculum, he saw a guard peering in, chuckling to himself and licking his lips as he watched the struggle within. Beyond him were four horses on the other side of the main door.

Phoebus thought for a moment, and wondered how he could distract the man. He was too far to take him by surprise. He looked at Remus and made a motion with his arm about the back of the domus. "Around," he commanded and the wolf set off to prowl around the other side of the building. Phoebus waited a few moments and then he heard it.

The horses squealed and reared in a panic, scattering up and down the street in both directions.

The guard at the window turned and saw the wolf, his yellow eyes staring through the dim dark at him, a low growl reaching out to squeeze the courage from him like the flesh from a rotten piece of fruit. The guard ran in the opposite direction and when he reached the corner of the building he fell.

Phoebus swung the broken pilum with all his might and took the man in the throat, knocking him to the ground where he slashed his pugio across his neck. He moved quickly to the window and peered in to see two men standing over Alma one trying to grab hold of her legs while the other urged him on. Phoebus knocked urgently on the window.

"What is it Drax?" the soldier nearest the window said, leaning close to look out through the cloudy glass. But the moment he did, the broken shaft of the pilum crashed through the glass and into his eye socket with such force that it lodged there.

The man pressing down upon Alma turned quickly to look back at his screaming mate and quickly flew forward to crash into the wall as she kicked him with all her might in the lower back.

"AAAH!" the man roared, but she was already running out of the room.

Phoebus kicked in the front door then, and the scene that met his eyes struck horror into his heart. *Paulus... Culhwch!*

The Praetorian standing over Culhwch by the fire immediately drew his gladius and swiped it at Phoebus who ducked and rolled, only to crash into the table in the middle of the room.

"Remus!" Phoebus shouted and in a second, as the man was about to hack at him, the enormous black wolf lunged from the doorway to clamp onto the man's thigh from behind.

The man roared and raised the gladius again to strike but Phoebus was already grabbing hold of his arm, wresting the sword from his grasp.

"NO!" Alma shouted, panicked as she set eyes upon the wolf, and threw herself over the body of her fallen son.

From the cubiculum, the other two Praetorians rushed Phoebus who parried the first attack with the gladius and drove the blade up into the man's head.

The second man, his eye socket bursting with blood where the pilum and taken his eye grabbed hold of Phoebus from behind.

"Remus, kill!" Phoebus said and the wolf turned from the flailing man whose leg he had and bit into the side of the one attacking Phoebus.

Remus shook his head violently, his fangs so deep in the man's flesh that they could hear it tear. The wolf brought him to the ground and tore out his throat.

"Cut me loose!" Culhwch roared.

Phoebus picked up his pugio and scrambled across the blood flagstones to cut him free.

Culhwch only just recognized him, but it was no time for greetings. He grabbed the pugio from Phoebus and, doing his best to shake the paralyzing numbness in his limbs, he took hold of the weapon with both hands and fell upon the wailing Praetorian, the point of the pugio poised above his throat. He looked to Alma and she nodded quickly. *Paulus is alive!*

Culhwch felt such relief then that he gave full weight to his rage. "Who sent you?" he demanded.

"We're...Praetorians..." the man winced.

"That's not good enough!" Culhwch could see his fellow villagers gathered outside the door, having been warned by Ula and Aina when Morna had reached them. "Keep all the children away from here!" Culhwch said through his swollen mouth before he turned back to the man who had beaten him and ordered the violation of his wife.

"Tell him!" Phoebus yelled. "Or I'll let my wolf tear you apart! Remus..."

The wolf left the body of the other soldier, blood dripping from his jaws, and came to look down on the man. The beast's growl made the man piss himself.

"Who sent you?" Culhwch demanded. "Why did you attack us?"

The prostrate Praetorian looked up at Phoebus and spied the dragons upon his arms. "We're here for him," he muttered, pointing at Phoebus with a shaking hand. "He's needed...in Rome."

"*Who* sent you?" Culhwch demanded one more time.

"The...the Emperor..."

Culhwch spat on him and quickly drove the pugio into his neck, killing him instantly.

"Remus, there." Phoebus pointed to a corner by the hearth, away from the others, and the wolf went and sat still.

"Alma," Culhwch said, his voice as close to weeping as he crawled to her where she was bent over their son. "Are you badly hurt?"

She shook her head. "He got here just in time." She looked at Phoebus. "Phoebus? Is it really you?" she asked.

Phoebus nodded and knelt beside them, his arm upon Culhwch's back.

"Paulus…" Culhwch said, grasping his son's shoulders where he lay upon his stomach. "Wake up, please…" he pleaded.

A moment later, a deep groan came from Paulus, and Alma, tears running down her cheeks, lifted him to rest in her lap. His eyes opened and he looked up at his mother and father. They were bloody and beaten, but they were alive.

"What happened?" Paulus asked.

"Phoebus saved us," Culhwch said, his arm around the younger man whom he pulled close. "Thank the Gods you arrived, Phoebus Pen Dragon." Culhwch looked to the corner where Remus sat staring at them. "You…and your wolf."

Phoebus smiled and reached down to clasp Paulus' hand. "It's all right now," he said with a great shuddering breath. "It's all right."

While the villagers, led by Cradawg, Culhwch's brother, cleaned up, scrubbed and purified the domus of blood, and disposed of the four bodies, Alma and Morna tended to Paulus and Culhwch in the other cubiculum which had remained untouched during the struggle.

Phoebus left them to it and sat outside at the back of the domus, leaning against the stone wall and gazing up at the shadow of the hillfort.

Remus dozed beside him in the dark, his ears still alert to every sound around them.

Phoebus wanted to weep for all the pain that his friends had endured. He had not seen them in many years, and they had always been true and brave friends to his family. Even so, their acquaintance with him and his family had brought them to this, to be attacked in their own home. "Gods…why punish such kind and generous people?" he said to the moon above. "They've done nothing wrong."

There was no answer, and as Phoebus watched the hillfort, his eyes extremely heavy with the great exhaustion that gripped him, he thought he could still see his old home on fire, the flames rising up to the sky as it all burned, as if the place still held the memory of that tragic night.

He did not see Alma appear beside him to place the woollen blanket over him, nor hear her hesitantly set a plate of food before Remus who watched her silently from where he lay.

When morning arrived at last, Phoebus awoke to Culhwch kneeling beside him. He was much older than he remembered. Many years had passed. His face was bruised and battered, but he still managed to smile the way Phoebus recalled when he was young, despite his cracked lips and one shuttered eye.

Culhwch looked down at Phoebus' arm and saw the dragon tattoo upon it. "The Dragon's son returns."

Phoebus rubbed his eyes, and noticed his hands were still stained with blood. He looked at Culhwch, his father's old friend. "I'm so sorry this happened to you." He buried his face in his hands, the shame too much.

"Hey…hey… Don't, Phoebus. You saved us last night. If you hadn't come…" He couldn't finish, for the fear of what was almost done to his wife and son was too much to bear. He looked around. "Where is your wolf…Remus, is it?" He looked at the empty platter.

"I sent him to range around the hillfort. He has to hunt, or he gets restless."

Culhwch shook his head. "As long as he hunts the rabbits that eat our vegetables, and not the villagers, then it's not a problem."

Phoebus laughed, feeling the stiffness in his ribs as he pushed himself up with a groan and stood before Culhwch.

"I never thought little Phoebus would be so tall," Culhwch said.

"Can I be 'little Phoebus' again?"

Culhwch's face grew sad and he put his arm on the younger man's shoulder. "Come. Let's get you cleaned up and then we can eat. Alma and Morna are preparing food." They began to walk inside.

"How is Paulus?"

"He has a headache," Culhwch said, grateful that that was all. "Oh, and my apologies for Morna."

"Why? I haven't even met her."

"Oh… I know…"

They entered the small domus and before Phoebus took three steps, Paulus' wife, Morna, was striding over to him, hands on her wide hips, her pale hair tied back in a long ponytail. She was short and had piercing, pale blue eyes that rested beneath rocky eyebrows that were much darker than her hair.

"So you're the one whose family caused all of this?" She wagged a wooden spoon with bits of porridge clinging to it in Phoebus' face.

"I'm sorry for what you have been through," he said.

"'Sorry' doesn't cover it!"

"Morna, that's enough," Paulus said from the small cubiculum.

She glanced to the dark doorway and shook her head. "My children almost lost their father last night! Have you any idea what that's like?"

Phoebus was silent. *Yes, I do know.* But he did not say it. "Are you children safe?"

"Yes. They are staying with the twins for now," Morna said, lowering her spoon.

"And how are Ula and Aina?" Phoebus asked. He remembered the older girls who had worked as cooks in their home on the hillfort, and who had whisked him and Calliope to safety the night it burned.

"They're fine," Paulus said from where he now stood in the doorway, squinting through the pain in his head as he smiled at Phoebus. "It's good to see you, my friend."

Phoebus turned to him and hugged him. He felt Paulus squeeze him tightly, all the relief of being alive evident in that quiet greeting. "I'm glad you're safe."

"Me too," Paulus said.

"No thanks to your family," Morna grumbled.

"That's enough, dear," Alma finally said, dropping her ladle back into a pot she had been stirring in the kitchen and then coming over to them. "Morna, please set out the bowls. I'm sure everyone is hungry."

Morna eyed Phoebus one more time before going to do as her mother-in-law asked.

Alma stood looking at Phoebus, her eyes betraying a deep mixture of sadness and gratitude. "I can't believe you're here. It's been so long."

Phoebus nodded and looked down, for he was unused to such kindness.

Alma hugged him tightly.

There was a sudden thump at the back door that made them turn quickly, and when they did, they saw that Remus had dropped two dead rabbits there for them.

"My Gods, Phoebus," Culhwch said. "How did you ever find such a companion?"

"That *is* a story."

"Is he going to eat us, or eat with us?" Paulus joked.

Phoebus smiled. "He's brought you some food. He does that."

"I don't dare pick them up in front of him," Culhwch said. "I might lose my hand!"

"He's fine," Phoebus replied. "He's probably already eaten five himself."

"Well…" Alma said, "let's get you cleaned up, and then we can eat."

Phoebus turned to Remus and pat his head. "Good boy." He then pointed to a spot outside the door. "Sit. Watch."

The wolf turned and settled himself outside the back door to watch the field between the village and the hillfort.

"I really have to hear that story now," Culhwch said.

The breakfast was delicious, the best food Phoebus had had in a long while - boiled eggs, porridge, fresh bread, and sheep's cheese with honey. He had not realized how much he had missed fresh, hot food that did not require gutting or skinning.

Alma made sure that Phoebus ate his fill, and did not stop offering more until he said he could no longer eat. "I still can't get over how grown up you are, Phoebus."

It had been an oddly comfortable meal, like the intervening eighteen years had winged by as quickly as the crows diving in the wind above the hillfort. But so much had indeed happened, and after Phoebus told them of his own travels and how he rescued Remus, he then related his family's journey back to Etruria, and then to Greece. They sat in silent shock at all that their friends had been through.

Culhwch shook his head and grasped Phoebus' hand when he had finished telling his tale. "We mourned for your father…" he swallowed, "…when we heard of his passing. He was my dear friend. When he was wounded in the Battle of the Dragon's Domus, I never thought I would see him again…when the barge took him down river to Ynis Wytrin."

"The 'Battle of the Dragon's Domus'?" Phoebus looked confused.

"That's what the villagers call the night we all fought the Praetorians when they attacked the hillfort," Paulus said.

"More violence thanks to his family?" Morna said.

Culhwch turned to her. "And we were happy to fight." He turned awkwardly so that he could look at her through his good eye. "The Dragon and his family brought life and care back to this land."

"And pain."

"We've had over fifteen years of peace here, Morna. We cannot complain." Paulus tried to calm his wife, laying a hand upon hers and squeezing. *She is still feeling the fear of last night.*

"It's true," Culhwch continued. "But the last time we saw your father...saw Lucius...he was much changed. He was filled with anger, and a thirst for vengeance that I feared would destroy him."

Phoebus wanted to weep, but he forced his eyes to remain dry, to maintain the facade of a stoic. He looked at Culhwch, wanting to put his mind at ease. "Before he disappeared...died...you should know that he had healed himself. Despite all that Rome did to us, he did not let himself be devoured by the hatred he felt."

Everyone was silent as they looked at Phoebus.

"But...whatever it was that he had been through, he could no longer stand the world. He...he no longer wanted to be with us."

"Ah, now there, you are wrong, my boy," Culhwch said. "Your father loved all of you. You were everything to him, and every fight he fought in life was not for Rome...it was for you, Calliope, and your mother."

"Then why did he leave?" Phoebus looked him in the eyes. "Without a word...without a reason?"

"Men...even dragons...have their allotted time. Only the Gods know how long and for what purpose. But he used his time well, protected those whom he cared for, and gave his might and strength to those who had none."

Phoebus began to shudder and, unable to hold back his tears any longer, he buried his face in his blood-stained hands and wept.

Alma and Culhwch closed in to comfort him.

"Let it out, lad," Culhwch said. "Be proud, and hold onto his memory. Know that in helping all the people you have on your travels, you have proved yourself his son a hundred times over."

"Thank you," he said, accepting the cup of beer which Morna now handed to him with a reluctant but earnest smile before she sat back down beside Paulus.

"But now, it seems that Rome is back," Culhwch eventually said. "And you need to get to safety."

"What did they want?" Phoebus asked, seeing Alma shut her eyes against the vicious memories of what had occurred only the night before.

"They just kept demanding to know where your father, mother, sister and you were. They also asked about your father's men."

"But why? My father and most of his dragons are dead."

"They didn't give their reasoning. They just demanded to know."

Phoebus was relieved Calliope was safe in Ynis Wytrin. "And why send Praetorians to look for us?"

Culhwch shook his head. "There is only one person to whom the Praetorians report."

"The Emperor?" Paulus asked.

His father nodded. "And you can bet that there are more than four of them looking for you."

"Phoebus?" Alma suddenly asked. "Where is your mother? Where is Adara?"

He looked at her and shook his head. "I haven't seen her in a few years. Have you?"

"No," she said sadly. "I haven't, despite wishing for it." *There's so much pain in his voice,* Alma thought. "You haven't seen her at all?"

"No. That's why I left Ynis Wytrin in the first place…to look for her. But no one has seen her, not Lord Einion in Dumnonia, nor the Lord Afallach in Dunpendyrlaw whom I visited. Their men have been looking for her, but have had no success."

"Poor Adara," Alma said, remembering how she had found a sister in her. "I pray to the Gods she is safe."

"Why did she leave Ynis Wytrin?" Morna asked.

Phoebus looked across the table at her and shrugged. "When my father disappeared, she was filled with anger and hurt. She didn't speak much, and I didn't listen. I was too caught up in my own grief to hear her, my sister, or my aunt. Then, one day, she was gone."

"Phoebus…" Culhwch began, his voice hesitant. "It is possible that…that she…"

"I know. But I can't give up searching for her. I already lost my father. I can't lose my mother as well."

"Phoebus, I know that this place holds many hard memories, but there are also, I suspect, many good ones, no?" Culhwch asked.

"Yes," Phoebus replied.

"Stay with us for a while," Culhwch said, ignoring the look of sudden dismay upon Morna's face. "The villagers here honour the Dragon and his family, and will always stand for you. You'll be safe here."

"But you won't be," Phoebus said. "Especially if Praetorians are hunting us. I have to find my mother before they do."

"We're willing to risk it," Alma said with all the selflessness, grace, and strength Phoebus remembered of her from his youth.

She is still a warrior, he thought. "I know you are, and I'm deeply grateful to you for it. But I can't stay. I ask only that you continue to watch over our home for us while we are away."

"Do you think the Dragon will ever come home, Phoebus?" Paulus asked, his own memories of mingled joy and death on the grassy mound rushing back unbidden.

"I don't know, my friend. But my father said there is always hope."

"That is the Lucius I remember," Culhwch said. "Until that time of hope, however, you need to get to safety. Lay low for a while. If you won't stay here with us, you should go to Ynis Wytrin and your sister."

"Or at least to Dagon, Briana and Einion in Dumnonia," Alma added. "Somewhere out of Rome's reach."

"Rome's reach is long," Phoebus said, "but I will try." He looked at each of them. "I'll head to Ynis Wytrin, and then continue the search for my mother."

"When will you leave?" Morna asked, unable to stop herself, or the feeling of dread in her chest.

"Tonight," Phoebus replied.

When darkness fell that evening, and the moon ducked out of sight behind grey whiffs of summer storm clouds, Phoebus and Remus stood in the field at the back of Culhwch and Alma's domus.

"Here," Alma said, handing Phoebus a linen bundle. "I've packed you some food."

"Thank you," Phoebus replied. "I...I enjoyed seeing you, despite the circumstances."

"We're family, Phoebus Pen Dragon," Culhwch said as he stepped beside his wife. "You always have a home here. Remember that."

"I will."

"Morna says goodbye," Paulus said as he joined them.

"Tell her I'm sorry."

"She knows I'd be dead if you hadn't come along."

"Nevertheless…"

"And here," Paulus handed him a long bundle.

"What's this?" Phoebus asked, undoing the folds to reveal a black pommel.

"One of the Praetorian gladii. I cleaned it and removed the emblems so it can't be recognized. You need a sword."

Phoebus smiled sadly. "Yes, I do." He hugged Paulus. "Thank you, my friend. I hope I can meet your children some day."

"Me too," Paulus replied, feeling somewhat sad that his wife had refused to bring them. *I understand her fear,* he thought. "Take care."

"I will."

"May the Gods protect you on the road," Alma said, hugging him and kissing his forehead.

"And may the Gods watch over you," Phoebus said.

"They always do," Culhwch said with a smile. "Farewell, Phoebus Pen Dragon. You…and your wolf…" He eyed the beast sitting beside Phoebus.

"Thank you again," Phoebus said, looking at the three of them one more time. Before he wept again, he turned and began to walk. "Remus, come."

The wolf turned and followed, and together they disappeared into the darkness of that summer night.

"I'm afraid we won't see him again," Alma said, her voice shaking. "Any of them."

Culhwch put his arm about her and held her close. "Only the Gods know for certain, love," he said, feeling deeply grateful that the Dragon's son had come to them, and that his Alma and Paulus were alive beside him.

.   .   .

The journey to Ynis Wytrin was not an easy one in the dark, especially as it had been so long since Phoebus had made the approach on the secret path through the southern marshes.

Thankfully, he was blessed with a clear night sky, the stars and moon lighting his way as he headed northwest across the plains, keeping away from the roads. He climbed the high, forested hills, and walked along the rivers that spread over that green land like veins about the beating heart of Ynis Wytrin.

The thought had crossed his mind to visit his grandparents in Lindinis, but he quickly dismissed the idea. It was too dangerous to venture into a town, especially if there were more Praetorians about like the ones who had attacked Culhwch and Alma's home. Truthfully, there were also other reasons why he did not wish to see his grandparents.

His grandfather, Publius, when last he had seen him, had said some very hateful things about his father, that he had only ever put their family in danger, abandoned them, and cared only for himself.

When Phoebus had wept for his father's passing, Publius had been glib, almost dismissive.

"'Perhaps now you can start to live your own life?' he had said.

Phoebus knew his grandfather had no idea what had truly happened to their family, to his father. He did not want to know. *It scared him too much to think of it.* Still, he thought it would have been nice to see his grandmother, Delphina, but in going, he could also be putting them in danger. Lindinis had proved to be a snake's nest. He knew he could not go there.

He felt the gladius which Paulus had given him. It felt wrong to hold it, an implement of persecution and death wielded by one of the men who had tried to kill his friends. "Paulus is right, though. I need a sword," Phoebus said to himself as he came down the last hill before the marshes stretched out before him. He stood there with Remus, peering into the thick mist that encircled the Isle and protected it from the eyes of the world. He stared at the maze of brambles and wild hedges, the rushes and tall marsh grasses that swayed in the early morning breeze that swept in from the distant sea.

He walked along the bank of one of the brooks for a while, searching for the way in, for he had not come that way in many years. After a time, he sat upon a fallen tree trunk, now unsure if he could find the way at all. He hung his head where he sat in the middle of that vast flood plain, the trickle of water in the dark all around him filling his ears.

"Far-Shooting Apollo," he said, his hands up to the sky. "Guide me, Lord… Help me to find my way…"

He felt the sun begin to heat his back as it rose in the east, its light spreading over the world like the slow return of warmth in spring.

Phoebus opened his eyes and watched the light travel along nature's battlements of green and brown and there, a short distance ahead and to his left, the sun briefly lit a gap where the tall grass and rushes seemed to sway like an open door in the wind. *Thank you, Apollo…* he said, standing and picking his way along the rippling water. "Remus. Come."

The wolf, who had been eating a duck it had caught, lapped quickly at the water, and then leaped over the brook to follow Phoebus into the labyrinth of the marshes.

It took the better part of the day to pick his way through that world of sun-speckled mist and swaying grass. Many pathways led nowhere, or to hidden deer nests. Eventually, however, the mist thinned and the path began to widen and rise. The tamped grass of the pathway grew less sodden, the scent of mud and mold giving way to the sweetness of grasses drying in the light.

"I think we're almost there, Remus," Phoebus said as he pushed forward, his arms plying their way through the sweetgrass until the path stopped abruptly and opened up onto a familiar field.

It winded him to see it again, the Isle of the Blessed. He had not realized how much he missed it, the tranquility, the safety, and the light. He closed his eyes and breathed in the air.

A scream rent the air, and Phoebus turned to see one of the young priestesses running from where she had been working the soil of one of the crops to his right.

"Wolf!" she yelled as her white form fled to the nearest dormitory. "Wolf!"

Several voices burst out in the golden, afternoon light, and eventually, several of the young priests arrived on the field with hoes and pitchforks, ready to meet whatever threat had intruded on the sacred grounds of Ynis Wytrin.

"Everybody calm yourselves!" Weylyn called out as he pushed his

way through the small mob. "It is Phoebus Pen Dragon!" The old druid
stepped forward, a smile upon his ancient face.

"Remus. Heel," Phoebus commanded as he stepped forward to meet
Weylyn, noting how much more heavily the old druid leaned upon his
staff. "Weylyn," Phoebus greeted him even as the old man reached out to
pull him close.

"I'm relieved to see you, lad," Weylyn said. "Thank the Gods you've
come back."

"It's good to see you. And to be back in Ynis Wytrin."

Weylyn looked down at the enormous wolf. "And you've come with
a friend?"

"This is Remus. I saved him from a baiting pit in the north, and he in
turn has saved my life many times over."

Weylyn lowered himself to look into those knowing, yellow eyes.

To Phoebus' surprise, Remus stared back as if trying to relate something to the druid. Suddenly, the wolf whined and licked his face.

Weylyn laughed and reached out to rub the wolf's neck. "He is a
good soul." He looked at Phoebus. "And a loyal companion to you,
Phoebus Pen Dragon." He looked at the dragons tattooed upon Phoebus'
forearms. "He has already seen many lives and-"

"And what?" Phoebus asked, having always been eager to hear what
Weylyn said about the world and the order of things. His teachings rang
just as true as those of Father Gilmore's about the Christus. "Weylyn?"
Phoebus asked, worried as the druid stared at the wolf who sat calmly by
Phoebus' side.

"Oh, ah… Sorry, lad. Remus is truly captivating," Weylyn found his
voice. "You must always keep him close."

"I do… I will," Phoebus replied, a little confused by the far-off look
in the old man's eyes.

"Back to your labours!" Weylyn called over his shoulders, scattering
the apprentices.

"Where is Calliope?" Phoebus asked. "I must see her immediately.
There are Praetorians hunting us."

Weylyn turned to him. "I know."

"You know?" Phoebus was shocked.

"Come. We must speak." Weylyn put a hand on Phoebus' shoulder
and led him past the crops and animal pens toward the ancient oak tree.

As they walked, Phoebus saw Father Gilmore staring at him from a group of his priests who had come to tell him of Phoebus Pen Dragon's arrival. The priest did not look happy.

"It is good to see you again, Phoebus Pen Dragon," Etain said from where she sat beside Weylyn beneath the broad branches of the oak tree a short time later. "You've been gone so very long."

"I've travelled far," Phoebus said. "But tell me, please... Where is my sister?" Phoebus stood before them, Remus laying in the early evening sun upon the grass, his yellow eyes straying to where Father Gilmore approached at a furious pace.

"Gilmore, my friend," Weylyn said. "Come and greet Phoebus. He has returned to us!"

The priest arrived with a scowl upon his face as he eyed Remus. "How could you bring such an evil beast into the safety of the Isle? He is as covered in blood-guilt as you are!"

"Be calm, Gilmore," Etain said softly. "Remus is one of God's creatures, is he not?"

"No. I'll not be calm! What if he attacks our flocks, or even our younger acolytes? What then would you say of his presence here?"

"He will do no such thing!" Phoebus said. "What's got into you, Gilmore?" There had been a time when he had admired the priest, his teachings, and what he had to say. But Gilmore had much changed over the years, grown more vigilant in his protection of Rachel and Aaron. Phoebus looked beyond the priest, but could not see them anywhere. He turned back to Gilmore, Weylyn and Etain. "I promise you, Remus will harm no one. He will remain with me the entire time."

"And how long will that be?" Gilmore demanded. "A week? Two years? Two nights? Ynis Wytrin is not a roadside taberna where you can simply lay your head, take food, and whore before setting off."

"How dare you?" Phoebus stepped forward, his hand upon his gladius.

Gilmore looked down and smiled. "You see? Quick to anger, and ignorant of the danger in which you place us all! This isle is sacred and must be kept safe from the eyes of the outside world, Phoebus Pen Dragon. Simply by being here, you put us all in danger, especially Aaron and Rachel!"

Phoebus shook his head and turned back to Weylyn and Etain. "How did you find out about the Praetorians?"

"Truthfully, we did not know they were Praetorians," Weylyn said. "But we did know men from Rome were coming. Lord Einion wrote to warn you and your sister."

"Calliope saw them in her visions," Etain said, extending her hand to Remus who padded over and sat beside her. She pat the beast and smiled at Gilmore as if to show him he was wrong about him.

"Where is my sister?"

"She is safe with Einion, Briana, and Dagon in Din Tagell. When he heard of the men hunting your family, Einion sent word that you should all go to him."

"At least *he* was thinking of the safety of Ynis Wytrin!" Gilmore said.

Phoebus ignored him. "Thank Apollo she is safe! Is my mother with her too? Has she returned?" he asked Etain.

She shook her head sadly. "I'm afraid not, Phoebus. No one has heard from her or seen her. Lord Einion has had men out across the land to try and find her, but they have been unsuccessful."

Phoebus sat down on one of the logs beside the High Priestess. "And you haven't been able to see her?"

"No. She is hidden from me."

"But there are Praetorians out hunting her!" Phoebus said.

They forgave his sudden outburst, saw the worry in his eyes.

"Did my aunt Clarinda go with Calliope to Din Tagell?" he finally asked.

"No, lad," Weylyn said. "She cannot go anywhere. She has…"

"What?" Phoebus looked worried.

Etain reached out to hold his hand. "The Gods have begun to take your aunt's mind."

"What?"

"She has descended into madness," Gilmore added abruptly.

Phoebus eyed the priest. "I want to see her," he insisted.

"I must warn you, Phoebus, she is not well. Madness takes hold of her in fits and starts. There are moments, between periods of raving, in which she is lucid. But those are few and far between." Etain squeezed his hands with surprising strength for one so old. *You must also go to Rachel and Aaron, for they need you more than ever!*

Phoebus wanted to recoil at the urgency in the thoughts that invaded his mind, but he felt in the warmth of Etain's hand a great sincerity and importance. "I would like to see my aunt nonetheless," he added.

"Very well," Etain said. "We will sit with Remus while you go to check on Clarinda."

Phoebus nodded and turned to go. "Remus. Stay," he said as he went to the guesthouse where his family had lived and where his aunt now dwelled.

"This is not a good idea," Gilmore said to Weylyn and Etain. "He will push her mind farther into the darkness."

Neither of them replied as they watched Phoebus approach the guesthouse, open the door, and disappear inside.

The inside of the guesthouse was dark and musty. A small fire burned in the hearth, and smoke from a burning chunk of incense upon a small plate snaked its way around the room.

Phoebus half expected to smell the resin which had been used upon his father's burns so long ago and which had constantly filled his nostrils in that room, but the scent was not present, only the memory of it. He tried to ignore the remembrances of his mother and sister there too, along with his father, when they had first come to Ynis Wytrin, when they had lived there in exile. Beyond the press of those memories, he saw his aunt's form laying still in her bed, the rise and fall of her chest very slight.

"Matertera?" Phoebus whispered. "Matertera Clarinda?"

The form upon the bed stirred slightly, then turned. Her eyes opened slowly and she smiled. "Lucius? Lucius, you've come home?"

"No, aunt. It is Phoebus. Your nephew."

"Lucius…" she repeated. "Did you bring Caecilius back with you this time? He's been wandering for so long in the dark along the river. He wants to come home."

Phoebus closed his eyes as he leaned upon the edge of the table, his foot accidentally kicking the strong box beneath. "Matertera… Uncle Caecilius died many years ago."

"I know," she began to weep.

"And so did my father, Lucius. Your brother."

She shook her head wildly. "No! No! No!"

He looked at the table before the fire and went to pour her a cup of water from the clay pitcher there. He then approached the bed where she was now sitting up. "Have some water, matertera." He extended the cup to her.

She took it with both hands and drank the way a child does when they are first learning to do so. When she was finished, the water dripped from her chin and she handed the cup back to him.

Phoebus set the cup back on the table and sat on the edge of her bed. "What is it, matertera?"

She grasped his hands with her bony, thin ones, and leaned in close to whisper to him. "Lucius," she said, her voice on the verge of tears. "Why did you leave me here alone? I trusted you! I needed your protection!"

"I'm Phoebus, matertera. Your nephew."

She shook her head. "No. You all leave me. You, Lucius…Caecilius…Calliope…Phoebus…Adara…our mother…and even father…"

"I am Phoebus," he repeated. "I'm here with you."

"No," she shook her head, silent tears streaming down her cheeks. "You are already gone." She looked away and smacked the sides of her head. "Lucius… Caecilius is waiting! I want you to go and bring him back!"

Phoebus felt his heart sink. *The Gods have taken her mind. She's already gone.* He stood up. Kissed her head, and cupped her face gently in his calloused hands.

She looked up at him with wide glassy eyes. "Promise me, Lucius? You'll get him?"

Phoebus tried to smile for her. "I will, sister. I will."

Clarinda laid herself back down upon the bed and closed her eyes, smiling as she did so. "That's good…" she muttered. "I'm glad you are back, nephew."

Phoebus looked at her for a few moments, unable to comprehend how this was the same person he had left behind with his sister. He opened the door and went back outside, gasping at the fresh air as he made his way back to Etain, Weylyn, and Gilmore who were still beneath the tree with Remus. "May I sleep in the roundhouse?" he asked them.

"Of course, lad," Weylyn replied. "Of course. You may stay as long as you wish."

.   .   .

Phoebus wanted desperately to see Rachel and Aaron, but he knew that he could not do so until they were finished with the tasks which Gilmore had set for them. So, he settled himself in the roundhouse and lit a fire in the pit before it to wait and think, about his sister, his mother, and his aunt who had, it seemed, descended into a type of madness from which there was little hope of her returning, even with Etain's help.

The darkness began to fall, and the stars to flicker in the heavens above. In the distance, on the other side of the Isle, the chapel bell began to toll, signalling the end of the rituals Father Gilmore undertook for their Christus, Mary, and his uncle, Joseph. The sound of the bell was strangely soothing in the falling twilight.

Remus looked up at the sound and let out a long, lonely howl that travelled about the Isle, causing the sheep and goats to bleat.

"Quiet, Remus," Phoebus said as he reached out to stroke the wolf's mane. "You don't want to scare them all to-" He stopped suddenly, for he heard their voices coming toward him, through the dim light by the crops and animal pens.

Rachel arrived first at a run. "Phoebus! You're back!" she said, so loudly that Aaron stopped and looked behind to make sure they were not being followed by Father Gilmore.

Phoebus stood up. "Remus. Stay," he said before taking a few long strides toward Rachel and picking her up in his arms and spinning her around. He felt her long hair fall about his face and shoulders like a warm blanket, and the scent of sweet clove and incense which clung to her filled his senses. He held her tightly, feeling a welling of joy and peace as she kissed his face and lips.

"I can't believe you're back," she whispered. "I missed you so much!" She held him tightly, not letting go as he put her down.

"And I missed you, Rachel. So much..." Phoebus forced himself to let go of her, and looked to Aaron who was now approaching, a knowing smile on his face. "And you, Aaron." Phoebus hugged him as well, and felt that true brotherhood revived.

"You were gone long, Phoebus!" Aaron said. "Why? Calliope was so worried."

"Did you find your mother?" Rachel asked, noting the immediate sadness that marred his beautiful features. She reached up to place her hand on his cheek and he closed his eyes.

"I didn't find her," Phoebus said, looking away.

Rachel could see the emotion in him that had been pent up for so long. She took hold of his hand and stepped closer to the fire where the enormous wolf sat, his eyes taking in the newcomers. "Will you introduce us to your companion?"

Aaron watched with a smile as Rachel approached the beast without a trace of fear. He knew Father Gilmore saw the wolf as a black demon in their midst but, then again, he believed Calliope and Phoebus were a danger to them all. "He's huge," Aaron said as he joined them.

Rachel approached within two arms lengths and stopped, smiling at the animal.

"This is Remus," Phoebus said, going to sit beside the wolf and petting his head. "He and I have been companions for a long time now, and he has saved my life many times."

"Remus," Rachel repeated as she knelt before the wolf and reached out to touch him.

The moment she laid her hand upon him, Remus' eyes closed and he leaned his head into her hand the better to feel her touch.

"He likes you," Phoebus said.

"He is beautiful," Rachel replied. "Such a handsome creature."

Aaron came to settle himself on Remus' other side, but he did not pet the animal.

Remus opened his eyes and stared at Aaron. His tail began to wag.

Aaron pet him then.

"Well, you both certainly have a way with animals," Phoebus laughed, thinking of all the people, including Gilmore, who were terrified at the first sight of Remus. "He senses the peace here, I think." Phoebus poked at the fire and when he was finished, Rachel stopped petting Remus and sat on the log beside him, her body pressed next to Phoebus'.

"Tell us about your travels," Aaron said. "Where did you go?"

"Everywhere," Phoebus grew serious. "I travelled beyond the wall of Hadrianus in the north to see Lord Afallach of the Votadini at his fortress... I climbed the mountains of the Brigantes and crossed the northern dales to the western sea where the water was as blue as in Etruria." His voice grew low, his look faraway into the fire as he remembered. "I ventured into the towns of Eburacum and Viroconium, and even Coria where my mother had taken us when we had travelled with the Empress years ago."

"It was dangerous going into the towns, Phoebus," Aaron said. "At least I assume it was, never having actually been to a town, that is."

"I had to try," Phoebus replied. "I asked in markets across the land, plied farmers with questions, and even dared to speak with soldiers at remote outposts who would not have posed a threat to me."

"And no one saw or heard of her?" Rachel asked.

"No. It's as if she's disappeared...the same way my father did."

Rachel grabbed hold of his hand. "You must not stop believing, Phoebus. Your mother is alive, of that I am sure. I feel it."

"But how? How can you know?"

"I just do."

He looked at her brilliant, brown eyes, lit by the fire, the broad smile that graced her lips. *I've missed you so much!* he thought, wanting her to hear him. They looked at each other for a few moments, until Aaron spoke again.

"What did you notice across the land? Do people speak of the Christus?"

Phoebus shook his head. "If they believe, they do not speak of it openly. What I did notice, however, was that people are suffering everywhere. They are tired, and hungry, and in danger of attack by those who would do them harm." Phoebus glanced at the gladius and pugio which leaned against the log behind him.

"And did you help them when you could?" Rachel asked.

"I did. But there were many who..." the memories flooded back, of the pain and wailing of those times he had been unable to save others. "I couldn't help everyone."

"But you tried," Rachel said. "Only God can help *everyone*, Phoebus."

"I know. But still..." He wanted to tell them of what had happened to Culhwch and Alma, of the Praetorians who were now hunting him and his family, but he decided against it.

"I wish we had been able to go with you," Aaron said. "It would be good to help others beyond Ynis Wytrin."

Phoebus shook his head. "The world beyond this sacred isle is beautiful, but it is also so very terrible and cruel. There is much suffering."

"All the more reason to go out into the world," Aaron added.

Phoebus looked at him. "You still long to do so?"

"I know that we cannot, for reasons that are still not entirely clear to me and Rachel." He looked at his sister. "But, the holy Apostles of the Christus did not spread his word by remaining in Judaea. They ventured forth at great peril to themselves."

"But doesn't Father Gilmore say you must honour their sacrifices by keeping yourselves safe?" Phoebus remembered Gilmore's vigilance when it came to the safety of his two friends. "Many sacrifices were made to bring you here and keep you safe, no?"

"Everyone makes sacrifices for their purpose," Aaron said. "Weylyn, Etain... Einion and Briana, and Lord Afallach in the north. And your father, Phoebus, I know he made great sacrifices to keep you all safe."

Phoebus grew quiet. *And then he abandoned us.* "My father is dead," he said flatly. "If he were not, he would be here with us. Our family would be united instead of scattered across the land."

From the shadows of the apple orchard nearby, Etain stood with Gilmore who had come to keep an eye upon his charges, wary of the returned Pen Dragon and the troubles he brought with him.

"This has gone too far," Gilmore muttered.

"What are you afraid of, my friend?" Etain asked him. "Bonds of friendship and love? For make no mistake, that is what lies between your sacred charges and the children of Lucius Pen Dragon."

"But they are no longer children, are they? I worry for the attachment they have developed, for it will only lead to heartache."

"And if it is God's will that they be so connected so that the sacred vine may continue to grow and thrive? You may try to keep them from the outside world, but the outside world will find them. Does not life find a way? Is that not the way of Creation?"

"I don't want to lose them," Gilmore whispered, pain in his voice. "I couldn't bear it, Etain. They *are* my purpose."

"I know," she said, her hand upon his where he gripped the trunk of an apple tree. "And you will not lose them."

"How do you know?"

"I know. I believe." She looked at him. "After all, it is written in the sacred text that 'now faith is the assurance of things hoped for, the conviction of things not seen.'"

"You do remember the most poignant words at the most inopportune moments, Etain."

"Inopportune for you, you mean," Etain replied with a smile.

"Yes." He could not help smiling. But it faded quickly. "I just worry for them."

"Do not let your worries outweigh your faith, Gilmore."

"It is not so easy, sometimes, especially when others depend upon you."

"You must also have faith in *them*." She nodded in the direction of the three around the fire. "They will all do what is right."

"I pray to God that it is so."

Etain left him there in the dark to contemplate his thoughts. She had said what she needed to say. *The rest is up to him,* she thought as she made her way to her room near the Well of the Chalice.

"Do you remember how free we felt when we were young?" Phoebus suddenly asked Rachel and Aaron as the fire continued to crackle, sending sparks up into the night sky. "Life felt so different then."

"We are free now," Rachel said.

"Are we? I don't know."

"We are," she said, her voice filled with conviction. "We are free to sit here and talk. We are free to breathe, to make friends..." She pet Remus who was now lying flat at her feet, pressing his head against her shins. "We are free to believe...to wonder at the world...to reminisce about the past...and to hope for the future."

"And to love whom we choose to love," Phoebus added, unable to stop himself from looking at Rachel.

And she met his gaze in equal measure.

"Love..." Aaron murmured to himself. "I wish Calliope were here."

Rachel and Phoebus did not hear him.

"But are you free to do so?" Phoebus asked her.

"Oh yes," she said. "To truly love another is to touch the face of God."

Phoebus felt his heart racing as he reached up to touch Rachel's face. When he did so, her eyes closed and a peaceful look graced her. It seemed that a light surrounded them. *I cannot put her in danger,* he thought.

The moment he thought it, her eyes opened and she pressed his hand harder to her cheek.

Aaron stood suddenly, lost in his own thoughts. He looked down at his sister and friend and smiled to himself. *The time is for them now,* he thought. "I'm going to walk up Wearyall Hill and sleep the night there," he said. "Good night."

"I'll remain here for a while, brother," Rachel said.

He nodded.

"Good night, Aaron," Phoebus added.

"It is good to see you again, my brother," Aaron said before turning and walking away.

"He loves Calliope deeply," Rachel said to Phoebus. "Since she left, he has been miserable."

"As I have been miserable away from you," he said. "I have missed you more than I can say."

Without another word, Rachel leaned in and kissed him, slow and lingering, full of the purest love and innocence.

Phoebus felt his heart lighter than it had been in a very long while, his fears and worries fading away to nothing, at least for a time. They remained like that for a while, safe, protected by their love.

Phoebus wondered at how much he cared for her, and thought that that is how very deeply his own father had loved his mother. *How could he walk away from such a love?* he wondered. *Not even death would keep me away!*

"You should go back to your dormitory," Phoebus suddenly said, a fear inching its way back into his heart.

"I have missed you so much, Phoebus Pen Dragon." She shook her head. "I would not leave you now. I know my heart."

"What do you mean?"

"I believe you know." Rachel stood then, no longer the little girl with whom Phoebus used to run and feed the animals, but rather a woman grown, a woman of faith and goodness. She moved to the door of the roundhouse and pushed it open. "Come."

Phoebus looked up at the night sky, brilliantly pocked with stars. He felt a cool breeze blowing on the back of his neck. For a moment, in his mind, he saw Venus standing beside the doorway with so much grace and care in her brilliant eyes.

All is well, Phoebus Pen Dragon, the goddess mouthed.

Phoebus placed his hand upon his heart and followed Rachel inside. "Remus. Guard," he said before closing the door behind him.

The wolf looked at the door and then sat up before the fire, his eyes scanning the darkness beyond.

Father Gilmore gripped the tree tightly as he watched Rachel lead Phoebus into the roundhouse. He wanted to rush in, to remove her. In his mind, he wanted to save her, but then he reminded himself that if the Magdalene had not had the courage to love, to sacrifice, then his purpose would be non-existent. Rachel and Aaron, to whom he had dedicated his life, would not exist.

He crossed himself and pressed his hands together in prayer. "God… Guide me in what is right. Let me not fail in my duty, but do honour to your divine house."

But Gilmore suddenly felt an urge to rush the roundhouse, uncaring of and ready to fight the sentry wolf, when a brilliant light filled the sky above him. He shielded his eyes from the divine light, trying desperately to see what it was.

He forced himself to open his eyes and there, above the roundhouse, he saw the shining, ethereal light of an angel hovering.

He fell to his knees then, crossing himself, and spread his arms wide to the apparition. "Merciful God… Gabriel, is it you?"

The archangel turned his gaze upon the priest and smiled serenely. He held a brilliant rose in one hand, and a scroll in the other which rippled strangely in the breeze. The archangel then bent over to touch the roof of the roundhouse with the rose, and the entire structure began to glow and pulse with life.

Father Gilmore felt tears burning his cheeks as he watched and prayed, and he felt gratitude to God for alleviating the fears he had been torturing himself with. He wanted to stay, to watch, to bathe in the heavenly light cast by the archangel, but he knew that it was not for him. And so he stood, wiped his eyes, and turned away to leave that humble domus of peace and love to itself and the loving couple within.

· · ·

Phoebus Pen Dragon's heartbeat woke him, like a slow and steady drumbeat that echoed throughout his body and mind. It was joined by the dewy sound of three mourning doves who were perched in the fruit-laden branches of a delicate olive tree above him.

He opened his eyes slowly, feeling the heat of a divine sun upon his face. He looked up through the silver-green leaves to see the brilliance of an endlessly blue sky, and he felt joy fill his being, an inner peace and clarity that made him want to weep with gratitude. He sat up in the long grass.

What place is this? he thought, though he knew the answer was not important. Rather, it was the moment.

He stood, supporting himself upon the olive tree which, when he touched it, sprouted new green shoots. He turned then to see a path leading away from the tree, through a field of tall grasses that swayed like dancers in a temperate breeze. He followed the path up and over one hill, and then over another from which the path stretched onward toward a third, taller mound in the middle of a forest glade of strong, gnarled oak and high, spear-pointed cypress.

At the entrance to the glade stood Apollo and the Christus.

Lords... What is this place? Phoebus asked. He felt no fear, no hesitancy.

This is the Knowing, Apollo said, his voice lingering on the air like the most beautiful of musical notes, the stars in the heavens pulsing in his godly eyes.

It is the Heart of the Matter, the Christus said, his voice filled with a kindness and grace that spread through the world with an endless peace. *It is the place of Faith and Hope.*

Enter, son, Apollo said, the stars burning more brightly as he smiled. *They await you.*

Phoebus stepped forward, between Apollo and the Christus, and followed the path upward, between the encircling trees. He reached a high mound, the banks of which were blanketed with blood-red roses, and lilies of purest white.

He walked slowly, his hands reaching out to the blooms to either side which grew more fulsome, more brilliant at his touch.

To his surprise then, he saw Aaron standing in the middle of the widening path, waiting for him. He wore a long tunica of purest white with golden waves about the hem.

It was then that Phoebus realized he wore a similar tunica, but one of deepest red with a golden meander.

You are here, my friend, Aaron said.

I am, Phoebus replied, feeling joy to see him there.

Come, Aaron prompted.

When Phoebus drew even with him, they walked side by side, farther up the path until they stood before twin thrones constructed of marble of purest white. They were shaded by a beautiful, broad-limbed olive tree, the leaves of which shimmered like silver in the sun.

Both men gasped and fell to their knees, for truest love sat upon those thrones.

On the left, Rachel sat, robed in white, and on the right sat Calliope Pen Dragon, robed in red. Both women were serene and brilliant, their eyes joyful each at the arrival of their twin, and their love.

Ivy and grape vines sprouted from out of the earth about their thrones to gather about their bare feet in bursts of emerald, and in each of their hands they held forth a golden chalice. Upon Calliope's chalice was etched a dragon, and upon that held by Rachel was a dove in flight.

Phoebus watched as Aaron stood and approached Calliope, his hands outstretched to accept the chalice she proffered. Inside, a golden olive oil shone, lighting his face as he pressed the cup to his lips to drink before handing it back to her.

Phoebus then looked to Rachel whose smile filled him with love and hope, the likes of which he never thought to feel.

Her olive arms extended to offer him the chalice which he slowly accepted. Inside, he saw crimson wine swirling, its reflection upon the gold like the setting of a red sun.

Phoebus drank and felt renewed as it pulsed throughout his veins, his body, his mind, and his heart. He handed the chalice back to Rachel and stood back to look upon her, beside Aaron who now gazed in adoration at Calliope.

The throned hill upon which they stood seemed to rise up, reaching through time from the peaks of Olympus to Heaven itself.

Far below, however, a ringing of dread horns shattered the peace of that valley of lily and of rose. With the tramp of harsh destruction, men came with deadly intent and hate in their hearts.

Phoebus looked down the long slope to see a lone warrior, an Amazon, standing with a sword in her hand, ready to face the invading darkness. She turned to look up and met his gaze with timeless love and selfless determination.

Mama! Phoebus cried out, the flowers about the slope fading and darkening the closer the attackers came. *NO!* he cried out as the woman charged, her battle cries echoing over the valley as she rushed to defend those whom she loved.

Phoebus rushed to help her, tripped, and fell headlong down the hill. The world spun in his vision, and the sounds of thundering hooves, clashing blades, and screams in the dark rang painfully in his ears.

All was still again, so still. Sunlight poured in at the window and the sound of mourning doves upon the thatched rooftop soothed the ears.

Phoebus opened his eyes and saw the peaked roof of the roundhouse above him. He tried to breathe slowly, in and out, to try to calm his racing heart, but it was only the touch of the woman beside him that managed to fill him with peace. He turned to look into her dark, loving eyes. He took in the soft beauty of her red lips which smiled at him with the greatest sincerity.

Beneath the blankets, she edged her naked body closer to press against his and kissed his eyes and tear-stained cheeks.

"I am here, Phoebus," Rachel whispered, her hand upon his heart, calming him, her touch burning away the darkness of his dreams like sunlight dispersing clouds after a storm.

"I love you, Rachel," he said as he turned onto his side, his rough hand stroking her long, dark hair.

"And I love you, Phoebus Pen Dragon," she replied as she laid herself upon his scarred chest and he held her tightly in his arms. "What dreams did your Gods torment you with that you would wake with tears in your eyes?"

He wondered how he could tell her, how he could possibly relate all that he had glimpsed in that otherworldly realm of dreams. The images were seared into his mind, and yet, he could not describe it in words if he tried. There, was, however, one thing he could describe. "I saw the coming of Rome...and my mother fighting for us..."

Rachel placed her hands on either side of his head. "You are not alone, Phoebus. And neither is your mother. God is with us...always."

God, and the Gods... he thought, remembering Apollo and the

Christus side by side. *The Knowing... The Heart of the Matter...* He shut his eyes tightly again against the image of his mother charging into darkness to protect them all.

"Phoebus..." Rachel said, her warm hand gentle upon his pulsing temple. "Be here with me."

He looked at her and saw her upon that marble throne, the golden chalice in her hands, the dove, the wine within. "Aren't you afraid of having sinned?"

Her face grew serious. He could feel her sweet breath upon his face. "What sin?" She smiled again, and the sight of it filled Phoebus with hope once more. "I love you, and you love me. There is no misunderstanding. I choose to be here with you, and you with me, yes?"

"Of course, my love."

"Then be here with me now, my love," she said, kissing him again.

Phoebus kissed her back and held her gently in his arms, and in their lovemaking, they were silently aware of their act of creation.

The moment echoed pleasingly in the olive boughs of the far-off realms of the Gods.

When they emerged from the roundhouse later that morning, the sun was already high and warm.

Remus still sat where he had been commanded to stand guard and when they stepped outside, he turned his eyes upon them.

"Good boy," Phoebus said, feeling relief that the wolf had remained there the entire time. He imagined that had Remus roamed around the Isle, the night might have been one of chaos instead.

"He is a beautiful animal," Rachel said, rubbing the wolf's mane.

Phoebus spotted Gilmore then, walking quickly toward them with purpose and intent.

The priest approached with a storm in his eyes, his jaw set as if cast in iron. "I would speak with both of you!" His voice was like the breaking of glass in a quiet wood.

Remus began to growl as Gilmore approached, but Phoebus but his hand upon the wolf.

"No, Remus. Quiet."

The wolf quieted and sat between Phoebus and Rachel.

"What have you done?" Gilmore demanded, looking around at the younger priests and priestesses who listened from the gardens and animal pens nearby.

Phoebus was about to protest, to proclaim his love for Rachel in defence of his actions, but before he could, Rachel stepped forward to meet the enraged and fearful priest.

"Father," she said calmly, her arm reaching out to take his hands.

Gilmore slowed immediately, clearly trying to douse the angry fire that burned him. His eyes were red with lack of sleep, and his taut jaw shook, making his beard quiver. "My child...you are in danger." As he looked upon her, he realized she was a woman grown, that he had refused to see it for many years.

"I am not, Father," Rachel replied.

"Yes, you are." He pointed at Phoebus. "You are in danger from Rome, for everyone who is close to his family is put in mortal peril."

"I am not afraid of Rome, Father," she said.

Phoebus saw her hold her head up high, and was awed by her courage and the complete lack of doubt in her words.

"Then of the sin you have committed!" Gilmore blurted, immediately regretting the words as if the archangel, in that very moment, turned his disapproving gaze upon him.

Rachel held his hands more tightly. "There is no such thing as sin, Father. Recall how you related to us that the Christus said that 'it is you who make sin exist when you act in accordance with the nature of adultery." She let go, and turned to go to Phoebus' side. "There is no adultery here, Father. Only love."

Gilmore closed his eyes, a desperate attempt to calm himself. "You would use the words of the Magdalene's teachings, her holy gospel, against me?"

Rachel smiled sadly at him. "I *am* her teachings, Father. Is that not what you have also said?" She turned to Phoebus and kissed his cheek. "I must get to my work now, but I will see you after."

Phoebus looked upon her with true love in his eyes, and in that moment he thought a light surrounded her that spread out upon the grass as she walked to see to her labours. "Fear not, Gilmore. I love her with all of my being, and I would marry her."

"You would, would you?" Gilmore said, his rage simmering beneath the surface.

"Yes," Phoebus replied, trying to meet the priest with the same, calm defiance with which Rachel had done so. "You wouldn't understand such love, I suppose."

Something changed in Gilmore's eyes that gave Phoebus pause.

"You have no idea what you are speaking about, Phoebus Pen Dragon, nor the forces arrayed against you."

"I know what Rome is capable of. I remember all too well what it has done to my family."

"I'm not speaking about Rome," Gilmore growled, but forced himself to calm down. *Lord, forgive me, but I hate what his family does to me!* "You think you are the only one who has ever loved?"

"Of course not."

"You think I have never loved?"

Phoebus did not reply then.

"I loved a woman once, and she loved me. I, like you and Rachel, believed that because we loved each other, it was not a sin. And it's true, it was not, and neither is it for the two of you." He hung his head, realizing the truth that his ward had reminded him of.

"Then why do you protest so much?" Phoebus asked.

"Because, it is not about sin. Neither is it about Rome...not completely, anyway."

"Then what, Gilmore? Help me to understand!"

"It is about the hate and evil that lurks in every shadow behind every good thing in this world. It is about what that wickedness is capable of, how it hunts heroes in roundabout ways, never directly, but with indirect attacks at those whom we love."

"And you are such a hero?" Phoebus tried unsuccessfully not to sound mocking. "Forgive me. I didn't mean it like that..."

"I am not, but I have tried to live a heroic life in my own way, Phoebus Pen Dragon...as you do...and, as did your father. A heroic life does not mean being flawless. It means continuing to try, to fight on, despite our mistakes and failings."

"What happened to the woman you loved?" He could see the haunted look in Gilmore's eyes. "Does Weylyn know of her? Does Etain?"

Gilmore met his eyes and shook his head. "I have never told anyone. But I am telling you now. In an attempt to get to Rachel and Aaron, men were sent to hunt for me, and to get to me, they found her. She lived in the hills outside of this sacred fortress of mist and light..." Gilmore's eyes grew teary. "She refused to give me, Rachel, or Aaron, up to the hunters, and so they killed her, and our...our unborn child..."

Father Gilmore collapsed upon one of the logs about the fire pit, his legs suddenly too weak to hold him up.

Phoebus looked at Remus who observed the priest closely, and then sat beside him. "I'm so sorry, Father. I didn't know."

"Nobody does. I couldn't face the shame of it. It was my fault that... Mary...and our child were slain."

"Was it Rome who sent the hunters?" Phoebus asked.

Gilmore looked at him. "Evil has many ministers. It uses whom it wishes. It could be an emperor or general, it could be a shopkeeper, or even an unknowing friend. By simply knowing me, Mary's life...our child's life...was ended, and I continued to live."

Phoebus reached down to touch Remus' fur as if the wolf were a talisman against the dark thoughts that intruded upon a day that had begun so brightly and full of hope.

Gilmore pushed himself to his feet. He remembered his vision of the night before and looked to the rooftop of the roundhouse where Gabriel had appeared to him. He stared at Phoebus. "Rome...Evil...is hunting you and your family, Phoebus Pen Dragon. Your union with Rachel may indeed be blessed. But your life together may not be."

Phoebus stared at the priest. He had no words of reply, only a sinking feeling in his heart, a feeling that what the priest told him was true.

Without another word, Father Gilmore left to go back to his toils and prayers, weighed down by much more than anyone in Ynis Wytrin could imagine.

Later that day, Phoebus found himself walking slowly along the path that led from the Well of the Chalice to the long avenue of oak trees and the Tor. He needed to think alone, for what Father Gilmore had said weighed upon him heavily indeed. It also angered him, for though he saw much beauty in many of the Christian teachings he had learned during his time in Ynis Wytrin, the tendency towards feelings of guilt was something Phoebus had trouble with.

He was capable of feeling guilt himself, of course. But he did not feel that guilt for laying with Rachel, for it was an act of true love and beauty, the goodness of which he could feel with every fibre of his being.

However, the idea which Gilmore had planted that Phoebus was putting her in mortal danger was something he could not rid himself of, like a man who has wandered inadvertently through a thick spider's web.

The fact that he knew Father Gilmore was right angered him even more. Over the years, he had grown to love Rachel, and Aaron was like a brother to him. There were things he did not understand about them, secrets, but he also knew that it was vital that those secrets be kept safe.

Rome is hunting our family. No one is safe who is close to us. It was a painful thought to revisit, and he walked faster along the sun-dappled pathway to the Tor as if trying to escape it, to flee from the images of Culhwch, Alma, and Paulus being tortured to get to them. He mulled over all that the Gods had shown him in his dreams the previous night, those haunting, beautiful, and terrible images that had filled him with wonder and dread simultaneously.

"I wish Calliope were still in Ynis Wytrin," he said to Remus who strode happily beside him through the grass. "She would like you, boy." He pat the wolf's head as they came to the steep path up the side of the Tor and began to climb, opting for the direct path instead of the lengthy, labyrinthine approach used for the ceremonies.

It had been years since Phoebus had climbed the ancient Tor that overlooked Ynis Wytrin, not since his father had disappeared. The world felt strange upon those grassy heights, as if sound and light were different at that threshold of the Otherworld.

Remus became more alert and ranged around the top as if searching for something he knew was there but could not see, even with his wolf's senses.

For Phoebus, it was a place of meditative quiet but, unlike Wearyall Hill, the Tor, for him, was also a place of simmering fear. *Why did I come up here?* he wondered, now that he was there.

He sat himself down upon the long grass and looked out over Ynis Wytrin, that blessed isle that had been a sanctuary to his family for so many years. He looked from the valley where the Well of the Chalice and its sacred waters had brought his father back from death, beyond the avenue of yews to the apple orchards and crops that fed the inhabitants of the Isle. He looked upon the ancient oak, its branches spread wide like the arms of a loving mother, and beyond it the Christian temple and the gentle slopes of Wearyall Hill where the Holy Thorn stood as a lone sentry against the outside world.

The outside world... Phoebus thought of his mother and sister who were out there, in danger, hunted by Rome. He thought of his father who had, long ago, fought for goodness and right with the might of the line of Anguis, the Dragon. He had not hidden in safety in Ynis Wytrin, but had toiled and fought in the world of men, the world of Rome.

"Dragons are not meant to hide, are they boy?" Phoebus said to Remus who had lain down beside him.

Phoebus looked up in the windy sky above to see the crows winging, falling and rising, turning and soaring like dry leaves. "That's what it feels like...living..."

And you must go soon, Phoebus... a voice said behind him.

Phoebus did not turn right away, but he recognized the heavenly voice, felt comfort in it. He turned slowly to see Far-Shooting Apollo standing before him, a translucent apparition between the distant cloud and sunlight. The crows that had been wheeling in the sky now came to land about his feet, all of them looking to him, their glossy black eyes filled with his light.

Apollo's cloak moved strangely about him, blowing in the opposite direction of the whipping wind on the Tor, and his starry eyes smiled to look upon the young man before him.

"Lord?" Phoebus turned and knelt before the god.

Your road has not ended, Phoebus Pen Dragon, and you cannot remain in this sacred place.

Phoebus felt his heart sink. "But...Rachel..."

Your time together is at an end. It must be, or else the hunters will destroy her and the hope she represents.

"Surely she is safe here," Phoebus said, his gut hurting at the thought of Rachel coming to harm.

Only if you are not. Apollo looked sternly upon his mortal grandson. *You have drunk of the cup, and now you must set it down.*

Phoebus' dream rushed back into his mind. "But why must I?"

To fight, and to protect, Apollo said. *The Darkness is closing in and would strangle the Light.*

"But if I die, I will not see her again! Her or our..." He dared not say it.

Apollo made no reply.

Phoebus hung his head, his hands supporting himself upon the steep, grassy embankment. "I must go to Dumnonia," he said, knowing the truth of it. "I must fight."

Yes.

"Then I need my father's-"

Apollo was already gone, and the crows soared once again on the rising wind.

Phoebus felt a great sadness. He did not want to leave, but he also knew that he could not leave Calliope and his mother, wherever she was, to death at the hands of the Romans.

"Apollo give me strength," he prayed, his eyes closed as he struggled to control his rising fear. "I am a dragon," he told himself, looking at his forearms, and remembering his father. "I am my father's son, and I will not hide." *Father, wherever you are in the Afterlife, help me and guide me so that I can save those whom I love, as you did...*

He paused, waited for a response, a sign of hearing from across the dreaded Black River, but none came, no echoing voice, nor the blowing of the boatman's horn. Not even an errant ray of light.

Perhaps I am alone? Phoebus thought.

He sat for a while longer, looking out over Ynis Wytrin, wanting to remember every inch of it, every tree and rock, every pathway and curving slope. His eyes rested on the thatched peak of the roundhouse where he and Rachel had lain together, the last place where he had ever felt, or ever would feel, quiet or peace.

"I don't want to leave this place," he said to Remus as the bell of the Christian temple began to toll. "But I know I must." Phoebus Pen Dragon pushed himself to his feet, turned, and began the trek back down the steep side of the Tor, his wolf by his side.

When Phoebus arrived at the bottom of the Hill of the Chalice, it was to find Etain and Weylyn waiting for him in the orange-gold light that suffused the limbs of the great oak tree.

In the distance, the bells of the chapel had ceased and the muted sound of Father Gilmore's evening prayers flowed out into the misting air along with the sweet tang of burning frankincense.

"Sit with us, Phoebus," Etain said. Her eyes were full of the kindness and warmth which had always made it easy for him to speak with her.

"Lady… Weylyn… I know that I need to leave," he said as he sat down with them. "I just don't want to."

"I know, lad," Weylyn said, his old, gnarled hand upon Phoebus'. "It is the way of things that the toils we must undertake are the ones we want the least."

"I'm afraid for my mother," Phoebus admitted. "Calliope is safe in Din Tagell, but my mother is…"

"She is alive, Phoebus," Etain said, her voice comforting, like a childhood song at bedtime. "I may not be able to connect with her, or see her, but I do not feel the lack of her in the world. She is out there… somewhere…"

"Should I go north to find her?" *I've already searched for so long!*

Etain shook her head. "Your way lies upon a different path."

"And that path leads to Dumnonia," Weylyn said.

Phoebus noticed something strange in the Druid's voice. "What do you mean?"

"Only that you must go there," Weylyn said, "to your sister, to Einion, Dagon, and Briana. Your father's dragons are there. And they are still strong. If Rome comes, you have them."

"And you must be there before the dying of the year at Samhain," Etain added, her green eyes boring into Phoebus'.

"Lady?"

She stood and reached up to touch the soft green leaves of the ancient oak above them, and spoke into the branches. "There, in the green, the hunters shall meet, and there will be an end of things…and a beginning…"

Weylyn observed her with awe-filled eyes, and laid his hand upon Phoebus' arm to stop him from speaking.

"The land will howl and roar as the Lord of Annwn rides out to deal death…to bring destruction…to…to…" Etain cried out, her face suddenly pained, and she collapsed, only to be caught by Phoebus who had jumped up as she fell.

"Lady, are you all right?" Phoebus asked as he laid her on the grass.

"Etain?" Weylyn knelt beside her, his hand upon her forehead.

Her breathing calmed and she opened her eyes to look upon Phoebus. "You must be brave, Phoebus Pen Dragon. Dig deep for your courage when the blood flows at Samhain."

Gwyn ap Nudd? Phoebus thought. *The Lord of Annwn?* He remembered years ago, finding out at long last from his mother what had happened to his father when he had gone to Dumnonia, when he had fought that dark lord, and nearly died.

Phoebus felt icy fear run along his spine when he saw the knowing look in the High Priestess' eyes. "I…I will, lady. I am the son of the Dragon."

"You *are* a dragon," she replied before closing her eyes, exhaustion overtaking her.

"Help me get her to her rooms," Weylyn said.

Phoebus bent and, getting his arms beneath Etain, hoisted her into the air and followed Weylyn toward the Healing House and Etain's rooms. "Remus, stay," he called over his shoulder as the wolf began to follow.

Remus sat immediately and waited, watching his master as he went.

"Olwyn," Weylyn called to the younger priestess as they approached.

She looked up from where she was cutting herbs in the garden outside the Healing House. "What is it, master Weylyn? What has happened?"

"A vision," Weylyn replied. "But she is fine. She just needs to rest."

Olwyn set her basket down and went to open the door to Etain's quarters.

Phoebus went up the stone steps and into the dark interior where Olwyn was already lighting lamps. He placed the High Priestess gently upon her bed and stepped aside for Weylyn.

"My friend, are you quite well?" he asked her, pressing a wet cloth which Olwyn handed him to her forehead. "What did you see?"

Her eyes still closed, Etain shook her head. "The hunters… They bring blood and rage… A clash of Eagles and of Dragons!"

Both Weylyn and Olwyn turned to look back at Phoebus.

He stood still in the middle of the priestess' quarters, the Druid, High Priestess, and young priestess staring back at him.

Etain opened her eyes then and, slowly, swung her legs over the edge of the bed so that she was sitting, supported by Weylyn and Olwyn. She pointed at Phoebus, the palm of her hand upturned as if welcoming him and sending him off simultaneously. "You have been welcomed, and so you must go into the dark with knowing and a full heart."

None spoke. None dared.

Phoebus looked back at her. "The Knowing. The Heart of the Matter."

Weylyn and Olwyn were clearly confused by the words he spoke, but not Etain. The High Priestess smiled at him and nodded. "Yes."

"I...I will leave at dawn, with the sun," Phoebus said as he bowed to Etain, backed up, and rushed out into the dusk light.

When he returned to the oak tree, he found Remus sitting with Rachel and Aaron who had finished their evening rites in the chapel and had come to wait for him.

"Is it true?" Aaron asked as he approached. "Father Gilmore says you are leaving Ynis Wytrin?"

Phoebus looked at Rachel and could tell that she had been crying. He wanted to as well, but he held back his tears. "I don't want to."

"Then don't," Rachel said, standing and throwing her arms about him.

"I must," he replied, holding her out so that he could look at her. "You are not safe if I stay here. No one is."

"Rome will not find you here!" Aaron insisted.

"You don't know that," Phoebus said. "And there are greater dangers than Rome in the world."

"God will protect us," Rachel said.

"As I must, my love," Phoebus said, kissing her lips and feeling the wetness of a tear as he did so.

Aaron looked away. "First Calliope leaves, and now you."

Phoebus turned to Aaron. "And you know I would not do so if it were not required."

Aaron did not reply, but crossed his arms and nodded.

Rachel wiped her eyes, sniffed, and stood tall, her arm laced through Phoebus'. "Father Gilmore told us the story once, of how the Magdalene had to flee, to protect more than herself, to protect the future. She underwent a world of hurt in order to protect Hope."

Phoebus looked upon her and her brother then, and in that moment, despite all the pain they would endure, he knew it was the right thing to leave, that his mind and heart now accepted the inevitability of leaving. "I'm sorry."

Rachel turned to him and, instead of wailing or weeping, she mustered a smile and laid her hand aside of his face. "Don't be, my love."

. . .

That night, Phoebus did not sleep, but watched the rise and fall of Rachel's breathing, burning the sight of her into his memory to be a light in the coming dark. His mind went back to the dream of her and Calliope upon those thrones, of him and Aaron standing before them as the darkness of battle approached from behind.

He kissed her brow. "God…please keep her safe. Keep *them* safe…" He placed his hand upon her stomach and in that moment, she opened her eyes which were lit by a nearby lamp.

Rachel reached up with her arms to hold him, and together they were grateful for those final hours before the boat would take him away from her, the same way it had taken the Magdalene away from her home so many years before.

Outside, the night was quiet and mist-filled, the Gods spreading a white cloak over the land to shield them and that blessed isle.

When the unwanted dawn of that day of departure arrived, Phoebus forced himself to rise from the bed where Rachel slept, where they had made love, where he had tried to imagine the life that might have been for them.

Gods… I offer myself up to you, if you will protect her.

He stared at her for a few minutes before dressing and packing his satchel for the journey. He gathered up the black gladius, his pugio, and took his ragged cloak from off the hook.

Rachel stirred and sat up in the bed. "Is it time?" she asked.

He nodded, unwilling to say the words.

"I'll walk you to the dock." She stood and dressed herself, pulling her long tunica over her body. After fastening her sandals, Rachel took her own cloak from where it had hung beside his, and he put it about her shoulders for her.

They kissed again, long and lingering, each breathing in the scent of the other, fingers seeking to remember the feel of each other's face and hair, like a blind man, before being sent away. There was little else to say. It all hurt.

"Come," she said.

He could see that she had found her courage, that she was forcing herself not to plead with him to stay, to forget about Rome and the battle she suspected awaited him. But it was not for herself that she did this, no. It was for him. It was for her love of him that she endeavoured to make it easier for him to go, though it was not at all easy.

Phoebus opened the door and together they stepped out of the roundhouse into the misty morning. "The Gods are cloaking my departure."

Rachel tried not to think of the evil that might be lurking in wait beyond the borders of Ynis Wytrin, the Romans who were hunting her love.

Remus, who had been sleeping outside the door, stood when they emerged, and nuzzled both of them. He whined a little, sensing the change to come.

"I know, boy. I don't want to leave either. But we have to." Phoebus pet him and closed the door behind.

"You will watch over him, Remus, yes?" Rachel said to the wolf as she laid her hands on his thick black mane and stared into his brilliant eyes.

The wolf stared back at her, blinking slowly, his breathing calm.

"I need to see my aunt first, before we go to the dock," Phoebus said, and they began to walk along the apple orchard, the branches of the trees laden with new fruit. They passed the vegetable crops, and the great oak, and followed the pathway to the guesthouse.

"Do you want me to come in with you?" Rachel asked as they came to a stop before the door.

Phoebus shook his head. "No. It's all right. I should go in alone."

"I'll wait here then."

Phoebus set his satchel down and took hold of the iron handle before turning it and going in.

"Matertera?" he said softly once inside the dark room where a low fire burned in the hearth. "Are you awake?"

"I'm here, Phoebus," Clarinda said.

He turned to see her sitting at the table where she had laid out the items contained in the strong box which his father had left behind.

"What are you doing up?" he asked.

She turned to him, her gaunt face making an attempt to smile. "Etain came to tell me that you are leaving today. Apollo has helped to calm my mind so that I may bid you farewell."

"Are you sure you don't want to come to Din Tagell with me?"

She nodded sadly. "I am sure. I'm of no use to you. Ynis Wytrin is where I will see out my days."

Phoebus felt a deep sadness then, seeing his father's younger sister so worn and resigned. "Please don't say that."

"It is the Gods' will, Nephew. I have accepted that, and so should you. We all have our assigned destinies to see through."

"Yes. We do."

"Will you be all right?" she asked. "I know that you and Rachel have grown close."

"I must go to keep you all safe. Rome is hunting us."

"I know," Clarinda replied. "But the necessity of your leaving does not lessen the pain of it, I'm sure." She remembered her brother, Caecilius, leaving Delphi with Lucius for the last time. She stood quickly and hugged her nephew. "Promise me you will be careful."

"I will. And I'll find Calliope and mother." He looked down at the table where all of the items had been laid out - his father's corona, his armillae, the deeds to their lands, the scrolls, and the bags of coin.

"I thought you might like to take something," she said.

Phoebus looked over the items. "The torc is gone."

"Calliope wears it."

He smiled. "Then I shall wear this," he said, taking up a silver armilla with dragon finials that he remembered his father wearing. "And some coin." He poured out a couple aurea and a few denarii and dropped them in the scrip on his cingulum. "The rest can stay here, in case someone else needs them…someday." His eyes then fell on a bundle of linen. He reached out to pull back the folds and revealed the dragon that had adorned his father's armour. The only thing to have survived the fires. "And this…" Phoebus ran his fingers hesitantly along the dragon's lines as if it might burn him to touch it.

"Not that," she said abruptly.

"Why not?"

Clarinda stared at the image that their ancestor had forged long ago from the stone given to him at Delphi. "The dragon must remain here, in case someone else needs it, someday." She laid her hand upon his arm and felt him pull it back from the image. She looked up at him. "There is no asphodel where you are going, Phoebus." A strange look invaded her eyes, a far-seeing one that gave him a shudder. "Be brave. You are your father's son."

"Thank you, Matertera."

"I will miss you and your sister, but do not worry for me. I am where the Gods see fit to place me."

He looked down at his aunt and hugged her tightly. He had never really known her when he was young, but in the years since they had returned to Ynis Wytrin, despite her madness, he had gotten to know those parts of her which the Gods had seen fit to preserve. He had come to know her as a kind, selfless woman who had loved her brother fiercely, and who had wanted nothing more than to serve the Gods to the best of her abilities.

Phoebus felt then that he would never see her again, and hugged her more tightly.

"I know..." she said, feeling him shudder. "I know. All will be well." She stood back. "Now. You must go. Go to your sister in Dumnonia and to safety."

"Thank you," Phoebus said.

But she shook her head. "There is no need to thank me. I will keep these here for when they are needed," she said, gesturing to the items on the table. "May Apollo guide you and guard you on your road, Nephew."

"And may he ever watch over you, Matertera." Phoebus bent to kiss her cheek, then turned, opened the door, and went out.

Clarinda smiled to see Rachel waiting for him and then closed the door again. She placed all of the items back in the strong box, locked it, and pushed it back beneath the table.

When that was done, she took a chunk of incense from a small cedar box upon the table and went to kneel before the flames of the hearth. Ignoring the pain in her knees from that hard floor, she placed the incense in the flames and turned her palms upward.

"Oh Shining and Far-Shooting Apollo... Please protect my nephew and niece, and their mother... Let them not come to harm. Guide them and guard them against the darkness. Show them the way..."

When Phoebus, Rachel, and Remus arrived at the docks, they found Aaron waiting there with Father Gilmore, Etain, and Weylyn.

"Did you visit your aunt?" Aaron asked. "Is she well today?"

Phoebus walked up to him. "She is brave."

Aaron did not say anything else about her. No one did.

Beyond the group that had been awaiting him, Phoebus spotted the small barge where four priests were seated to row him across and out of Ynis Wytrin.

Father Gilmore approached him first. "You are making the right decision, Phoebus Pen Dragon."

Phoebus looked back at the priest. A part of him wanted to shout at him, to shove him, but he knew in his heart that Gilmore was kind, that his only concern was for Aaron and Rachel, and that was something to admire. He now knew how much Gilmore had suffered and sacrificed for the twins, and for the Isle, and it was not his place or right to undo that. "Know that I love her with all my heart," he whispered into the priest's ear. "Thank you for guarding them."

"And thank you for leaving them," Gilmore replied. "May God protect you."

Phoebus nodded, and turned to Weylyn. "Thank you."

"There is nothing to thank me for, lad. You and your family have done more for this isle and this land than you can possibly imagine. May the Gods give you strength in the fight to come." Weylyn found himself feeling great empathy for the younger man before him, a man who had taken a titanic weight upon his shoulders in trying to live up to the memory of his father. "You honour your family line, Phoebus Pen Dragon," he said, glancing over Phoebus' shoulder at Rachel, "and I pray the Gods give you the strength you need."

Phoebus nodded and then turned to Etain who walked down the dock with him a little.

"Olwyn has packed food for you for the journey. It is in the barge," she pointed at the boat, paused, and then spoke again, her voice grave. "The hunters are abroad," she said, "and more are coming." She looked at the gladius that jutted from his satchel. "Arm yourself, Phoebus Pen Dragon, against your enemies, and against the dark. I will be watching you from this side of the mist," she said.

"Thank you. And, if you see my mother, will you please-"

"I will send her to you in Dumnonia," she finished. "Of course. I have not given up my searching, nor will I." She took his head in her hands and kissed his brow. "The blessings of Ynis Wytrin go with you."

He nodded, and looked to Aaron and Rachel who were waiting with Remus a little farther down the dock.

"They are safe," Etain said. "*All* of them." Her green eyes were brilliant and excited. "Know that."

"I know," he replied before going to join Rachel and Aaron and walk with them to the end of the dock where the barge bobbed gently up and down on the dark water.

"Farewell, Brother," Aaron said, hugging Phoebus tightly. "May God keep you safe wherever you go."

"And you, Brother," Phoebus said with a sad smile. "For that is what you are."

"I know." Aaron looked down at the boat and the cowled priests there who waited to take Phoebus away. "When you see Calliope, please tell her that…that I love her and miss her and that she is ever in my thoughts and prayers."

"I will. And you take care of each other," Phoebus said, taking Rachel's hand.

Aaron nodded and stepped aside to pat Remus one more time.

"I don't want to leave you," Phoebus said, unable to comprehend the aching he then felt in his heart.

As if sensing it, Rachel placed her hand upon his chest and breathed with him. "I am with you. And I shall ever be with you." She pressed his heart. "In here."

"I will only ever love you. You, and no one else," he said, his eyes and throat burning.

"And I you," Rachel said, her big brown eyes growing as glassy in the misty light as the smooth water that was about to take him away. "Stay safe, my truest love, and may God watch over you on the road."

Phoebus took her to him and kissed her, their lips wet with tears.

"There is no love more pure than that," Etain whispered to Gilmore and Weylyn who stood to either side of her.

"I wish I could take away her pain," Gilmore said, "but I know that I cannot. It is not my place."

"Have you not said before, my friend, that pain and sacrifice can lead to healing, restoration, and new beginnings?" Weylyn looked at Gilmore.

"Yes," the priest replied. "But that does not mean I wish for those whom I love to suffer."

Etain smiled and gripped each of their hands. "Let us pray for the family of Pen Dragon."

The three of them then turned and left the dock to wander back into the holy places of Ynis Wytrin, each to pray, to offer, and ask for the grace of all their gods for those who had protected their sacred isle.

"Go now, Phoebus," Rachel said as she pulled herself away. "Before I lose the courage I have mustered to be able to let you go." Her voice broke, and she kissed him again.

Phoebus nodded and wiped his eyes. "Remus," he said. "Inside." He pointed into the boat beside the bundle of food. "Sit."

The priests shifted uncomfortably as the wolf settled in amongst them.

Phoebus took Rachel's face in his hands one more time, kissed her, and then pulled himself away to get into the barge.

The dark water all around the barge rippled as the rowers pushed off.

The mist began to move in quickly to swallow them, and Phoebus Pen Dragon watched as Rachel and Aaron waved one last time before they disappeared from sight.

Phoebus put his head in his hands and wept silently. He knew in his heart that he would not see them again and, though he should have been used to goodbyes after so many in his life, this time it felt like his heart was being ripped out.

PART III

THE HUNTED

BRITANNIA A.D. 229

XIII

MATER UMBRAE

'The Shadow Mother'

The wind had howled all night in the wild lands of Venedotia. It shouted among the thick trees and jagged, lichen-covered rocks, and ripped at the surface of the river in the valley. There had been no rain, but the gale which the Gods hurtled down from the heights of the snow-capped mountain to the west had been incessant and made it difficult to track.

When the sun finally emerged that morning to take its vengeance on the dark night, the mist began to rise up and flee into the sky, held back by the clawing branches of the gnarled and knowing trees. The dawn chorus of robins and blackbirds began, more pleasant to the ear than the roar of the local mountain gods.

In this early dawning of a day of blood, the rider reined in her white gelding and stopped to listen, her head cocked to the right. Her brilliant green eyes scanned the valley below. Her brown leather breeches and boots creaked as she dismounted, masked by the birdsong around her. The ropes of her long, braided black and grey hair shimmered like snakes upon her head in the morning light as she tied them back and out of the way.

"Stay here, Aegis," she said to the horse, stroking his neck and slinging her moss-green cloak over his back to cover up his brilliance in the dark forest.

She stepped forward to the edge of the gully to look, to listen, and after a few moments, she spotted her, the young, red-haired Ordovician woman, as she picked her frantic way along the rocky river far below. *Keep going, girl!* she thought as she watched her clamber over the rocks where they narrowed.

She then looked back, behind the young woman, scanning the terrain and spotted them, the bloody splashes of the red legionary tunicae that pursued her. Their voices crashed in the still morning, harsh and uninvited, like a rusty scythe blade in a field of green spring wheat. She counted the men. *One...two...three... Where are the other two?* She looked around quickly to see if they were following her now, but they were not. *They must be trying to get ahead of her!*

She knew she had to move quickly.

She had been pursuing the five Roman deserters from Isca Silurum for days, ever since they had raped and slain a Silurian mother and her two children. Another crime committed by the Romans as they fled north, away from their posts. There had not been an opportunity for her to take them safely, but now that they had fixed their eyes on another quarry, safety was no longer her primary concern.

What the young Ordovician woman had been doing alone in the wilds, she did not know. What she did know, however, was that if they caught up to her, she would suffer the same fate as their previous victim.

She would not let that happen.

Something sounded to her right and she wheeled, her pugio shooting out from the cingulum that belted her brown tunica.

No one was there, but there were urgent voices in the air, shimmery-sounding, as if under water, but all she saw was the sparkle of morning sunlight as it graced the trees.

She turned back to the river and could see the three men moving closer, their harsh laughter chasing the young woman who had not yet noticed how close they were.

She took her yew bow and quiver of arrows from off her saddle bags and set off along the ridge overlooking the gully.

The Ordovician girl bent over, gasping as she leaned upon a slippery rock in the shallow but rushing water of the gully. Her heart felt like it would burst, she had been running for so long. She splashed her face and drank, choking a little as she did so. A flock of birds shot into the air to her left, high on the rocks above.

She closed her grey eyes for a moment, her red hair plastered against her freckled cheeks. "Spirits of the forest and glen... Protect me and guide me home. I beg of you..."

You must keep moving! the whispers hissed on the air where the sunlight sparkled about her.

The girl nodded and pushed herself up to make for the far end of the gully.

"There she is!" barked one of her pursuers behind her, his voice urgent like that of an excited hunting hound when it has picked up the scent of a doe. "After her!"

"We've almost got her, boys!" another shouted gleefully.

She looked back and saw the three Romans in red picking their way over the rocks and water, ripping away moss and lichen as they clawed their way toward her.

"Come here, pretty!" the third shouted, casting his eyes to the heights where the other two of their party had moved to intercept her. "Let us show you a bit of Rome's might on the point of my pilum!"

"No!" the girl moved on, climbing nimbly over and around the rocks, falling, slipping, and splashing through the frigid, earth-brown water.

She went under, but pushed up off the muddy bottom and grabbed hold of a ledge to pull herself forward, but as she rose up, like a water nymph daring to peak above the surface, she was knocked off her feet against the flat of a great boulder. The impact was hard, so hard that she felt she might not be able to move ever again. Her eyes focussed and she saw one more Roman directly in front of her. It was he who had back-handed her, and she felt a trickle of blood from where his iron ring had cut her cheek.

"Ha!" the Roman before her shouted. "I'm first!" he called to his mates. He grabbed hold of her jaw and pinned her against the rocks as he raked over her body, her form showing beneath her soaked clothing. "You've given us quite a hunt, girly! But now, it's time to pay up!"

The girl grasped for a small knife tucked in her belt and made to stab at him, but she was too slow and he slapped the blade away so that it fell beneath the surface of the water.

"Nice try!" He grabbed at her clothing, his hand pressing her painfully against the rocky surface.

"NO!" she shouted and struggled, kicking as hard as she could against the bulky Roman.

"Oh, yes!" he growled and grunted as he worked down his bracae.

He was about to thrust when the girl saw a flash behind his left shoulder and heard the thump of a bowstring.

A second later, a barbed arrow pounded into the side of his head and he dropped sideways into the water.

"Hey!" one of the three others rushing toward them shouted, accompanied by the slither of their gladii.

The girl turned to see an armed woman rushing toward her, looking past her to the other three Romans.

The woman nocked another arrow and the subsequent scream echoed around the gully as another Roman fell. "Quickly! Run!" the woman said to the Ordovician girl, just as a pugio flew out of nowhere to catch her bowstring, making the bow straighten suddenly and fly from her hands. She rushed past the girl, her gladius rising up to meet the other two.

The urgent and harsh clang of steel sounded loudly in the gully and it seemed that the overhanging saplings shuddered at it like a sensitive crowd in an amphitheatre.

The girl looked over her shoulder as she made to escape and saw the warrior woman slash the throat of another Roman before the third punched her in the side of the head, sending her sideways onto a jagged rock where her ribs cracked audibly.

"AAAH!" the woman cried out in pain, making to rise up, but only to have her neck grabbed, and her head forced beneath the dark water. She struggled and flailed, felt around for a loose rock with which to strike.

"Looks like we'll have two eh, Quintus?" the man pinning her beneath the water said.

The girl turned suddenly and felt the air go out of her entire body as a fifth Roman punched her in the gut. She doubled her over, a fire in her lungs as she gasped. She felt her hair pulled harshly and as her head was wrenched back she saw the warrior woman's legs flail.

"I'll still fuck you if you're freshly dead, bitch!" the man holding her growled.

She felt his blade against her neck. *Forest spirits help us!*

The water closed in and her vision of the world above grew blurry as the woman struggled.

Goddess give me strength! she thought.

Then her hand felt the handle of a knife on the bottom. She grabbed hold of it and thrust upward, feeling it pierce soft flesh. The grip on her neck loosed a little and she withdrew the blade and thrust again.

The Roman holding her clawed at the bleeding wounds beneath his chin, his eyes agog.

She pushed him aside quickly, rose out of the water and threw the knife.

The blade planted itself in the fifth man's eye. He screamed and dropped the pugio he had at the girl's throat.

The Ordovician girl took up the pugio and drove it into his neck at the collarbone, landing on top of him as he fell backward into the water. Wailing, she drove the blade into his body again and again and again.

The woman saw her collapse, and then she too fell over, pain wracking her body, her breathing desperate and inadequate to keep her conscious before she fell against the flat of a boulder.

It was as a dream, teetering on the edge of willful death, wondering if it was time to give up on life's toils. Her mind raced through myriad memories, of joy and despair, of the truest of loves, and of the deepest of losses. All of it wavered in her vision.

Then, the sun's chariot reached its zenith and shone onto the gully where the blood of the battle was already washing away. The birds resumed their song, joined by the carrion birds who had perched themselves in the trees above in anticipation of the feast to come.

Death continued to tempt her and she could feel the waters of the black river rising up her legs to swallow her.

But the light would not allow it, for it grew brighter, warmer and in that moment a chorus of love-filled voices accompanied flickering lights about the woman's head.

She opened her eyes and gazed upon the winged creatures, mortals in miniature. They moved quickly, in a sort of calm frenzy as they touched her brow and tickled at her neck in an attempt to wake her and pull her away from the dark shore which she gazed upon.

The Ordovician girl appeared before her, her tunica stained with blood. She still grasped the pugio. She spoke in words the woman did not understand, but the gestures were sufficient.

The woman nodded and let the girl help her to her feet.

The lights about her head scattered and returned to the mossy embankments to observe them from a safe distance.

The woman grunted painfully as her broken ribs groaned beneath her skin. "Aaah!" she cried as she leaned upon a rock.

"Rhaid i ni fynd!" the Ordovician girl said. "We go!" She pointed to the north, out of the gully.

The woman nodded, her senses returning, her head clearer now, despite the lacerating pain. "Are you all right?" she looked at the girl, her eyes glimpsing down. "Did they harm you?"

The girl shook her head. "Diolch," she said, kissing the woman's hands. "Diolch yn fawr."

"You're welcome," the woman said. She pointed to her gladius and the bow which rested against the side of the gully.

The girl tucked the pugio in her belt, went to retrieve them for the woman, and handed them to her.

"What is your name?" the woman asked the girl, pointing at her, not sure if she knew any Latin, and doubtful that she was even aware of Greek.

"Vala," the girl replied. "Vala ydw i."

"Vala?" the woman repeated, and then put her left hand upon her own chest, her right using the bow to support herself. "I am Adara… Adara Pen Dragon."

The girl's eyes fixed on the ring on her left hand, two intertwined dragons with a fiery ruby where their heads met. "Dewch," she said, trying to lead the woman away. "To…home…"

The woman nodded and followed. When they reached the end of the gully, she pointed up. "I need to get my horse." The girl helped her up the steep slope to the forest path above. The woman whistled and her call was answered by an urgent neighing and the clip clopping of hooves.

Soon, the gelding appeared on the path, her cloak still clinging to its back. The horse went to his mistress and nuzzled her gently, his nose sniffing at her wounds.

"I'm all right boy. Just a little broken up," she said, her head leaning against his neck for a grateful moment. "This is Aegis," the woman said to the girl.

The girl pat the horse and offered to help the woman up.

She shook her head. "I can't ride right now."

The girl insisted and pointed at the fur-covered saddle.

The warrior nodded and set down her bow and gladius. She then gripped the saddle, and let the girl hoist her. She cried out in pain but made it, settling herself on top.

Vala handed her the bow and gladius again and pointed to the northwest where a titanic snow-capped mountain loomed above in the sky. "Yr Wyddfa," the girl said, then motioned beyond it. "Seg-ontio."

"No!" the woman said quickly. "We can't go to Segontium! There are more Romans there."

Vala nodded that she knew and made a gesture indicating going around the mountain, away from Segontium. "To Mon... Ynys Mon..." Vala said. "Domus...home."

"Your home is on Mona?"

The girl nodded. "Home...Mona..."

The woman nodded. "Yes. All right."

The girl named Vala nodded and began to lead the way north.

As Aegis began to follow her, Adara looked back at the gully where the small creatures flit about the sun-bright rocks and the carrion birds now glided down to the bottom to clear away the corpses of the dead.

It was a long journey for Adara Pen Dragon, painfully so because of her broken ribs and the fever that had begun to set in.

Vala led them out of the forests on the lower slopes of Yr Wyddfa, through the glens where rivers ran through and the moss and heather-clad terrain tumbled northward toward the sea.

Adara had checked the rough map she had with her, a remnant from Lucius' campaigns, and could see that Vala was indeed leading her around the mountain to the sea where they would have to cross what the girl called Afon Menai, the straights between the mainland and Mona.

It made her nervous to be so close to the base at Segontium, for there were five hundred troops said to be based there, the men of I Sunicorum Cohort. After all, she had just slain five of their fellow legionaries, deserters or not.

But she knew she could not travel and that her fever would only get worse. She needed to rest and heal in a safe place and, though Rome had long ago sacked Mona and slaughtered all of the Druids there, it had remained, as far as she was aware, peaceful in recent decades. The threat it had faced more recently was from Hibernian raiders rather than Rome, though, she doubted Vala saw it that way.

Adara observed the girl as she walked stalwartly before her and Aegis. She appeared strong and stubborn. *I wonder why she left her home?*

Eventually, the scent of the sea filled their senses and, as evening was falling, they arrived on the shores of Afon Menai.

Adara felt herself sweating, her shaking having grown worse, but she knew she could not let herself sleep, especially as Segontium was so near now. They crossed the Roman road that led from Canovium to Segontium, and she felt that by even touching the paving stones she was exposed.

At last, they came to Afon Menai, taking a fern-covered forest path down to a rocky shore where the island of Mona stretched out before them on the other side of the swelling waters. It was late in the day, but the summer sun was still relatively high, casting orange and pink light over the rippling waters, belying the dangerous currents that lurked beneath the pastel surface.

Vala helped Adara down slowly from off of Aegis' back and turned to look up and down the beach.

"Are we crossing here?" Adara asked, indicating the other side. "Now?"

Vala shook her head. "Pwll Ceris... Dangerous now. Later."

Adara nodded. She was glad Vala knew at least a little Latin, for otherwise she would not have understood a word of her strange Brythonic tongue.

"Cwch," she said, pointing to some of the beached fishing boats as she gestured that she was going down shore to find a vessel.

As Vala went to a group of three fishermen who chattered together in the light of the resting sun, Adara leaned against Aegis' bulk. Her ribs ached and she dared to pull up her tunica to look. Her left side was swollen with welts of angry purple, black, and blue. She tried to ascertain the damage, wincing as her finger felt her ribs. Three appeared to be broken. "Gods, help me..." She sighed. "Wherever this girl is taking me, I hope it is soon."

Suddenly, she heard Vala cry out as one of the fishermen groped at her. "Hey!" Adara shouted at them through her pain. She drew her gladius from where it was tucked beside the saddle. "Leave her alone!"

She saw Vala slap the man while his friends laughed at him. Adara began to walk toward her and saw that a third fisherman followed. She levelled the blade at him.

The old fisherman, a man of about sixty years or so, put up his hands. "It's me, child… Tomos. I know your father."

"He help us," Vala said, her freckled cheeks flushed from the unpleasant interaction with the others. "Cwch." She didn't care whether she knew the man or not. She just wanted to get them over the water.

Adara looked the man over, and he did the same to her. "Roman?" he asked her.

"No," Adara answered.

He looked doubtful but shrugged. He pointed to the scrip at Adara's belt and rubbed his fingers together.

"Denarii," Vala clarified. "Want coin."

Adara nodded and put up one finger.

The man shook his head and put up three fingers.

"No."

The gold of her dragon ring caught his eye, and he lit up. "That!" he pointed.

"This is sacred to me. No."

"Then denarii!" he grunted, holding up three fingers once again.

"Fine." She did not have the strength to haggle with him. "We leave now."

"No," the man said, pointing at the straits. "Pwyll Ceris… The swells…too dangerous. We wait." He began to walk farther along the beach.

Vala gestured that they should follow and took Aegis' reins while Adara, leaning on her stringless bow, went after.

The fisherman stopped at a long barge which was covered with drying nets. He looked at the westering sun down the straits and began to fold his nets.

"My horse won't be able to go in the boat," Adara said to him, her head spinning.

"No horse," the man replied, pointing at the water. "Swim."

Adara felt her stomach drop. She had no idea how strong the currents were. Vala and the fisherman had displayed sufficient caution to make her worry about it. "He'll drown."

"No," the man said. "Later cross and swim." Once his nets were set aside, he pushed the long boat to the shoreline where the water was already receding slowly. "We wait." He then went back to the where the trees ended and leaned against one.

After a little over an hour, with the sun falling more quickly now, the man got up from his resting place and went to push the boat to where the water had reached its lowest point. He indicated that they should come with him. "Off," he pointed to the saddle bags and furs on Aegis' back.

Vala set about taking everything off Aegis and put it in the bottom of the boat which was scattered with dried fish guts and lengths of kelp. She then helped the fisherman to push the boat into the water.

Adara stood back, stroking Aegis' forehead. "You can do this, boy. Follow us." She began to pull the horse forward by the reins.

Aegis balked at first, but Adara soothed him. "I need your help," she whispered, and his ears pricked up.

Together they walked along the soft, shell and seaweed-strewn sands of the low tide. The crossing was much narrower than it had been, but Adara had no idea how deep it was, or if Aegis could swim through the current at all.

The fisherman gestured to the sun, and made a frantic motion at the narrowed straits.

Adara led Aegis to the water's edge. "Follow me, Aegis." *Epona, keep him safe,* she prayed as the sound of the water filled her ears.

Vala helped Adara climb into the boat and settle.

The fisherman put out his hand for the coins he had negotiated.

Adara turned stiffly and placed two in his hand. "You get the last one when we're on the other side."

He grunted and slid the two silver coins into a pouch that hung from his belt. That done, he pushed with his long barge pole and the boat slid into the water.

Immediately, they swung to the right, carried in the current.

Adara looked back to see Aegis rearing and pacing at the shore, reluctant to cross. "Come on, boy!" she shouted "Come!"

Aegis raced down the shoreline, following their direction as they pulled farther away toward the other side and the vast, flat green lands of the isle of Mona.

"We have to go back!" Adara shouted.

But the fisherman pressed on, shaking his head as he strained against the pole.

"Aegis!" Adara called out.

The gelding raced back and forth neighing loudly a few times and then, with an intense burst of energy, he leapt into the water and followed them. His nostrils flared and his head strove against the current as he went after his mistress, willing himself to the other side.

"You can do it!" Adara called, straining to look back.

For a moment, when the straits were at their low tide deepest, Aegis began to get swept away, but he powered through and soon his long legs touched bottom again and he drew even with the boat, charging for the far shore and dry land.

The boat came to a sudden stop on the sandy shore of Mona.

Adara got out of the boat with Vala's help and went straight to Aegis to take the reins and stroke his forehead while his panicked breathing calmed. "You did it," she soothed.

Meanwhile, Vala had removed all of their belongings from the boat. When that was done, she turned to watch Adara and Aegis, hoping that the woman would be able to make the rest of the journey. Suddenly, she felt hands clawing at her breasts and hips and turned to push the fisherman away.

He gave her a toothless smile and came at her again. She shouted and slapped him.

He slapped her back and she fell. He made to try again to feel her young body, but was met by the point of Adara's blade at his throat.

"Get away from her," Adara growled, ignoring the excruciating pain in her side.

"My coin," he demanded, his hand out for the last third of his payment.

Adara shook her head and pressed the blade forward. "Get out of here, or I'll cut you!" She felt her anger rise, and knew she would have done it if he came again. She'd had enough of such men, pathetic and weak ones who thought a young girl was an easy target.

He looked at the dried blood on her blade and backed away. "You'll regret this, woman," he growled, looking at her over his shoulder before he turned his boat around and pushed it back into the water.

Adara watched him go back, carried by Afon Menai's current, and when he was away, she turned back to Vala. "I need to rest," she said, her vision swimming before her.

Vala rushed to her side and led her away from the water to the tree-clad embankment at the top of the beach where Aegis was cropping at some of the long grasses. She then took up Adara's cloak, fur saddle, and saddle bags, and placed them beside Adara. "We wait...morning. One day riding."

Adara shook her head. "Take me now. Please..."

Vala looked to where the sun was setting and wondered if they could make it in the dark. "Yes. We go to Traeth." She set about placing the saddle and bags on Aegis' back. When that was done, she fastened Adara's weapons also, and then turned to help her up.

Adara shook her head. "I...I can't..."

"Must!" Vala insisted. "Almost home." She bent to help Adara get her foot in her cupped hands and then hoisted her.

Adara cried out, and fell onto Aegis' neck, holding on with what little strength remained to her.

Vala brought the reins up, and then climbed up to settle herself in front of Adara. "Hold," she said, placing Adara's arms about her waist. When she felt her squeeze, she clicked her tongue and kneed Aegis forward along the beach to where a path went up into the thicket and the darkening dirt road northward.

They rode through the night, the wind howling among the forests of oak, beech, and birch.

As Vala pushed Aegis forward along the pathways she remembered, ever onward toward the home she called 'Traeth', Adara fell in and out of consciousness.

She dreamed dark dreams in that land of angry and pained memory. She heard cries and lamentations on the wind, and saw the coming of Rome's legions with fire and death.

The island of Mona remembered the slaughter that Rome had once wrought there, when the Druids had been massacred and their sacred groves burned and bloodied with their people's lives.

At one point, Adara thought she could hear Vala weeping as they rode through the dark, but she was too weak to ask anything, focussing only on clinging to the girl as Aegis trotted along.

When the sun finally rose, the sound of the sea once more entered their hearing.

Adara felt Aegis' pace slow and come to a stop. She opened her eyes as she leaned on Vala's back and saw the brilliant morning sun sparkling on the sea. She stared down a track that led to a walled enclosure with several structures, including a large roundhouse from which smoke rose into the early morning to be whisked away. Beyond the enclosure, the land dropped away to a bay where a long, curving beach of golden sand slept beside crystal blue water.

"Traeth," Vala said, pointing to the enclosure and the beach beyond. She kneed Aegis down the path and called out as they approached the gate in the low stone walls. Within the enclosure was a covered woodpile to the right, and animal pens with goats and sheep to the left. Beyond that, to the left, was a small roundhouse which stood opposite a square, thatched structure from where the sound of hammering emanated. At the far end, a large roundhouse rose up, its thatched peak contrasted against the blue morning sky. Beside this was a well, and wooden racks where drying fish danced in the sea breeze as though they were still alive on the line. "Tad!" Vala called out. "Helpa ni!"

The hammering stopped and a big man with a red beard and red hair the colour of Vala's came rushing out. "Vala?" he called. "Vala!"

Adara watched as the man came up to them, his face ablaze with concern and relief and just as he was about to speak more, the world went black and she felt herself falling…

The pain cut and bit, like a pack of rabid dogs that tear at an unconscious body they've come upon. It reached out to the senses and grappled with them from far off, through the haze of thoughts and memories. Even as Adara's soul strolled once more along the thick, lapping waters of the black river, the pain kept her in the world of the living. She heard tender and worried voices, and felt the distant warmth of angling sunlight.

Just as she began to turn away from the water, her side exploded in agony as bones were moved and cracked and braced. Rough hands held her fast and she tried to scream, but it was as if from some other realm where no one could hear her.

The faces of her children swam before her eyes and she tried to call out their names, to tell them to run, even as the black water tide rose up to lick at her ankles and soften the rough sand at her bare feet.

It was the deep quiet that woke her, the silence playing strangely about her ears for a while until it was joined by the soft hum of the sea, like the trumpet of a conch when pressed to the ear.

Adara opened her eyes slowly, with great discomfort as her lids stuck together and her arms were fastened to the sides of a small bed. She tried to strain against her bonds, but was unable to move due to her bindings.

She gave up for the moment and allowed herself to look around. She was in a small roundhouse. She could tell from the wood and thatched conical roof above her. The smell of woodsmoke was strong, and there was also the scent of her own stale sweat. But there was something more, something rotting.

She began to panic and wondered if her wounds had turned gangrenous for they felt strange, swollen.

Her eyes fell on the small window in the stonework above her where the sunlight filtered in, lighting the pink and yellow flowers of mallow and rock rose that had been placed on the sill. The colour and light calmed her, even as she began to feel the dizziness return to overcome her.

She wanted to close her eyes again, to sleep, but she heard the sound of an iron latch and a door creaking. Her heart raced as she saw the form of a bearded man come into the small house. He closed the door behind him and came to sit upon a stool beside her bed.

Gods protect me, Adara prayed, frustrated by her inability to move.

"You are safe," the man's soft, deep voice said.

"Untie…me…" she croaked. "Let…me…go…"

"I cannot do that. It's not safe," he replied in Latin.

Adara turned her head a little to look at him. He had a thick beard and red hair the colour of copper. He was burly, with think arms and strong, rough hands. She would have expected him to harm her in that moment except for the kindness in his eyes and the relief in his smile when he placed his hand upon her brow.

"Good. Your fever has broken." He lifted her head gently and pressed a clay cup to her lips. "Drink. You need to drink."

Adara sipped at the fresh water and felt it soothe her dry throat. She drank again and felt him lay her head down on the straw pillow. "Where am I? Who are you?" she asked.

"You are at Traeth. My home. You've been in a fever for three days now."

"How did I get here?"

"You don't remember?"

She shook her head.

"My daughter, Vala, brought you here. You saved her. Don't you remember?"

Adara thought back and the memories of battle returned, led her thoughts to the injuries she had sustained. She nodded. "Yes. I remember now. Is…she well?"

He smiled. "Vala is well, thanks to you. She and her step-mother argued and she ran away. I never…" His voice broke for a moment. "I never thought I would see her again. Thank you for helping her, Adara Pen Dragon."

Adara looked up suddenly at the mention of her name.

"Vala told me your name."

"And…what is yours?" she asked, suddenly very tired.

"I am Killian."

"Why have you tied me up, Killian?"

"I have reset your bones and bandaged them with a poultice of symphytum. If you move, the ribs will break again. Thankfully, they were clean breaks and should heal."

"How do you know?"

"We had a lot of injuries in the copper mines to the north. I learned. It's crucial that you don't move."

Adara wanted to argue, to rail against her confinement, but she didn't have the energy.

He stared at her, a sort of wonder in his eyes. "You have many weapons, Adara Pen Dragon… How many other women and girls have you saved?"

His face wavered in her vision as her eyes grew heavy.

"Many…" she said before she fell back into her healing slumber.

XIV

VENUS OBDUCTA

'Venus Shrouded'

The olive grove was at its most peaceful in the early hours, the morning mist still clinging to the trees like a lover reluctant to leave the bed. Mourning doves sang their dirge as the sun's light fell over the top of the mountain and tumbled down its steep slopes to set every drop of dew alight upon the grass.

Adara breathed deeply as she roused from her slumber, her chest rising and falling without pain as she filled her lungs with fresh morning air. She felt the softness of the couch beneath her, and the flutter of the folds of her blue stola in the mountain breeze, the swaying of her long hair over the edge of the lush pillow.

I'm home? she thought, recognizing the rising slope of Hymettos, the villa behind her, and every part of the olive grove where she had once played, free of the world's cares, before love…before anger.

Through the thinning mist, she saw her then, a golden figure in purest white walking among the trees. Her face was veiled, but a golden light shone from beneath. With every step of her bare feet, flowers sprang from the grassy ground, and wherever she placed her hand upon an olive limb, green shoots sprouted.

Adara swung her legs down from the couch and felt the cool, wet grass on her bare feet. She watched as the veiled figure came toward her, the light about her growing brighter.

When the figure stopped before her, the veil fell gently to the ground like a leaf in autumn.

Adara fell to her knees and wept for joy as she looked up at the Goddess Venus…Love.

Do not weep, Adara Pen Dragon…

I cannot help it, Lady. My heart has done nothing else.

Love smiled and laid her hand upon Adara's head, suffusing the mortal with a sense of calm and comfort. She then bent to raise her from the ground and held her close, her breathing like a soothing song, her touch a salve for the soul. *You cannot give up on life, child. You have much to fight for.*

I have lost so much... Adara fought the song, the calm. She clung to the anger and sadness that had been driving her, eating away at her and feasting on her goodness.

Love released her and looked upon her. *Do you remember when I came to you here?*

Yes.

When I revealed your impending motherhood to you?

Yes. I do. I remember the joy, the absolute love that filled me.

You are a mother still, Love said, her voice firm but full of care. *Your children need you yet.*

They are better without me.

Love looked sad at that, the light of her long, golden hair flickering. *No. They are not. They need you...your nurture...your light.*

Adara shook her head. *I am too full of anger, Lady. I am...so lost.*

You are not, Love insisted. *You are journeying through your knowing. Do you forget the birth of your Love, the source from which your children have come?*

The green pools of Adara's eyes flooded with tears beneath her creased brow and anemones sprouted where they fell at Love's feet. *He left me...my Love...my Life...*

He will never leave you.

Adara nodded and looked Love in her starry eyes. *He is dead. Gone from this world without us...without me.*

He is dead to the world, yes. Love's eyes too rimmed with tears then. *But you must not forget. You must forgive, Adara...in your heart...for you...for your children.*

I cannot.

Love's visage grew dark in that moment, as sad as a neglected garden in the throes of winter. She kissed the mortal upon the forehead, and her light returned. *You have been mother to many upon your road, Adara Pen Dragon... No amount of the blood of the wicked will fill the void you perceive. However...it will soon be time to fight for those who love you, whom you love, no matter how dark and full of anger your heart has grown.*

Love then urged her to lay herself down upon the couch where she closed her eyes and wept herself to sleep. The goddess set her brilliant hands upon her side and then was gone, into the light among the trees and flower-strewn ground of the mountainside...

You are not alone...

Her face was wet in the dim light of the small, round hearth at the centre of the roundhouse. The grove was gone, as were the sunlight, and the pervading sense of love and memory which she had resisted. The beams of the conical roof rose up into the darkness above where bunches of herbs dried and swayed. Outside the small window, it was dark and thunderous, the sky iron grey and sad.

Adara made to wipe at her face, half expecting her hands and legs to be tied still, but they had not been fastened for many days. She had not left the roundhouse. She had been still and sleeping while she healed, and her body ached from the lack of movement, and from her bruises. She sat up and stared at the low fire in the midst of those loose stones.

The only faces she had seen were the girl, Vala, and her father, Killian, though she had heard several other voices. She did not hear any of them now, all sounds muffled by the thunder and rain.

Adara pushed herself up slowly and went carefully to the bucket which sat behind a curtain on the other side of the small roundhouse. After relieving herself, she poured water from the clay pitcher that had been set upon the table opposite the low door. It had been flavoured with chamomile flowers and honey. It tasted good.

She then pulled back a piece of linen which covered a copper plate and saw dried apples, a piece of black bread, and goat's cheese. She sat herself down slowly and ate. She thought about her situation, wondered how long it would be before she could ride or fight. She then thought of Aegis whom she had not seen since she was brought there.

"Today, I'll go to see him," she said to herself as she gazed at the fire. She knew he was being cared for. Vala had been good with him.

Her dream rushed back to her then, and her heart sank, tears beginning to rim her eyes as she felt, remembered, her rejection of Love's comfort.

Forgive me, Goddess, she thought, reaching out to the divinity. *I am not myself. I have lost myself.*

There was a knock on the door and it opened slowly.

Killian's red head came in first as he bent to go through. He smiled when he saw her sitting at the table. "You're up? Good. That is good."

"I feel very strange."

"You should. You've been lying down for many days," he replied as he approached with a fresh bandage, and another pitcher of water. "I'm glad to see you eating also."

She looked at him, this burly red-haired man with the kind face and voice. *Why would he help me so much? What does he want?* She was endlessly suspicious, and had been so for many lonely years, but something told her that the help Killian offered her was sincere and born of deep gratitude for her saving his daughter's life.

"I brought new bandages," he said. "It's been a couple of days since they were changed."

Adara looked at him and then felt her left side where the ribs had been broken. She breathed deeply, hesitantly, and found that the pain was much reduced, almost gone. She nodded.

"It will be easier if you stand," he said. He suddenly realized she was not wearing her breeches. "I can get Vala to do it, if you prefer. She's milking the goats."

Adara thought for a moment and shook her head. "It's fine. You do it." She lifted her loose tunica to just below her breasts to reveal the think layer of bandages which Killian had wrapped about her. "Gods, it smells," she gasped, fearing infection.

He smiled as he began to unfasten the bandage. "It's all right. I changed the poultice last time to one of onion and dandelion to help reduce the bruising. May I?" he asked.

She nodded.

Killian began to unwind the bandage which had been wrapped about her ribcage several times. When the last layer fell away, he took a cloth and poured some of the clean water over it. Gently, he wiped at the dried paste from the poultice until her skin was clean. It was his turn to gasp.

"What? What is it?" she asked as she looked up at the ceiling, her long hair falling down her back.

"Nothing...nothing. It's good. The poultice has never worked this well. There is barely any bruising left, and the swelling has gone down fully." He turned to take up the new dressing.

Adara looked down at her ribs and, with shaking fingers, reached out to touch the skin. *Thank you, Goddess...*

"Don't press hard on your ribs. The bones will take much longer to set and heal than your skin," Killian said. "I never saw any of the men in the copper mines heal as quickly as you have, Adara Pen Dragon." He began to wrap the new bandages about her.

The feeling of his hand upon her skin where he held the end made her feel uneasy, but it was strangely pleasant. It had been so long, years, since someone else had touched her. Suddenly, however, it felt wrong, though he was only seeing to her wound.

"I...I can do it," she said quickly, her hands almost pushing his away.

"I'm finished," he said, his face now almost as red as his hair. He tucked the end beneath the folds snuggly and stepped back. "There."

Adara let her tunica fall quickly. "I need to wash," she said.

"There is no better bath than the sea here," Killian said.

"The sea?"

"Yes. We are a short distance from the traeth, the beach. The storm should pass by the end of today. Tomorrow, you can go down and wash. It's cold, but you will feel clean afterward."

"I'll do that," she said, and after a moment she asked something that had been on her mind. "How did you come to learn Latin?"

Killian shrugged as he folded up the old bandage. "Roman traders often came to the mines for copper. I picked it up. I tried to teach Vala, but she is stubborn. She knows a little. Definitely more than she lets on."

"And your wife?"

"Mair?" he said.

"Vala's stepmother?"

He nodded. "She knows some, but refuses to speak it. Nor will she allow our boys, Mil and Merin, or our daughter, Vanora, to speak it. The anger with Rome runs deep here, but I have taught them some Latin anyway."

"I understand," Adara said.

He looked at her at that. "Are you not Roman?"

"My father was...is. My mother is Greek."

"And yet you go by the name 'Pen Dragon', which is the language of the Britons."

"It's a long story," Adara said, looking away.

Killian did not press. "Well, perhaps you can tell us over the evening meal?"

She looked up quickly.

"Now that you are able to move, there's no need for you to stay locked up in here. Besides, Vala insists."

Adara smiled. "Perhaps tomorrow. After I have had my sea bath?"

"Very well." Killian made to go to the door.

"May I see Aegis?"

"Of course. He's beneath the shelter in the animal pen next door. All he's done is watch this house from there."

Adara felt guilty at that, but knew it could not have been any other way. She also felt confident that Vala had taken good care of him.

Killian was about to open the door when Vala stepped in, her hair wet from the rain.

"You're up?" the young woman said as she rushed across the floor to Adara and put her arms around her in a great embrace.

"Careful with her, Vala. Don't squeeze too hard. She is a warrior, but she is still injured."

"I...am happy...that you are well," Vala said, her Latin much better than it had been.

Adara could not help but smile as she looked at her. "And are you all right?"

Vala nodded. "Very good." She turned to her father. "But Mair is refusing to cook one of the chickens for our meal tonight."

"It will be tomorrow, now," Killian told his daughter. "The lady wishes to bathe in the sea first."

"Please..." Adara said, "call me Adara."

Killian nodded and looked directly at her green eyes. "Very well... Adara." He looked to his daughter who was smiling at him. "Vala, get her a pair of sandals which she can slide on more easily than her riding boots, and then take her to see Aegis."

"Le, Tad," she said, reverting to Brythonic.

"Now that Adara is conscious, let us speak Latin in front of her," Killian said, eyeing his daughter.

"Yes, Father."

Killian smiled and went out.

When he was gone, Vala turned back to Adara and hugged her once more.

This time, Adara returned the hug, patting the girl's back and hair. She suspected that she had not told her father all that had happened to her, nor how far she had gone to flee her stepmother.

It felt strange, almost otherworldly, to be outside again. Despite the low, grey clouds that raced over the isle of Mona, Adara had to shield her eyes from the brilliance around her. She had been bed ridden for close to a week. Her muscles felt weak, and her balance was a little off.

"Take my hand," Vala said as she led Adara out of the roundhouse toward the animal pens.

Aegis looked up from the hay he was eating beneath a rough lean-to.

As they walked, Adara looked around. Killian's home was well-tended, the thatch of the workshop, and main, large roundhouse fresh and sturdy, the same as the one she had been occupying. Rocky pathways radiated like a small network of roads from the main gate to each building, traversing the mud where chickens roamed.

A woman watched from the doorway of the main house as Vala led Adara to the animal pens. She stood with crossed arms, her long brown braid bouncing as the wind played with it.

Adara waved, but the woman simply nodded and went inside.

"That is Mair," Vala said without looking back.

"Your stepmother?"

"Yes. I don't like her. But she keeps a good home."

Adara stopped halfway to the animal pens, needing to rest a little. "Why did you run away from here, Vala?" Adara asked. She knew the irony of her question, for she had run away from her own children. But she was curious.

Vala glanced at the big roundhouse and then looked at Adara. "Mair tried to beat me."

"Why?"

"Because I refuse to…to marry a dirty farmer of pigs." She pulled a face that made her look ten years younger than she was.

Adara smiled.

"I try to go to *my* mother's family among the Demetae… I want to marry for love, like my mother and father did." She looked sad.

Adara took her hand. "What happened to your mother, Vala?"

The girl looked up, something haunted in her eyes. "When…when I was ten years old, Hibernian raiders came and attacked our home to the north, near the mines. My father was underground when they came, but I was with my mother." Vala paused and looked to the sky for a moment. "Fy mam…my mother…she was warrior like you. When they attacked our home, she tell me to run while she look for my younger brother."

"What happened?"

"I run like she tell me, but she stay to fight. She killed two of them, but the others kill her…and my brother…"

Adara's heart went out to the girl and she put her arm about her. "I'm so sorry, Vala."

"Me too. Father stopped working in the mines, and moved us here with Mair. Her husband killed in the attack. They marry, but not for love."

"Marrying for love…" Adara began, "…can be filled with pain also."

Vala looked at her. "You marry for love?"

"Oh, yes. I did." Adara stepped away then and went to where Aegis was stretching his neck over the fence toward her.

Vala followed after her, wondering what happened. "I take good care of him. Ride him on the traeth…the beach."

"Thank you, Vala," Adara said, relieved that Aegis was in such good form. "Hello, boy," she said softly, pressing her forehead to his soft muzzle.

Aegis closed his eyes as he felt his mistress near again and leaned into her from his side of the wooden fence.

"He miss you," Vala said.

"He is my only friend now," Adara answered.

"Not only one," Vala replied as she leaned on the fence beside her.

From the door of the smithy across the way, Killian watched his daughter with Adara and smiled to himself. He sighed, knowing what was coming. He knew what Vala was thinking. He did not mind in the least.

Her first day out of doors exhausted Adara, and she slept soundly that night. The throbbing in her side had nearly faded to nothing. She was almost bothered more by the lingering feeling of Killian's hands on her torso as he wrapped the bandages about her. Every time the memory returned, she immediately pushed it away, not wanting to deal with it and all that it dug up. As she sat on the edge of the bed early that morning, she held her gladius hoping it would remind her of her purpose. The only problem was, however, that her purpose was not entirely clear to her.

She remembered the olive grove in her dreams…Love's words…

It will soon be time to fight for those who love you, no matter how dark and full of anger your heart has grown.

"I'm so tired of being angry," Adara said to herself as she sat there, alone in that small, dark roundhouse. "I'm also tired of being dirty!" She then slid on the sandals Vala had given her and, gladius in hand, made her way outside to go down to the beach.

Nobody was stirring yet as she walked past the well and fish-drying racks to the smaller gate in the wall. Beyond a long row of ferns and grass, she could see the broad crescent of a sandy beach below where the morning tide was coming in, rippling gently in a series of small, white-crested waves that slowly caressed the shoreline.

The sky was blue and expansive, and Adara felt that she had not seen a sky like that for an age. The morning sun cast its light upon the water and there were flickers of fire as if they had been cast off of from the wheels of Helios' chariot.

Adara followed the path of trampled grass and fern until she came to a sandy access point that led down onto the beach. The sound of the sea was soothing and she paused a moment to breathe deeply, its fresh air cleansing her lungs.

Her eyes opened wide a second later as she panicked, wary of being set upon as had happened so many times in the past.

But there was no one there. She was alone.

Adara bent slowly to remove the sandals and walked barefoot along the curve of the beach. She had not felt soft sand on her feet in so long, she sighed when she felt it and the icy cold kiss of the tidewater about her ankles.

"Gods, grant me some peace…" she said as she looked out to sea toward the brilliant morning sun, its rays stretching out to her, warming her face and arms.

Adara set the gladius and sandals down, just out of reach of the water. She looked around one more time and, when she was certain she was alone, she pulled her long brown tunica up over her head. She then began to unravel the bandages about her torso and set them down on top of her tunica.

She stood there, naked, the sea's breeze rippling about her, goosebumps covering her arms and legs, pulling at the strands of her black and grey hair. As she stood there, she remembered long ago days when she had lain naked in the sun upon a pink-pebbled beach with Lucius. The memory only served to churn up hurt, like iron raking the coals of a dying fire.

The past is the past, she thought as she looked at the entwined dragons on her finger, her hand making a fist as if to strangle them.

You must forgive... Love had told her.

But she did not know if she was capable of that.

Taking a deep breath, she waded slowly into the icy blue water of the bay so that it rose slowly up her body, past her knees and thighs, her groin, and up her healing torso to her breasts. She dropped quickly to go underwater, and gasped as she came up, the cold hitting her as if she had been punched. She went under again, scrubbing her skin with handfuls of sand which she grasped from the bottom. She scrubbed at her hair and scalp too, feeling the oil and grime wash away.

When she felt clean, she dove and swam farther out, her memories of childhood joys by the sea rising to the surface as she opened her eyes to explore Neptune's realm of brilliant blues and greens, the sun's light pulsing all around her naked body as she swam.

She shivered from the cold, but she did not care in that moment, for it soothed her aching body and focussed her mind such that she did not think on the world of angry regret that harried her the long hours of every day.

Adara floated on her back, her arms and legs outspread to the sky, her eyes closed as she allowed the waves to gently urge her back toward the shore. When she reached down with her arms and felt the sandy bottom again, she stood up, shivering quite violently then. She wrung out her hair as best she could, and went to slip her tunica back on. She sat down for a few minutes to watch the sun and the water, and it was then that she noticed a figure watching her from the wall surrounding the roundhouses.

Killian waved to her, his red hair lit by the sunlight.

She waved back, wondering how long he had been there. She realized she did not mind. For the first time in a long while, she felt that her cares and worries were less burdensome. Even if it was for a short time, it felt wonderful.

Later that day, Vala came to fetch Adara to bring her to the main house for the evening meal.

When Adara opened the door, she found the young woman there smiling at her, the wind outside pulling violently at the strands of her red hair. She laughed. "The weather here doesn't last, does it?"

Vala entered and brushed her hair back. "No. It is…changeable. You come to eat?"

Adara nodded. "Yes."

Vala looked admiringly at the leather breeches, tunica, and cingulum. "You meet Mair now."

"Lead the way," Adara replied and closed the door behind her to follow Vala along the stone pathway, avoiding getting muck on the small sandals they had given her to wear.

Until then, Adara had only seen Killian and Vala. Mair had remained at a distance, and though Adara had heard the children, they had not been allowed to speak to her as yet.

Adara understood the distrust. She was a stranger, and to them at least, a Roman. A part of her would have preferred to remain in her small roundhouse, but she knew she could not avoid it. She had been their guest for many days now, eaten their food, drunk their water.

The main roundhouse was much larger than the one in which she had been recuperating. It rose up like a behemoth of thick stone and straw, its peak reaching up to touch the sky. Beneath the low overhang of cut, tightly-packed straw, firewood was piled, awaiting use, and there was a bench to the left side of the main door which was made up of four sturdy, oak planks. To the right of the door was a hollowed-out log that served as a basin.

"Vala," called Killian who was coming from the well to the left with a bucket. "Here is fresh water," he said, smiling at Adara as he approached. "Welcome to our home."

"Thank you," Adara replied, remembering him watching her on the beach. She reddened and he looked away quickly.

"Vala. Tip the old water."

Vala lifted the edge of the basin and the old water ran out to fall into another bucket to be given to the vegetables which they grew.

Killian then emptied the new water into the basin. "To wash," he said.

Vala washed her hands first and then went straight into the maw of the roundhouse. Adara did the same before bending and following her through, and Killian came last, closing the door behind him.

When Adara stood up inside, she was surprised at how vast it was, how warm, and earthy. Directly ahead, the focal point of the entire home was a great, round hearth surrounded by four tree trunks covered in furs. Over the fire was an iron frame from which three copper pots hung, the contents of which boiled and steamed and smelled delicious. About the perimeter of the roundhouse were bundles of wool in baskets out of which drop-spindles poked. There was also a table with pieces of leather and tools. The largest table was for food preparation and upon it were clay bowls filled with vegetables and various greens. Above the table several bundles of herbs dried and swayed in the breeze that gently circled the home. The floor was covered in a mixture of dried dirt and wood shavings.

On the other side of the fire, at the far side of the house, was a ladder that led to an upper floor that went around the structure. On this level of wooden planks supported by wooden pillars, the family's sleeping pallets radiated about the edges of the house with a close view of the thick framework of beams and thatch which was more grey than yellow due to the accumulation of smoke which slowly seeped through the straw to the sky.

Adara could see Mair standing at the far table, chopping food. She did not turn, and Adara thought to go over to her when Killian stood beside her.

"Mil, Merin, Vanora… Come and meet our guest!" he called.

Two young boys poked their heads out from the gallery above and slid down the smooth wooden ladder to rush over. They were followed by a young blonde girl who slowly, and methodically, made her way down the ladder after them.

"Wait for me!" she called out rushing to join her older brothers who stood before their father and the newcomer. The boys elbowed each other a couple of times then stood still, as though they were troops ready for inspection.

"These strong lads are Mil," Killian began, "and Merin. And this little one is Vanora."

"Hello!" Vanora said with a toothy smile, her face framed by wisps of blonde hair.

"Hello," Adara returned.

"Rydych chi'n bert!" Merin said in Brythonic, his brother giggling beside him.

"He say you pretty," Vala told Adara.

"It's been a long time since anyone has called me that!" Adara laughed. "But thank you, Merin."

"All right, you two. Go on!" Killian poked each of the boys who ran off giggling, looking backward at Adara with cheeky smiles and instinctively knowing the path they could take without slamming into anything.

Vanora remained, rocking back and forth on her tiny feet and smiling up at her father and Adara.

"Yes?" Killian asked as he knelt before her.

"Nothing," she replied, her eyes straying to the woman with the dark hair.

Adara began to kneel to speak with the girl when Mair spoke from the table where she worked.

"Vanora. Come here and get the vegetables for the pot," she said over her shoulder.

"Go on," her father whispered to her, and she ran off.

"You have beautiful children," Adara said as she stood again.

"Thank you," Killian replied, his eyes looking at his wife. "Mair, our guest has arrived.

Adara thought she heard a disgruntled sigh as the woman wiped her hands on a cloth and turned away from her work to come and greet her.

Mair's long, brown braid was fraying a little, and her eyes looked tired, no doubt from the work which her children put her through. She was younger and slightly plump, but possessed of a simple beauty which she carried well. Her skin was smooth and vibrant and free of scars, unlike the woman who now stood in her home.

"You are…better?" Mair asked Adara, her hands on her hips.

"Yes," Adara replied, forcing a smile. "Thanks to your care."

"Killian and Vala's care," she corrected, eyeing Adara up and down.

"I am grateful to you all," Adara said.

"You liked the sea?" Mair said, eyeing her husband.

Adara looked from Mair to Killian and back. "Yes. It was good to wash. The sea was…bracing."

"Not for Roman ladies." There was disdain in Mair's voice.

Adara ignored it. "Not all of them," she replied. "But I liked it."

"Food is ready," Mair said. "Sit. Eat." She motioned to the fire and Adara stepped over one of the logs to settle herself while Vanora came with a wooden bowl and emptied chopped vegetables into one of the copper pots.

Vala sat beside Adara, across from Mair who brought a stack of wooden bowls to the fireside. Vanora sat beside her mother, the boys to their left on a log of their own. Killian sat by himself on the log between his wife and Adara.

While the vegetables cooked in one pot, Mair ladled out a fish stew into the first bowl and handed it to her husband.

While her mother served the soup, Vanora went around with chunks of rough, dark bread in a basket so that everyone could take some.

"It smells delicious, Mair. What is it?" Adara asked. "I haven't had fish from the sea in a long time."

"Good fish. From morning catch," Mair replied, continuing to hand the bowls out to her sons, herself and Vanora, and then to Vala. She gave Adara the final and smaller portion.

Killian eyed his wife sternly and then turned to Adara. "Here, take mine. I'm not that hungry."

Adara shook her head and held on to her bowl. "I'm fine, really. My appetite is still quite small."

"You're certain?" he asked.

"Yes, of course." Adara replied. When the others began eating, she began too, dipping the hearty bread into the broth and picking up chunks of fish with her fingers, as the others did. "Hmm. Very good, Mair," she said, but the other woman made no reply.

"Where from, lady?" Vanora asked shyly from the other side of the fire.

"I was born in Graecia," Adara said, a hint of sadness in her voice.

"It is far?" Vala asked beside her.

"Very far."

"Farther than Isca?"

"Much farther."

"Farther than Londinium?"

Adara smiled. "Oh, yes."

The boys looked at each other when their father translated, their eyes wide with incredulity.

"Graecia is farther than Rome, is it not?" Killian then asked.

"Yes," Adara replied.

"But you are a Roman?" Mair's eyes accusing and filled with distrust.

Adara could not figure out if she distrusted her because she thought she was Roman, or because she was a woman. "I am half Roman."

Mair stared at the ring on Adara's finger. "You are married? You have man?"

"I did," Adara said, lowering her bowl from her lips, already finished the meagre portion she had been served. "He is dead."

"Killed by Rome?" Mair asked. "My husband was killed. Now Killian *my* husband." She ate some of her fish, continuing to stare at Adara. "Where do you live now, with your man?"

Adara stared back at her. "As I said, my husband is dead. And we lived in many places."

"And now? Your home?" Mair pressed.

"I have no home," Adara replied.

Killian watched her, a sadness on his face. "It is not right, not to have a home. Was your husband from Graecia also?"

Adara shook her head. "My husband was Roman." Adara stared into the fire. "Rome tried to kill him."

"Romans killing Romans?" Vala asked.

Adara turned to look at her. "Yes."

Vala squeezed her hand.

Adara would have wept but for the continuation of Mair's questions.

"You have children?" Mair asked.

"Yes. Two."

"Are their names Phoebus and Calliope?" Killian asked.

Adara looked shocked. "How did you know?"

"In your fever, you spoke their names aloud many times. You sounded very sad."

"They are dead?" Mair asked bluntly.

Adara stared back at her. "No." *Gods, protect them.*

"How old are they?" Vala asked.

"Older than you, Vala," Adara said. "Now they are…" she thought for a moment and was shocked. "Twenty-five summers... Much older than the last time I saw them."

"What mother leaves her children?" Mair asked, her tone accusatory, disdainful.

Adara did not answer.

Vala reddened and shot Mair a deathly stare. "What kind of mother tries to beat her daughter for not wanting a pig farmer?"

Mair shot her a dark look, but the girl held her gaze.

"That's enough!" Killian said to his wife and daughter. "We have a guest." He turned to Adara. "I am sorry."

"No...no... Mair is right to ask. What kind of mother am I that I would leave my children, though they be older?" Adara looked around the fire at that family, the kind father, the jealous wife, the naughty boys, and the darling girl. She looked at the rebellious daughter beside her and smiled sadly. She missed such family atmosphere, the warmth of a fire at home, the mingled sounds of disagreements and laughter. She sighed. "My heart was broken..." Adara said, her voice low. "And...and I turned away from my children when I should have stayed...when we should have found comfort in each other."

The guilt pressed down upon Adara's shoulders such that she felt she would fall into the fire before her, a pain ripping through her chest and in the pit of her stomach.

Vala put her arm about Adara and reached out to wipe away the tear that had run down her cheek.

Adara coughed and sat up. "Forgive me." She shook her head.

"Have soup," Vala said, taking Adara's bowl and serving her from the other pot, ignoring Mair's angry stare.

"Thank you," Adara said, taking her bread and dipping it into the bowl, more to avoid looking at the others than out of hunger.

A while later, everyone had finished eating and the pots were removed by Killian so that Mair and Vanora could clean them. The boys chased each other about, in and out of the roundhouse, while their mother kept their younger sister at her side.

"Vala!" Mair called angrily. "Help Vanora!"

Vala rolled her eyes and went to help her younger sister with the drying.

Killian bent to build up the fire with some logs he had fetched from outside the door, and soon a bright, wood-scented blaze rose up to warm them all. When that was done, he settled himself on the log beside Adara, leaning on his knees and gazing into the fire while he poked it with an iron.

"You have a beautiful family," Adara said.

He nodded. "Thank you."

"I am sorry if my presence has upset Mair," Adara said.

"She is like that. Don't worry." He turned to her. "You saved my daughter. I owe you everything… Vala is my world." His voice was low so that Mair could not hear him.

"I understand," Adara said. "My children are everything to me."

"Why did you leave then, Adara Pen Dragon?"

Adara thought about it a moment, then turned to him, her green eyes big and bright and filled with regret. "To keep them safe…and…because it became too painful to see their father's face in theirs…"

"Where are they?" Killian asked. "I have never been south."

Adara wondered whether she should give specifics or not. Ynis Wytrin was a secret place, open only to those who were permitted to enter. "They are near Lindinis."

"I have not heard of this place."

"It is near the border of Dumnonia," Adara lied. She wasn't sure why.

"I have heard of Dumnonia," Killian nodded. "Many mines there." He did not speak for a moment, but then turned to look at her. "You said you do not have a home now?"

"That is correct. I move around a lot." Even as she said it, memories of all her homes flashed in her mind - Athenae, Etruria, the hillfort, and Ynis Wytrin.

"Does that not make you sad?" he asked.

"Yes…it does."

"Well…" Killian was about to speak when Vala joined them again.

"You stay with us!" she said excitedly, looking from Adara to her father. "You said she will take long time to heal!"

"Yes," Killian answered. "You must rest and get strong again."

"Rest here!" Vala said. "For as long as you want!"

On the other side of the roundhouse, Mair spun and stared in their direction.

"Oh, no. I couldn't," Adara said.

"Yes. You must!" Vala insisted. "You cannot ride yet."

"It is too much," Adara smiled at the girl.

But Killian was shaking his head. "No. It's not too much. You saved Vala's life. The Gods sent you to us." He turned to Adara. "Please stay. Heal and grow strong."

"I cannot simply stay and sleep and eat your food."

"You can help with the animals, and spinning this year's wool," Killian said. "I would say you can cook too, but Mair would not allow it." He winked at his glaring wife, but she only shook her head angrily at him.

"You can also teach me to fight like you!" Vala was very excited now.

Adara looked from Vala to Killian and back. Obviously, Mair was not thrilled with the idea. She would have to win her over in some way. She knew that she should leave, but there was a part of her that did not want to. She also knew that her ribs were in a fragile state. One fight or fall, and the healing could be easily undone. She needed time and rest. "Very well," Adara said.

Vala clapped and jumped up, her face beaming with joy in the firelight.

"But I insist you let me help," Adara said to Killian.

He waived her off. "Yes, of course. But first you heal and grow strong. Swim. Then, you help."

Adara smiled, and the act of it mesmerized him.

"Thank you," she said to the father and daughter.

Over the following weeks, as the warmth of summer wore on, Adara fell into a comfortable routine as she became a part of Killian's family. She spent her days in the same way by rising early to make her offerings in the hearth fire of her small roundhouse, then going down to the sandy beach to stretch, run, and then wash and swim in the icy waters of the Hibernian sea. Some days, she brought Aegis down with her so that the gelding ran back and forth along the shore while she swam.

It felt good to let go of her worries, at least momentarily, to stop looking over her shoulder. She had not realized how much of a burden she had placed upon herself by seeking out those who sought to harm others. She knew she could not change the world, or punish every wrongdoer across the land. Her forced recuperation had made her see that.

Eventually, she became strong enough to help with feeding and milking the animals, and mucking out the pens. She brushed, cleaned, and spun the year's wool, and then helped to dye it in various bright and earthy tones which Mair would eventually weave into new clothes for her brood.

In the evenings, when she shared meals with Killian and his family, she tried not to remember the past, the rural family idylls of a golden Etrurian summer, nor the warmth of the great, round hearth fire in the hall she and Lucius had built. The beautiful memories brought nothing but pain now, and so she had thrown herself into her healing, and the shared labours of the small farm with that adoptive family.

Despite this new life, and the busy comfort of her routines, when Adara lay herself down every night, Venus' words came to her, reminded her...

You must forgive, Adara...in your heart...for you...for your children.

The goddess was there, in her heart and mind, whispering to her in the quiet, unguarded moments of night.

It will soon be time to fight...

But not yet, please... Adara would pray.

Over the weeks there, she also trained Vala, teaching her the parry and thrust, and a variety of attacks which she in turn had learned from Briana years before.

The girl was adept at it, and Killian watched with great approval as Vala adopted the ways of their warrior ancestors.

Mair did not approve, and she made her feelings known to Killian, and this often gave birth to a new shouting match in the Brythonic language they shared.

It was after one particularly harsh argument between Killian and Mair, just after the evening meal, that Vala stormed out into the night, leaving Adara sitting alone with the warring couple.

"I'll turn in for the night," Adara had said awkwardly when the argument abated a little.

"Yes! You do that!" Mair shouted at her.

"Stop it, woman!" Killian shouted at his wife. "Go see to the little ones!" he said, pointing to the upper floor where the younger children could be heard weeping for all the fighting.

Adara made to leave, and Killian followed.

"I'll walk you back," he said, leaving the fireside and going out into the starry night.

As they walked along the path to the small roundhouse, Adara looked up at the sky. The stars were brilliant, and the constellations shifted before her, their flickering fires calm and hypnotic. "It's so beautiful here," she said as she reached her door.

"Yes, it is," Killian said, his deep, gruff voice calm as he stood in front of her, staring into her eyes. "As are you, Adara Pen Dragon."

Adara looked back at him. She could feel his breath gentle upon her face, feel the warmth that emanated from his strong body which now stood so close to her.

"I should go soon," she said. "I've cause too much trouble for you."

"I don't want you to go," Killian said, his voice a tortured whisper.

Adara felt herself shaking, from fear, from heartache. "I...I don't want to leave but I must-"

Killian was already leaning in, his lips pressed to hers, his hands caressing her face.

For a brief moment, she kissed him back, but then her hands were upon his chest.

He felt her tears running down her cheeks onto his rough hands and he looked upon her, even as she gently pushed him back, shaking her head slightly. Her eyes were filled with brilliant, summer starlight.

"I have fallen in love with you, Adara," he said, stepping back toward her and laying his forehead against hers. "I never thought to feel this way again."

"You can't, Killian," she replied, her eyes closed. "We can't. You have a family. As do I."

"Your husband is gone, and your children grown. You said so yourself."

Adara felt her heart ache painfully then, and her tears flowed more freely as she sobbed.

Killian held her close, his hand stroking her long hair. "We could be happy together. I do not love Mair."

"But I love my children, and my husband."

"And he is long dead. You must allow yourself to *live*."

He said it with such fervour, so much care for her that, were she any other woman, she might have given in to the fantasy. But she was Adara Pen Dragon, and that meant something to her, and the realization that struck her was stronger than anything else in that moment.

"Some things never die, Killian," she said, her hand now upon his bearded cheek. "I shall ever be grateful to you."

"Let me come in," he said, his voice soft and longing.

She shook her head. "I can't. Please go. Find Vala. She will be on the beach." Adara, her face wet with her tears, stepped over the low threshold of the small roundhouse and slowly closed the door.

Killian stood there on the other side, wishing she would open it again.

Inside, Adara pressed against the door, willing herself to keep it shut. She searched her heart for the forgiveness she so desperately wanted to give - which the Gods urged her to give - and which she had forgone for so long in favour of unending anger and hurt.

When Killian heard the bolt slide home, he turned away from the door and went to find his daughter. She too would be saddened by the fact that Adara would soon be leaving for, in her, Vala had found a new and loving mother.

That night, when Adara laid herself down upon her bed, she turned onto her side to gaze at the fire in the hearth. Her tears blurred her vision as she thought of Phoebus and Calliope, the worries they must be experiencing, and the angry words they had said in parting, about her, about Lucius.

"Lucius..." she said to the flames. "I'm sorry. I know you did your best for us. I love you, and I miss you." She closed her eyes, and as she fell asleep, she whispered. "I forgive you, my love..."

XV

MORS ET NAUTARIUS

'Death and the Boatman'

Throughout the summer, the Praetorians of the Blood Eagle century continued their sweep of Britannia in search of the Dragon, his family, and his men. Dispatches were sent back and forth between Nemesianus in the north and Carcer in the south each informing the other of the regions they had covered, but none of the men had discovered anything.

Bored and frustrated, many of the men had caused disturbances wherever they went, stealing from farmers, harassing the locals, and drinking the tabernae dry.

And there was nothing anyone could do about it.

People appealed to the praetors in Londinium and Eburacum, Gaius Junius Faustinus Postumianus and Calvisius Rufus, but they had received orders directly from the Augusta, Julia Mamaea, in Rome, that they were to allow the men under Aurelius Nemesianus to carry out their mission unhampered. Their hands were tied.

The people of Britannia worried over this rogue century of Praetorians, where they would arrive next, and the methods they would use to extract answers to their questions.

Frustratingly, for the men of the Blood Eagle century, there were stories of dragons across the land, and yet, no one ever saw one, or knew the location of a lair, a relation, or even offered some sort of description.

"Gods damn this cold and inhospitable land!" Evander said to the two soldiers with him. "And they call this summer here?" He felt the rain falling sideways into his ears as the wind blew it like unwanted kisses from a toothless whore. He had been in a foul mood ever since he had left Nemesianus in Coria, for he had hoped for a larger, more intimidating group of men to go with him to the lands of the Ordovices.

Instead, he had got two of the smallest men in the century, a gambler named Manus who had been jailed for killing two opponents in the Suburra of Rome, and a little man named Inek who had been set for execution for pickpocketing senators outside of the Curia in the Forum Romanum.

Their constant chatter did not help either.

"Maybe the rain will break soon?" said Inek, crouched so low beneath his cloak that the horse appeared riderless.

"Sit up, soldier!" Evander shouted as he kicked his horse eastward down the road that led from the fort at Segontium, along the coast to Canovium.

"Where did the tribune at Segontium tell us we could cross?" Manus, a dark-haired and brooding fellow, rode up beside Evander to ask.

"He said there was a taberna somewhere along the coast, facing Mona, at the narrow crossing point." Evander squinted through the rain as they rode, not seeing the coast yet, nor any sign of a taberna. "He better not have lied to us!"

Unfortunately, Evander, Manus, and Inek had found the tribune of the fortress supremely unhelpful. He had looked down his aquiline nose at the three of them and sent them on their way. When Evander had asked for new supplies, the man had scoffed. "Try staring down your nose when it's bent sideways!" Evander had shouted at him before slamming his fist into the tribune's face.

The soldiers about the tribune had not done a thing, for Evander had waved the imperial pass in their faces. Only after the tribune's face had been flattened did he provide some useful information.

"If he lied, we'll have to go back and pay him another visit!" Manus said.

Evander grunted and kicked his horse into a gallop down the forest road.

An hour later, the rain stopped and the wind blew away the clouds to reveal patches of blue in the sky above. They began to catch glimpses of the rushing waters of the straits through the wall of trees that separated the road from the beach below. The sun was setting, and the water shimmered in hues of orange and purple.

"I'm hungry," Manus growled as they searched for a path that led down to the shore.

"I don't want to hear it!" Evander shouted. He was still angry at the measly supply of oat cakes which the tribune had reluctantly given them. *Maybe I* will *go back and see him!* he thought.

Eventually, the cliffs flattened out and the rock and sand shore of the straits became more visible. They found a path through the trees and Evander steered his horse through the thicket of oak, birch, and rowan until they came out into the open.

"There it is," Evander pointed across the water. "Mona."

"Are we sure we have to go over there?" Inek asked. "One of the men at Segontium told me that the air is thick with the shades of Druids slaughtered by Rome all those years ago."

Evander turned on him. "Let me put it this way… If we don't follow Nemesianus' orders, we'll be dead."

"I didn't think you were afraid of him?" Manus asked with a playful chuckle.

Evander's thick arm shot out, serpent-quick, and knocked the man out of his saddle and onto the beach. "I'm not afraid of him! I'm following orders! And if you two don't want to go back to those prison cells you were living in, you'll do the same!"

Manus glared up at Evander from the ground, rubbing his jaw as he got up. "Fine." Manus climbed back up onto his horse and adjusted his gladius at his side. "Where's this taberna then? At least we can eat before we cross."

"The tribune said it's along the beach. Let's ride. We can eat and hopefully find someone to take us across." Evander kicked his horse and the other two followed, Manus staring daggers into his back as they went.

It wasn't long before they came to a run-down taberna at the top of the beach where several boats were lined up along the shore in front of it. The tide was coming in, and so the boats were pulled up all the way, each one tied to a tree or one of the many pylons that stood outside the raucous establishment.

"Tide's coming in," Evander said. "Let's bring the horses around to the roadside. The beach is going to be flooded soon."

They rode around the side of the wooden taberna to the road above. They dismounted with a tired grunt and tied the horses to the posts out front. They then removed their saddle bags and went inside.

It was dark in the taberna, which was lit only by a few scattered lamps burning smokey seal oil. The place was packed with fishermen who drank beer from clay cups, and picked at the bones of fish which they had brought in to be cooked by the taberna's proprietor. They were singing songs of the sea, the sort fishermen sang when darning their nets at the end of a long day.

But when the three Praetorians entered, the lamps flickered with black smoke as the door opened and closed behind them. The singing died away, and the men stopped eating.

All eyes were upon them, but the Praetorians were undeterred. They met the locals' gazes directly and looked around for a free table.

When Evander spotted one in a corner of the taberna, he walked over to it, followed by the other two, their hobnails thumping heavily on the wooden floor planks.

The proprietor came over to them with three cups of beer. "Greetings to the men of Rome," he said, his hand shaking slightly as he set the cups down.

Evander stared at him and before he could get away, he grabbed the man's tunica sleeve. "Our horses are out front. I want them brushed, fed, and stabled. Do you have someone who can do that?"

"Ye…yes, sir. My son." He waved to a young man behind the broad counter that stood between the seating area and the kitchen. "Three horses out front. Take care of them!" he shouted.

The boy nodded to his father and rushed outside to find the soldiers' horses.

"We also need rooms," Manus said.

"We have one big room where everyone sleeps."

"We'll have it for ourselves," Evander stated.

"You can't do that!" the proprietor said.

"Yes. I can." Evander produced his imperial pass and procurement paper. "I can do anything I want. I can kill you all if I want to."

The proprietor stared at the scroll with the red seal upon it. He could not read it, but he assumed what the Praetorian said was true. Besides, some travellers had already told him tales of the horrific actions of the Praetorians moving across the land. They were not ones to be crossed.

"Very well. I'll let the fishermen know they cannot sleep here tonight."

"Good. Now, get us food, old man," Evander said.

The man nodded and went away quickly.

"I could get used to this," Manus said as he took up his cup and downed his beer.

"Don't get too comfortable," Evander said. "We have a job to do."

"At least we can eat first," Inek said.

Evander stood up from the small table, ignoring his two men, and went to the centre of the taberna. He filled the space, making the patrons uncomfortable, standing like a statue of Ares in their midst, his eyes angry.

"We need someone to take us across the straits as soon as possible."

The fishermen all looked from one to another of them, all avoiding looking at the Romans in their midst.

"We're willing to pay for information too!" Manus said out loud.

Evander glared at him, but was calm in a moment, for he noticed that several of the fishermen stopped talking and now looked to him.

"Information about what?" someone called out.

"We're searching for dragons," Evander said.

He was met with laughter and chuckles.

"We are looking for a family of dragons," Evander continued. "They go by the name of 'Pen Dragon'. The family of one 'Lucius Pen Dragon'."

There were a few whispers and confused looks that Evander could see, but no recognition.

"No 'Pen Dragons' here!" someone shouted.

"What about his warriors?" Evander asked, his voice growing more annoyed. He began to realize that they were not going to help, even if they did know something. "No dragons? Are you certain?" Slowly, he drew his blade and began to walk slowly among the tables, eyeing every person there, he and the bloody eagle upon his chest staring down at them. "No one? Nobody wants to save the others here from dying?"

"We can't tell you what we don't know!" someone protested.

Evander walked over to the man who had said it and smiled at him. "I know." In a flash, he took the man's head and smashed it down onto the table which was immediately covered in a spray of blood as his skull cracked on the surface.

Another man made for the door, screaming, but Manus' pugio flew across the room to take him in the ribs, sending him careening into a post and knocking himself unconscious.

"Anyone else want to test how serious we are?" Evander asked the stunned and silent room.

On the far side of the taberna, near the end of the bar, a lone hand raised up above all the other heads there.

"You!" Evander pointed to an older fisherman. "You want to run too?"

The man stood up, shaking on his legs. He cleared his throat.

"Sit down, Tomos!" one of the men with him hissed. "You'll get us killed!"

"What is it?" Evander demanded. "What do you know?"

"Is…is there a reward for information?" the fisherman asked.

"Reward?" Evander replied. He shrugged. "Yes. I'll give you a reward if it leads to something."

The fisherman named Tomos looked in the direction of the table where Manus sat cleaning his pugio beside Inek.

"Please," Evander said. "Join us." He made his way back to the table followed by the fisherman.

Everyone watched Tomos go to join the Praetorians and, when he was seated with them, they went back to their conversations gratefully while the proprietor got two of his men to help clear the body and blood from the one table, and to help the man by the door who was bleeding from the wound in his side.

"So?" Evander said to the man who now sat between him and Manus, with Inek sitting across from him. "What do you know?"

Tomos gulped. "You asked about dragons?"

"Yes." Evander stared into his eyes.

"I saw dragons…on a golden ring."

"A ring?" Evander asked, already disappointed and shaking his head as he drew his pugio from his side and pointed it in the man's face. "Are you trying to get yourself killed, old man?"

"No. I swear by Manannan!"

"I don't know who that is. Just tell me what you know!" Evander growled.

"Several weeks ago," the fisherman began, "I ferried two women with a white horse across the straits to Ynys Mon…I mean, to Mona. The one woman was younger, a red-haired Ordovician, a local."

"So?" Inek said. "You saw a local? That doesn't help us."

The fisherman continued, trying to work the spit in his drying mouth.

"The older woman she was with…she was hurt…and she had a golden ring with two dragons and a ruby. I saw it when she paid me, or, when she paid me only half of what she owned me!" He hit the tabletop with his bony hand, remembering the insult the women had offered him. "She had a sword, a gladius that she pointed at me to avoid paying!"

Evander looked at Manus and Inek, and then back to Tomos. "Was this woman, the older one…was she a local? Ordovician?"

The fisherman shook his head. "No. But when I asked her if she was Roman, she said she was not. She was lying to me."

"You are sure of this?" Evander pressed.

"Yes." The old man relaxed a little. He licked his wrinkled lips and stared at Evander's cup of beer. "May I drink?"

Evander looked at the cup and smiled. "Go ahead."

Tomos took the cup and gulped thirstily at the beer. When he finished, Evander looked at the other two and spoke again.

"Tomos… That is your name, yes?" Evander asked.

"Yes."

"Do you have a boat?"

"Yes."

"Can you take us across to Mona?"

The man nodded.

"Do you know which way they went?" Manus asked.

"They took the road up the east coast of Mona. There is a small farm by the Traeth…a beach. They went there."

"You are certain?"

He shrugged. "Yes."

"If you are wrong, we'll come back and kill you." Evander eyed him closely.

"I'm…I'm sure. Yes. They went there."

"We'll go tonight," Evander stated.

The old man shook his head. "Dangerous. Pwll Ceris too dangerous."

"What's that?" Evander asked, bringing his pugio close to the old man's quivering face.

"The…the currents. Too strong now. They will drown us. We wait until morning. Then, safe."

Evander lowered the blade and smiled at Manus and Inek.

. . .

"Ready now… Pull the string back to your ear and look down the arrow's shaft. Breathe out…and…loose."

Adara watched the concentration in Vala's eyes and stepped back, smiling.

Vala took aim at the sandy tuft of grass at the back of the beach and let her arrow fly.

"Excellent!" Adara laughed. "You see? You did it!"

Vala raised the bow in the air above her head and spun around, her bare feet making joyous marks in the sand. "It is much easier than I thought!" she said.

"It's all in the breath," Adara added. "The sinew your father found for the string helps also."

Vala grinned. "When you teach me to fight with gladius?"

Adara looked to where her gladius lay across her cloak on the sand nearby. "Another day, I can show you."

Together they went to sit on the sand and gaze out to sea. It had been a glorious late summer morning with very little wind and a blue expanse of sky set ablaze by Helios' golden rays.

When Adara had risen to brush and feed Aegis, a chorus of birdsong from the hedges surrounding the enclosure filled the early morning air. Shortly after, Vala had quietly slipped from the main house to ask if she wanted to go for a swim.

It had been exactly what Adara was thinking, and so the two women had walked along the path to the beach smiling and laughing.

Adara had been getting stronger by the day. Her ribs had mended well, unusually well according to Killian. Her mind had also healed much in her time at the Traeth. She had begun to feel a measure of joy again, to allow herself to laugh, to smile, and to take time away from the world of worry and guilt which she had carried with her for so long.

Mair had softened toward her too, happy that Adara, when she was well enough, contributed a great deal to the work of their family home. Though she was not overtly friendly toward the woman, she was no longer angry at her presence. "The Gods have sent her to us for a reason," she said to Killian one night when they lay down to sleep. "Just please do not forget me, my husband."

Killian kissed his wife at that, and made love to her, forcing himself to remember all that was good about her.

And so, as Adara shared meals with that Ordovician family, she was happy to answer their questions about Graecia, a land whose ways and mysteries were a constant source of wonder to the children, and to Vala, who also wished to know more about Adara and her own children. She imagined the latter to be as brave and beautiful as their mother.

They asked about Ynis Wytrin, which she eventually told them of, for they had only heard spoken of it in whispers, as if it were some magical, far-off place, as unattainable as Olympus itself.

Killian noted that Adara spoke little of her husband, Lucius Pen Dragon, and wondered whether the pain of his loss was too great to bear, or whether he had been a brutal man of war, unable to love a woman such as her. A part of him, though unvoiced, wished for the latter, but he suspected the former was true and kept that to himself. Still, he could not fully push aside the feelings he had developed for the woman who had come into their lives like a welcome storm after a drought.

Of all the family, however, it was Vala who had grown most fond of Adara.

Killian could see plainly that his daughter admired her, and he dreaded the day that she would have to leave, for leave she must. He knew it to be so, though he hoped it would not be for a long while.

"I feel safe with her here, Tad," Vala said to him one afternoon as she helped him in the forge. "She is unlike anyone I've ever met, except for Mam."

"She is," he agreed, kissing his daughter's red hair. "But she will have to go back to where she came from soon."

"But she has nowhere to go!" Vala protested. "I think she would like to stay with us!"

"To do what?" he asked, setting his hammer down and crossing his arms.

"Well..." she looked away for a moment. "Maybe you and she could...marry."

Killian had felt his heart jump at such a thought, but he shook his head. "I am already wed to Mair, Vala. You know this. We are a family."

"Tad, I've seen how you look at her, how happy you are when she is near, and when she speaks."

"Oh, my girl... It is a fantasy. That is all. Her heart is with someone else, though he be long dead. Some things do not change."

"But *I* have changed!" Vala protested. "I am alive because of her. I am happy for the first time in years because of her." She shook her head. "I don't want her to leave."

"Nor do I, Vala. Nor do I."

Vala remembered that conversation with her father as she and Adara sat on the beach that bright and sunny morning, their hair wet from the sea, the light warming their faces, arms, and legs. "Do you love my father, Adara?"

The question was sudden, and it took Adara by surprise. She did not answer right way, but looked at the hopeful face beside her. She knew Vala was young, still naive about some things, love in particular. "I have grown to love all of you," she replied.

Vala shook her head. "That is not what I mean." She sat up and turned to face Adara, her legs crossed on the sand. "Do you love him? Could you if he loved you?"

Adara remembered Killian standing at her door, so many nights ago, how his heart beat in his chest as she pushed him away, despite the urge to bring him in. "It's not that easy, Vala."

"Why not?"

"Because," Adara grew quiet, her eyes distant as memories flooded back, breaking the dam she had built up to protect her heart, the dam which she had hidden behind in her time there. "Because my heart... though it is broken...belongs to my husband."

"To Lucius Pen Dragon?" Vala said, feeling slightly guilty that she had used the name to press her point, that Adara's tears fell at the mention of him in that moment. "I'm sorry!" she said, leaning forward to kiss Adara's hands.

Adara shook her head. "Yes, Vala. I know that you may find it difficult to believe that one can love the dead, but the bond which I have... had...with Lucius, was something beyond the world, beyond time. It is unbreakable, though that does not mean that it does not hurt. It can hurt more than anything else, but it can also bring joys that outshine the darkest of days."

"I don't understand. You do not love my father?" Vala looked devastated.

Adara reached out to place her hand on her cheek. "He is a wonderful man, and that is shown in the wonderful young woman you have turned into." She searched for words to provide comfort, but found that she could not, not in the way she knew Vala wished for. "I have been blessed to know you and your family."

"But not enough to stay?"

The question hung there between them, uncomfortable, the answer unknown. Because Adara had begun to feel some degree of normalcy again in that far corner of Britannia, she had avoided thinking of leaving. She also knew that if she remained for too long, she might never leave, might give in to the feelings she did have for Killian.

She also knew that she could not ignore Venus' warning, that she would soon have to fight for those who loved her, and whom she loved. In her time on Mona, she had healed both her body and her mind, but she had also found the forgiveness to which Love had urged her.

Adara realized that then, on the beach with Vala, and she wept in the sunshine as the girl knelt and hugged her tightly, her tears falling into the water as the tide rose about them.

"We better go back," Adara said, wiping her eyes.

"Please do not be angry with me," Vala said. "Forgive me," she said as they picked up their things.

Adara smiled and kissed her cheek. "There is nothing to forgive. You have helped me more than you know and, if things were different, I would remain here with you and your father, and be a proud mother to you."

"But things *are* different, yes?"

"Yes."

Vala smiled sadly. "Perhaps one day, you can bring your son and daughter here to see us? I would like to meet them!"

"I would like that," Adara replied. It had been a very long time since she had had such an urge to see Phoebus and Calliope, and she could feel the pull of Ynis Wytrin once again as it called to her from behind its misty veil. "Come. I'll race you to the far side of the beach!" Adara said suddenly before she bolted.

Vala squealed and chased after her, carrying the bow and quiver of arrows, her copper hair flying in the wind like the mane of some magical horse.

Adara laughed as Vala's youthful form blew past her on the way to the path that led back to the enclosure. Then, she stopped, skidding to a halt in the sand to see a flash of fire and smoke. She wondered if the forge had caught fire, but the smoke was rising from the far end, higher and higher until it formed an aquila in the sky.

"Adara! Are you coming?" Vala called from down the beach, brushing the strands of her hair aside from her face.

"Don't you see it?" Adara pointed in the direction of the farm.

Vala turned to look and then back to Adara. "See what?"

Adara shook her head and looked again, but all she saw was the blue of the sunlit sky above the grassy cliffs and the peak of the large roundhouse reaching up to it. She smiled. "It's nothing," she said as she joined Vala again. "I might have won if I had not stopped," she joked, her arm about Vala's shoulders.

"I know, Adara," Vala said with a wink. "I know."

Clouds began to roll in as Adara and Vala walked together along the pathway from the beach back to the enclosure. They laughed as Vala related the unfortunate time when she had met the pig farmer that Mair had intended for her.

"He hadn't even washed before he appeared with a brace of pig's feet for me!" Vala said.

Adara wrinkled her nose. "I mean, if he had been a horse breeder, he might have smelled better, but pigs!"

"Very stinky!" Vala pinched her nose.

More laughter, but it died in their throats as they rounded the far end of the enclosure, and Adara pulled Vala quickly to the ground.

They were not greeted by the boys running after each other in the mud, nor by Mair doing her usual utmost to teach Vanora how to spin the wool, or tie the fish to the drying rack. They did not hear the chorus of Killian's hammer in the small forge where he was constantly repairing a blunted knife edge, or making tools for the neighbouring farmers.

When they rounded the corner of the Traeth it was to find Mil, Merin, and Vanora crying as they shook beneath Mair's protective arms and bowed head to which was pressed a black gladius blade held by a short, grinning soldier.

Before them, Killian was upon his knees in the mud, his face bleeding profusely from a wound to his head. Above him stood an enormous soldier whose gladius was pointed directly at his throat.

"What is happening?" Vala hissed, but Adara clamped her hand over the girl's mouth as they peered over the low stone wall into the enclosure.

"Roman soldiers..." Adara whispered. Her heart raced to find a way of saving the family, of taking out the soldiers before they harmed anyone. For a second, she thought they had come because she had killed the deserters who had attacked Vala but, instinctively, she knew they were there for another purpose. *Apollo, guide me...*

"See anything Manus?" the big soldier called out.

"There's definitely someone staying in here!" a muffled voice called from the small roundhouse, followed by the crash of furniture.

"There's a third one!" Adara said into Vala's ear.

"We have to do something!" Vala hissed back, but Adara pressed her lower to the ground lest they should be seen.

The big soldier faced Killian directly, his deadly blade point pressed to the manubrium at the bottom of his neck. "Listen here, ginger knob... Tell us where the woman is."

"I told you I haven't seen any woman," Killian replied, staring up at the brute he had heard the others call 'Evander'. "I live here with my wife and three children. There is no one else here. I've never heard of an Adara Pen Dragon, or others by that name. I've never seen any 'dragons'."

"You see," the soldier said. "I just don't believe you. I have information to the contrary. I have it on good authority that you have another daughter, a red-headed beauty, who crossed the straits with another woman. That woman was wounded and refused to pay the fishermen who took them across. He was quite descriptive in his anger, wasn't he, Inek?"

The soldier with his blade above Mair's head looked over at Evander. "He also said she had a white horse." The short soldier pointed to the animal pens where Aegis was. "The old shit was very angry!"

"So angry," Evander repeated, "and when people are angry and scared, they talk."

"That man is only trying to cause trouble for us. He's a liar," Killian said, looking the soldier in his cold eyes. "That horse is mine, I told you, and there has not been any Roman woman here."

The big soldier smiled. "I never said she was Roman."

Killian felt his heart sink. "I just assumed..."

"You assumed you could lie to me!" Evander pressed the blade so that it broke the skin of Killian's neck very slightly, a trickle of blood running down his chest. "Tell me where Adara Pen Dragon is."

"I don't know who that is," Killian said.

Evander grabbled hold of Killian's hair and wrenched him around to face Mair and the children.

By the smaller roundhouse, the third soldier emerged eating an apple and watching from the entrance, his crunching unusually loud in the tensity of the moment.

"We have to do something!" Vala pleaded into Adara's ear.

Adara nodded, her mind searching for a strategy. "Take the bow and run to the far end of the enclosure."

"The bow?" Vala asked, panic in her eyes.

Adara put her hands upon her face. "You can do this, Vala!" she hissed. "Run low so they don't see you this side of the wall. When I come out, you shoot the big man and I'll go for the one holding Mair. We have to act fast."

Vala was shaking.

"You can do this. You are strong!" Adara said. "Now go, quickly!"

Vala took up the bow and quiver of arrows and set off, her bare feet padding silently along the dirt path beneath the stone wall.

Adara drew her gladius in her right hand and took up her pugio in her left.

"All right, smith," Evander said into Killian's ear as he held his hair in his fist, forcing him to look at his family. "Tell me where she is, or I'm going to kill your wife and children before you, one by one."

Mil, Merin, and Vanora screamed with fear and huddled to their mother.

"Please don't!" Mair shouted. "They're here! The girl and woman!"

"Mair, no!" Killian shouted.

"I'll not sacrifice our children for them!"

"Where are they?" Evander demanded.

"The beach!" Mair pointed over the wall toward the beach below the low cliffs. "Swimming!"

"Mair, no!" Killian shouted.

"Take them away!" Mair pleaded. "Leave us alone!"

Evander let go of Killian's hair and smiled, his blade levelled at his face. "You see? Not difficult to co-operate, is it?"

Killian did not speak, but his eyes searched for a weapon, anything he could use to fight. He spotted the hammer on the woodpile beside the door to their home.

"Think you can get out of this, Ordovician? After we kill your wife and children, and then you, of course, I think we'll wander down to the beach and have a little fun with your daughter and the Roman before we truss them up and bring them back to Rome. How does that sound?"

Evander looked at Inek and gave the nod.

The short soldier raised his gladius to strike at Mair who threw herself over the children as he was about to swing down. But he froze for a moment and then fell backward, a pugio buried deep in his eye socket.

"Attack!" Manus shouted from the small roundhouse, tossing his apple to the ground.

The thump of a bow echoed from the far end of the compound and Evander howled as an arrow planted itself in his left shoulder.

Killian kicked out at him, knocking him to the ground and ran for his hammer on the woodpile.

Vala screamed as Manus turned and charged directly for her. Panicked at his attack, she shot again, but her arrow went wide.

"Vala!" Killian shouted, running as fast as he could and swinging with all his might. He took Manus in the side and knocked him off balance so that he slammed into the fence of the animal pen.

Killian threw himself onto the man and they struggled. He grunted as he grabbed the soldier's sword arm and tried to pry the blade away. "Help Mair!" Killian shouted to Vala.

Vala hesitated, wanted to jump to help her father as he struggled with the soldier, the goats and sheep running about the pen in a frenzy, Aegis rearing angrily.

"Go!" Killian shouted again.

Vala ran toward Mair and was almost tripped by Evander who had groaned to his feet.

But Adara had lunged in and hammered the pommel of her gladius into the big soldier's head. He stumbled sideways, past Vala who joined Mair and the children and hurried them away and out of the enclosure.

"Who are you?" Adara demanded, her blade poised over the soldier. "Why are you looking for me?"

From his sprawled position in the mud, he eyed the woman with the long lair, her loose, wet tunica and bare legs and feet. His eyes fell upon the glimmer of gold on her finger where he saw the intertwined dragons. "You're her, aren't you?"

"Tell me who sent you!" Adara demanded, slashing at his shin and making him growl.

"The Emperor, that's who!" Evander said, his hands grasping in the mud to the side of the stone pathway that led to the main roundhouse.

"Why?"

"To bring you back to Rome!"

Adara looked confused.

"We were sent to find your husband, Lucius Pen Dragon!" Evander shouted the name.

"My husband is dead!" Adara shouted back, the rage in her limbs like fire. She wanted to slay him right then, but she wanted to know more. "Why does the Emperor want my husband?"

"If you come to Rome with us…you, your husband, your children, and his men will all get a pardon!"

Adara's mind raced. "Don't you mention my children!" she shouted and slashed at his other shin.

"Bitch!" Evander shouted, his hand finally grasping the paving stone he had been working at. He hurled it at her and took her in the side of the head, sending her flying backward into the mud.

Adara lost the grip on her gladius as she fell. She saw the big soldier push himself up, pick up his own blade, and come for her.

Gods protect my children! she screamed inside as the sword began its descent toward her.

"Adara!"

There was a flash of red and iron as Killian hurled himself into Evander and the two of them fell sideways onto the body of Inek, punching and grappling.

Adara, her head still spinning, grabbed her gladius and pushed herself up. She charged for the struggling men. "NO!" she screamed as Evander pulled the pugio from Inek's face and slammed it into Killian's neck.

Evander wheeled to face her, but when he held up his hand to block her swing, she cut through his arm and planted her blade deep in the side of his head, sending him to the ground, his face confused, his body convulsing.

"Killian, no!" Adara leapt over Evander's body to Killian's side.

Blood spurted from his neck as he gasped, his eyes searching.

"TAD!" Vala shouted as she flung herself to her knees beside him. "Tad, no! Please no!"

His eyes blinked rapidly, and he smiled a bloody smile as he looked his last upon her, his shaking fingers reaching up but falling just short of touching her cheek.

Killian was dead.

A ringing started in Adara's ears as her head swam and her eyes flooded to see Vala wailing over her father. *Gods, why?* she demanded, but there was no answer, only the sound of the wind from off the sea, the desperate cries of Mair who tried to stop her children from seeing their dead father.

"Tad..." Vala whimpered as she lay upon his bloody chest. "Tad, na... Peidiwch a'm gadael... Don't leave me!"

Adara felt the world fall away from her, the claws of panic and fear digging deep into her guts and her heart. She felt Death's fist gripped about her neck as it made her look at the bodies of the three Praetorians who had come to kill her, who had slain Killian, and who had come to Britannia to hunt their family. *Not again!* she pleaded. *Gods, please not again!*

As the indecisive sun broke through the dissipating clouds, Adara rallied herself and went to Vala's side. "Vala..." she said. "He is gone. Come... Come with me."

Vala violently shrugged off Adara's shaking hands. "Leave me alone!" she shouted. "Why did you ever come here? I wish you had let me die in that valley!"

"Please don't say that," Adara said.

"I curse the day you came into my life!" the girl wailed, her tears falling freely from her shut eyes. "Just go! Leave us alone! I don't ever want to see you again!"

"I'm sorry, Vala," Adara said, glancing to where Mair lay upon the ground beside the roundhouse, her children crying about their grieving mother. "I didn't mean for this to happen. I'm sorry."

"I hate you!" Vala turned, looking up from her father's body. "Just leave! Go!"

Adara stood frozen to the spot, watching the girl she had saved shudder and wail beneath the weight of a world of pain. The family before her, the family who had helped her, had been destroyed, never to be the same again.

And it's my fault!

She felt numb, uncertain.

"Leave now!" Vala shouted one last time over her shoulder. "Please...go!" she cried.

Adara picked up her blood and mud-covered gladius, turned, and went back to the small roundhouse where she vomited outside the door.

As Mair went to Vala's side, the children still wailing upon the grass beside their home, Adara went inside to gather her things, her jaw set and her mind and heart fortified against the pain that sought to consume her just as the freezing tide engulfed the beach below.

In that moment, she understood Lucius in a way she had never expected, for despite the very best of intentions to protect those whom we love, it is not always possible.

I'm so sorry, Lucius, my love... I understand now...and I forgive you.

She filled her satchel, dressed, and armed herself, and when she was ready, she emerged from that small house of pain and healing to see Vala, Mair, and now the children all leaning over Killian's body. She was outside their circle now, an unwelcome intruder.

She wiped her burning eyes and turned from the keening scene to go to where Aegis stood beneath the shelter in the animal pen among the frenzied flock. "We need to fly, boy," she said, reaching up to stroke his neck and calm him.

Phoebus...Calliope...I'm coming...

XVI

FILIA QUAE REDIIT

'A Daughter Returned'

It was always an unpleasant surprise to find how short the summer months were in Britannia. Spring was a generous season to be sure, green and melodious with new life. Yes, it was wet, but the sun often emerged to warm the budding trees and the river that ran through Lindinis.

Summer, however, was like a long hoped-for visitor who came unannounced and who, shortly after arriving, quickly decides to leave.

And suddenly, it is autumn, the end of the year for the native Britons, the time of harvest before the time of slaughter.

Publius Leander and Delphina had noticed over the years that the local Britons grew more wary and suspicious, more superstitious, at the outset of every autumn. As the wind grew colder and the leaves upon the trees began to brown and yellow before blanketing the land, it was as if the people began to fortify themselves for the coming months. They rallied their families and their hearts for the coming of the Wild Hunt which, they claimed, raged across the land at Samhain at the very end of October.

Delphina felt a chill when, in the market, she heard everyone from children and their mothers to burly warriors speaking in whispers about the imminent return of Gwynn ap Nudd, the dark god of their strange otherworld which they called 'Annwn'. They spoke of the turnips they grew which they would carve and set alight outside their homes in the hopes that they would protect them from the ranging Lord of Death and the Hunt. It reminded her of the Jews she had been friends with in Athenae who had told her how their ancestors had painted their doors with sheep's blood to protect them from the Angel of Death who plagued the Egyptians.

In Athenae, the autumn had been a beautiful season when the vines burst with colour and the grapes and olives were harvested. But, in Britannia, it was a season of uncertainty when both fear and hope vied for men's hearts. Even the wind that blasted over the land and along rivers seemed to change its tune such that a note of menace was ever present.

The Romans in the crowd at the market were either blissfully unaware of the impending threat, or arrogantly dismissive of the warnings the local Britons gave them, despite the fact that the omens were always darker in those dying days of the year.

As Delphina shopped for lettuce, leeks, and parsnips in the market on a wet and windy day in late September, the leaves gathering about her feet, she listened to a couple of Durotrigan women speaking.

"I'm afraid this year," the older of the women said to the other.

Delphina glanced sideways at her while she picked through the parsnips.

"I've heard some of the priests saying that the omens have not been good. Carrion crows have been amassing in the sky as if preparing for something. Animals have been dying of a falling sickness, and the bodies of slain warriors have been seen scattered over the land, though there have been no battles. They even say that farther north, there have been great tremors in the earth."

The younger woman's eyes bulged. "The Gods are angry."

They each turned toward the turnip seller's stall farther down. "We'll take two each," the older woman said.

"It's a bit early this year," the old farmer said to the two women. "I can't understand why everyone has an urge to get their protectors so soon." He shrugged. "I'm happy to oblige though."

"Can't be too safe!" the younger woman said.

"No you can't, dear," the farmer replied as he accepted the coin from each of them. "Take care of yourselves, ladies."

Delphina watched them leave.

"Good day, lady," someone said from her other side, making her jump. "Forgive me, Delphina. I didn't mean to startle you," he said in a low voice.

Delphina turned to see Trevor Reghan standing beside her. He looked over the produce, but did not look at her. "We haven't seen you in a long while, Trevor," she said. "Is everything well? Are your wife and children all right?"

It had in fact been many weeks since Delphina had seen or spoken with Trevor, and Publius had only seen him at the Ordo meetings. Never outside.

"I have been keeping my distance."

"Have we offended you in some way?" she asked, worried that they had lost yet another friend.

"Not at all. There is a Praetorian in town who has been watching you and your husband."

She looked to him suddenly, but turned away quickly. "Why?"

"He was with the man who came to your home…Aurelius Nemesianus. He's been here the whole time since then, waiting."

"For what?"

"My guess is to see if any of your family come to see you. When Publius accidentally revealed your identities to Nemesianus, the danger set itself up at your doorway."

"What do we do?"

"Act normal, as you have been. Have Adara or your grandchildren come to see you?"

She looked down. "No."

"That is good. They will be in danger if they come." He picked up an apple and looked at it. "Be wary," he warned. "I'll let you know if I hear more." Trevor Reghan paid for his apple farther down from Delphina, and then walked away.

The vegetable seller made his way to her after helping another woman. "Are you ready to pay?" he asked.

Delphina nodded. "Yes."

He added it up in his head. "That will be one semis," he said.

Delphina pulled out a small leather pouch and handed him two bronze quadrantes. "Thank you," she said before placing her vegetables in her linen sack with the bread she had already purchased. She cast a glance about the centre of town, her eyes searching for anyone suspicious. When she did not see anything, she turned to go home and bolt the door.

.   .   .

"Publius, did you know we were being watched by one of those Praetorians?" Delphina looked at him across the low table in the triclinium as they ate their cena of vegetables and cured pork. All day she had been worrying over what Trevor Reghan had told her. She also wondered why Publius had not told her of the danger they were in, for surely he knew. "Tell me."

Publius Leander set his plate down on the table and looked at his wife. "Yes. I knew. Trevor told me weeks ago."

"And you didn't think I should know about the danger we were in, even as I walk about town?" She brushed back her white hair, her hand shaking.

Her tremor has got worse, he thought sadly. "My dear, I did not want to worry you unduly."

"Unduly?"

"Please don't fret." Publius sat up and tried to reach for her hands. "Delphina. All will be well. I promise."

She pulled back. "You can't promise that. Not even poor Lucius could promise that."

"*Poor* Lucius?" he grunted. "Don't speak to me of him," he said, his hands up. He was finished.

The light from the small brazier in the corner of the triclinium danced along the pale orange of the walls and the half-finished paintings Delphina had begun so long ago, of an olive grove where the charcoal outlines of a man and woman sat beneath a tree while two children peeked from behind the trunks of trees.

At the time she had begun the work, she had not realized she was painting the life she had hoped for, of living with her daughter's family on the slopes of Hymettos where her grandchildren could have played freely and without worry. It was around that time, on the edges of that realization of a life lost, that Delphina's hands had begun to shake and she had stopped her work. Now, the outlines of that family were a half-reality, faded and translucent as though that grove were a veil and they peered at her from the other side.

She began to weep silently as she looked upon it, as she struggled to remember. "I miss them, Publius," Delphina said.

He had been watching her, listening to the flicker of the flames as he fought his own tears. "I know. I do too."

"We can't go to Dumnonia, can we?" she asked, though she knew the answer with utmost certainty.

"No," he said. "We can't."

She covered her face with her hands and wept.

Publius stood from his couch and went around to sit beside her, his arm about her. "I'm so sorry. I should have told you we were being watched."

"It's no matter," she sniffed. "Not now. We have to stay here, to distract the Praetorian, to keep his eyes on us."

"If we were to go to Dumnonia, he would follow us and then Calliope, Phoebus, and Adara would be in danger."

"If Einion has found Adara," Delphina said. "She's still out there… our girl…our beautiful girl…"

They held each other and wept for some minutes as the realization that Lindinis, that small domus, would remain their entire world. As her head rested upon her husband's bony shoulder, Delphina stared at the faint outline of her daughter upon the plaster wall. *My beautiful girl…*

October spread over the land in the southwest of Britannia as the leaves of oak, ash, beech, and birch tumbled like spilled mosaic tesserae across the grassy fields and forests. The nights grew colder, and the clouds darker. Cattle and pigs were slaughtered, their meat prepared for the coming winter, and wood was cut in the surrounding forests to supply fuel for homes and for the great Samhain bonfires across the land.

For Publius Leander, frustration was the order of the day, for he had been pushing to have the colonnade built before winter. Unfortunately, only the outline of the foundations had been laid. Due to a hold-up at the quarry near Sorviodunum, they would not receive the shipments of limestone blocks and columns until the following spring.

The quarrymen had sent word that, for an extra fee, they could try and speed things along, but Publius' fellow Ordo members said that there were no more funds to allot to the project.

The added worry about the Praetorian hidden in their midst did not help matters or moods, as Publius and Delphina began to feel as though they were living with a menacing shade who followed them wherever they walked in town, watched them as they ate, and observed them when they tried to sleep.

They kept the light burning brightly in the lararium at all hours, praying that the Gods had not abandoned them, and that they protected Adara, Phoebus, and Calliope, wherever they were.

It was a lonely existence and, in it, they found themselves waiting out their days, giving in to cruel nostalgia in the silence of their meagre domus.

One night, close to the ides of October, as a cold rain poured down, hammering the tiles of the rooftop, Publius and Delphina were awoken by a timid knocking at their door.

At first, they each thought it was a dream, but the knocks did not stop, coming every ten seconds or so in groups of three.

Eventually, each of them emerged from their cubicula on either side of the small garden.

"Is someone knocking?" Delphina whispered, looking fearfully at her husband through the rain that fell in through the garden roof.

"I think so!" he said before going back into his cubiculum and picking up the pugio he kept to hand.

They both walked to the atrium where the lamp in the lararium cast its light onto the floor.

The knock came again, making them both jump.

Publius held the dagger up at the black oak door. "Go lock yourself in your room, Delphina. Stay there."

She shook her head and put her hand on his back. "I'm staying with you."

"Who is it?" Publius called out. "Go away!"

The knock came again, but no one spoke.

The pugio shook in Publius' hand as he reached for the latch of the small iron door hole to peer outside. *If he puts his face close, I'll stab quickly!* he thought. He opened the door hole to see a cloaked figure standing in the street outside. "What do you want?" he demanded, the pugio poised to strike.

The figure spoke from the cowled darkness of their hood. "Baba... it's me!" the person whispered.

"Adara?"

"Let me in, quickly," she prompted.

Publius dropped the pugio and, with trembling hands, he slid the iron bolt and opened the door.

Adara rushed in, closed the door behind her and locked the door again.

Publius and Delphina stood absolutely still for a few moments, unsure if it was a dream or not, whether the Gods were toying with them.

But when the woman before them removed her sodden cloak and hung it on one of the pegs, she turned to embrace them both at once.

"My girl, my beautiful girl!" Delphina wept with relief into her daughter's mass of braided hair.

"I'm here, Mama," Adara said. "I'm here."

The long interval of time that had stretched between that moment and the last time they had seen each other fell away as they hugged each other and wept at the joy and relief that brought.

Time made its point, however, when they looked upon each other, for Adara barely recognized the two aged people before her. Their hair was white and thin, their bodies and the way they moved belying a frailty which had not been there before. She saw her mother's hands shaking, but did not say anything. At the back of her mind, she detected a slight anger at seeing them so old, but she pushed that down. *They are alive.*

For Publius and Delphina, the shock was even greater, for they barely recognized the woman standing before them, more of a battle-hardened Amazon than the beautiful, stola-draped daughter they had brought up.

What happened to my little girl? Publius wondered. "What are you doing here?" Publius said as he and Delphina looked upon their eldest daughter. "There are Praetorians in Britannia. They've been asking about you, Phoebus, and Calliope. Even demanding to see Lucius!"

Adara nodded. "I know. I ran into some of them."

Delphina stepped forward again to put her hands on her daughter. "Are you all right? Are you hurt?"

Adara held her hands. "I'm fine now, but...they killed someone I cared for."

Publius and Delphina did not ask more, did not want to upset her. They were still shocked by her transformation in the intervening years. It was obvious that loss had hardened her.

Delphina knew that Adara had always been strong, that she was capable of meeting any challenge the Gods set her, including coming through the death of her husband. In that moment, however, they were relieved just to see her alive, to hold her, to hear her voice, for they had missed her more than anything.

"Lord Einion has had men out searching for you across the land," Delphina said. "We've all been so worried."

"I needed to be alone," Adara stated. "But I'm back now."

"You can't stay, Adara," Publius whispered.

She frowned. "Why not?"

"Because we're being watched by the Praetorians." He picked up his pugio which he had dropped. "Let's get away from the door." He then led her through to the small triclinium where he lit the brazier.

Delphina went into the kitchen and brought a small plate of cheese, apple, and bread which she put on the low table. She then brought a pitcher of water and a cup for Adara.

"Thank you, Mama," Adara said, and it felt good to do so.

Delphina smiled, her eyes bright in the dim firelight.

"Who is watching you?" Adara asked after she finished chewing a piece of bread and drunk some water.

"One of the Praetorians. Trevor Reghan warned us."

Adara looked from her father to her mother.

"The man who leads them... His name is Aurelius Nemesianus. He's..."

"What, Mama?" Adara pressed.

Delphina grasped her hands together so they would stop shaking "He is an evil man. I could see it in his eyes and hear it in his voice when he came here."

"He was here?"

"Yes," Publius said. "He lied to me about wanting to help Lindinis. Then he told me that the Emperor and Augusta sent him to search for Lucius, for you, Phoebus, Calliope, and any of Lucius' men who still live."

Adara hung her head. "Even after Lucius' death, they still won't leave us alone!" She rubbed her face and looked up. "What else did this Nemesianus say?"

"He said that the Emperor and Augusta want Lucius, along with his men, to return to Rome to take up the mantle of the Praetorian Praefectus and protect the Emperor. In return, he promised a full pardon for Lucius and his men, and the return of all our lands, the structures to be rebuilt at imperial expense."

"And you believed him?" Adara asked, ready to be angry.

Publius shook his head. "No. It is a trap…though…for a brief moment, I had hoped it was true, that we could have our old life back."

"There is no going back, Baba." Adara sat straighter. "And my Lucius is long dead and-" She stopped herself. *No more tears.*

"Lord Einion sent word of this Praetorian force," Delphina said.

"How did he find out?"

"I don't know," Delphina replied. "He did not say."

"Too dangerous," Publius added.

Adara was thoughtful. "Dio. It must have been Senator Dio. Lucius must have arranged the connection between him and Einion before he… Anyway, Dio always liked Lucius."

"Lord Einion said we should all go to Din Tagell for safety. Calliope is already there."

Thank the Gods, Adara thought. "And Phoebus?"

"Lord Einion said he had men looking for you and for Phoebus." Delphina was quiet.

"Did they find him?"

"We don't know," Publius said. "We can only assume he was looking for you, Adara. You left."

"Because I had to."

"I understand," her father said.

"No. You don't."

"Your children were still grieving when you left."

She looked at her father squarely. "And so was I. And they were not children. They were grown. They had the beginnings of their own loves, and hope. What did I have?" Adara shut her eyes and fought back the tears, the weakness. "They were safe in Ynis Wytrin, but I could not stay there, not without Lucius."

"But where have you been all these years? You didn't send word, didn't show your face…" Publius gripped the edge of his couch. "We were so worried."

"I was fighting."

"Against whom?" her mother asked. "For what, my girl?"

"For some slight measure of the goodness I once knew…for myself…for my children…for…for the memory of the man I loved, and still love."

Delphina sat beside her daughter and put her arm around her, though hesitantly. She did not like the look that came across her husband's face.

"For the man who put us all in danger? The man who abandoned you in Delphi, causing you to lose your child, and then abandoned you again here? The man who ruined all of *our* lives? He's dead, and yet he is still putting us in danger!"

"Publius, that's enough!" Delphina shouted at him, releasing her hug on her daughter.

"I shouldn't have come here," Adara growled. "This was a mistake."

"Please don't say that," Delphina pleaded.

Adara shook her head, staring at her father. "You never understood. You refused to."

"Understood what? Eh? Tell me!" Publius was on his feet then, an angry old man grasping at raindrops in the wind. "That Lucius was some kind of god? Pfft! What sacrilege! He was more like his hateful father than anyone realized."

"Please stop," Adara said. "You don't know what you're saying."

"I know perfectly well what I'm saying! If he was a god, then why did he leave? Where is he? Why is he allowing Rome to continue to persecute us? It's all ridiculous, a fantasy you've all created to act as a salve for the great disappointment you all feel!"

"Publius!" Delphina's hands began to shake more.

"I wish he had never come into our lives, that you had never met him. At least then, we would still have our family and our home in Athenae. Instead, your mother and I are exiled to this, this place, alone, without a visit from our grandchildren, or a word from you!"

"That is your fault, for what you thought, for the hateful things you said."

"Now I am persecuted for the things I think?" Publius put his arms up. "Oh, the death of Democracy has come! That I should *think*?"

"That is not what I mean, and you know it!" Adara stood now too.

"What I know is that you are clinging to a fiction while the world around you falls apart. While a Praetorian spy lurks in the streets outside waiting to kill us all."

"I can't do this anymore," Adara said, feeling a great exhaustion come over her.

"I'm going back to sleep," Publius declared. "I suggest you don't stay long." With that, he stormed out of the triclinium and slammed his cubiculum door.

Adara stood frozen in the middle of the room, only then noticing her mother's attempt at painting upon the walls. She saw the faded image of herself, her children, and of Lucius, and for a moment, it all did feel like a fantasy, a dream from another life, and that was like a knife to her heart. "I'm so tired."

"Then sleep, my dearest girl," Delphina said softly. "Rest here, and we will speak more tomorrow."

Adara turned to her mother. "I'm sorry, Mama."

"You have nothing to be sorry about. It's your father. The life the Gods have given him is not what he envisioned, nor what he wants. He has not dealt very easily with the changes wrought upon us."

"You mean the changes *we* forced on you. I'm so sorry."

"Don't you say that, Adara. Don't you dare!" Delphina's old hands gripped her shoulders. "Your father chooses to blame everything on Lucius, all of our ills, our hurts, and our losses. He *needs* someone to blame in order to explain it all. But I see…I know…that it's because of Lucius' sacrifices that we *are* still alive, that you are here with me, that Phoebus and Calliope have grown to adulthood. There is no greater love."

"I miss him so much, Mama."

"I know," Delphina nodded and hugged her again.

"I was so angry with him for so long-"

"I know… I also know that you have honoured his sacrifice by fighting on, but you cannot continue to torment yourself."

Adara was quiet.

"But your father was right about one thing… You cannot stay here. You must get to Din Tagell to be with your children, to help them. They need you more than anything."

"What about the Praetorian in Lindinis?" Adara wondered if she should leave then, perhaps lure him away from her parents and kill him outside of the town.

"We'll talk of that tomorrow. For now, rest. Sleep." Delphina stood and took a wool blanket which she sometimes used from a small table in a corner of the room. "Would you like my room?"

"No," Adara said even as she removed her weapons, set them upon the stone floor, and laid herself down on one of the dining couches. "I'll sleep here."

Delphina covered her with the blanket and kissed her forehead.

Adara's eyes grew heavy quickly and soon closed, but not before taking one last look at the faint images upon the triclinium wall.

Adara slept into the next day and it was not until midday that her eyes opened slowly, her senses tingling from the scent of fresh bread and meat which her mother had set out for her on the low table beside a cup of watered wine. She sat up and rubbed her eyes. She wished she could visit the baths in town, but knew that it was too risky. She had to do something about the Praetorian. They weren't safe.

She was glad that she had thought to stable Aegis at the farm of a Durotrigan family outside the town, and hoped that they were caring for him well. They said they would for the coin she had offered them.

She remembered the night before, and a great sadness came over her. The words she and her father had shared had been hurtful, filled with an anger that served no purpose but to drive them farther apart. *Oh, Lucius,* she thought. *Gods give me the strength to help my children,* she prayed. *Help me to get to them before the Praetorians do.*

She picked up the cup of wine. *Oh, Venus and Apollo... Guide me in the days to come...* She tipped some of the wine onto the floor, and then drank, swirling the fresh liquid around in her mouth before swallowing. She had almost forgotten the taste of wine.

"Do you like it?" Delphina appeared at the triclinium door, smiling as she looked upon her daughter. "Lord Einion has been generous to us. Once a year, he sends us wine and oil from the Middle Sea. He said he thought it would be a comforting reminder of home."

"It is a reminder," Adara said.

"May I sit with you?" Delphina asked.

"Of course, Mama," Adara replied, feeling sad that she should feel the need to ask to sit with her.

They were quiet for a few moments, each of them enjoying the other's presence.

Adara sighed and turned to her mother. "I'm so sorry I didn't come to see you more often, Mama. I left you and Baba here alone."

Delphina shook her head. "Do not apologize. It was our choice to be here rather than in Ynis Wytrin with all of you."

"You mean it was Baba's choice." Adara shook her head. "I suppose he has left for the day? To work, as usual, rather than stay and speak with me?"

Delphina looked down at her clasped hands, a sad, resigned smile on her face. "Your father has always been happiest when working, whether on Rome's business, or for the good of the people of Athenae. It's how he derives joy from this brutal life."

"Even here, in this nest of vipers?"

Delphina nodded again. "Even here." She reached up to stroke her daughter's long tangle of loose braids. "I'll be back," she said, before standing and going out of the room.

Adara ate a bit of the meat and bread and when her mother returned she saw her holding a small phial of oil and a brush. "Mama, you don't need to…"

"Oh, let me. Please. I can do this for you." Delphina, worked slowly with shaking fingers to undo the braids, one by one, until Adara's hair tumbled down her back in a rough cascade of black and grey. "It's been so long," she said as she set to it with her boar's bristle brush.

Adara smiled to herself as her mother ran the brush over her hair, slowly, methodically, picking out bits of leaf and pine needle that had attached to her during her nights in the wild.

"Remember when I used to comb your hair for you after you were out on the slopes of Hymettos, running or riding along the paths of the pine forest?"

"Of course I remember."

"Those were some of the happiest days of my life," Delphina said.

"I know, Mama. I'm sorry."

"Stop it. You cannot apologize for growing and living your life the way you see fit."

"I know… It's just…this is not the life I envisioned when I was young, when Lucius and I were wed." Adara tried to prevent her mind from going back to that flower-strewn day of light and joy on the Palatine Hill. She had never been happier. But now, the memory of it, the longing, served only to resuscitate years of hurt.

"The Gods hide their plan for us so that it is ours to discover. I'm sure Odysseus and Penelope did not envision life as it turned out, but they made the journey. They chose from among the pathways the Gods lay before them."

"Perhaps I have chosen poorly, then." Adara regretted the words immediately.

"No," Delphina said. "You experienced a love that few are privileged enough to have. You raised strong, beautiful children. And you have shown a strength that few possess. How many have you aided in your travels? How many people continue to live because of you?"

"Some have also lost their lives because of me." Killian's face hovered in her mind and she had to close her eyes against it. Only her mother's touch upon her hair as she oiled it brought her back.

The air in the doorway shimmered and there, faint, a part of the air itself, stood Love. *Hear your beloved mother...*

Adara gazed upon the goddess, her beauty, her majesty, her kindness. *Listen...*

"Everyone dies, Adara. It is the way of things. But while we are alive, it is up to us how we honour the Gods' blessings, by our thoughts and deeds. The Gods made their own sacrifices, and underwent their own trials, as we must. But on the other side of that struggle is..." her voice faded.

"Mama?" Adara said, turning slightly to look up at her.

Delphina still held Adara's hair in her hands, the oil glistening in the faint light.

"Mama, are you all right?"

Delphina blinked. "Oh, sorry, my dear." She continued oiling Adara's hair and stood back. "I forgot what I was saying." She sighed and sat across from Adara. "It happens more these days." She took a small piece of meat and chewed slowly.

Adara looked beyond her to the doorway, but nothing was there.

"Adara," Delphina began. "Before you leave-"

"I can't just leave you here, Mama."

"You must. For now, at least." There was no room for negotiation in Delphina's voice.

That did make Adara smile.

"But before you do go, I would ask that you make peace with your father."

"He doesn't want to talk."

"He does, my girl. He is proud and grasping at nostalgia. It is the only way he can survive in this place, the only way he can go on. But if you leave and all he has to hang on to are the angry words you shared last night then…I fear it will finish him. I also worry about what it will do to you."

"I've been filled with so much anger these past years, I'm not sure I remember what it's like not to be."

"We must let go, and allow goodness to fill our hearts." Delphina paused before saying the next thing she wanted to say. "Poor Lucius…he understood that in the end."

"But too late."

Delphina shook her head. "It is never too late."

Adara thought of her father, how loving he had been the entirety of her life, how optimistic and hopeful. She remembered how happy he had been for her when she had met Lucius, how filled with jollity he had been on the day of her and Lucius' nuptials. "I'll speak with Baba tonight."

"Thank you, Adara."

"First, Mama. Can you do something for me?"

"Anything."

Adara smiled. "Can you braid my hair? I can't fight when it's loose."

Delphina beamed. "Yes. I can do that." She sniffed. "And when I'm finished, I'll wash your clothes for you. They need it."

They laughed together at that, and it felt good.

Diagonally across the street from the small domus of Publius Leander, the Praetorian named Dis sat patiently in the quarters he had commandeered from an old, retired soldier whom he had paid handsomely to go away for several weeks.

The trooper, who had formerly been in the employ of one of the Ordo members some years before, had jumped at the opportunity to make some extra coin and get out of Lindinis to spend time in Aquae Sulis. "It's all yours, Praetorian," the man had said before leaving. "Just don't kill anyone in here."

"I do my killing wherever I need to," Dis had replied, his nose almost touching the other's.

"Whatever," the man said, unafraid. "You enjoy this shit hole town. I'm going to take the waters and visit a clean lupanar."

It had been months since Aurelius Nemesianus had left Dis in that provincial outpost to watch the old couple in the hopes that their daughter or someone else related to the Dragon would show up. Months of waiting, and sleeping, and eating while the rest of the men were out fighting, looting, and whoring as they searched across Britannia for any sign of Pen Dragon.

Things had gotten more difficult of late when he realized that he was being watched. By whom, he did not know, but he suspected the Durotrigan Ordo member, Trevor Reghan.

The old man, Publius Leander, had proven disappointing, for all he did every day was see to his boring Ordo business and the slow building of his colonnade.

When Dis realized this, he took to going to the bathhouse to soak and listen for any gossip whispered in the steamy guts of the caldarium. He would then wait by the window of the small domus where he was staying to see when the old man would return at the end of the day. When he did, Dis would step out to stand in the street near their door and listen to what he and his wife discussed inside, if he could hear, that is.

He also watched for visitors, or messengers who might come to the domus, especially during the night. However, as the weeks and months dragged on, and no one came, he began to grow increasingly bored and frustrated. So much so that he considered just killing the old couple and being done with it.

I could always tell Nemesianus that they died in their sleep and that there was no point in staying any longer, he thought. But he decided against it. Besides, with the approach of October, and the cold wind and rain that accompanied it, Dis thought it better to remain warm and dry where he was rather than travelling upon the roads of Britannia.

And so, he waited and waited. Then, on that rainy night at the end of September, he heard a redundant knocking in the street outside, barely audible above the sound of the falling rain upon the cobbles. He went to the small window and peered out into the darkness to see the faint form of a cloaked figure for a split second before it disappeared into the domus of Publius Leander.

"And who are you?"

.   .   .

It was early evening when Publius Leander returned home. There was a frantic working at the lock with his key, and then he burst into the atrium, spun, and locked the bolt again. He leaned against the door, panting, and waited until he caught his breath.

The lamplight from the lararium cast shadows onto the floor at his feet. The light drew his eyes and he looked to see the images of the Gods staring back at him. "Gods protect us…" he said beneath his breath.

Publius had been acting normally as he went about his business in town, meeting with other Ordo members, confirming numbers with the tile manufacturers, and asking after the quarry work for the stone. All the while, he was panicked inside. He could feel the shadow of that Praetorian closer all the time, and now that Adara had returned, his fear was more acute.

It was that fear for her safety, and the presence of the Praetorian, that had caused him to spew all the regrettable, hateful words the previous night. He had never been so disappointed in himself. He had lost sight of who he was, of who was important. The truth was, he had behaved more like Lucius' horrible father, Quintus Caecilius Metellus, than poor Lucius ever had. *At least Lucius did all he could to defend his family!* he told himself. *Even though it meant his own demise.*

At some time during the pointless day, Publius Leander resolved to make amends with his beloved daughter, to apologize to her and to his wife, for his behaviour toward Delphina had also been something he regretted.

"The threat of death is a fine tonic," he muttered as he hung his cloak upon the wall beside his daughter's. "Delphina? Adara?" he called out, immediately lowering his voice. "Are you here?"

"Publius?" Delphina called. "We're in the triclinium!"

He walked the few paces to the triclinium and found his wife and daughter on the couches, the table between them set for the cena. There was water and wine in two pitchers, and clay cups for them all. A clay platter sat in the middle of the table with a small, roasted chicken in the centre, surrounded by boiled eggs on a bed of lettuce.

"I've also made some fresh bread," Delphina said.

The sight gave Publius pause, and brought tears to his old eyes as he looked at his wife and daughter sitting together.

Adara saw this. She immediately got to her feet, went over to him, and hugged him tightly.

Publius hugged his daughter back and felt such warmth and love that his strength seemed to be renewed.

"I'm sorry, Baba," she said into his shoulder.

He shook his head vigorously. "You have nothing to apologize for. It is I who am sorry, with all my heart, my girl. I have been unfair to you, Phoebus, and Calliope…and to our dear Lucius. I should never have said the things I said, and I pray you, and the Gods, forgive me for it. I beg your forgiveness."

She could feel him shaking, see the world of regret in his eyes as tears ran into the whiteness of his beard.

"I let my fear get the better of me," he continued, glancing at Delphina who looked up with watery eyes at them. "I promise to be on your side, no matter what. You are stronger than I have ever been, a survivor, and I am so proud of you." He hugged Adara again and, this time, it was her tears that wet his shoulder.

In the relieved silence that followed, the three of them settled on the couches, Publius and Delphina together, and Adara on hers, her back to the triclinium wall where the faint images of her and her family remained.

Delphina gazed at the wall behind Adara. *I must try and finish the mural, for it in, I can at least gaze upon my daughter and grandchildren.*

They ate together that evening, going over the myriad good memories that had made up the majority of their lives, for in doing so, they dispelled with the once-prevalent perception that life had been but a series of tragedies. And while there had indeed been great tragedy visited upon all of them in some way, shape, or form, the blessings of the Gods had been numerous.

The lamplight flickered on their smiling faces, masking the worries that were etched upon them. They ate, and drank together, and enjoyed the act of doing so, for it had been years since such a thing had occurred.

However, the knowledge that Adara would have to leave imminently, to go to her children in Din Tagell, if they were both there, hung between them like an unwanted guest at dinner.

Eventually, Adara relayed to them all that she had done on her travels, the people she had tried to help, the things she had seen, both beautiful and terrible, across Britannia. After she had told them about Mona, about saving Vala, and of Killian, she was silent.

"You cannot blame yourself, my girl," Delphina said. "Had you not come into their lives, the girl would surely have fallen to those Romans."

"But Killian would have lived."

"But only with a broken heart that would never mend," Publius added. "No parent should outlive their child, and you ensured that that did not happen."

"But the Praetorians came to Mona *because* of me!" Adara protested, feeling the darkness closing in on her mood.

"If what Einion said is true, there are Praetorians searching all over, not just for you, but for Phoebus and Calliope, and all of Lucius' men."

Adara sighed, felt her heart sick at the memory of Killian's passing in the bloody mud at the Traeth. "I know." Adara finished her watered wine. "I must go and find Phoebus and Calliope, be it at Din Tagell, or in the wilds. I have to get to them before the Praetorians do."

"It is all that matters," Publius said. "And though it pains us to see you leave, the children's safety is first and foremost."

After a few moments of silence, the joy of their meal having run its course, Delphina stood up. "I have some honeyed pastries for us. I'll get them." She went out to go to the small kitchen.

"I'm sorry I have to leave, Baba," Adara said when her mother had left. "Will you and Mama be all right?"

"We'll be fine. No one is interested in us. We'll be more use to you here, drawing their eyes, than we would were we to come to Dumnonia."

"You enjoy your work for the Ordo so much?"

He shrugged. "It keeps me busy, and keeps my mind off of things I should not dwell upon."

"The past has a way of sinking its claws into us and not letting go, doesn't it?" she said.

He smiled sadly. "It certainly does, my girl. It certainly does."

Delphina returned with a plate of honeyed pastries filled with goat's cheese. "Something sweet to round out our cena."

"Oh, lovely!" Publius smacked his lips.

There was a loud knocking then.

"What was that?" Delphina asked, setting the plate down.

It came again.

"Someone is at the door," Adara said, her senses tingling. "Are you expecting visitors?" she asked her father.

"No," he said gravely. "I am not."

"Publius Leander!" a deep voice called out from the street outside, followed by more knocking.

"Do we ignore it?" Delphina asked.

"If it's the Praetorian," Adara said, "he won't go away easily."

"What do we do?" Delphina asked, a rising panic in her voice.

"Mama, stay here," Adara said as she and her father went to the atrium.

Publius drew the small pugio that he now always kept at his cingulum.

Adara took her gladius and pugio from the wall behind her, and rushed to the atrium to join her father who was about to answer the door.

"I know you're in there!" the Praetorian shouted.

"Of course we're in here!" Publius shouted through the door. "This is our home and you have disturbed our meal. Off with you!"

"Open up, in the name of the Emperor!"

"The Emperor is in Rome!" Publius retorted.

The street outside was silent again and Publius leaned closer to listen, not daring to peer through the door hole just yet. He looked back at Adara and Delphina in the atrium door. "I think he's-"

There was a great crack and splintering of wood as the black door crashed inward, knocking Publius off of his feet and back across the atrium into the small garden.

The Praetorian went directly toward him but Adara attacked from where she had been standing to the right of the door.

Her gladius shot out, but the soldier parried.

"Hmm. There you are, bitch!" he growled, his big fist shooting out and sending her backward into the wall.

She moved immediately, his gladius point chipping the plaster where he had thrust. Her own blade slashed out to take him in the side of the arm and he roared at the pain.

The Praetorian rushed her, knocking the gladius from her hand with a swing of his own, his left hand shooting out to fasten about her neck as he lifted her off of the ground. "Where is your husband?" he demanded.

"Dea...dead," Adara gasped, her legs kicking at him only to strike his armoured chest and greaved shins.

"Leave her alone!" Delphina shouted.

"Tell me where the Dragon and his men are hiding, and I won't kill her!"

"She's telling the truth!" Delphina wailed. "He is dead! They're all dead!"

"Wrong answer!" the Praetorian said, turning back to see Adara's eyes rolling in her head.

"Get away from my daughter!" Publius suddenly shouted, running at the back of the Praetorian and driving his pugio clumsily at his head and striking off his ear.

"AAAH!" the Praetorian howled, and his grip released on Adara. He wheeled on Publius and was about to strike him when Adara grabbled hold of his sword arm, and wrenched his blade free. She struck him in his other ear with the flat of her hand and slashed at his thigh with his own blade, making him stumble to the ground.

She charged again to finish him, but his hammy fist pounded into her gut, sending her gasping for breath against the wall.

Grasping at his leg and missing ear, the Praetorian fled for the doorway and the darkness of the night.

"Publius!" Delphina ran over to her husband. "Are you all right?"

He lay gasping on the floor, pointing at the broken doorway. "Adara, don't let him get away!"

Adara took up her gladius which had fallen in the corner and rushed out into the street. "Ach!" she screamed, startled by the appearance of Trevor Reghan beside her with a long bow drawn to his ear.

Trevor shot down the street into the darkness at the edge of town, and the snap of the bowstring was followed by a shout of pain. "Come!" he said to Adara and the two of them rushed along the street, following the trail of blood that appeared like quicksilver in the cold moonlight.

"We can't let him get away!" Adara said as they ran, her lungs heaving as she gulped at the cold night air.

"Wait!" Trevor said as he slid to a halt and looked at the ground. There, at their feet was the arrow he had loosed. He picked it up and held it to the moonlight to see the blood on the barb. "Damn it!" he growled.

Adara looked around for the body, her sword poised before her in the darkness. "He's gone. I have to track him!"

Trevor reached out to grab her arm and stop her. "No. Don't! It's too dangerous. There are many more of them across the land. He could be running to the others."

"But he's going to warn them that I'm here. He knows about Din Tagell!"

"Yes, he does. And so does Aurelius Nemesianus. I've had word that he's recalling his men to Isca Dumnoniorum."

"What?" Adara asked.

"A century of Praetorians," Trevor said. "Adara, they're preparing to go into Dumnonia. You can't waste time chasing him. You have to warn the others!"

Adara stared down the street out of the town, into the darkness of the road flanked by wood and field. A cold wind blew about them, the dead leaves skittering about their feet.

"Come," Trevor Reghan said. "We need to get your parents to safety. Are you injured?" he asked, looking her over.

"I'm fine," she said, her only thoughts then of Phoebus and Calliope and the force of Praetorians seeking their deaths.

When Adara and Trevor Reghan arrived back at the domus, they found Publius sitting with his back to one of the four columns about the garden, Delphina dabbing his head with a wet cloth.

"Baba!" Adara said, rushing to his side. "Are you injured?"

He shook his head. "It's nothing." He looked up at her. "Did you get him? Is he dead?"

"He got away, Publius Leander," Trevor said, his voice grave.

"No!" Publius hit his thigh with his fist.

"From all the blood on the street, he was badly wounded," Trevor said. "He may die on the road."

"Or he may report back to Aurelius Nemesianus!" Publius said.

"Yes. He may."

"I have to go to Dumnonia," Adara said. "Phoebus and Calliope are in danger. I need to warn Einion and the men."

"Don't leave now," Trevor said. "It's not safe. You should ride out at first light. Do you have a horse?"

"Yes. I stabled him with a Durotrigan farmer outside of town, along the north road."

"I know the man. You can trust him," Trevor said. "Tomorrow, I'll put the word out that bandits attempted to break into your parents' domus and that your father fought them off. That will explain the broken door and blood in the street. I'll also have my men fix and secure your door tomorrow."

"What if they come back here?" Delphina asked.

"You may stay with me until this is finished," Trevor offered.

"Until what is finished?" Publius asked.

"All of it," Adara added, her face grave and determined. "Are you sure it is safe for you to do so, Trevor? You've done so much already."

"I am happy to do what I can." He smiled at Adara. "You know…the people across this land pray for your family. They remember the Dragon."

"I…I don't know what to say."

"Say nothing." Trevor looked around. "I'll go search the street again, in case he has come back."

"Thank you, Trevor," Adara said.

"You are welcome," he replied. Before leaving, he turned back to Adara where he stood in the broken doorway. "We all miss him…Lucius, that is."

Adara nodded sadly.

"May the Gods protect you, Adara Pen Dragon," he said before disappearing into the night.

When Aurora awoke the next morning, her gaze painting the sky in warm yellow, cool blue, and bursting orange, Adara stood in the atrium among the debris of the previous night's fight. She gazed upon the Gods in the lararium, her palms upward as she prayed. The smoke of the incense she had offered wafted about the small shrine, floating out to surround her as she breathed slowly, in and out.

"Gods… Please guide me on my path that I may get to my children in time. Please protect us against those who seek to do us harm. I don't know where this path will lead, but I pray to you for the strength to fight on and see it through to the end, whatever that may be." She closed her eyes and thought of Lucius, remembered the love in his eyes, the light that she had always seen in him. "Lucius…my love… Wherever you are in the Afterlife…please give me the strength and skill to protect our children. I miss you, and I still love you, with all of my heart and soul…"

She wiped at her still-shut eyes, breathed deeply, rallying her courage, her determination. She looked to where the packed saddle bags sat on the floor beneath her hanging cloak.

"Here," Delphina said behind her.

Adara turned to see her mother and father standing there, tears in their eyes.

Delphina held out a small sack to her. "I've packed you what food we have for your journey. You need to keep up your strength."

"Thank you, Mama," Adara said, taking the sack and kissing her mother's cheek. "When this is all done, perhaps we can all celebrate Saturnalia together?"

"That would be wonderful," Delphina said.

"For now, you stay safe, my daughter," Publius said, stepping in to hug her fiercely. "I am proud of you, and I believe in you."

"Baba," Adara fought the tears again. *I need to be strong!* "Promise me you will both stay safe. Do not take risks. If it comes to it, go to Ynis Wytrin. Please."

"We will," Publius said. "And you promise to stay safe too. Do whatever you must to protect yourself, Phoebus, and Calliope."

"Tell them we love them," Delphina said.

"I will," Adara replied before turning to take up her cloak.

Her father took it gently from her and draped it about her shoulders. "You have your weapons?" he asked.

"Yes."

"Then I suppose this is it," Publius Leander said, his voice quavering.

"Ride to your children, my dearest daughter," Delphina said, her tears falling freely now. "May the Gods protect and guide you."

"Don't worry about us," Publius added. "We'll see you at Saturnalia."

"I would like that," Adara replied, hugging him again, squeezing with all her might. She turned to her mother and hugged her the same, one more time, before she took up her saddle bags and turned to the door. "I love you both."

"We love you too," they said.

Adara looked one more time upon her parents and, feeling that it was perhaps the last time she would see them, she smiled and then tore herself away, to run down the street and out of Lindinis, the wailing of her heartbroken parents fading behind her as she went.

XVII

SUB SUPERFICIE

'Beneath the Surface'

The year, to the Britons, was in its death throes. Samhain approached, and with it the menace of the Morrigan's envoy, Gwynn ap Nudd, Lord of Annwn. And as the night of the Wild Hunt on Samhain grew nearer, there was a trembling in the air, a shiver in the light. The sun grew dimmer at times, and the clouds that crawled over the land from the sea grew blacker and more jagged.

The people of Dumnonia felt this shift as it approached, they expected it. And so, they fortified their hearts and homes for that dread night of the turning of the year, the death of the old one and the birth of the new. Wood to feed the bonfires throughout the long night was stockpiled like weapons before a battle. Guardian faces carved into the stubborn, hard surfaces of turnips were readied to defend doorways, and baskets of apples were brought out so that their skins could be offered to the flames along with prayers to the Gods.

And then, there were the dreams that came, like morning mist upon the moors. They tested and harassed mortals as they slept, and clung like cobwebs to their minds during the shorter days. For those who dared to travel upon the moors, their ears were pained by the echo of howling, as if the dead were clamouring at the gates of Annwn, anticipating the slaughter to come when they and their lord would bring terror across the land. Soon, the peaks of the rocky tors that bubbled out of the earth from the Underworld would be aflame with fiery crowns.

It was three days before the coming of Samhain, three days before the Wild Hunt's pitiless ride, and the day dawned with a new and welcome light in the air that warmed the moorlands. Flowers stretched to their extents to reach that light, creatures emerged suddenly from their burrows to be warmed by it, and in the sky, birds wheeled and soared in its full, brilliant bloom.

On the shores of the Sacred Pool, removed from most mortal eyes, the horses of the wild herds splashed and galloped in the shallows, their voices raised to the light that danced upon the surface like a million jewels tossed down by the Gods.

In the roundhouse on the shore of that place of peace, Elana, the Guardian of the Lake, was roused by distant music, a song she had not heard in a long while. Her bright, watery blue eyes opened where she lay sleeping upon her fur-covered bed.

It is time, she thought.

And then, she sensed it...the burning of the ancient dragon brand upon her chest.

She sat up and stared into the flames of the hearth at the centre of the roundhouse. She stood and, smoothing her white robes down over her naked body, she listened as the horses - her wards - suddenly stilled about the dark waters. The birds winged quietly in the blue sky, and all creatures sat quietly to watch every motion of he who stepped across the grassy carpet to Elana's door.

Music followed him, laced through the air like a drop of honey in warm water. He stood before the door, his blue cloak billowing in a breeze that did not exist on that plane.

But Elana...she could feel that breeze, and hear that music. She always had when it neared, even in her eternal exile at the edge of the Sacred Pool that was her tiny and timeless realm. She walked to the door of her home and opened it to see Apollo standing a few feet away, his star-whirling eyes gazing into the watery depths where the heavens showed on the still surface.

She walked toward the god, her feet bare upon the grass, and came to stand beside him. "Lord Far-Shooter..." she said, bowing to Apollo. "To what do I owe this honour?"

Apollo turned to the nymph and raised her up, brushing aside the long stands of her crow-black hair. "To your sacred duty," he replied, the reeds along the shore shivering at his voice. "The Dragon's family is in danger. Men are coming to kill them."

"I have sensed it," she said. "Who are they?" A pang of fear cut at her heart when she observed the worry in his divine eyes.

"Men of Rome."

She hung her head. "Have they not been through enough?"

"Death is approaching, and the time of The Change is here for them." The words Apollo uttered were dreaded, and rarely spoken.

A tear breached the shores of Elana's water-blue eyes. "My lord… Why do you not protect his family and slay these evil men of Rome? In battle, in time before, you intervened on behalf of your son. Why not his family?"

"When the Morrigan entered battle against him in the world of men, I was permitted. But I cannot always intervene in the affairs of mortals. They must choose to fight, or surrender, to live…or to die. The answer lies hidden in each of their hearts." Apollo looked from Elana to the watery depths of her sacred charge. "It is for them to decide, to suffer and learn through their adversity."

She could see the sadness in his visage, the memories of heroes past, of battles fought and won or lost. "Haven't *they* suffered enough, my lord?"

He looked to the heavens, as if gazing to the far-off peaks of Olympus. "No. Not if they are to reach what awaits them."

"And what awaits them?" Elana asked, feeling a shiver run up her body, like ripples when a stone is thrown into still waters.

"Everything…and nothing…"

Elana was silent, amazed, even after so many ages, that the Gods could be so cruel, even toward their own. *But I know I must obey, and do what I am commanded to do,* she thought.

"Yes," Apollo said, hearing her thoughts. "You must."

"I will, my lord."

The sun shone down more brilliantly then, illuminating the pool where Apollo gazed, such that it appeared as a bowl of fire set in the vast moorlands. "The Dragon's son is coming. He seeks. You must give him succour and strength, for his heart is filled with hurt. He must be prepared for the coming fight."

"And if he wants what he cannot have?" she asked, full of pity for all that she had seen in time.

"He must be allowed to try, for even in the deadly attempt, even if he fails, there is strength and learning to be gained."

The light upon the water began to fade and he turned to face her again, placing his fire-warm hand in blessing upon her cool brow.

Elana's eyes closed as she listened to his final words.

"Your sacred duty here, the time of your guardianship in this place, has only just begun, Elana. You have a role to play in this land…in other times…with other heroes…"

She opened her shocked eyes to look upon Apollo again.

He looked back at her, the constellations bright in his gaze. "It is a land of dragons, after all…"

Then, he was gone, and the light faded and the clouds darkened at once.

Elana found herself standing alone again on the shore of the Sacred Pool, its dark water lapping at her pale feet.

The wind rippled the water's surface, and the reeds shivered and swayed. On the far side, the horses reared and charged, the birds screeched in the sky, and the animals dove into their burrows to escape the falling rain.

Elana, the rain wetting her hair and face, turned to gaze up the path that led down from the moors and the world beyond her borders.

I am here…and you are always welcome…

It was cold, and the wind over the moors gusted with gnashing teeth. It had been thus for Phoebus Pen Dragon ever since he had left Ynis Wytrin.

He and Remus had travelled due west over the moors, leaving the lands of the Durotriges behind and plunging into those of the Dumnonii where the River Uxella narrowed enough to cross. Because they travelled mostly at night and avoided any of Rome's roads, it was slow going, but Phoebus knew he could not afford to go anywhere near the line of fortlets running north from Isca Dumnoniorum.

The Praetorians who were hunting him were out there. He could feel it, sense the menace in the air as he journeyed and the October days wore on.

After crossing the Uxella, the climb over the Cantuc hills began as he and Remus picked their way over the rock and forest pathways that were exposed to the cloud-choked sky. From there, Dumnonia and its vast, wild moors stretched out before them.

As Phoebus stared down onto the expansive green world of mist and rock, he remembered when he had travelled through by road and wagon with his family as they attempted to leave Britannia. Now, he journeyed into that mysterious land on his own by unknown pathways, blind to what lay ahead.

He knew where he wished to go, but not how to achieve it. "We must trust in the Gods, Remus," he said to the wolf who stood beside him, eyes staring into the distance, his hackles rising as if sensing the coming danger. Phoebus knelt down and pat him. "We can do this. We must."

He looked at his father's armilla on his wrist, and felt the black gladius at his side.

In the distance, clouds rolled in off of the sea to rush over the moors, breaching the Hercules promontory, where the ocean ended and the channel began.

"We'd better get off of these hills before the storm comes," he said to the wolf as he began the descent.

It was then that the rain started and did not stop.

A few times, as they travelled, Phoebus had spotted riders and, briefly, had thought they might be Einion's men. However, he had remained in hiding as they passed, crouched on the ground beside streams and on forest pathways to observe them. They all turned out to be small detachments from the fortress of Isca Dumnoniorum, patrolling along the Isca river. There was no sign of Praetorians that he could see, but he gave them a wide berth nonetheless.

In Phoebus' mind and memory, the land in which he found himself was different. When his family had last come that way, it had been in summer, when the hills were a deep green, and the sun and sky teased the senses with orange and pale pink light. Herds of deer had grazed and thundered before them then, but now, all life appeared to be in hiding.

Maybe they all sense the threat? Phoebus wondered, unable to keep his mind from thinking of the tales Einion had told them of white giants sleeping upon the hillsides, awakening only to go in search of maidens to devour. *Could Remus and I defeat a giant if we had to?*

But no giants appeared, and as they came to the abandoned Roman fort near Nemeto Statio, no Romans appeared either. The land fell farther toward the sea, the forests tapering off as if scythed by the giants who lay sleeping after their destructive labours.

Phoebus was constantly ready for a fight but, even as he slept, hidden by the natural shield of the roadside hedges, while Remus stood watch, the only aggressors Phoebus had to face were the long, cold, wet nights.

The wind howled in concert with the banshees who, though unseen, acted as heralds for the coming of the Wild Hunt.

This played upon his mind, drawing him back to the days before he had wielded a sword, and violence had assailed his childhood.

After weeks of wandering, the trees and hedges thinned out and the expanse of the dark moor lay before Phoebus and Remus. Ancient tracks led them past stone circles where Einion and Briana's ancestors had made sacrifices to their gods in the shadows of the rocky tors that rose out of the damp earth. Shelter became more scarce, and the nights were filled with apprehension and doubt.

Three nights before the coming of Samhain, despair began to strangle Phoebus. His memory had betrayed him, and he had lost his way. He wanted to scream to the sky and slash at the earth with the black Praetorian gladius Paulus had given him. Instead, he sat against the bole of a thin, windswept hawthorn that stood just beyond a circle of nine standing stones that jut up toward the sky.

"Remus, hunt," Phoebus commanded, and the wolf rushed off to feed himself. He felt his own stomach growl with hunger, for he had long ago finished his own supply of food.

The rain eased and, as the sun fell beneath the curtain of the clouds to light the moors and the lichen-covered surface of the standing stones, Phoebus' eyes began to grow heavy with exhaustion, his heart weighed down by despair. "Apollo…Venus…Epona… Help me. Guide me and give me strength."

The standing stones before him shimmered and wavered in the dimming light as he tried desperately to stay awake, his back against the fairy tree, his eyes upon the circle as they closed.

You will not survive, Dragon…

The voice Phoebus heard was mocking, filled with disdain, but also with pain.

Phoebus looked to the centre of the stone circle and there he saw a tall, dark, lithe warrior with long hair. His movements were feline, his eyes dreadful. He clutched at his stomach and was upon his knees. He looked directly at Phoebus, and blood poured out of his mouth as he spluttered.

You are already dead! he said, laughing in his pain. *All of you! The*

Hunt is coming for you! He turned quickly and was struck by some unseen force that shook the stones about him, staining the grass with his blood.

Phoebus' eyes shot open, his hand drawing his gladius, but the circle was empty, the blood swallowed by the earth. The moon's silver light peeked from behind the wind-torn clouds, and lit the stones, their surfaces glinting as if set with jewels beneath their lichen cloaks.

All was still but for the weaving of the wind.

Phoebus felt warmed by the tree at his back, and he let the warmth lull him again, his exhaustion getting the better of him as he closed his eyes once more.

Then, as if the sun were rising in the night, a milky, ethereal light began to grow inside the circle, lighting Phoebus' shut lids.

He opened his eyes slowly and there, before him, glowing in the light cast by Selene's orb was a brilliant stallion.

It stepped from the circle, his hooves light upon the mossy ground, barely making an imprint. He nodded his great head and black and silver mane, his dappled coat aglow.

Phoebus pushed himself to his feet, his hand shielding his eyes from the brightness. "It can't be..." he said, his voice quavering. "Lunaris?"

The stallion approached to stand before Phoebus who reached up with a shaking hand to stroke his neck and cheek which were cool to the touch, like spring water in the moonlight.

"I thought you were gone." He leaned into the stallion's neck and hugged him. He remembered when his father had first gone into Dumnonia to set Einion upon his throne, Lunaris had not returned with him, having died in battle against the great wyrm upon the moor. "I missed you, boy. Are you real?"

The stallion suddenly backed away and began to walk westward into the darkness of the moor, surrounded by a puddle of milky light. After a few paces, he stopped and turned to look back at Phoebus.

"You want me to follow?"

The stallion stomped at the ground and continued to walk.

Phoebus followed, listening in vain for any sign of Remus who ranged somewhere on the moor. He turned back to the stallion. "Lunaris, where are you taking me?"

But the stallion walked on, and Phoebus followed his light into the dark, trusting that it was not some trick of the spirits in that place to lead him to his death in the bogs.

For miles, Phoebus walked in the dark, following the white light of the apparition, stumbling over the rocks that bubbled out of the grassy ground. The trickle of a nearby stream accompanied him as he went, but he could not see it, for the moon was now hidden from his sight.

He only saw Lunaris, trusted him, followed him. At one point he worried whether the dark warrior he had seen had conjured the apparition to try and lead him into a trap, but his heart told him otherwise.

They continued on into the night, passing through a larger stone circle, and then on to the ford of a river protected by a long wall of trees.

The stallion waited for Phoebus on the other side of the river which he had, impossibly it seemed, walked over in mid-air.

Phoebus descended the nearest bank and clambered up the other side, grabbing onto roots and rocks until he achieved the top. On the other side of the river, he turned around, for he felt suddenly strange. The way he had come was shrouded in an impenetrable mist as if the river had been some liminal borderland.

And suddenly, it was early dawn, and the sun's light began to reach to Phoebus' feet.

The stallion, now fading into the sunlight, turned to look at Phoebus, his great glassy eyes taking in the mortal man.

Farewell...

Phoebus heard the thought, and felt his heart tighten as Lunaris disappeared in the morning light.

He found himself standing on a wet, dirt track that appeared to be sunk into the moorland. He looked around, his gaze reaching out beneath the ceiling of low, grey clouds as the rising sun skipped beneath them.

Phoebus wondered if he was dreaming, whether the entire walk had been a dream, but then he felt Remus appear at his side, the wolf's fur a comfort beneath his hand. He looked down at the beast. "Did you eat?"

Remus licked his mouth and stared ahead.

Phoebus looked too and suddenly, he felt he recalled the place, the feeling of it. A part of him recognized the high walls of grass and rock, the road, and the trickle of water as it led the way downward, almost eagerly to a place in the near distance. It felt familiar, like a recurring dream in childhood suddenly emerging from the recesses of the mind.

"I've been here before!" he said, his voice almost a gasp.

He began to walk and then, he heard it, the sound of thunder upon the earth.

Remus' ears perked up and his eyes searched about for the source of the shaking when, above them, came the sound of a herd of horses charging by, their bodies a blur of wild manes and rearing heads.

"With me, Remus," Phoebus commanded, smiling to himself as relief filled his body. "We've made it."

The hidden track fell away, the water rushing more quickly at their feet as they walked on. The world about them moved differently, the light flickering within itself at times. There was a faint echo of excited voices, but no one to be seen. The air smelled of damp and peat, of sweet clover, and wet rock.

Soon, the track widened to reveal the misty lake, its banks dark and languid, bristling with reeds shivering in the strangely warm wind. On the far bank, herds of horses charged and splashed, frolicking freely and without a care.

Phoebus strode to the water and stood staring out over the calm surface. He remembered now the last time he had been there with his family, with his mother and sister, his father still among the living, though he had been filled with anger. The recollection made Phoebus want to weep, but he was not there for sadness or self-pity. He was there for that which would allow him to defend his mother and sister.

"Welcome back, Phoebus Pen Dragon..." a gentle voice said, like a mourning dove at dawn in an olive grove. "I've been waiting for you."

Phoebus turned to see Elana standing along the shoreline, her feet bare beneath the hem of her white robes, her black hair like a raven upon her shoulder.

At her feet, Remus had sat himself silently to gaze up at her. She reached down to lay a hand upon his enormous head.

"Lady Elana," Phoebus said as he turned to walk slowly toward her. "How did you know it was me?"

She smiled, her brilliant blue eyes like a clear sky after weeks of cloud. "Did I not tell you many years ago that you are always welcome?"

"You did." He bowed his head.

"And so you are." She looked back to the roundhouse at the side of the lake where she lived. "Come inside. Eat and rest. You have had a long journey."

Her voice was like a song he had long forgotten but which, at its utterance, gave instant comfort.

She approached him and took his hand. "Come." And together, they went into the roundhouse while Remus laid himself down outside the door to stare calmly out at the water and the rushing horses on the far side.

It was warm by the hearth fire inside the roundhouse, warmer than Phoebus had ever thought to feel again after his weeks in the wild. As his clothes dried beside the fire, he sat wrapped in a blanket, eating a bowl of stewed moor greens, turnip, and wild garlic which Elana had given him along with a crust of spelt bread. Nothing had tasted so good as that in a very long while, and he ate it with gratitude as he stared into the flames of the same hearth where he had sat with his exiled family so long ago.

Elana prepared a tea for Phoebus, her back to him as she worked at her table.

"Lady?"

"Yes, Phoebus?" she said, her back still to him.

"Have you seen my mother and sister? Please tell me that they are safe, that they have passed this way."

She paused in her actions, set her pestle down, and tipped the contents of the mortar into a broad, clay cup. She turned to face him then. "Your sister is safe. She passed this way with Einion, Briana, and Antiope on the way to Din Tagell. She is there now, waiting for you."

Phoebus sighed, the relief clear on his face. "Thank the Gods." He set his empty bowl down. "And my mother? Have you seen her?"

Elana's face saddened. "I have not. Nor has Etain. She has been hidden from our sight for too long, cloaked by her anger."

"I dreamed of her when I was in Ynis Wytrin."

"Tell me of your dream," she said.

Phoebus told her of Apollo and the Christus, of the twin chairs with Calliope and Rachel and the grails they offered to him and Aaron. He spoke of the appearance of his mother and the dark army she faced, how he was unable to help her.

Elana listened intently, only able to guess at the Gods' plan in showing him, but feeling a rising awe in her ancient heart. *He is so young to be burdened by so much!*

Death is approaching, Apollo had told her. *Men of Rome are coming to kill them.*

She wanted to give Phoebus what he wanted, what he needed for the coming fight, but she remembered Far-Shooting Apollo's command…

He must be allowed to try…

"Why are you here, Phoebus Pen Dragon?" she asked, her voice more stern than she had wanted to be.

He stared into the flames, unable to meet her gaze. "There are Praetorians hunting my family, and my friends. My father…he…he is dead. He left us many years ago."

In that moment, Elana saw the young boy Phoebus had once been, sitting beside her fire, looking for comfort or hope in the face of great adversity. She wanted to hold him, to give him succour, but it was not for her to do so. Pity filled her being, for him, for the impending doom Apollo had warned of.

Phoebus looked up at her. "I am so tired of the hurt I feel… Why did he abandon us?"

"The Dragon…your father…was crushed between worlds after his trials, Phoebus…after his apotheosis. Yes, he was the son of Apollo. You know this now." She took the cup of herbs from the table and ladled hot water from a pot over the fire into it. She set it down to steep and then sat beside Phoebus. "You must know that he had to leave, and when someone great leaves the world behind, the pain of their departure echoes across the land and in the hearts of everyone who holds them dear."

"But in doing so, he upended our lives!" Phoebus said loudly. Our family is scattered now, destroyed! We were safe in Ynis Wytrin."

"Did you not choose to leave the Isle of the Blessed?" she asked.

"Yes, but only to find my mother who also disappeared."

"Your mother also chose to leave, did she not?" Elana said. "You both had the freedom to choose your paths, and that freedom…your choices…are what have led you to this moment in time."

"It was not my choice for my father to die, nor for our family to be torn apart."

"I know…but had it not been so, think of all the people you would not have helped in your travels, or the wolf who is now your greatest friend. Despite your pain, you chose to help rather than destroy."

"And now, I must fight and kill."

She said nothing to that, but for an instant, as the firelight flickered upon his skin, she could see him covered in blood. She reached out and took up the tea she had made for him. "Drink this."

"What is it?" he asked, taking the cup from her.

"It will help you."

He sipped at the bitter liquid once…twice…and a third time. "What will it do?"

She smiled and took the cup from him as his lids grew heavy and he laid his head upon her lap. "It will help you to sleep…and to see…"

Phoebus nodded off with Elana in his eyes, looking down at him, her hand gentle upon his brow, her voice soft in his ears.

"Sleep, Phoebus Pen Dragon. Rest for the coming storm." She then began to hum and, somewhere beyond consciousness, the notes of Apollo's lyre filled the air…

Phoebus found himself standing naked at the edge of the lake, staring at the dark depths while all around him, snow floated gently down to melt on the surface. He reached out to catch some like an excited child in winter, but he frowned when he rubbed it between his fingers, discovered that it was ash.

There were harried voices on the air, and the sounds of screams and of battle.

Though the sky was iron grey, the surface of the water reflected the constellations of heaven, Pegasus…the Bear…the Dragon…all turning, writhing in star-fire.

Then, across the water, a beacon of light as pure as the silver moon in full bloom appeared.

Phoebus shielded his eyes as he tried to look upon it, and there he saw Apollo staring back at him, the black water a great divide between them.

Apollo pointed at the watery depths and there, in the deep, a light formed and dissipated the stars' reflection upon the surface.

Phoebus began to walk, drawn by the light. The black water rose higher and higher, up his strong, scarred body, slowly engulfing him, pulling him down beneath the surface.

He tried to fight it, but he found himself going deeper and deeper until the light began to fade and metamorphose into his father's face, a bright but pained visage.

Phoebus reached with all his might out to him, but he could not manage. *Father!* He tried screaming, but his throat filled with icy water and he was pulled backward to the surface, the apparition fading farther and farther out of sight…

Phoebus' tear-filled eyes shot open and he looked up to see Elana's face, her own eyes weeping to look upon him as she stroked his forehead and hair. He wept then, shutting his eyes against the fleeting dream.

"What did you see?" Elana asked.

He told her.

"You are haunted by pain and hurt, Phoebus. But only you have the ability to overcome them."

He sat up and wiped at his face, staring into the fire. "Did…did my father die in water? Did he come here to die?"

"No, Phoebus," she replied. "But what is death, but the start of a new beginning?" She laid her hand upon his shoulder. "Just as at Samhain, the old year dies and gives way to the new."

"All I know is that my father is gone, never to return."

"The death of one life is the start of another."

"That is of little comfort when death leaves such a gaping hole in the lives of the living."

"But a part of him *is* here," she said.

He thought about that, about the dream the Gods had just sent to him. "Why would Apollo show me my father drowned?" He pressed his palms to his eyes as if to erase the vision. Then, he looked up. "Unless… he was not showing me my father! He was showing me the very thing I came here in search of."

He must be allowed to try… Apollo's voice said to her.

He wants what he cannot have! Elana replied. *He could die!*

"I need my father's sword, Elana," Phoebus finally said. "That is why I came here. I need it to defend my family…to defeat Rome."

A great sadness filled the nymph's features, and she felt that her heart would break for the young man beside her.

"Where is it, Lady?" he asked.

"You know where it is, Phoebus Pen Dragon."

He looked toward the door, and saw the lake beyond it, dark and foreboding. "Can you get it for me?"

"I cannot."

"Then I must do it myself."

Elana stood and went to the small window to look out at the Sacred Pool of which she had been guardian for ages. "You will not find what you are looking for down there, Phoebus."

"That sword is my birthright. I have to try!" Phoebus turned to her and felt fear at the look in her eyes, the resignation in the hanging of her head. Beneath the hem of her robes, he spied the dragon imprinted upon her breast. "You know I must do this, don't you?"

She nodded and stood. "I do," she replied as she kissed his forehead. "The choice is yours."

Phoebus nodded, then picked up his cloak, and wrapped it around himself before going out the door.

Outside, the morning mist still clung to the surface of the surrounding moors. The black forms of crow shadows flit in the milky white light where the horse herds grazed on the far side of the lake.

Remus stood immediately as Phoebus emerged from the roundhouse with Elana. The wolf went to his side and licked his hands.

Phoebus knelt and pat him. "I'm going in. You stay here."

Remus looked at the water and then back to Phoebus. He whined.

"I'll be fine," Phoebus told him before walking slowly to the water's edge and a little distance along the shore. His feet were bare, and he could feel the icy cold of the water, biting at his ankles.

Elana followed close behind him. *I cannot dissuade him,* she thought. *I must not.*

Phoebus stared silently across the water for a few moments, his eyes searching for Apollo, for the light, but all he saw was the cold wind upon the black water, and the nervous rustling of the reeds along the shore. He felt the cold take hold of him as he removed the cloak and let it fall to the ground. His skin prickled and the dragons upon his forearms were dark against his skin in the early, grey light. He turned to look at Elana.

She gazed from him to the watery depths. "You are your father's son," she said, looking at the dragons.

He nodded and stepped into the water. His heart began to race, and he fought back the fear that still lingered from his dream. *I must do this now!* he told himself, breathing in and out, filling his lungs. *Apollo, guide me...*

Phoebus waded into the black water, deeper and deeper, as it crawled up his body. Then, he took a last deep breath and plunged beneath the surface.

It was dark in that watery underworld, strands of grasses flowing up like a forest from below, or like the hair of a Titan maid who lay sleeping on the bottom.

Phoebus Pen Dragon pulled at the water, harder and harder, pushing for the centre of the lake, searching for any sign of the light he had dreamed.

But the blackness went on, and he saw nothing.

Father, please! his heart cried out in that liminal world.

Deeper and deeper he went, despair beginning to set in as his lungs burned, and the pressure upon his body increased.

Then, he saw it, a faint light.

Phoebus swam toward it and then, suddenly there before him, upon the bottom of the lake was an ancient, algae-covered altar with a bundle fastened to it.

But what he saw shocked him to his core for, beside the altar, for a moment, his father's face hovered in the darkness, pale and lifeless.

Time stopped in that second, but then the eyes opened and the mouth gaped as if to shout, to warn him of danger.

Phoebus' vision began to waver. Panicking, he took hold of the bundle. But he could not dislodge it. He set his feet upon the altar and pulled and pulled, screaming in the depths. His lungs burned, and his ears began to ring as his entire body strained against the ropes.

Then, the ropes snapped.

He felt his vision fading entirely, his mind wandering to somewhere beyond consciousness.

Swim, Phoebus! To the light! a voice shouted.

In that moment, the morning sun dawned over the moors and cast its light upon the surface of the Sacred Pool.

The bundle held fast in one arm, Phoebus pushed off of the altar toward the sunlight, even as water began to fill his mouth, and choke his lungs. He pushed harder, and harder, seeking to evade Death as it reached out with painful claws to pull him back.

The light! To the light!

As abruptly as a bolt from Olympus, sunlight warmed his face and filled his eyes as he broke the surface. He gasped, unable to breathe, all of his senses filled with water and his iron grasp of the bundle he dragged with him.

There was a loud splash as Remus plunged into the water, his jaws grasping Phoebus' arm and pulling him onto the muddy shore.

Phoebus fell face down and, for a moment, he could see his breathless end, but then he coughed and heaved and purged the water from his body. He wept and pounded the earth as he lay naked upon it, no strength left.

In the distance, the sound of horses' hooves echoed.

I'm too late, Phoebus thought, fearing that the Praetorians had found him.

Remus began to howl.

"Elana, run!" he gasped. "Leave me!"

The nymph did not move. "You are not alone, Phoebus Pen Dragon," she said.

Phoebus felt his consciousness wavering as he strained to look up at the approaching rider, too weak to stand and fight. He pointed at the white horse rushing toward him, and looked up at the rider, unable to comprehend what he was seeing.

"Phoebus!" a woman's voice shouted as the horse skidded to halt. "I'm here!"

The tears burned in his eyes. "Mama?"

"I'm here, my boy!" Adara said as she fell at his side. "I'm here!"

Elana watched, her own tears falling onto the muddy shore of the lake. *It is happening...*

XVIII

ARMA DEORUM ET HEROUM

'The Weapons of Gods and Heroes'

"Phoebus!" Adara Pen Dragon said as she knelt in the mud beside him. "I'm here." Quickly, she observed the scars on his body and she felt a stabbing pain in her heart.

Elana handed her Phoebus' cloak and she covered his shaking body with it.

After a few moments, he opened his eyes and looked up at Adara. "Mama?" There was doubt in his voice, as though he had indeed fallen through the dark gate of the Underworld and was looking upon a shade. But then, he felt the cool moorland wind upon his face and heard the swishing of the reeds along the shore. He perceived his tight grip upon the heavy bundle which he clutched to his breast. "I saw him…I saw father drowned," he wept, a mixture of deep sadness and anger.

Adara's eyes blurred as she stroked the wet hair off his forehead. She turned to look up at Elena.

"We need to get him inside by the fire," Elena urged.

Phoebus looked at her again, a great confusion upon his face, a delirium setting in. "You're here?" he demanded of his mother, flashes of his long journeying to find her rushing by in his mind. "Why did you leave us?"

"I'm sorry," Adara wept, unable to hold back now as she bent to kiss his forehead. "I'm so sorry."

"He's dead, Mama. He's dead!"

"I know, my dearest boy…I know." Adara wiped her eyes and, with Elana's help, pulled Phoebus to his feet. "Come. We need to get you warm."

As they walked slowly back to the roundhouse, Remus and Aegis following them, the sky began to darken and the wind to blow.

Elana looked up at the sky, her senses tingling, alerting her. *The hunters are gathering,* she thought, feeling the dread taking hold. "Quickly. Inside!" she said to Adara. "I will see to your horse."

Inside the roundhouse, Elana pulled one of the cots close to the hearth fire and added fuel to build it up. At a look from her, the flames rose higher and hotter. She then took the soaking bundle from Phoebus' grasp and put it on a log on the other side of the fire. They laid Phoebus upon the furs and then covered him with another fur and blankets, tossing the wet cloak aside for the moment.

"I'm here now, Phoebus," Adara whispered as she sat beside him. "And I'm not leaving again."

"I...I've been searching...for...you..." he mumbled before his exhaustion overtook his shaking body.

Adara looked up at Elana, panic in her eyes.

"Let him sleep," Elana said. "I will prepare a tea for him. He took himself to the very edge of exhaustion. He needs rest."

"Why did he go into the Sacred Pool?" Adara asked.

"For that," Elana said, pointing at the dripping bundle.

Adara gazed across the flames at the bundle, soaking and covered with algae. Then, it dawned on her what it was, and she looked at the guardian nymph. "Is it?"

Elana nodded. "He must be the one to open it," she warned. "I will see to your horse..."

"Aegis."

"Aegis," Elana repeated with a smile. She went to the door and opened it to find Remus staring inside, whining. "This is Remus," she said as the great wolf looked at his master. "Go to him, Remus."

The wolf walked in, sat beside Phoebus, and rested his head on his chest. The yellow eyes looked at the woman sitting with him, and then turned to look upon the prostrate man.

"Have you been watching over my son?" Adara asked the animal.

The wolf's eyes looked from Phoebus' face to hers, and then back to his master.

"Thank you," Adara whispered as she took her son's hand.

That evening, the second day before the coming of Samhain, the wind grew cold, and a menace laced the air that tore over the moors. The horses charged frantically about the shores of the Sacred Pool, and the voices of the dead grew louder as they assembled at the gates of Annwn for the Hunt.

Elana stood outside the door of the roundhouse, uttering prayers to Apollo.

"Far-Shooter...Lord of Light, Prophecy, and of Healing... Your children have need of you now, more than ever. Rome is coming. I can feel it in the earth and on the wind...I can see it in the waters... Give them the strength they need for the coming fight. Their hearts are pure and good."

She looked up at the night sky where a million stars burned beyond the curtain of clouds, hope beyond the darkness. And there, among the constellations, Anguis burned brightly, the Dragon, and as she gazed upon it, she could hear a great roar and clash of battle that she had not heard since the battles of Gods and Giants.

"Lord...what are you showing me?" she asked, expecting to see Apollo emerge on the other side of the lake.

But he did not appear.

I am to be tested as well, she thought.

She looked down at Remus, who sat beside her, and stroked his head. "I will see to your master now." Elana then turned, opened the door of her home, and went inside to see Phoebus sitting, furs wrapped about his shoulders as he sipped the healing tea she had prepared for him.

He stared across the fire at the bundle which he had not yet dared to open. He did not look upon his mother where she sat near him. When Elana was seated with them, he spoke. "Why did you leave us without a word in Ynis Wytrin?"

Adara could hear the anger, fear, and great hurt in her son's voice. She did not answer immediately, but breathed through her own whirling emotions before speaking. "It was not about you or your sister, Phoebus, I swear. I was..." She leaned upon her knees to gaze at the fire, to try and find the words to properly relay a world of painful emotion in just a few sentences. "I was angry...so angry I didn't know what to do. Life had lost its light for me, even in Ynis Wytrin with you and your sister. Your father was my life...I mean...of course you and Calliope are as well." She smacked her thigh, frustrated that the words were not sufficient. "I felt abandoned...I felt a sadness that I had never felt before...so deep that it strangled my every thought, every action."

"We all felt abandoned," Phoebus said, shaking his head and staring at his mother now. "And you made that doubly so for me and Calliope."

"I know," Adara said, "and I'm so sorry." She took a cup of tea which Elana handed her. "After your father returned from the east, when he came back to us…changed…so different…I was angry with him…for what he had put us through, for the loss of our child. I blamed him for all that had happened. I was cold toward him, trying to figure out how to love him again. But my anger was…it was…" Adara sighed. "I was too weak, too stubborn. And then, just as I was coming to terms with our new life, and the *person* your father had become, he left."

"And so did you."

"Not immediately, but yes. I left. I couldn't stay in Ynis Wytrin any longer, a dark cloud in that blessed place. I needed to stay busy and distracted from all the pain I was feeling, and so I set out to help others, as your father always had done."

"You mean to put yourself in danger."

"That also." She looked at Elana who sat there listening intently, her hands clasped in her lap, great pity in her eyes. "A part of me thought that if I was in danger, that Lucius would somehow come back to me. Then, I started to feel good helping others, giving aid where I could."

Phoebus shook his head. "But *we* needed your help! Me and Calliope!"

Adara looked upon her son. *He is a man now, filled with his own anger.* She felt her heart fill with sadness then, the weight of a world of regret. "I'm sorry, Phoebus."

"Why did you come back now, after so many years?" he asked.

"I wanted to, for a long time. I…I just didn't know how to. I knew I had hurt you and your sister too much by leaving. Perhaps my shame kept me away. But then, when I was on Mona with…with friends…we were attacked by Praetorians. I found out they are here in Britannia hunting us."

"I know. They attacked Culhwch and Alma's home."

Adara looked up quickly, fear in her eyes.

Phoebus put his hand up. "They're all right. Remus and I arrived in time to…help them."

She relaxed a little. "Thank the Gods. On Mona, I…I was not able to save everyone. When the Praetorians arrived to take me, they demanded to know where you and your sister were, where your father was."

"All our lives, they've hunted us and harassed us," Phoebus growled, his eyes resting on the bundle across the fire again.

"And they are here now," Elana said suddenly.

Phoebus and Adara looked at her.

"In Dumnonia?" Adara asked.

Elana nodded. "Yes. And you must prepare to meet them. You must get to Din Tagell where Calliope is waiting with Einion, Briana, and the dragons."

"I'm ready," Phoebus said. He stood and picked up the bundle. He sat back down with it across his knees. "And if we're going to meet the Praetorians in battle, we're going to need these." He looked down at the bundle and began to unwind the ropes.

"Are those…" Adara looked at Elana.

The nymph nodded. "I have kept them safe for you…until you needed them again."

Adara grasped her hand and smiled. "Thank you."

"It was Lucius' wish."

Adara's smile faded. She turned to Phoebus who was removing the layers of sodden, waxed and oiled leather, and the wool blanket beneath. But his smile faded when he pulled back the final layer to reveal just two swords. "What? This can't be it?" He looked at Elana and then back at the swords.

Adara looked too and there she saw Lucius' ancestral gladius with the eagle upon the pommel and the Pegasus upon the hilt. Her husband had given it to their son and he had, at far too young an age, slain another with it.

Phoebus drew the blade and held it up to the firelight. It was untarnished, and still sharp. It had seen many a battle across the Empire in his father's hand, and his great-grandfather's before him, but it was not what he had come there for.

"May I?" Adara asked her son as she looked upon the hilt of the gladius which Lucius had had made for her by the mysterious smith, Terdra.

He held it out to her and she took hold of the walnut pommel adorned with golden images of horses and Epona. She smiled sadly as she ran her fingers along the antler handle to the hilt with golden dragons which sprouted from the deep green sheath with acanthus leaves. "I never thought to hold this again," Adara whispered, pressing the hilt to her forehead.

"Where is it?" Phoebus suddenly demanded of Elana. His voice was harsh, accusatory. "Where is my father's sword? The one my mother gave him...the one given by Apollo?" He held up the now empty bundle of leather. "Someone has stolen it!"

"No one has entered the lake, Phoebus," Elana said. "The swords have lain in wait until you needed them."

"But not all of them!"

"Phoebus, be calm," Adara said, but the look he shot her silenced her.

"Do you have it?" he demanded of the nymph.

"I do not," Elana said calmly.

"Then who does?" He threw the leather across the room to land on the dirt floor. He looked with disdain on the blade that had been given to him, refusing to touch it until he had answers. "I need my father's sword to fight the Praetorians!" For weeks Phoebus had been focussed on retrieving the magical blade, the dragon-hilted sword that no other blade could match, that would help him in the battle he knew was coming. "Where is it, Elana? I must have it!"

Elana stared back at Phoebus from the other side of the fire, her brilliant blue eyes growing stern as she thought back to the moment, years before, when she had placed the swords upon the altar at the bottom of the Sacred Pool. "Listen to me, Phoebus Pen Dragon," she said. "I have not touched the swords since they were entrusted to me."

"Then where is it?" he demanded.

She stood and looked down at him. "The weapons of gods and heroes appear when they are needed, to whomever needs them."

"And I need it now!"

"Yes," Elana replied. "And you have your sword, and your mother has hers. You have what you need for the coming fight."

He looked away from her gaze, unable to hold it any longer. "I...I don't understand..." His voice was softer now, resigned and disappointed. "How could someone steal it?" He balled his fists and looked at her again. "You have failed in your guardianship, Elana."

She seemed to grow in stature then, filling the space in the roundhouse, brighter, beautiful and terrible at once. "No. I have not. You have received what the Gods believe you are deserving of. That is all."

"Phoebus," Adara finally said, turning to her son. "It is the sword your father gave to you. That is a sacred thing. And that gladius has been wielded by your ancestors without fail. It is a good sword."

"But not as good as the one you gifted to him."

"They have all seen battle, and all remained true."

"The strength of the sword is in the intent of the one who wields it," Elana said suddenly. "Ask yourself, Phoebus Pen Dragon… What is your intent?"

"I want to defend my family and friends," he stated without faltering.

"Then do that," Elana replied.

"We will do that together, Phoebus," Adara added, gripping his arm. "By Samhain, we will be with your sister and our friends again in Din Tagell, to stand together."

Phoebus looked at both of them, his jaw set, his eyes frustrated and desperate. He stood without a word and stormed outside into the night.

"I am sorry, Elana," Adara said.

"There is nothing to be sorry for. His pain runs deep, and he is still trying to prove himself worthy of his father."

Adara smiled sadly. "I think we all are." She held her own sword across her lap and felt her tears burning. "I feel my heart breaking all over again."

Elana sat beside her, and placed her arm around her. "You are stronger than you think, Adara Pen Dragon. I knew that the moment I met you. And Lucius knew that too."

"He was my true love, Elana," Adara said, wiping her eyes. "I don't know if you are permitted to understand such a love, but it is all-encompassing. It is a life force that drives and inspires one so."

"I…I do understand," Elana said, her voice low and thoughtful. "All too well."

Adara looked at her.

"I also know that Death is not so powerful as to erase such a love."

"No. It isn't," Adara agreed. "But Death did come for Lucius." She tried not to think of her love drowning as Phoebus had seen.

"You will be with him again," Elana said, her voice low and fearful.

Adara stared at her, her hand gripping her sword, feeling the familiar weight of it, remembering when she had slain the man who had burned her husband and destroyed their home. She nodded. "I am ready, even if it takes the Praetorians slaying me to be reunited with my love."

Oh to have such a love! Elana's heart ached.

"I must speak with Phoebus," Adara said as she stood, took up her son's gladius, and went out.

Elana was alone before the fire then, as she always was. She leaned forward to stare into the flames and there saw an army of dark riders with hatred and death in their eyes. "Gods…do not abandon them now."

Outside, Adara saw Phoebus' silhouette against the silvery backdrop of the lake. Moonlight fell between the cracks in the clouds and she stood for a moment to watch him, her son, now grown into a man, shouldering all of the burdens that that entailed.

Have I failed him? she wondered. *He had no Diodorus to guide him, no safe or permanent home to guard him.*

He had our love… a voice replied in her head, and she felt her heart flutter.

I'll be with you soon, my love, Adara replied, and in that moment, she felt an overwhelming sense of peace that she had not felt in a very long while. She had, she realized, finally set aside her anger.

Adara walked over to join her son at the lake, his wolf turning to observe her approach. "Are you all right?"

"No," he replied, staring out at the water where he had almost drowned, where he had seen his father drowned. "This is not the life I envisioned."

"It never is, my son. Trust me. If I had seen how things would turn out, had I the power of seeing like Etain or Elana, then I would have done some things differently."

"Even Etain and Elana can't see what the Gods have in store for us. And if that is the case," Phoebus turned to his mother, "what hope is there for any of us?"

Adara leaned against him. "If your father taught me anything, it is that there is always hope, even at the darkest of times. And though… though we may feel like it, we are never truly alone."

Phoebus looked upon his mother, a once glamorous woman now turned warrior.

She held up the gladius that was now his, the sword which he had pulled from the Sacred Pool before them. "The past is the past. There is nothing we can do to change it. But what we can do is see to our intent with sincerity, and take whatever action we can in the name of goodness and what is right."

He took the sword from his mother and held it up to the moonlight, its blade glinting in the darkness. "I intend to fight the evil men who have come to kill us."

"And I will do the same, my son," she said.

The moon disappeared then, and darkness closed in around them. The wind began to groan, and a fox screamed somewhere out on the moors.

Remus stood up and stared into the darkness across the lake, a low groan in his body.

"Come," Adara said. "We should rest. Who knows what this eve before Samhain will bring."

It was a night of darkness and ill-omen, a prelude to the night of Samhain when Gwyn ap Nudd would ride out to terrorize the land of the living. Out on the moor in the falling night, beyond the safety of the Sacred Pool, tors loomed like giants against the sky. Dogs howled and cats hissed at the faint shapes of banshees circling high above as they uttered their dreadful chorus. Beasts and birds cowered in their dens and in the branches of trees, and the people of the moor prayed in their hovels, awaiting the dawn so that they might travel to the safety of their lord's keep in Din Tagell for the death of the year.

Inside the roundhouse, Elana prepared food while Adara kept the fire fed. Remus sat facing the door, listening to the restless horse herd about the lake and the building chaos beyond its shores.

Beside the fire, Phoebus Pen Dragon held his father's gladius up to the light after sharpening it. He thought of all the battles his father had fought with that blade, from Parthia to Numidia, and the bogs and glens of Caledonia. It was not the sword he had hoped for, but it was what he had, and he was now glad of it. However, the thought of his father's god-made blade being stolen, held by the hand of a thief, lost forever, gave him great grief.

I'm sorry, Father... he thought. *I did not get here in time.*

The wind outside raged and tore at the thatched roof of the round-house, found its way inside to pull at the hearth fire.

Across from her son, Adara looked over the sheath and blade she had never expected to see again. She turned it over in her hands, sending reflections of firelight into the rafters. "This will be a long night," she muttered.

"It always is," Elana said. "But you must rest, both of you." *For I have had a glimpse of what awaits you.* The thought hurt the nymph's heart, for the Gods had made her feel deeply the days of her long life. *How many more will there be in the ages to come?* she wondered as she handed Phoebus and Adara their bowls of stew and cups of tea.

"Thank you, Elana," Adara said, setting the sword aside and accepting the bowl. "You have always been so kind to us."

"It is my honour to aid the Dragon's family," she said. *Though I cannot keep Death from you.* She turned away, not wanting them to see the tears rimming her eyes.

Phoebus and Adara ate in silence, each alone with their thoughts, their fears, and the memories which emerged from the blades they now possessed.

"I must sleep," Phoebus said, yawning. "I…I'm so tired."

"As am I," Adara said.

Without a word, Elana took their empty bowls and cups and led them each to a bed where they fell into a deep slumber, despite the chaos outside. "Rest," she said as she covered them with blankets.

She then took their swords and sat with both across her lap before the fire. With her hands over them, palms down, Elana prayed. "Far-Shooting Apollo… Divine Goddess Venus… Epona, Goddess of the Sacred Herds… Be with the Dragon's family tomorrow. Imbue these weapons with your might, and fill those who wield them with strength in battle. Guide them. Protect them, I beg you. Do not let the darkness drown out the light." Her hands shook as she breathed in and out, attempting to weave protection about the sleeping forms behind her.

Remus looked over his shoulder at them and at the nymph.

"You must protect them tomorrow," Elana said to him.

The wolf blinked slowly and laid himself down in front of the door.

The sound of horses' hooves woke them the next morning. But it was not the sound of the free and rollicking herds of the Sacred Pool. There was the loud jingle of tack, and the harsh voices of men calling to each other in the morning mist beyond the lake.

Remus stood up suddenly, his growl low and wary.

Elana moved from where she had been keeping vigil through the long night, and went to the small window to look out.

The world was shrouded in mist, but the faint glow of torches accompanied the muffled voices on the moorland breeze.

"They are here," she said before turning and going to wake Phoebus and Adara. She laid her hand upon each of their brows to wake them with a calm that belied her own growing worry. "It is time, my friends. Wake."

Phoebus opened his eyes. He had been dreaming of Rachel.

Elana felt great pity for him then, for she could feel the heartache that beat within his breast. "All will be well, Phoebus. But you must wake now."

Adara sat up too, and rubbed her face. "Is it time?" she asked, turning to Elana.

"Yes," the nymph said. "You must rise and prepare."

Remus began to growl more intensely.

"What is it, boy?" Phoebus asked, standing and stretching.

"Rome," Elana said.

"What?" asked Adara.

"They are here."

There was a pained screech somewhere across the lake, and then another, followed by a pounding of horses' hooves.

Elana grabbed at her chest in pain. "They...they are slaying the herd!"

"No!" Adara said as she and Phoebus dressed hurriedly. "We must stop them!"

Elana shook her head. "No! You must ride! Ride as quickly as you can for Din Tagell!"

Adara turned to the nymph. "Come with us!"

Elana shook her head. "I cannot. I must stay and guard the Sacred Pool."

"But they will kill you!"

"I will slow them to give you time to get away," Elana said, handing each of them their sword. "Go now! Aegis is waiting for you."

Phoebus and Adara looked about the roundhouse, trying to still the useless, rising panic each of them felt. Then, they stopped and looked at Elana.

"Thank you," Phoebus said. "With all my heart, thank you."

"Go now, Phoebus Pen Dragon. May the Gods protect you." She kissed him on the cheek and opened the door.

Outside, Aegis stood before the door, already saddled.

"Remus, with me," Phoebus said.

The wolf's hackles were up as he peered into the swirling mists toward the horrific sounds of slain horses.

Inside, Adara turned to Elana. "Will we meet again?"

Elana smiled sadly. "Only the Gods know. If we do not, know that you are not alone. Love follows you…always." She kissed Adara's forehead and then went outside with her.

The wind was picking up and the morning sun burning through the mist. On the other side of the lake, on a distant rise of the moor, black banners with a bloody eagle appeared, jutting up from a mass of horsemen. Their black armour was dull in the pale light, their presence there a sacrilege.

"Go now!" Elana shouted as Adara and Phoebus got on Aegis' back.

They looked down at Elana to see the dragon upon her chest begin to glow in that morning light.

Elana strode to the shore of the lake, facing the distant Praetorians. She looked back one more time. "Ride!" she shouted before spreading her arms wide and raising them to the sky.

A great wind began to circle the lake and a thick mist formed on its surface.

The horse herds fled into the mist, away from the blades of those hateful soldiers who had invaded their sanctuary.

Adara put her heels to Aegis and together, they and Remus, charged away, northwest onto the misty, windswept moor.

When Elana saw that they were away, her sea blue eyes widened with a rage she had not felt in an age. The wind and rain lashed at the enemy, tearing their banners from their poles, and frightening their horses such that they reared and charged in all directions, away from the Sacred Pool.

"There they are!" the voice of their commander shouted into the wind. "After them!"

Ride, Dragons! Elana's heart screamed. *Ride!*

The thunder of horses' hooves charged violently, and unceasingly across the moor, toward night…toward death.

XIX

TEMPESTAS ADVENIENTIS

'The Coming Storm'

The urgent call of gulls as they encircled the fortress of Din Tagell woke Calliope Pen Dragon where she slept on the northern side of the fortress. She had grown used to their incessant song over the months she had been living there, their need to raise an alarm at daybreak as they soared above the rocky cliffs and chasms of the fortress of Einion.

She had also grown accustomed to the constant groan of the roiling sea which, day and night, lashed the high, rocky walls, filling the bay of the Haven with its violent tide. The sea never calmed in that place as Samhain approached, as if both sea gods, Manannan and Neptune, laid siege at once to the land.

But it was not the sea that had tormented Calliope's slumber, nor the babe that had been growing inside of her for the past six months and more. There had been dread omens across the land that night, she was certain. She had felt them, seen them in glimpses of fire, heard them on the howling winds. They had been vague at first, in the days prior, hovering at the periphery of her senses but, that night, the omens had cut deeply, violently.

At first, she had wondered if it was the fearful talk of Einion's people about the impending arrival of Gwyn ap Nudd, the Lord of Annwn, who had attacked their lord's hall years before. However, she believed that there was more to it than that.

Thunder rolled in the distance, though the sun reached into the guest-house that morning.

Calliope wiped at her eyes and felt the salt crust of her dried tears. She had wept again in her sleep, though she knew it was not for the omens she sensed. She could not recall what made her weep, and wondered if the child inside of her was trying to tell her something.

"Aaron…" she whispered her love's name and tried to smile, as she did every morning before she rose. She pushed herself up slowly, her hands caressing her belly. "It will be all right, little one," she said. "I'll protect you." She had heard from the people of the land that every Samhain, it was not uncommon for pregnant women and animals to miscarry, blood offerings to the Lord of Annwn and his hunters. She tried not to listen to them, and wondered why anyone would say such a thing to her.

Gwendolyn, Einion's queen, told her that people said it in the hopes that the utterance out loud would prevent it from happening.

After relieving herself, and then washing her face in a basin that sat upon a table beneath the small window, Calliope stepped into her leather slippers and slowly slid her new, larger white tunica over her head. She then took up her thick, grey cloak. As she did so, a wave of nausea rushed over her and she made for the bucket that served as her privy to vomit.

Throughout the initial stages of her pregnancy, she had vomited constantly, but now it only happened in the mornings.

Einion and Gwendolyn had suggested that one of their servants sleep in the guesthouse with her, to care for her if she required anything, but Calliope had insisted that she preferred to be alone, that she wished to have quiet during her prayers and meditations. In truth, she did not want someone present when she wept to herself in the lonely firelight of the guesthouse. She missed Aaron deeply, as well as Rachel. She found herself worrying about Phoebus, and wishing that her mother was with her, to help her and guide her through pregnancy. Briana had comforted and reassured her as best she could, but it was not the same.

Daily, Calliope tried reaching out to Phoebus and her mother, but she could not see or hear them. And that worried her.

From beyond the mists, Etain had tried to allay her fears, and Elana, when she had seen her, had said that she felt certain that they were still alive, though where they were was hidden to her own powerful sight.

After drinking some water from the clay cup she kept on her table, Calliope went to the low door and opened it. When she emerged into the morning light and wind, a crust of bread in her hand, she breathed deeply of the fresh sea air, and it cleared her head immediately.

There was a throaty squawk nearby, and she turned to see Corvus perched on the low bench beside the door, his dark eyes blinking up at her.

"Good morning, Corvus," Calliope said as she reached out to stroke his bobbing head. "I hope the gulls have been leaving you alone this morning."

He squawked again.

"Good." She crumbled the crust of bread on the bench and he immediately began to peck at it. She then looked around the grass and along the walls of the guesthouse, searching for the last of the wild flowers, and spotted a small bunch of red valerian at the corner of the squat stone house. She walked over to pick it. She turned to look back at the house where she had been living, sunk into the ground, its slate rooftop slick with sea mist and moss. Every time she looked upon it, she remembered the first time she had stayed there with her family, when her father was still healing from his wounds, when he was still alive.

She felt again where she had dried her tears of the night before. She turned then to look down the narrow, winding path that led across the plateau of the castle rock to the stone altar that looked out over the cliffs to the sea. She stood before the altar, breathing slowly and deeply of the salt air.

Storm clouds gathered out in the distant ocean, making their lumbering way directly for Din Tagell.

Calliope looked from them to the altar where she laid the valerian flowers upon it, like droplets of crimson blood or wine. She held her hands up, palms toward the sky, and closed her eyes.

"Oh Gods… Apollo, Venus, and Epona…protectors of our family. Keep us safe through this long, dark night of Samhain. Shield us from those who seek to harm us. Protect my mother and brother, wherever they may be. Guard me and my baby from the evil that ranges abroad this night and-"

Her prayers were interrupted by a distant chorus of thunder and she turned to look south over the moors. There, a mass of black clouds boiled above the land, lightning flashing, as if a godly battle took place within.

Calliope Pen Dragon stood there alone, the wind swirling about her, pulling at her cloak and hair as she watched with a sense of impending doom. *Gods, please help us,* she prayed. *Baba…I miss you…I need your strength…your protection.*

Suddenly, in her mind, the men of the black ship she had seen long before were marching over land, all that they rode over shrivelling to black, dead at their touch.

NO!

"Calliope?" an urgent voice called out, faint at first, and then louder. "Calliope, are you all right?"

Calliope opened her eyes to find she was laying in the green grass before the altar. Above her, she saw Antiope and Nisien, the eldest son of Einion and Gwendolyn, his black hair blowing in the wet wind. Corvus stood perched on the edge of the altar, squawking as he looked down at her.

"Sit her up," Antiope said to her cousin and together they helped Calliope to sit against the altar.

"I must have fainted," Calliope said, her hand to her head.

"Corvus alerted us," Antiope said. "He made quite a fuss in the hall."

"Lady, you must eat something," Nisien said, his grey eyes worrying over her. "My mother always says she would eat first thing when she was pregnant."

"I know," Calliope replied. "But I did not faint because of hunger. I saw them, the black army."

Antiope and Nisien looked at each other.

"We're in danger," Calliope said, her eyes straining to look out to the moors where the black clouds were indeed gathered.

"Let's get you into the hall," Nisien said. "There is food."

They helped Calliope to her feet and, each holding an arm, and guided her over the bumpy ground to the path that led to the great hall.

There was much activity on the summit of Din Tagell. Samhain was upon them and people were flooding in from the countryside, making for the safety of their lord's fortress so that they might celebrate the new year in safety, together. A steady flow of people wended their way up the path from the great rope bridge carrying baskets of apples and bundles of firewood. They brought bread, and cheese, and bales of wool for, once again, it had been a prosperous year under the protection of Lord Einion.

The stables on the landward side were filled with the carts, horses, and pack mules which people had travelled on, though most had arrived on foot from across the moors and down the coast.

All spoke of the omens of the previous night and that fear belied the joyous smiles and laughter upon people's lips as they arrived at last to set up their individual watches around the great hall of Din Tagell.

As Calliope walked with Antiope and Nisien along the pathway to the hall, the three of them were greeted by groups of Einion's people. There were women and children, some holding tightly onto their young ones, keeping them from the cliffs, while others cradled their babes, hoping for a blessing from their lord. Old women and old men caught up with friends and reminisced about the dark years when Einion's wicked uncle ruled, and then expressed gratitude for the years of prosperity since Einion retook his stolen throne. And while they prepared the bonfires for the long, dark night, and readied the apple offerings for the Gods, the rest of the men, and some women, stood guard at the land-ward fortress of the narrow entrance, and along every pathway of Din Tagell.

It was widely rumoured that Rome was abroad in the land, hunting dragons, and Lord Einion refused to be caught unawares, or to see his people harmed in any way.

Besides, it was the night of the Wild Hunt, a bloody night many still remembered, when battles were fought and when Gwyn ap Nudd had darkened the doorway of Din Tagell's hall.

It was the recollection of this last memory that was front of the people's minds as they watched Calliope Pen Dragon walk with Prince Nisien, and the Princess Antiope. They smiled and bowed to the daughter of the Dragon, the 'Pen Draig', the warrior who had helped their lord retrieve his throne and then done battle with the Lord of Annwn himself.

"Blessings on you and your child, lady!" one woman said to Calliope as she passed.

"Thank you," Calliope replied, smiling at all of the faces turned toward her.

"Hail to the Dragon's daughter!" an old man called out from another group.

Calliope nodded to him and smiled, and did the same to all the others who looked upon her as she passed with their prince and princess on their way to the hall.

"Good morrow, Lady Calliope," said one of Einion's captains at the main entrance to the hall.

"Good morning, Edern," Calliope said, noting the many voices that emanated from the hall.

"The Dragons have returned," he said, his face unsmiling.

"And?" she asked.

Edern shook his head, his dark hair falling to hide his face as he opened the double doors. "My Prince. Princess," he addressed Nisien and Antiope.

"Thank you, Edern," Antiope said as she helped Calliope over the threshold and into the hall.

Lord Einion's hall bustled with life. His warriors and their wives and children were all gathered there about the tables set with food and drink. The hearth fire burned brightly and the scent of roasted meat tickled the senses and rumbled the stomach.

Einion, who sat upon the great stone throne at the far end of the hall, stood when he saw Calliope enter with his son and niece. He was a formidable man, his long hair and beard still dark, his frame strong and quick. He wore a golden torc about his neck, and a thick bear-skin cloak covered his deep green tunic. At his side, as ever, hung his father's longsword.

Near Einion stood Arthrek, the captain of his guard, as well as Ewella, both of whom, along with Edern, had fought beside their lord on that Samhain night years before.

Gwendolyn, Einion's queen, sat beside him on a slightly smaller throne, flanked by her women, Caja, Ebrel, and Melwyn. Gwendolyn whispered something to Caja and the latter quickly cleared a space for Calliope at the table immediately to the right of the dais where the thrones sat.

"Calliope!" Dagon waved to her. "Look who is here!" He stepped aside to reveal Brencis, Dima, Magar, Boas and Deva who had all been at the court of Afallach in the north at Dunpendyrlaw.

Calliope walked between the filled tables that flanked the aisle to the dais where her father's men stood waiting to see her. She remembered their faces, weathered and battle-worn, from when she was a child. They had all been a part of their familia at the hillfort, so long ago. "It's good to see you all," she said, her hand straying to the dragon torc about her neck. "I'm relieved to see you all safe."

"It does us good to see you, Calliope," Brencis said, smiling more with relief than joy, his hand upon his heart as he bowed to her, the others following suit. "Lord Afallach sends his wishes to the Dragon's family."

Briana arrived at Calliope's side with Dagon, while Antiope and Nisien went to sit at the table nearby.

There was a familiar jingle of scale armour and Calliope turned to see Barna, Akil, Shura, Hipolit, and Taboras, all the surviving members of her father's Sarmatian cavalry ala.

They bowed to her as well and saluted Lord Einion.

"Any sign of them?" Einion asked, his voice grave.

Barna shook his head. "Nothing, Lord Einion."

Calliope turned back to Brencis. "Did you hear anything of my mother and brother?"

Brencis stepped forward. "Phoebus did show up at Afallach's court many months ago, but since then…nothing."

"None of you has had word of my mother?" Calliope asked, her hands covering her belly.

"I'm sorry, lady," Brencis said. "We did slay some of the Praetorians who were hunting her and your brother."

"And how many more Praetorians are there?" Calliope asked, trying not to remember the dreams and visions that had tormented her.

"We have heard that it was a century of Praetorians," Magar put in. "Half of them landed in Horea Classis. The other half at Isca Dumnoniorum."

"Erm," Shura cleared his throat, wiping the dust from his face, for he had just returned from patrol. "From what some of the farmers and miners have told us, Lord Einion, the Praetorian forces rejoined at Isca."

Einion looked to Gwendolyn. "It's happening," he whispered.

She nodded gravely. "Do you think they will come here?"

Einion did not answer.

Calliope looked behind the throne then and was surprised to see the dragon standards of her father's men prominently displayed. Their fanged maws gaped, and their terrifying eyes looked out over the gathered crowds. The long red and gold wind socks hung, swaying in the cold breeze that reached into the hall from the sea outside. "Why are the dragons displayed?" Calliope asked Dagon, but it was Einion who answered.

"Because, Calliope… This night, of all nights, your father's dragons do not hide. We honour him and his memory."

Calliope felt a chill as all the warriors turned to her, memories of battle and of honour reflected in their eyes. She wanted to thank them, but found she could not speak. She could not take her eyes from the statue of the great, stone dragon with outspread wings that towered over the thrones and standards at the back of the hall.

Einion had commissioned the statue from the sculptors Emrys and Carissa years ago, before they had gone to start a new life in Gaul. The statue served as a permanent monument to the Dragon's legacy of honour, courage, and sacrifice.

Calliope stood there in silence, looking upon the dragon.

Briana took her hand. "Come. You should sit. Rest and eat." She smiled. "You need to feed both you and your child." She led Calliope to the table to sit.

"Arthrek," Einion called as the men gathered before him.

"Yes, Lord?" the younger man said.

"I want the main gatehouse on the other side of the chasm heavily fortified and our horses kept saddled and ready."

"All of them, Lord?"

"Yes." Einion looked at his warriors, his people and his friends. "If the forces of Rome, or even the dread riders of Gwyn ap Nudd, dare to attack us this night, I want us to be ready."

Outside, thunder rumbled in the distance and a moment later, Edern came into the hall from his post at the door. He marched up the aisle, through the warriors, to Einion. "My Lord!"

"What is it, Edern?" Einion asked.

"A storm on the moors. Clouds as black as pitch turning in the sky like a maelstrom at sea!"

Einion descended the dais and went down the length of the hall to look for himself, Gwendolyn and the men crowding behind him.

They all looked into the distance to see the black clouds swirling with bursts of lightning flashing within. They spread across the moors, darkening the sky like pitch across a floor of white marble.

"Light your fires now!" Einion called to the people gathered outside. "The night is racing towards us!" He turned to Arthrek. "Go to the gatehouse. Have them light their beacons to signal to everyone else across the land. The fires must be lit! Add pitch to them so that the rain won't drown them out."

"Yes, my lord!" Arthrek said before marching off to carry out Einion's orders.

Einion turned to look at the frightened faces of his people gathered outside. "Do not worry!" he called to them. "You are all safe here!" He turned to Dagon. "Has the Lord of Annwn allied himself with these Praetorians?" he whispered.

Dagon stared out at the spreading storm. He knew Einion was thinking of that night of blood and battle so many years before, for he was as well. "If they are allied against us, my friend, then there is little time."

Einion turned to the warriors about him, Dumnonians and Sarmatians alike. "Arm yourselves, my friends. We have to protect our families, friends, and the people, from what is coming."

"These Praetorians are bloodthirsty," Brencis said gravely. "They won't show any mercy."

Einion looked at him. "Then neither will we."

They watched as the bonfires on the plateau of Din Tagell were lit, and then the great fires above the gatehouse on the other side of the chasm. And soon, bonfires began to appear down the coastline and across the land, deep into the moors where their brave flame keepers stood sentry against the rushing night, the armies of Rome, and of the dead.

As the sky darkened, Calliope sat at the table, surrounded by Einion and Gwendolyn's younger children, extended family, her father's dragons and their families. And though she was not alone, she had never felt more so.

"What is it, Calliope?" Briana asked. She sat opposite her and reached across the table to take her hands. "Have you had another vision? What have the Gods shown you?"

"I've had so many, I can no longer discern between them and reality, Briana. I feel like something is closing in on me. Time is moving strangely."

"I felt at odds during my own pregnancy. It is normal."

"It's not that. I..." She caressed her swollen belly and breathed.

"Are you unwell?" Briana asked, her voice low.

Calliope shook her head. "I...I wish my mother was here for this."

"There is some time before the child comes. Adara may yet arrive."

"I'm scared for her and Phoebus. Something is happening." She sipped at her cup of water. "And I feel guilty for not telling Aaron about his child."

"I know," Briana said before standing and coming around the table to sit beside her. "You have to remember that it is safer for Aaron that he does not know. He and Rachel are also hunted by Rome, Calliope. You know how special they are."

Calliope looked around and nodded. "Father Gilmore has often alluded to the reason, and I have heard him speaking of it with Weylyn and Etain."

"Then you know that Aaron cannot leave Ynis Wytrin. Ever. And if he found out you were with child, I feel certain he would stop at nothing to come to you."

"I know." Calliope sighed. She tried reaching out to Aaron, to Phoebus, and to her mother, but all that met her thoughts was the racing wind and the blackness of the building storm outside. It was as if the Gods deliberately blinded her. *Gods... Apollo, Venus, and Epona... Please keep them safe.*

The day was long and dark. The rain held off, battering the heart of the moors instead where, it seemed, a battle continued to rage in the dark sky above. The unease among the people was deep as well, for Einion's men, including the dragons, went about armed and ready for whatever fight might come.

By then, it was widely whispered that there were Romans abroad in Dumnonia, Praetorians who hunted the Dragon's family, and his men.

The Dragon's men, over the years, had become a part of their community. At Lord Einion's side, they had protected Dumnonia and its people from Hibernian raiders. Now, they would have to defend it against the Empire.

"Has there been any word?" Calliope asked Einion where he stood at the bottom of the dais, speaking with Dagon.

A crack of thunder sounded outside.

Einion looked up for a moment before turning to Calliope. "Not yet. But we are keeping a watch. And the fires have been lit across the land.

The brave souls manning them have been instructed to send word if they see anything."

"Some things cannot be seen," Calliope mumbled to herself. She wavered on her feet and Einion and Dagon grabbed her arms.

"Calliope, you should rest," Dagon said. "The night is still several hours away."

She shook her head. "I just need some fresh air," she said. "It's stuffy in here with all the people. I'll be back." She tried to smile at them, her father's friends, but she knew it was forced. "Yes, fresh sea air. That will help."

Calliope walked down the aisle, past the hearth where a whole sheep was roasting, and carried on out of the hall.

"I worry for her," Einion said to Dagon. "She usually sees so much, but now…it's as if something harries her."

"I know. I don't like it," Dagon said. "I'll go with her." He turned to go, giving Briana a look as he passed.

The wind outside was vicious and even the gulls were now huddled in the crevices of the castle rock, no longer able to soar in the sky above where clouds raced across the sky like eager armies on their way to battle. In the sunken areas about the plateau, large groups of people were huddled together against the wind, their bonfires already burning but struggling to stay lit, and those that were lit blew sideways as if some god deliberately sought to extinguish them.

Outside of the hall, Calliope stopped and breathed deeply of the air, her left hand pulling her cloak close about her, her right hand rubbing the dragon torc about her neck. Even after many months, it felt strange to be in that place without her family, for the memory of their flight from Dumnonia, from Britannia, was something that haunted her. It was the subsequent series of tragedies that ultimately led to the destruction of her family.

Had I been older, I would have stopped it, appealed to my father! she sometimes thought, naively, she knew. Then she remembered Father Gilmore's lessons on free will and how it is considered a gift from God. *Odd that he should say such things when Aaron and Rachel are not free to leave Ynis Wytrin. Baba did his best to protect us in the way he knew best. He chose.*

But she knew that the cost had been great.

A great shiver ran through her body and she began to walk along the pathway from the hall. People greeted Calliope as she went, their faces peering out from beneath the hoods of their woollen cloaks, smiling, some even bowing to her, the Dragon's daughter.

She made her way to the postern gate and stepped through it to stand on the windswept terrace that overlooked the harbour of the Haven. No ships were anchored there beside the squat stone warehouses of the Iron Gate far below. She remembered when her family had left from there, so many years before… She had later found out that her father had intended to slay Emperor Caracalla. She also remembered the pride that had swelled in her when she discovered that he had chosen not to do that. So many people feared him then, when he returned, but she did not. Her hope had been rewarded.

"I miss you, Baba," she said, her voice lost on the wind.

"Calliope!" Dagon said as he approached from the postern gate. "You should be careful out here. The wind is liable to pick you up!"

"I'm all right," she replied.

But he could not hear her, and motioned for her to follow him back inside the walls of the fortress. "You need to be careful," he said, his arm about her as he led her back up the stairs and along the path toward the southern entrance.

They walked slowly, able to speak now.

"Adara and Phoebus will be all right, Calliope," Dagon said. "I can feel it."

"I cannot," she replied. "It's as if my reserves of hope have been used up, Dagon. I feel dread most of the time lately." She looked up to see Corvus winging along the stone walls, following her, shielded from the winds. "How has it come to this? Why did Baba have to leave?"

"Maybe he did not have a choice?"

"There is always a choice," Calliope replied, her voice uncharacteristically bitter.

They arrived at the gatehouse where the bridge stretched over the chasm to the landward defences. There, they could seen Einion's men standing guard in the whipping wind, their eyes turned toward the moors and the angry, bubbling clouds where lightning continued to burst within.

"I remember when I first met your father in Numidia. My uncle, Mar, and I, greatly admired him. He was not just a Roman tribune and soldier. He was something more. I knew it from the moment I met him." Dagon smiled to himself.

Calliope looked at him, the mixture of joy and sadness as he recalled.

"What struck me was his selflessness, how he led and cared for his men. I had never seen that in a Roman commander before. And then, when you and your brother were born, that selflessness became all-encompassing. He cared even more for you, Phoebus, and your mother. But he also knew fear." Dagon looked at the ground. "It was that fear of any harm coming to you that led him down that dark and bloody road."

Corvus came to land beside Calliope and stood upon the rock beside her.

She reached out to pet his black head and continued. "I was so happy when he returned to Ynis Wytrin, whole again...healed. I never thought such joy was possible."

"We were all relieved," Dagon recalled.

"But then...he left us...for good." Calliope's voice wavered. "And now he's dead. He'll never see his grandchild...he'll never-"

Dagon pulled her close as she wept, feeling his own eyes burning, his throat tighten. "What I do know is that Lucius would not have left if he could avoid it. His pain, though not visible, must have been unimaginably deep for him to leave." Dagon looked to the sky and felt the wind on his face.

Calliope stood and walked a few paces to the end of the rope bridge which swayed in the air above the abyss and crashing sea below.

Dagon stood beside her and together they looked out over the moors to see the beacon fires fighting against the storm. "You are the Dragon's daughter, Calliope. He loved you with all his being. Never forget that."

Night fell fully now on that night of Samhain. The rains had come and gone in waves, though the winds continued to blow fiercely. Despite this, Einion's people persisted in their efforts to keep their fires burning in the deepening dark. Apart from the brave keepers of the bonfires that dotted the coastline and crowned the rocky tors out on the moors, the majority of Einion's people had successfully made it to Din Tagell. In fact, more than had been expected came, driven there by the recent omens across Dumnonia, omens which many claimed could not be held back by the carving of any turnip, no matter how fierce its visage.

Einion's troops huddled around their own bonfires, their keen eyes staring into the windy land beyond. On the fortress rock, masses of people gathered together to warm themselves, the men telling tales and exchanging news, the women and children peeling the harvest's apples, tossing the peels into the flames as offerings to the Gods. Each had a piece of warm bread, meat, and cheese from their lord, and beer to grant them courage over the long night.

With so many fires burning, it was as if the land reflected the shrouded stars above, the way a calm sea does on a starry night, only more violently.

Inside Einion's hall, the people stood shoulder to shoulder, the warm glow of firelight on their faces as they ate, drank, sang, and laughed together in defiance of the threat without. They celebrated that Samhain night almost twenty years ago when Einion, son of Cunnomore had taken back his throne from his uncle, Caradoc. They never forgot their fallen brothers, fathers, sons, and friends who had lost their lives in the battle with Caradoc's men in that very hall, the floor of which was still stained with their blood.

And yet, simmering beneath the surface of jollity which they all displayed, was the deep and abiding fear of Gwyn ap Nudd, the Lord of Annwn, who would lead the Wild Hunt that very night to terrorize and slaughter with his army of dead. They remembered that dark faery lord appearing in their midst after the battle, leaping over the blood-soaked floor, and the fear and awe they felt when the Dragon had chased after him.

Those who had fought and lived now stood there, as they did at the dying of every year, and looked at each other, nodding silently, acknowledging each other's courage and the price paid for each young and smiling face.

Einion especially recalled his night of vengeance as clearly as his own reflection in a clear, calm pool of water on the moor. Now, surrounded by Gwendolyn, Briana, all their children, Dagon, and the last of the Dragon's men, he went over the events of that night in silent pilgrimage. *This is what we fought for,* he thought as he looked out over his people, his family, and his friends.

Then, Einion, son of Cunnomore, Lord of Din Tagell and Dumnonia, stood to address the hall, his father's longsword in his left hand, and a cup filled with wine in his right.

"Silence for Lord Einion!" Arthrek called out from the far end of the hall.

The voices died down and all turned toward the dais where Einion stood from the great stone throne, Gwendolyn beside him.

Calliope turned slowly in her seat at the first table before the dais, Briana and Dagon on either side of her. She felt unwell again, dizzy in the crowded heat of the hall.

"Are you all right?" Briana whispered, noting the sweat beading on Calliope's brow.

"I'm fine," Calliope replied, shaking her head. "Just a little dizzy. It will pass." She looked up at Einion, blinking to try and see him more clearly, focussing on Briana's touch as she gripped her hand.

"My friends!" Einion said. "On this blessed Samhain night, we are gathered here about our fires to celebrate our harvests, and the end of yet another year. Our land...by the grace of the Gods...has thrived once again. And though the storms rage all around us - even now - I know that we are blessed in each other."

There was applause about the hall, and cheers for Lord Einion and his men who had kept them all safe.

Einion put up his hands and everyone fell silent again. "But even as we celebrate, we remember..." His voice wavered for a brief moment, but he recovered quickly. "We remember my father, Cunnomore, and my mother, who lost their lives to my wicked uncle. We remember all those who fell to Caradoc's tyranny. We remember our friends and family who died to help me take back this land...this throne..." He looked down at Calliope then and saw the tears welling in her eyes. "This night, we remember Lucius Pen Dragon, my brother and friend, who aided me at his peril, and who is with us no more..."

All were silent in the hall then as Einion held his cup aloft and they followed suit.

"To the Dead!" the lord of Din Tagell shouted.

"To the Dead!" the people, young and old, echoed.

Einion then stepped down off of the dais to stand among his people. He paused, and turned slowly about, the light from the hearth fire lighting his face as he spoke...

. . .

"To the immortal Gods, to the thinning veil,
    To the ancestors who walk with us tonight.
    By fire and shadow, by earth and star,
    May we be blessed with wisdom and sight."

Calliope pushed herself to her feet then, turning to gaze at Einion and the fire behind him as he continued…

"Raise your cup, let voices ring,
    For those who've gone, for those who will be.
    May Fortuna smile and Vesta's hearth be bright,
    May we be alive next Samhain night!"

Einion raised his cup and tipped some wine onto the fire, and people did likewise about the hall. "To the Dead!" he shouted.

"To the Dead!" they all replied.

Suddenly, a great scream rent the air in the hall and the flames in the hearth rose upward to the rafters.

All turned to the source of the dreadful sound to see Calliope Pen Dragon pointing at the flames.

"He's coming!" she shouted. "The Lord of Annwn!" She then collapsed upon the ground, only just caught by Antiope and Nisien who had been standing nearby.

Einion turned about quickly, his mind racing back to that fateful night. "To arms!" he shouted to his men.

Children began to cry, and women huddled about their young. Men turned on the spot, searching for a threat as thunder erupted outside, its fury felt in the bones of the rock beneath their feet.

Calliope pushed herself to her feet again, a look of terror upon her face as people stepped back from her. "The river gateway!" she shouted, staring into some far off place. "Mother! Brother!… An army!… DEATH HAS COME!"

Einion and Dagon looked to each other. "The river!" they said in unison.

A great howling rent the air outside, and there were screams about the plateau of Din Tagell as people gazed up into the dark sky in terror to see the forms of banshees, those otherworldly scouts, soaring around the edges of fang-like clouds.

"Arthrek!" Einion shouted. "Form up the men! Prepare for battle!"

"Yes, my lord!" Arthrek returned.

Einion then turned to Dagon, Briana, and Gwendolyn. "It must be the Praetorians."

"What do we do?" Briana said.

"We fight!" Dagon growled, turning to Einion. "The Dragons are ready."

Einion looked to where Dagon stood before Brencis, Barna, Akil, Shura, Hipolit, and Taboras. "Raise your banners my friends! Let your dragons roar!"

The Sarmatians immediately went to retrieve the draconaria that had been standing sentry behind the throne. They each touched the dragon statue and then rushed to stand at the doors of the great hall.

"My people!" Einion called out to the fearful crowd about the hall. "We will ride to meet the threat. Keep you fires burning bright and hold fast to your courage!"

"We can fight too, Uncle!" Antiope said to Einion as she and Nisien arrived, their swords drawn.

"I need you here with Gwendolyn to defend the hall and the people. Can you do that?"

"Yes, Uncle!" Antiope said.

Einion smiled at her and looked to his son. "Nisien?"

"I'll die before I let anything happen to our people, Father!" Nisien replied.

Einion was about to answer when he noticed someone missing. He turned to Briana. "Where's Calliope?"

They all looked around, searching the crowd, the hall, but Calliope Pen Dragon was nowhere to be found.

Mama? Phoebus? Hurry! Death is coming!

Calliope's soul cried out as she rushed down the slippery, twisting pathways of the plateau, her hands grasping at the stone walls until she reached the great rope bridge, plunging past the guards toward the other side.

"Hold, lady!" shouted one of the guards who recognized her. "It's not safe!" But she had already disappeared into the darkness.

The bridge was flung violently side to side in the building gale, and Calliope clung to the rough ropes as tightly as she could, her hands bleeding, her feet slipping as she raced across the planks.

Above her, Corvus cawed frantically as he spun in the wind, following her across the dark chasm.

She could feel her mother and brother near, feel the great danger nipping at their heels like a slavering hydra in the darkness. "Mama! Phoebus! NO!" she shouted as she reached the other side.

"Calliope, stop!" Einion, Dagon, Briana and others shouted far behind her as they pursued. "It's not safe!"

No time to waste, she plunged past the guards on the landward side who stood beside their fires, and raced down the dark road toward the stables. There, she paused, exhausted, holding her belly as she panted. She scanned the stables and went to one of the horses she had ridden previously which, like the others, was already saddled as Einion had commanded.

"Lady Calliope! I can't let you go!" said one of Einion's men as he reached up to grab the horse's bridle.

Calliope turned on him. "My mother and brother are out there! At the river gateway! I'm going to them!" she shouted and kicked her horse so hard that it wrenched itself away from the man's grip and shot off like an arrow in the dark, the cold rain lashing her face, her eyes squinting into the blackness ahead.

"Wait! I'll go with you!" the guard called after her, but she was gone.

"Calliope!" Dagon shouted as he and the others arrived with Lord Einion.

"My lord!" the guard said. "She took a horse and rode off! Something about the 'river gateway'!"

Dagon and Einion looked at each other. They knew all too well where she was headed.

"Dragons!" Dagon shouted. "Mount up!" He climbed up onto his horse and raced off with Briana and the Sarmatians, their draconaria screaming into the night. "Sarmatiana!" he shouted.

"With the dragons!" Einion shouted to his men who were now mounted. "To battle!" he cried, kicking his horse and galloping off into the dread night. "Din Tagell!"

XX

AD MORTEM

'To the Death'

"After them!" Aurelius Nemesianus shouted to the men around him as they rode after their quarry, wiping angrily at his mud-spattered face and looking at the centurion, Carcer, beside him. "Three aurea to the first man who takes one of them down!"

"Fine for you to say, Nemesianus, but unlike your Patrician ass, most of us aren't used to sitting atop a horse at speed!"

Nemesianus looked to his left and right to see the Praetorians of the Blood Eagle century spread out across the windswept moor like an army of black ants following a blood trail. But the woman on the white horse far ahead of them was too good a rider, even with the man behind her. And then there was the mist, rain, and wind, all of which hampered their pursuit and which had followed them since the lake where they had found them.

He would never say as much to anyone, for the men were already skittish in that strange landscape, but he was not sure how they had found them. It was as if some god had led them there over the moors to that very spot where they had been hiding.

For months they had been combing Britannia without Fortuna's favour. Several of his and Carcer's men had disappeared without a trace, and on that very day as they rode, several horses had snapped their legs on the rocks or been swallowed by hidden bogs, their riders injured or killed in the falls such that a path of bodies was left in his wake as he rode.

No matter how close they got, nor how fast his men rode, something hampered them at every step. Some unseen force pushed that white horse onward, as if the land itself worked against him and his men in their offensive.

We've still got more than enough men to finish them when we catch them! he thought. *And we will catch them!* He believed it. He could feel it. After so long on the hunt, he was ready to wet his blade and taste dragon's blood.

They pursued that blur of white across the moor the length of that long day. Then, the darkness fell, suddenly and without warning. Lightning crashed over their heads, spooking their horses and scattering his men.

"Damn it to Hades!" Nemesianus cursed into the biting wind and rain. "We can't let them make it to that fucking fortress!" He recalled the grim elation he had felt when Dis had appeared at Isca Dumnoniorum, missing an ear and wounded in the thigh and one arm, to say that he had found the Dragon's wife. But now, he felt that dark joy slipping away, and so he kicked his horse harder and faster in a suicidal ride across the moor as fires seemed to explode from the peaks of surrounding hills. "Ride on! Faster!" he shouted at the Praetorians under his command. "Any man who stops, is dead! And someone kill that wolf!"

At the command, Carcer, Tarchon, Rhesus, Segundo, Manus and the others managed to form up around him as they rode on into the darkness, their sights set on the speeding white form of the horse and two riders racing away from them in the distance.

"You can't escape, Pen Dragon!" Nemesianus screamed. "Death is coming for you!"

"Death is coming for you!" the muted voice shouted in the dark far behind them, among the clatter of weapons and thunder of horses' hooves.

"They're still on us!" Phoebus said to Adara as she drove Aegis deftly on over the moor, northwest toward Din Tagell. "Remus, come!" Phoebus shouted to the wolf who had been following the entirety of the day, taking out the occasional horse and rider who got too close.

The wolf leaned into his run, his tongue lolling out the side of his bloody jaws.

Exhaustion clawed at all of them like Furies threatening to overwhelm them at any moment.

Adara had no idea how Aegis was able to pick his way over that landscape of rock and bog so quickly, but she was grateful for it, even as she expected them to be slammed to the ground at any moment. Even so, the Praetorians behind them were fast and, she felt certain, would not give any quarter when they inevitably caught up with them.

When the night crashed upon them, the ride became more treacherous and, as fires burst to life across the moor, a shrieking could be heard in the sky above that sent a chill through Adara and Phoebus.

"What was that?" Phoebus asked.

"Don't listen to them!" Adara shouted, perceiving black, winged shapes on the verges of the storm clouds above.

When they burst onto the open grassland between two tors, Adara lost her sense of direction. In the lightning that flashed around them, a long line of standing stones glittered like silver-specked sand on a moonlit beach.

"Look!" Phoebus pointed a short distance away to where the ethereal form of a dappled horse raced ahead, leading them down an ancient avenue that had been hidden to them. "It's Lunaris!"

Adara leaned forward, squinting in the rain to see the ghostly form like a beacon of light in the dark. She kneed Aegis after him. *Epona, guide us to safety!* she prayed, grateful for the horse's shade in that moment.

Then, suddenly, out of the darkness, two Praetorians appeared to either side, their spears extended, aiming to stab Aegis' flanks and down them.

"Faster!" Phoebus shouted to Adara as he drew his gladius and turned to parry a spear thrust. He grabbed hold of the Praetorian's spear shaft and was suddenly wrenched from off Aegis' back.

"Phoebus!" Adara shouted as she turned Aegis, her sword blade flashing in the dark.

Phoebus rolled away from the stomping hooves of the Praetorian's horse and stabbed upward, taking the beast in the neck and sending its rider tumbling backward.

The second Praetorian closed in quickly, but his horse veered suddenly when Remus growled and tore at its leg. The rider fell near to Phoebus and was about to slash at him when Adara's sword sang through the air and took off his head.

"Quick! Get back on!" she shouted.

Phoebus jumped up onto Aegis once again and then they were off, the other Praetorians closing more quickly now. "Remus! Come!" he called, and the wolf followed, fresh blood upon his snarling muzzle.

Adara kneed Aegis, the horse's lungs gulping at air, his nostrils flailing desperately as he instinctively followed the otherworldly horse before him. They reached a large stone circle and, suddenly, Lunaris disappeared as quickly as he had appeared, but not before lightning glimmered on a lake to their right and the land rose upward. "Keep going, Aegis!" Adara shouted as she focussed on the faint track that led northwestward.

The lightning ceased for a few moments and, behind them, the screams of Praetorian riders crashing into the lake could be heard.

In the midst of flashes of lightning above, and the raging bonfires around, a ringing began in Phoebus and Adara's ears, louder than the thunder of Aegis' hooves. The air began to waver before their very eyes in odd shades of green, and the wind grew more violent, taking on a life of its own. And on that wind, there was an incessant howling of thousands punctuated only by the sound of a dread horn that struck terror into their hearts.

"It's the Lord of Annwn's hunt!" Phoebus shouted as he held fast to Adara. "He's coming for us!"

Gods help us! Adara prayed, unable to stem the tears that ran from her eyes as they pressed on.

Soon, a line of trees appeared in the green darkness, the trickle of water unnaturally loud in their ears.

Adara made for the trees, Aegis' pace slowing, even as his breathing was laboured. "He can't go on!" she said, her voice desperate as she dismounted. "We can't make it to Din Tagell!"

Phoebus could tell his mother was on the verge of tears, but that she would not give up. *I won't let anything happen to her!* he told himself, reaching out to touch Remus' soaking coat beside him in reassurance.

The sound of the Praetorian horses ranging over the moor sounded closer and closer.

Phoebus looked about. "It sounds like we've reached the river," he said, vaguely remembering one from before. "Maybe we can slow them."

Adara pat Aegis and drew her sword again. "Hurry!" she said and they walked along the edge of the forest of oak, ash and beech until they found a path in that strange light that seemed to be faintly suffusing the world around them.

"It's too steep here!" Phoebus said as he peered over the thicket of hazel and holly. "Aegis won't make it."

Adara turned and looked behind, still hearing the oncoming Praetorians, their voices angry and enraged, out for blood. Now, was when the fear threatened to take hold.

But she held fast, for her son, for her daughter who was safe in Din Tagell.

Adara quickly unfastened Aegis' saddle and let it fall to the ground. "Go, boy! Run!" she said to the horse. "Thank you," she said, laying her hand upon his sweating, heaving bulk. "Get away from here!" she said, slapping his rump.

Aegis looked back and made his way up the river, along the narrow, tangled path that ran along the top of the small gully.

When he was gone, Adara turned to Phoebus and Remus. "Let's get across to the other side!"

They drew their swords and hacked their way through the thick and thorny underbrush to clamber down the steep slope of rock and root until they splashed into the riverbed below.

The water rushed about their ankles, its current strangely warm. The walls of the gully rose up steeply to either side. At their feet, the sand and rock seemed to sparkle, lit by some unseen source of light, and on the embankments, the trees shivered and swayed opposite to the direction of the howling wind.

"What is this place?" Phoebus said, but even as the question was upon his lips, there was the thud of a bowstring and Phoebus was knocked sideways into the rushing water. "Aaah!" he shouted.

"They're here!" a man's voice called out.

Remus shot off and a moment later was tearing at the flesh of the Praetorian who had loosed the arrow.

"Phoebus!" Adara said, kneeling beside him to see where the arrow had grazed his left shoulder, his blood leaching into the river water.

"I'm all right," he said with a grunt, his right hand grasping for his sword which he had dropped.

Adara looked her son in the eyes as the Praetorian voices closed in.

"There's no escape, Pen Dragon!" the voice of the Praetorian leader called out from beyond the trees. "Your family must surrender! The Emperor demands it! *I* demand it!"

They were hacking at the undergrowth now, the sound of dozens of blades cutting through to them.

"Mama?" Phoebus said. "You go. Get to Calliope. Remus and I will hold them off."

Adara shook her head. "I'm not leaving you!" *Perhaps this is where it ends?* "If we're to die here, it will be with these swords in our hands, and Calliope safe!"

Phoebus nodded and she helped him up.

"Mama?" a voice called out from high on the other embankment of the river. "Phoebus!"

A crow cawed in the trees above and they both turned and looked up to see the silhouette of a cloaked figure climbing down to them.

"I knew you were here!" Calliope Pen Dragon said, her voice reaching out to them, hunching over when she reached the riverbed.

"Calliope!" Adara cried, rushing to her daughter's side. "My girl what are you doing-" Adara stopped when she saw Calliope holding her belly. "By the Gods!"

"I could sense you both coming!" Calliope said, falling into her mother's loving embrace. "Death is here! The Lord of Annwn is almost abroad!"

"What?" Phoebus said, his eyes widening at the sight of her. "Calliope, the Praetorians are upon us!" Phoebus scanned around desperately for a way up the other side. "Quickly, you have to get out of here!"

"NO!" Calliope cried. "I'm not leaving you!"

"There they are!" a man shouted from the other side.

They looked up to see several black forms lining the opposite embankment, their gladii and pila points glinting in the greenish light, all pointed toward them.

Remus stepped in front of Phoebus and growled.

From among the Praetorians, one man stepped to the front, his high, black crest bristling like the hackles of an angry boar. "You cannot escape, Adara Pen Dragon!" he said. "You've given us quite a chase, but your time is up. This is where it ends."

"Where what ends?" Phoebus shouted back.

Aurelius Nemesianus laughed. "Why, your lives of course." He looked to the men to either side and they began to spread out and down into the riverbed. "You didn't really think you could escape us, did you?"

"We've done nothing wrong!" Calliope said, just as Corvus landed upon her shoulder.

Nemesianus climbed down slowly, a smile upon his face as he anticipated the coming moments. It was these moments before a kill that he had always relished, the sudden impact and finality of his actions making him feel all-powerful, undefeatable.

"Let my mother and sister go, Praetorian. If you have any honour, and want the Gods to spare you, you will take me and let them go."

"Phoebus, no!" Calliope shouted.

"Do you think I care about honour?" Nemesianus landed in the water before Phoebus and spat. His gladius was drawn, pointed at all of them. "I was supposed to bring you back to Rome, but as the Dragon is dead, and I'm tired of chasing you all over Britannia, I think I'll just kill you all here and now and be done with it! Your heads will be enough for the Augusta."

Other Praetorians lined up to either side of Nemesianus then, and upon the embankment behind him.

Nemesianus looked to his side where one Praetorian with a bandaged head grumbled and eyed Adara. "Before we kill you, though, I think I'll let Dis here play with your mother, boy. He owes her. And maybe we'll have some fun with your pregnant sister too. Do you want to watch? Or do you want to die first?"

The Praetorians' laughter echoed in the gully, even as the wind picked up and the trees pulled violently from side to side.

In that moment, a great thunder rent the air, and the ground around them began to shake.

Nemesianus, Dis and the others stared at Phoebus, Adara, and Calliope.

"Time to die!" Nemesianus said suddenly as he rushed in.

But Phoebus was fast, and his blade parried the Praetorian's attack.

There was the whistle of an arrow and suddenly, Dis fell sideways, a shaft through his face as he twitched in the water.

"Sarmatiana!" Dagon's battle cry came from the top of the embankment behind Phoebus, Adara, and Calliope and suddenly, a hail of arrows and spears filled the air above, soaring from both sides, along with the screams of men and the fall of bodies from both heights.

"Din Tagell!" came the other cry as Lord Einion and his men arrived, charging from up river to engage the Praetorians.

Chaos suddenly reigned in the gully and all along the river as men and horses screamed, swords clashed, and barbed shafts tore into flesh.

"Phoebus!" Dagon cried out as one of Nemesianus' men bore down on them.

Phoebus parried wildly, and pushed the man back enough for Remus to sink his jaws into his groin.

Adara turned to shield Calliope beside her where another Praetorian emerged, his blade seeking their deaths. As she fought him, another came from Calliope's other side, ready to swing but was stopped by Corvus who had taken flight and was pecking at the man's eyes, slowed enough for Brencis to reach them in time and slay him.

Men were everywhere, fighting in the water, on the embankments, and on horseback in the riverbed, and their blood was offered up to the dying night.

More Praetorians arrived, late in their flight across the moor, and joined the rest of the Blood Eagles in the fray, pushing back the men of Din Tagell who fought alongside the dragon warriors in their leather and scale armour.

Adara cried out as a blade found her side and knocked her against the rock face of the gully beside Calliope.

The Praetorian who had hit her rushed in to finish her but was knocked sideways by Aegis who had suddenly appeared and was rearing, his forelegs kicking out to crush the man's skull in.

A flight of arrows pounded into the horse's side and neck and Aegis screamed, rearing before falling hard into the water.

"Aegis, no!" Adara cried, before being thrown sideways by another man who tried to get at Calliope.

"Down, lady!" Arthrek shouted to Calliope as he jumped from the heights of the embankment onto the attacker, his blade jammed through his neck, only to be kicked by another Praetorian whom Phoebus rushed in to stab.

Phoebus helped up Arthrek and they formed up in front of Adara and Calliope.

Dagon and Briana joined them, their longswords slashing at the growing number of Praetorians closing in.

Remus tore at many of the enemy, wreaking terror along their lines, but even he could not overwhelm them and, as he tore out the neck of one, he suddenly cried out as a spear from Nemesianus' hand planted itself into his hind leg, taking the beast down.

"Remus, no!" Phoebus shouted, rushing forward to take Nemesianus when someone pulled him back.

"Stop, Phoebus! There are too many!" Einion shouted as he held the younger man fast.

Nemesianus gave them a blood-spattered grin before driving his gladius into Remus' neck, killing the wolf instantly.

"For the Dragon!" Dagon shouted to his men, and Brencis, Barna, Akil, Shura, Magar, Boas, and Deva formed up with their lord, standing over the bodies of Hipolit, Taboras, and Dima who lay dead at their feet.

Somehow, the Praetorians had formed up too and faced Einion and Dagon's forces, pressing in to cave the flanks and push them back against the gully wall, close to crushing the Dragon's family behind them.

The clang of steel was deafening as the fight along the front became more desperate.

"Stand behind us, Calliope!" Briana shouted as she pressed shoulder to shoulder with Adara and Phoebus.

Adara met her gaze and there saw the regret and resignation of imminent death. "I'm glad to die with you, my friend," Adara said, pressing her forehead to Briana's. "I'm so sorry."

"Don't be," Briana said.

The battle line in front exploded in blood and the battle cries of the Sarmatian and Dumnonian warriors.

In the chaos, they did not see Calliope Pen Dragon step forward to the front of the line, the trembling, bloody water about her legs as she raised her arms to the sky.

Aurelius Nemesianus smiled and stepped forward, his black gladius raised high above his head to slay her. Yet, something gave him pause.

The trees above them began to crack like thunder, and the water all about them began to boil.

Calliope, tears streaming from her closed eyes, held her arms aloft as if welcoming death.

"NO!" Adara shouted, trying to push her way to her daughter with Phoebus and Briana beside her.

"DEATH IS HERE!" Calliope shouted, her voice a powerful echo in the gully, louder than the wind and rushing waters.

The earth began to shake, and the air filled with a great, green and blinding light from out of a great opening downriver. The sound of a thunderous horn blasted from the green maw of that opening and Aurelius Nemesianus turned from the pregnant girl before him to look upon it.

The scream that exploded from the Roman tore his throat, his blinded eyes wide in terror as a deafening roar and wail of thousands filled the air.

XXI

DOMINUS ANNWNENSIS

'The Lord of Annwn'

The dead poured from the blinding light of that broken veil, driven on by the sound of a dread hunting horn that pierced the ear and shattered the courage of the living like iron against glass. Such a gale rushed from the gateway that it knocked men off of their feet and pushed them through the river water as they clawed at the rocks. All along the embankments, the trees and forest scrub suddenly burst into green flames that set the crystalline sand of the riverbed aglow.

Hardened men screamed like children in a nightmare in the dead of night, as a thousand shades charged on ghostly mounts to tear into the Praetorian ranks with gnashing teeth and jagged, slashing swords. The Romans screamed in terror as their bodies were torn asunder, burned, and broken to pieces, their eyes still seeing even as their heads tumbled into the roiling river water to be engulfed in the ensuing chaos.

The men of Din Tagell and Sarmatia watched the absolute slaughter, swords up in shaking arms, their tools of war useless, as in a dream when one is helpless.

Calliope Pen Dragon walked through the chaos toward the light, and her brother and mother ran to shield her.

"NO!" Briana shouted to them in terror, on her knees beside Dagon as the dead rushed all about them.

Seeing them go, Aurelius Nemesianus ripped his helmet from his head and ran after them, his men being massacred all around him. "Die Dragons!" he yelled as he made to slay at least one of the Dragon's family where they huddled together screaming, their gleaming swords raised to meet the crazed Praetorian's attack.

It was then that an explosion of sunlight erupted from the gateway, a brilliant, blinding light that burst painfully in mortal vision.

A roar louder than any creation of fearful dreams erupted from that light and, with a great rush of wind and fire, Aurelius Nemesianus was set alight, his body cloven in two by the flash of an otherworldly blade that cut like adamant through water.

ALL HAIL AND FEAR THE LORD OF ANNWN! the voices of the dead hissed in every living man and woman's ears in that moment.

Adara, Calliope, Phoebus, Einion, Briana, Dagon and all others who yet drew breath fell to their knees in the water to await death as they clasped hands and weapons at the end of all things...

But Death was not there for the good, the honourable, and innocent.

The army of the dead, their screams, their bloody howling faded out into the night as they ranged over the countryside, about the Samhain fires across the land, to wreak terror on the moors, fields, and mountains for the time permitted to them.

In the green glow of the river, however, the living, still trembling, slowly opened their eyes.

Einion and Dagon stood slowly and stepped forward, ready to meet Gwyn ap Nudd once more, to slay or be slain. But as they stood to defend their friends and family, they froze as though the gorgon, Medusa, stared them in the eyes.

Coming toward them all from down the river was a massive figure upon a brilliant, white, winged stallion. The horse reared and spread its wings wide.

The rider, high atop its back, glowed in the darkness like a morning sun.

But he said nothing.

Slowly, each of them stood and stared, and the fear that had such a hold of them moments before suddenly fell away in that heavenly light.

Other riders appeared behind the winged horse, the warrior dead who had ridden out with their lord. Their bodies glowed with images of gryphons, and boar, horses and serpents. And there were dragons...many dragons.

"It...it can't be," Dagon said, his eyes burning. "Hippogriff? Lenya?" His throat caught. "Barta?"

But there was no answer, only the silent recognition and returned gazes of the dead whose unblinking eyes looked upon the mortals before them, their memories and emotions hidden behind an unseen veil.

Adara, Phoebus, and Calliope stood up, their weapons lowered now, limp at their sides.

Einion, Briana, Dagon and the gathered warriors rushed to stand with them, all of them struggling to see, to comprehend for the tears in all of their eyes, for the blinding light.

The winged stallion stepped in front of all the forces of the dead, over the corpses of the slain Praetorians, to tower over them all.

The rider's sword was still drawn, the blood of the Praetorians running down it.

They shielded their eyes from the light, trying to look more closely.

"The sword…" Phoebus muttered. "I know that sword!"

Everyone froze, and it was then that the light began to fade in intensity and spread about the gully like soft morning sunshine across a field.

"Baba?" Calliope said suddenly, stepping in front of her brother, her hands protectively around her belly. "Is it really you?" her voice wavered.

The winged stallion knelt then, and his rider slid down from off his broad back, the water growing still at his touch. Despite the blood, his skin was flawless and godlike, his body powerful. He wore a tunica and bracae of brilliant white that was spattered with the enemy's blood. The sleeves and hem were bordered with glowing, blue images of horses, eagles, and dragons that appeared to move. But true recognition dawned when, beneath the collar of the tunica, the image of the dragon radiated upon his muscled chest.

And then, he smiled. It was in that moment that they could all see the stars whirling in his eyes.

"Yes, my girl," he said to Calliope, with a voice like music after an endlessly silent exile. "It's me." He sheathed his sword at his back and took his daughter and son into his arms. "I'm here."

Phoebus and Calliope clung firmly to their father, hoping with all their hearts that it was not a dream, but that somehow, the Gods had blessed them with a new reality.

And yet, there was something different, beautiful and terrible, about that moment, for the dead massed behind him, awaited him, honoured him.

"Lu…Lucius?" Adara said, one hand to her mouth, the other, trembling, reaching out to him. "It can't be. You…you were dead." She could not stop the tears that blurred her vision then, could not stopper the storm of emotions that threatened to overwhelm her.

"I could not come…until now. I tried," he said, stepping toward her. "You have been in my heart…always." He did not approach her then, but waited for her to come of her own free will.

Adara stood staring at him for a few moments, searching for the man she had loved in those star-clad eyes, the man who had been the source of her greatest pain but, more so, of her greatest joys and deepest, truest love from the moment they had met all those years ago.

He blinked slowly and, for the briefest of moments, there were tears in his own eyes as he looked upon her.

"My love!" Adara said as she embraced him. In that moment, she felt all the pent up pain and heartache she had been harbouring fall away to nothing, like blood in the runaway water.

He wrapped his arms about her and held her tightly, all others looking on in bewilderment, awe, and incredulity. "How I have missed you."

"My love…" Adara said again, suddenly afraid the moment would not last. "Please don't leave us again."

He shook his head. "I will not. But I cannot remain here."

She looked confused.

But Lucius turned from her and his children and approached the mortals behind them, his friends. He looked upon Einion, Dagon, Briana and the warriors gathered about them. "Thank you for protecting my family."

They stood in stunned silence, taking in the sight of the man they had once known, an injured man, an infinitely changed man who had returned to them in their hour of need.

It was Dagon who stepped forward. "Anguis? Is it really you?"

Lucius smiled. "Yes…and no, my friend."

"Where have you been all these years?" Briana asked.

He smiled and looked to the sky and stars above, the distant sun. "There are many mysteries in this world and the next that are beyond our understanding… Some things cannot, and should not, be explained." He looked back at them, familiar and yet impossibly distant. "Know only that I am with you, always. *We* are with you." He looked back to the lurking dead, those who had fought with them and against them in life. "We are connected by a heroic past, and a hopeful future."

Einion stepped forward. "How do we go on, Lucius Pen Dragon?"

Lucius looked him in the eyes. "By protecting the land and its people in this world…while I do so in the other." He looked beyond them to the shimmering green gateway in the river.

"You can't leave us again!" Adara said behind him. "Lucius, you can't leave *me* again!" She was close to weeping, her strength nearly fully sapped.

"No. I cannot. I will not," he said with a strange calm. "You may come with me, if you so choose." He looked at his wife and children.

"Where?" Phoebus asked, his eyes straying to the light.

"Into Annwn."

"I don't want to die, Baba!" Phoebus said.

But his father shook his head. "It is not death, my son. It is a beginning."

Just then, Corvus alighted upon Lucius' shoulder.

"Corvus?" Calliope said, confused for a moment, but then filled with understanding as her father smiled. But that smile faded as he turned to look sadly upon the fallen forms of Aegis and Remus in the bloody river water.

Adara and Phoebus followed his gaze, and they too understood, felt the sadness of loss.

In the distance then, the sound of wind and of horses' hooves erupted, and the screams of the dead and dying rose and faded.

Lucius turned to the dead behind him and spoke. "The Hunt is nearing its end, as is the long, dark night. Gather our fallen brothers, and bring them."

The dead moved slowly to pick up the bodies of Hipolit, Taboras, Dima and others while the living looked on.

"What will you do with them?" Dagon asked.

"They will *be*," Lucius replied as he watched the dead file back into Annwn. He looked up and listened, a calm expression upon his face that gave them all a measure of peace in their hearts on that dread night. He then held out his hand to Adara and, after a moment, she took it in hers.

"Adara?" Briana said, shaking her head and stepping toward her, tears running down her blood-stained cheeks.

But Adara turned to her with joy upon her face. "I'll be all right. All is as it should be," she said. "You have my love, all of you." She looked at Briana, Dagon, and Einion.

Phoebus and Calliope began to follow their parents, their steps slow and reluctant as they walked through the water after them, followed by the winged stallion.

"Lucius Pen Dragon!" Dagon said loudly as he stepped forward.

Lucius, still glowing, turned to his old friend.

"We'll join you again, in time, and drink to that day in the desert when we first met."

Lucius smiled and placed his hand upon his chest. *Yes, my friend. But for now, live…*

And Dagon heard him.

Lucius turned to his children, Adara standing beside him.

Phoebus and Calliope stood in the space between their parents and their friends who had risked their lives for them.

Adara looked at her children and they looked back at her. She smiled and nodded. "It's all right." And she seemed herself again, joyful, caring, and filled with light.

Phoebus and Calliope held hands and looked to each other.

"The world has changed, Phoebus," Calliope said, one hand upon her belly.

"Our friends are not safe with us around," Phoebus added. "Rome will never stop." He looked at the bodies of the dead Praetorians surrounding Remus.

Calliope squeezed her brother's hands and then rushed to hug Briana. "Thank you!"

Tears in her eyes, Briana held her tightly, and Dagon too.

"There is something of the Gods' devising drawing us into that light. We will be safer there," Calliope said, the dragon torc about her neck beginning to glow strangely.

"May the Gods watch over you, always," Briana said with love in her heart as she gripped Dagon's hand tightly for courage.

Phoebus and Calliope looked upon them all and, after a moment, tore themselves away to join hands with their parents.

As the winged stallion went past them into the otherworldly gateway, followed by Corvus who took flight from Lucius' shoulder, Lucius turned to his wife and children.

"Don't be afraid…" he said.

And together, they walked into the light, reunited at last.

Cumae, A.D. 230

The sky was especially blue that day, a late spring blue that filled the eyes with the promise of hotter days ahead. The sea that lay spread out like a jewelled carpet before the coast of Cumae sparkled, the waves laughing as they played upon the sandy shoreline like children in the summer sun.

Cassius Dio sat at a broad table in the tablinum of his sprawling villa. He faced the open terrace where a fire burned in a large, bronze tripod that looked out over the olive and citrus groves to the acropolis of Cumae, the temple of Apollo, and the Sibyl's cave.

"Such a place…" Dio muttered to himself. "It will be difficult to leave in some ways, Ampyx," he said to his freedman who was busy packing scrolls in a back corner of the room.

"Yes, Dominus." Ampyx looked at his master's hunched back where he leaned on the marble of his table, hands on his head. The last scroll of his *Roman History* lay spread out before him, awaiting the final words. Over meals, they had discussed the best way to end it, if one even could 'end' the history of a place that was, to some, eternal. He looked at Dio's feet where they had come off of the pillow he rested them upon, and then went to adjust them for his master. The winter had been especially bad on his health. "Dominus, may I?" Ampyx asked as he knelt beside him.

"Oh, ah, yes. Thank you, Ampyx," Dio replied somewhat absently, allowing his feet to be lifted back onto the pillow. "Please bring me some wine."

"Right away, Dominus," Ampyx said as he also adjusted the pillows behind his master's back. "I shall return."

Dio nodded and continued to stare outside. He closed his eyes and inhaled deeply of the scent of the lemon blossoms that rode the warm air into the tablinum. It was a lovely, comforting smell, and it helped to calm his mind as he tried to focus on his work.

"So near the end," he said as he tore his eyes from the groves and the sea beyond to look at the papyrus before him. *A forced end…sadly…* he thought, with not a little regret. But he knew the truth of it, for just as he knew spring was about to give way to summer, autumn, and then winter, he also knew that his own time upon that mortal plane was nearing its end. He could feel it, and could almost see it. *Perhaps that is the price of living in this place of prophecy where Aeneas went into Hades?*

Ampyx returned with a silver pitcher of watered wine and a silver cup. "Here you are, Dominus. This is the last of the wine, which we have not yet packed, that is." He poured and the splashing sound was pleasant to the ear.

"Thank you, Ampyx," Dio said. "You may take a rest from packing. I should like to be alone for a while."

"As you like, Dominus," Ampyx replied. "I'll be in the corridor if you need anything."

"Good lad," Dio replied without looking up.

He closed his eyes again and felt the sea breeze upon his face. He would soon be back in Bithynia, his homeland, to end his days where his life began. His eyes shot wide again. "No more distractions, Dio!" he chided himself. "Focus."

He took a sip of the wine Ampyx had poured, dipped his bronze stylus into the ink pot, and began to write…

But as the malcontents evinced displeasure at this, the Emperor became afraid that they might kill me if they saw me in the insignia of my office, and so he bade me spend the period of my consulship in Italy, somewhere outside of Rome. And thus later I came both to Rome and to Campania to visit him, and spent a few days in his company, during which the soldiers saw me without offering to do me any harm; then, having asked to be excused because of the ailment of my feet…

Dio stopped writing and thought on what a kindness it was for the Emperor to have sent him away. Alexander had warned and protected him when few others would, and for that Dio was grateful. As a result, he would be able to end his life peacefully, on his own terms, not ignominiously with a knife in the back.

Peace is a rare luxury these days, he reminded himself. And he knew Alexander's peace would not last, for the Sassanians, under Artaxerxes of Parthia, were making noise again. War was brewing in the east. "And so the wheel of war and violence continues to turn…" Dio said softly, such that it was almost a whisper. *Poor Alexander…*

There was a knock upon the tablinum door.

"What is it?" Dio called.

Ampyx entered, a distraught look upon his face. "Forgive me, Dominus. But a messenger just arrived from Rome with a letter from the Augusta."

Dio half-turned to look at Ampyx. "Well, give it here then!" He worried immediately. *Have I tempted fate by my gratitude?* he wondered as he broke the seal and unfurled the missive. "Leave me."

"Yes, Dominus," Ampyx said, turning and going out once more.

When he was gone, Dio looked down at the scroll and began to read…

To Senator Cassius Dio

From Augusta Julia Mamaea,

I trust that this finds you well, Senator. I shall be brief.

In short, our mission to find Metellus has failed. All of the Praetorians who went with Aurelius Nemesianus have disappeared. There is no word of the Dragon, his surviving family, or his men, and so the Emperor, my son, is left unprotected. You need not worry about finding men to guard him. I shall do that.

I do wonder if you did all that you could to find Metellus. Admittedly, at times, I have wondered about your loyalties, Dio, about where you believe yours should lie. I was contemplating your death upon receiving news of the failed mission to eliminate the Dragon and his kin, but Alexander intervened on your behalf and assured me that you have always been a loyal servant of Rome.

And so, you may live out your days. I hope you will make offerings and prayers to the Gods for Alexander's safety in the days to come, for he has risked much for you.

Farewell, Senator.

Julia Avita Mamaea

.   .   .

Dio set the scroll slowly upon the table where it curled quickly in upon itself. He stared at it, the way a man walking looks back to see an asp he has nearly trod on.

"She didn't even try to hide the fact that she *did* send assassins." He smiled to himself. *I was right. My warning got through.* The wave of relief he felt was overwhelming and made him sigh aloud. He took another, longer sip of the wine which, somehow, tasted sweeter than before. Though he felt more tired and ill than ever, he was indeed comforted by the fact that Lucius' family, his men and, perhaps, Lucius himself, yet lived. Dio had always known they had been blessed by the Gods.

He looked toward the acropolis of Cumae again, and then down at his work. He had been writing his history for much of his life. *I pray that it will keep the truth alive.*

He thought of Lucius and his family again, his relief still palpable. "But some truths must remain hidden."

With a renewed sense of purpose, Cassius Dio turned back to his work and re-read what he had last written.

"Pfft! I cannot end writing about my feet!" he laughed, shaking his head. "Think, Cassius. Think!"

And then he remembered a dream he had had, not long ago. He looked out to the Sibyl's cave and the sea as he searched his memory for it it. "Yes!" he said loudly, quickly dipping the stylus in the ink pot again and writing…

…I set out for home, with the intention of spending all the rest of my life in my native land, as, indeed, the Heavenly Power revealed to me most clearly when I was already in Bithynia. For once in a dream I thought I was commanded by it to write at the close of my work these verses:

"Hector anon did Zeus lead forth out of range of the missiles,
Out of the dust and the slaying of men and the blood and the uproar."

With those last words written, Dio set down his stylus in its tray, and leaned heavily back in his cushioned chair. "And so ends my History," he said, a lump in his throat. "After so long...it is done."

He looked once more at the Augusta's curled message. There was much to be grateful for that day...his work...his life...and the lives of his friends.

Gods grant that I have managed some good in this life, he thought.

Dio then pushed himself painfully to his feet and stood, leaning upon the cold marble of the table. The sea breeze flapped his loose tunica about him as he rounded the table and opened the cedar box of sandal-wood incense. Choosing the largest chunk, he limped over to the tripod, placed the incense in the flames and raised his palms to the sky.

"Far-Shooting Apollo... I thank you for guiding me through my History over the years of my life... I am filled with gratitude... I also pray to you for the protection of Lucius Metellus Anguis...Lucius Pen Dragon...and his family. Wherever they are, may they be safe, vibrant, and joyous, and may they have the long fought-for peace that they are so deserving of..."

Dio did not know why, but he felt tears form at the rims of his eyelids. *I have not known suffering as they have,* he thought, rebelling against the pain in his feet and legs as he stood there. He then went back to the table, picked up Julia Mamaea's letter, and returned to the tripod where the smoke of his offering rose up into the sky.

He could not help but smile as he dropped the missive into the flames. "A fitting offering," he said to himself, "and the end of my office."

He then limped over to a nearby couch on the terrace and reclined to look out at the sun and sea.

Had I the time, he told himself, *I think I might have written a history of Rome's dragons. But that is not my story to tell.* "Gods...but I do believe in dragons..."

THE END

Thank you for reading!

Did you enjoy *The Hearts of Heroes*? Here is what you can do next.

If you enjoyed this adventure with the Pen Dragon family, please post a short review on the web page where you purchased the book or on the Eagles and Dragons Publishing website.

Reviews are a wonderful way for new readers to find this series of books and your help in spreading the word is greatly appreciated.

If you would like to find out what happened to Lucius in Annwn, the story continues in Book VIII, *The Lord of Annwn*. More Eagles and Dragons series novels will be coming soon, so be sure to sign-up for e-mail updates at:

http://eaglesanddragonspublishing.com/newsletter-join-the-legions/

Newsletter subscribers get a FREE BOOK, and first access to new releases, special offers, and much more!

To read more about the history, people and places featured in this book, check out *The World of The Hearts of Heroes* blog series at the link below:

https://eaglesanddragonspublishing.com/the-world-of-the-hearts-of-heroes/

AUTHOR'S NOTE

I started writing the Eagles and Dragons series over twenty-five years ago in the twilight days of 1999. As we were getting ready to bid farewell to the twentieth century, I typed away in the confines of my graduate residence room at St. Andrew's University in Scotland. It all developed slowly, the story and characters of what, unbeknownst to me, would become an epic family saga set in the Roman Empire. I wrote without a thought for the awards, 'bestseller' labels, or the wide appeal the series would eventually have among both male and female readers, lovers of ancient history and mythology.

I simply felt compelled to write a story about a young, idealistic warrior from an ancient, once-powerful family.

After countless drafts and input from various people over the years, the first book, *Children of Apollo*, was eventually released in 2012. That seems like a very long time ago now.

The family of Lucius Metellus Anguis (who would later become 'Lucius Pen Dragon') became my family. Over the years, as I added more books to the series, we grew up together, suffered together, toiled together, and experienced both victory and defeat together. When I finished the sixth book, *The Blood Road*, about five years ago, there was a haunting sense of finality about it, a lingering sadness. Some of my readers wrote to check if Lucius was truly dead, if that was the end, the final book.

In my heart, I didn't want it to be the final book. How could I say goodbye to my 'other family'? In reality, however, I felt that I had given everything I had to *The Blood Road*, and so I wondered whether my readers' instincts were correct. Perhaps it was the last Eagles and Dragons series novel? After all, I had many other books I wanted to write, stories to tell.

I have told those other stories, and continue to do so.

But, as Delphina reads in this new novel "we are addicted to nostalgia", and I fully admit to that when it comes to myself. It is one of the perils of loving history so much.

In the years after *The Blood Road*, I thought often about the Metelli (aka the Pen Dragons). I wondered how the rest of the characters were doing after Lucius' disappearance. How were they coping with the loss?

What did that sense of emptiness drive them to do? I started to plot out possible fictional storylines that could be woven into the historical timeline of the period. After a short time, the plot for *The Hearts of Heroes* emerged, born out of my nostalgia for the world and characters of the Eagles and Dragons series.

Historically-speaking, *The Hearts of Heroes* takes place more than ten years after the events at the end of *The Blood Road* when Caracalla was murdered and his mother, Julia Domna, committed suicide. Macrinus, Caracalla's Praetorian Prefect, who conspired to murder Caracalla, ruled for just a year with his son, Diadumenian. Macrinus was subsequently defeated by the forces of Julia Maesa, Julia Domna's sister, at the Battle of Antioch in A.D. 218. Julia Maesa's grandson, Elagabalus, was proclaimed Emperor and ruled from A.D. 218 to 222. His rule was marked by religious controversy and sexual debauchery that might be compared to the time of Caligula. In fact, Elagabalus was so bad, so detrimental to the Empire that Severus had built, that his own grandmother had him and his mother, Julia Soaemias, murdered by the Praetorian Guard. Luckily for the Empire, the 'false-Antoninus', as Cassius Dio called him, was no more.

And so, Alexander Severus, the son of Julia Mamaea, Julia Maesa's other daughter, was set upon the imperial throne in A.D. 222 at the age of fourteen. Things were looking up for the Empire once more.

I first came across the name of Alexander Severus when I saw the triumphal arch dedicated to him in the ruins of Thugga, Tunisia, that is, Roman Thysdrus.

Alexander Severus appears to have been the opposite of his older cousin, Elagabalus, and if he turned out to be a 'good' man, it was because his mother who, according to the historian, Herodian, "kept Alexander from taking part in activities so disgraceful and unworthy of an emperor. Privately, she summoned teachers of every subject and had her son trained in the lessons of self-discipline; since he devoted himself to wrestling and to physical exercise as well, he was, by his mother's efforts, educated according to both the Greek and Roman systems."

Julia Mamaea was a lioness when it came to her son, protecting him with all of her power, and her gold, with which she was indeed obsessed! She kept the troops and Praetorians loyal by paying them with what she took from nobles whom she deemed to be her enemies. Mamaea and her son ruled the Empire until A.D. 235 and, with their subsequent murder, the dynasty begun by Septimius Severus was at an end.

When it comes to primary sources for the period, I have once again relied upon Cassius Dio and Herodian, both of whom do not mince their words about Elagabalus, and are profuse in their praise of Alexander Severus.

Cassius Dio and Herodian both make for fascinating, and sometimes salacious, research. For those who wish to read these primary sources, they are available to access online for free. Cassius Dio's *Roman History* is available on the Lacus Curtius website by Bill Thayer of the University of Chicago, and Herodian's own *Roman History* (he used Dio's text) is available on Livius.org.

As readers will know, I am quite fond of Cassius Dio, perhaps because he is a fellow historian. He has been a character in the Eagles and Dragons series from the beginning and so I thought it fitting that he should have a more prominent role in *The Hearts of Heroes* which takes place toward the end of his public life. According to Dio himself, during this time he was indeed Consul of Rome for the second time. By his account, Alexander Severus was kind to him and tried to protect him by sending him to Campania, away from the lion's den of Rome where he was sometimes at odds with the Praetorians. Though Dio does not specify where in Campania he lived, I chose Cumae as his home because of that place's connection to the Eagles and Dragons series and, of course, to Apollo and the Sibyl. Once Dio's consulship was at an end, he did indeed retire to his birthplace of Nicaea, in Bithynia, to live out his days. He died there in A.D. 235, the same year year in which Julia Mamaea and Alexander Severus were slain.

If you read Cassius Dio's *Roman History*, you will see that I have used his exact words at the end. His words about Hector being led out of range of danger by Zeus seemed a fitting end to our story.

Admittedly, it is going to be strange to say goodbye to the Severans. They are among the most fascinating people in Rome's history and, at least in the time of Septimius Severus, ruled the Empire when it was at its greatest extent. If you would like to learn more about the Severans, I highly recommend the book *The Severans: The Changed Roman Empire* by Michael Grant.

Readers will note that there are a greater number of references and images to Christianity in *The Hearts of Heroes*. This is not only a continuance of a theme that was begun in *Isle of the Blessed*, but it is also setting the groundwork for future books in the series. Ynis Wytrin is representative of a harmony between the ancient Pagan and newer Christian religions.

Astute readers, before the mention of the 'Pen Dragon' family, have pointed out the emergence of Arthurian themes in the Eagles and Dragons series. Those readers have been correct in that assessment and, indeed, Ynis Wytrin (Glastonbury), the hillfort (South Cadbury Castle), the Sacred Pool (Dozmary Pool), Din Tagell (Tintagel Castle) and the River Gateway (Slaughterbridge) will all play a central role as the story evolves.

For me, the Arthurian age, sometimes referred to as the 'Dark Ages', has always felt like a sort of liminal period in history, bridging the Classical and Medieval eras or, if you will, the Pagan and Christian worlds.

In *The Hearts of Heroes*, I have also introduced some new locations in Wales that have always fascinated me. The island of Mona, or 'Ynis Mon' in Welsh, is the island of Anglesey off of the north coast of Wales. This island was where the Druids held up when Rome invaded Britannia and attacked Anglesey around A.D. 60 under the Roman general Suetonius Paulinus. The location of Killian's home where Adara heals of her wounds is at a place called Traeth Bychan on the east coast of Anglesey.

As for the place where Adara saves Vala from the Roman deserters, that is set in 'The Fairy Glen' at Betws-y-Coed on the eastern edge of the ruggedly beautiful region of Snowdonia in Wales. Ever since I saw a picture of this magical place years ago, and drove through Snowdonia on a research trip, I have wanted to use it as a setting in one of these books. The country of Wales, with its kind people and its landscapes filled with myth and legend, is truly magical.

The other new location in the book is Viroconium Cornoviorum, today's Wroxeter, near the border between England and Wales. Not only was this one of the most prosperous cities of Roman Britain, but today it is a fantastic archaeological site to visit. In addition to its Roman past, Viroconium is presumed to have a connection to the tyrant, Vortigern, in Arthurian legend, whose name is engraved on the nearby Pillar of Eliseg over the border in Wales.

Readers will also have noted that I have opted to use modern Welsh as the language spoken by Vala and Killian. Welsh is indeed an ancient Brythonic language and, though I used modern Welsh in the story, it remains close to the ancient usage of which I studied very little in graduate school. Any errors in the usage, however, are entirely my own. To me, Welsh is a beautiful language, and I do feel that it adds to the story and the sense that Adara is very far from 'home'.

As always, we explore more fully the history, people, and places in this novel in the blog series *The World of The Hearts of Heroes*.

Lastly, fans of the Eagles and Dragons series should not worry at the ending of this seventh book in the series. Yes, things will evolve and change, as all things do. But, I am happy to say that, unlike the doomed Severan Dynasty, the world of Eagles and Dragons will continue for many adventures to come!

Thank you for reading.

Adam Alexander Haviaras
Stratford, Ontario
October, 2025

ACKNOWLEDGMENTS

In the early days of the Eagles and Dragons series, there were a great many people to thank who helped me with advice and input as I set about starting my writing career. As time has passed and I am more at ease in my craft, my acknowledgments are more to those who have inspired me. As always, there are several people to whom I would like to express my gratitude.

First of all, I would like to thank the fans of the Eagles and Dragons series who have stuck with me over the years. I love to hear from you, about how you've enjoyed the books. I'm also humbled by your own stories about how the series has inspired you and helped you to get through difficulties in your own lives. I am truly blessed to have such fans and will continue to endeavour to earn the time you spend reading my work.

When it comes to fans, I am deeply grateful to our amazing patrons on Patreon who continue to support me, my work, and Eagles and Dragons Publishing. Your generosity is truly appreciated and I greatly enjoy our chats and interactions. Special thanks to our patrons at the time of publication, Edwin K. Gwaltney, and Greg Hancock.

As always, I am so very grateful to my amazing, and now award-winning editor, A. Diassiti, at Beautiful Ink Editing. She certainly keeps me sharp, and constantly improving. If ever I tend toward getting lazy in my writing, she brings me back to a level that is worthy of the stories I am trying to tell. The fact that she is my wife does not get me any brownie points. With her editor's hat on, she's tough as nails!

When it comes to support on the home front, constant love, and inspiration for every story I tell, I cannot give enough credit to my wife Angelina, and our amazing daughters, Alexandra and Athena. I am grateful for them every day of my life, and I thank the gods that they are on this amazing journey with me. It is no easy thing to live with a writer, someone whose mind is almost always half-present. Their gentle jibes remind me that I am indeed a mortal man, and their never-ending love, compassion, and understanding make me strive to be the hero they deserve.

At its core, *The Hearts of Heroes* is a story about loss and grief, and how we, as mortals, deal with it.

When it comes to grief, I am in awe of my resilient mother, Jeanette, and my strong and stoic brother, Aaron. Ten years ago, we all began the arduous journey of dealing with the sudden loss of my father, Stefanos Policarpos Haviaras. I have been in awe of my mother's ability to soldier on, to smile at times, and to remain vibrant, even in the face of the loss of her life's partner.

To my younger brother, Aaron, I am grateful for his strong, silent, and reliable person. His memory of our father, with whom he spent many long hours talking, while I was on the other side of the ocean, has been a true comfort over time. And now that we are on the other side of the grief, laughing together again, it does indeed prove to me that there is always hope.

I would also like to acknowledge the life of my late godfather, Dennis Tini, who passed away a year ago. Not only was he my own father's best friend - he felt the loss acutely himself - he was also a second father to me, and a great artistic mentor. He was always supportive of my writing career, buying copies of the books for himself and for the special forces men he trained with. He was always laudatory when it came to my artistic endeavours, and showed his pride as if I was his own son. When I attended his memorial service in Farmington, Michigan, I was shocked to see hundreds of people, including countless other artists there. The cars for the service filled the entire old, downtown of Farmington, and every teacher, musician, student and others had a story about how he had mentored them, and inspired them to be the very best at what they did. The eulogy, which was given by Uncle Dennis' good friend, Mitch Albom, was something that I will never forget; it inspired us, made us weep and smile and remember. We all left filled with gratitude for having known him. I miss him dearly, but it is a comfort to know that he and my dad are now smiling down at me from Heaven, the one with a glass of Sambuca, the other with a glass of Ouzo - it was always a debate between them, which drink was better!

Lastly, I would like to acknowledge the people to whom this book is dedicated...

A couple of years ago, our dear friends Jean-Francois, Heather, Jessie and Leo Lamontagne experienced a family tragedy that changed their lives forever. What happened to them would have destroyed most people, and though they have struggled to deal with the result of a senseless act of violence, they continue to fight on. In the middle of great tragedy, they remain adaptive and hopeful, strengthened by their faith, and love for each other. They continue to fight and persevere on a level that most people could not possibly comprehend. They are truly one of the bravest families that I know and, in my opinion, they are true heroes.

My friends, this story is for you…

Thank you for reading.

Adam Alexander Haviaras
Stratford, Ontario
October, 2025

GLOSSARY

Greek and Latin

adyton – the innermost sanctuary or shrine in the cella of a Greek or Roman temple

aedes – a temple; sometimes a room

aedituus – a keeper of a temple

aestivus – relating to summer; a summer camp or pasture

agora – Greek word for the central gathering place of a city or settlement

ala – an auxiliary cavalry unit

amita – an aunt

amphitheatre – an oval or round arena where people enjoyed gladiatorial combat and other spectacles

anguis – a dragon, serpent or hydra; also used to refer to the 'Draco' constellation

angusticlavius – 'narrow stripe' on a tunic; Lucius Metellus Anguis is a *tribunus angusticlavius*

apodyterium – the changing room of a bath house

aquila – a legion's eagle standard which was made of gold during the Empire

aquilifer – senior standard bearer in a Roman legion who carried the legion's eagle

ara – an altar

armilla – an arm band that served as a military decoration

augur – a priest who observes natural occurrences to determine if omens are good or bad; a soothsayer

aula – a forecourt or waiting area

aureus – a Roman gold coin; worth twenty-five silver *denarii*

auriga – a charioteer

avia – grandmother

avus – grandfather

ballista – an ancient missile-firing weapon that fired either heavy 'bolts' or rocks bireme – a galley with two banks of oars on either side

bracae – knee or full-length breeches originally worn by barbarians but adopted by the Romans

caldarium – the 'hot' room of a bath house; from the Latin *calidus*

caligae – military shoes or boots with or without hobnail soles

caracalla - a long, Roman military cloak

cardo – a hinge-point or central, north-south thoroughfare in a fort or settlement, the *cardo maximus*

castrum – a Roman fort

cataphract – a heavy cavalryman; both horse and rider were armoured

cella – the inner chamber of a Greek or Roman temple

cena– the principal, afternoon meal of the Romans

cetus – (plur. ceti) a whale

chiton – a long woollen tunic of Greek fashion

chryselephantine – ancient Greek sculptural medium using gold and ivory; used for cult statues

civica – relating to 'civic'; the civic crown was awarded to one who saved a Roman citizen in war

civitas – a settlement or commonwealth; an administrative centre in tribal areas of the empire

clepsydra – a water clock

cognomen – the surname of a Roman which distinguished the branch of a gens

collegia – an association or guild; e.g. *collegium pontificum* means 'college of priests'

colonia – a colony; also used for a farm or estate

consul – an honorary position in the Empire; during the Republic they presided over the Senate

contubernium – a military unit of ten men within a century who shared a tent

contus – a long cavalry spear

corbita – a large, Roman merchant ship capable of carrying very large cargoes

cornicen – the horn blower in a legion

cornu – a curved military horn

cornucopia – the horn of plenty

corona – a crown; often used as a military decoration

cubiculum – a bedchamber

curule – refers to the chair upon which Roman magistrates would sit (e.g. *curule aedile*)

decanus – (plur. *decana*) head of a *contubernium* of eight men in the later Empire

decumanus – refers to the tenth; the *decumanus maximus* ran east to west in a Roman fort or city

dediticii – a class of persons who were neither slaves, Latin allies, or Roman citizens

denarius – A Roman silver coin; worth one hundred brass *sestertii*

dignitas – a Roman's worth, honour and reputation

domus – (plur. nominative *domus*) a home or house

draco – a military standard in the shape of a dragon's head first used by Sarmatians and adopted by Rome

draconarius – (plur. *draconarii*) a military standard bearer who held the draco

eques – a horseman or rider

equites – cavalry; of the order of knights in ancient Rome

exedra – a hall or room for conversation or debate, sometimes on a balcony

fabrica – a workshop

fabula – an untrue or mythical story; a play or drama

falcata – curved, single-edged blade capable of delivering extremely heavy blows

familia – a Roman's household, including slaves

fasces – the emblem of office of a Roman magistrate with *imperium*, carried by each of his lictors. Fasces consisted of a wrapped bundle of rods with a protruding axe head that enabled the magistrate to deliver corporal punishment

fibula – a Roman brooch that functioned like a large safety pin

flammeum – a flame-coloured bridal veil

forum – an open square or marketplace; also a place of public business (e.g. the *Forum Romanum*)

fossa – a ditch or trench; a part of defensive earthworks

frigidarium – the 'cold room' of a bath house; a cold plunge pool

funeraticia – from *funereus* for funeral; the *collegia funeraticia* assured all received decent burial

garum – a fish sauce that was very popular in the Roman world

gladius – a Roman short sword

gorgon – a terrifying visage of a woman with snakes for hair; also known as Medusa

greaves – armoured shin and knee guards worn by high-ranking officers

groma – a surveying instrument; used for accurately marking out towns, marching camps and forts etc.

hasta – a spear or javelin

horreum – (plur. *horrea*) a granary

hydraulis – a water organ

hypocaust – area beneath a floor in a home or bath house that is heated by a furnace

imperator – a commander or leader; commander-in-chief

insula – a block of flats leased to the poor

intervallum – the space between two palisades

itinere – a road or itinerary; the journey

khol – a popular cosmetic in the ancient world made from lead sulfide

lanista – a gladiator trainer

lararium – a household shrine or altar to the gods, usually in or off of the atrium

lar – (plur. *lares*) tutulary or domestic deities among the Romans

lemure – a ghost

libellus – a little book or diary

liburna – a small, swift galley used in the Roman navy

lictor – the bodyguard of a Roman magistrate who held *imperium* (e.g. a Consul had a bodyguard of twelve lictors)

lituus – the curved staff or wand of an augur; also a cavalry trumpet

lorica – body armour; can be made of mail, scales or metal strips; can also refer to a cuirass lupanar – (plur. *lupanaria*) a brothel; prostitutes were nicknamed *lupae*, or 'she-wolves'

lustratio – a ritual purification, usually involving a sacrifice

manica – handcuffs; also refers to the long sleeves of a tunic

mansio – (plur. mansiones) a hotel or pensione

marita – wife

maritus – husband

matertera – an aunt

maximus – meaning great or 'of greatness'

missum – used as a call for mercy by the crowd for a gladiator who had fought bravely

mortarium – wide Roman kitchen vessel used for grounding, mixing and pounding food

murmillo – a heavily armed gladiator with a helmet, shield and sword

nomen – the gens of a family (as opposed to *cognomen* which was the specific branch of a wider gens)

nones – the fifth day of every month in the Roman calendar

novendialis – refers to the ninth day

nutrix – a wet-nurse or foster mother

nymphaeum – a pool, fountain or other monument dedicated to the nymphs

officium – an official employment; also a sense of duty or respect

onager – a powerful catapult used by the Romans; named after a wild ass because of its kick

oneraria – a Roman merchant navy ship

optio – the officer beneath a centurion; second-in-command within a century

palaestra – the open space of a gymnasium where wrestling, boxing and other such events were practiced

palla – a woman's cloak or mantle which could be used to cover the head

palliatus – indicating someone clad in a *pallium*, a sort of Greek mantle or coverlet pancration – a no-holds-barred sport that combined wrestling and boxing

parentalis – of parents or ancestors; (e.g. *Parentalia* was a festival in honour of the dead)

parma – a small, round shield often used by light-armed troops; also referred to as *parmula*

pater – a father

pausator – a drummer on a Roman ship who kept time for the oarsmen

pax – peace; a state of peace as opposed to war

peregrinus – a strange or foreign person or thing

peristylum – a peristyle; a colonnade around a building; can be inside or outside of a building or home

phalerae – decorative medals or discs worn by centurions or other officers on the chest

pilum – a heavy javelin used by Roman legionaries

plebeius – of the plebeian class or the people

pompa funebris – a funeral procession

pontifex – a Roman high priest

popa – a junior priest or temple servant

primus pilus – the senior centurion of a legion who commanded the first cohort

promanteia – the right to be first to see the oracle ahead of others, granted to individuals or groups such as cities

pronaos – the porch or entrance to a building such as a temple

protome – an adornment on a work of art, usually a frontal view of an animal

pteruges – protective leather straps used on armour; often a leather skirt for officers

pugio – a dagger

quadrans – (plur. *quadrantes*) a coin that was a quarter of a bronze *as*

quadriga – a four-horse chariot

quinqueremis – a ship with five banks of oars

retiarius – a gladiator who fights with a net and trident

rosemarinus – the herb rosemary

rusticus – of the country; e.g. a *villa rustica* was a country villa

sacrum – sacred or holy; e.g. the *via sacra* or 'sacred way'

salve – a common Roman greeting, literally 'be well' or 'be in good health'

schola – a place of learning and learned discussion

scutum – the large, rectangular, curved shield of a legionary

secutor – a gladiator armed with a sword and shield; often pitted against a *retiarius*

semis – a coin that was half a bronze *as*

sestertius – a Roman silver coin worth a quarter *denarius*

sica – a type of dagger

signum – a military standard or banner

signifer – a military standard bearer

skene – the theatrical backdrop of an ancient theatre

spatha – an auxiliary trooper's long sword; normally used by cavalry because of its longer reach

spina – the ornamented, central median in stadiums such as the Circus Maximus in Rome

stadium – a measure of length approximately 607 feet; also refers to a race course

stibium – *antimony*, which was used for dyeing eyebrows by women in the ancient world

stoa – a columned, public walkway or portico for public use; often used by merchants to sell their wares

stola – a long outer garment worn by Roman women

strigilis – a curved scraper used at the baths to remove oil and grime from the skin

taberna – an inn or tavern

tablinum – a personal office or study

tabula – a Roman board game similar to backgammon; also a writing-tablet for keeping records

tepidarium – the 'warm room' of a bath house

tessera – a piece of mosaic paving; a die for playing; also a small wooden plaque

testudo – a tortoise formation created by troops' interlocking shields thraex – a gladiator in Thracian armour

titulus – a title of honour or honourable designation

tor – Celtic word for a hill or rocky peak

torques – also 'torc'; a neck band worn by Celtic peoples and adopted by Rome as a military decoration

trepidatio – trepidation, anxiety or alarm

tribunus – a senior officer in an imperial legion; there were six per legion, each commanding a cohort

triclinium – a dining room

tunica – a sleeved garment worn by both men and women

turma – (plur. *turmae*) a unit of cavalry within an *ala*; generally consisted of about thirty-two riders commanded by a *decurion*

ustrinum – the site of a funeral pyre

vallum – an earthen wall or rampart with a palisade

venator – a hunter

Venedotia – Latin name for Gwynedd region in the north-west of Wales

veterinarius – a veterinary surgeon in the Roman army

vexillarius – a Roman standard bearer who carried the *vexillum* for each unit

vexillum – a standard carried in each unit of the Roman army

vicus – a settlement of civilians living outside a Roman fort

vigiles – Roman firemen; literally 'watchmen'

vitis – the twisted 'vinerod' of a Roman centurion; a centurion's emblem of office

vittae – a ribbon or band

vomitorium – (plur. *vomitoria*) the entrance and exit passages from amphitheatres and theatres

Welsh

Afon Menai – the Menai Strait between mainland Wales and Anglesey

Betws-y-Coed – the 'Fairy Glen' in the Snowdonia region of Wales

cwch – a small boat

diolch yn fawr – thank you

mam – mother

Pwll Ceris – the 'Swellies', the currents in the Menai Strait
Rhaid i ni fynd – we must go
tad – father
traeth – literally means 'beach'
Yr Wyddfa – Mount Snowdon, the highest mountain in Wales

Become a Patron of Eagles and Dragons Publishing!

If you enjoy the books that Eagles and Dragons Publishing puts out, our blogs about history, mythology, and archaeology, our video tours of historic sites and more, then you should consider becoming an official patron.

We love our regular visitors to the website, and of course our wonderful newsletter subscribers, but we want to offer more to our 'super fans', those readers and history-lovers who enjoy everything we do and create.

You can become a patron for as little as $1 per month. For your support, you can also get fantastic rewards as tokens of our appreciation.

If you are interested, visit the website below to go to the Eagles and Dragons Publishing Patreon page to watch the introductory video and check out the patronage levels and exciting rewards.

https://www.patreon.com/EaglesandDragonsPublishing

Join us for an exciting future as we bring the past to life!

ABOUT THE AUTHOR

Adam Alexander Haviaras is a bestselling and award-winning author and historian who has studied ancient and medieval history and archaeology in Canada and the United Kingdom. He currently resides in Stratford, Ontario with his wife and children where he is continuing his research and writing other works of historical fantasy.

Historical Fiction/Fantasy Titles

The Eagles and Dragons Series
The Dragon: Genesis (Prequel)
A Dragon among the Eagles (Prequel)
Children of Apollo (Book I)
Killing the Hydra (Book II)
Warriors of Epona (Book III)
Isle of the Blessed (Book IV)
The Stolen Throne (Book V)
The Blood Road (Book VI)
The Hearts of Heroes (Book VII)
The Eagles and Dragons Legionary Box Set (Books 0-I-II)
The Eagles and Dragons Tribune Box Set (Books III-IV-V)

The Carpathian Interlude Series
The Carpathian Interlude - Complete Trilogy Box Set
Immortui (Part I)
Lykoi (Part II)
Thanatos (Part III)

The Mythologia Series
Chariot of the Son: The Story of Phaethon
Wheels of Fate: The Story of Pelops and Hippodameia
A Song for the Underworld: The Story of Orpheus and Eurydice
The Reluctant Hero: The Story of Bellerophon and the Chimera

Mythologia: First Omnibus Edition

Heart of Fire: A Novel of the Ancient Olympics

Saturnalia: A Tale of Wickedness and Redemption in Ancient Rome

The Etrurian Players
Sincerity is a Goddess (Book I)
An Altar of Indignities (Book II)

Killing a God - Novels of Alexander the Great
The Asp of Saqqara (Book One)

Titles in the Historia Non-fiction Series
Historia I: Celtic Literary Archetypes in *The Mabinogion*: A Study of
the Ancient Tale of *Pwyll, Lord of Dyved*
Historia II: Arthurian Romance and the Knightly Ideal: A study of
Medieval Romantic Literature and its Effect upon Warrior Culture in
Europe
Historia III: *Y Gododdin*: The Last Stand of Three Hundred Britons -
Understanding People and Events during Britain's Heroic Age
Historia IV: Camelot: The Historical, Archaeological and Toponymic
Considerations for South Cadbury Castle as King Arthur's Capital

Eagles and Dragons Publishing Guides
Writing the Past: The Eagles and Dragons Publishing Guide to
Researching, Writing, Publishing and Marketing Historical Fiction and
Historical Fantasy

Stay Connected

To connect with Adam and learn more about the ancient world visit www.eaglesanddragonspublishing.com

Sign up for the Eagles and Dragons Publishing Newsletter at www.eaglesanddragonspublishing.com/newsletter-join-the-legions/ to receive a FREE BOOK, first access to new releases and posts on ancient history, special offers, and much more!

Readers can also connect with Adam on Twitter @AdamHaviaras and Instagram @ adam_haviaras

On Facebook you can 'Follow' the Eagles and Dragons page to get regular updates on new historical fiction and non-fiction from Eagles and Dragons Publishing.

To watch Eagles and Dragons Publishing's mini documentaries and other fun videos, be sure to follow us on TikTok and subscribe to our channels on YouTube or Rumble.

More from

EAGLES AND DRAGONS PUBLISHING

START A NEW ADVENTURE TODAY!

Do you enjoy stories set in Ancient Rome?

If so, then you will love our marquee *Eagles and Dragons* historical fantasy series!

Start your journey today with the #1 best-selling and award-winning novel, *A Dragon among the Eagles*, and experience the world of the Roman Empire like never before.

The Winner of the 2025 NYC Big Book Award for Historical Fiction, *A Dragon among the Eagles* is the first prequel novel in Adam Alexander Haviaras' ground-breaking Eagles and Dragons series. If you like books set in the ancient world, then you will love this historical series that combines adventure, romance, and the supernatural.

Step into the world of the Roman Empire today!

Step into the world of the ancient Olympic Games!

A Mercenary… A Spartan Princess… And Olympic Glory…

Heart of Fire is an award-winning book for all those who struggle to make their dreams come true.

Start your adventure today and set off on a gritty, mysterious, and emotional journey into the heart of Ancient Greece.

Available from all major retailers and public libraries in e-book, paperback, and hardcover editions, or direct from Eagles and Dragons Publishing at:

www.eaglesanddragonspublishing.com

Step into the world of Ancient Rome with the Etrurian Players!

Sincerity is a Goddess is a heartwarming story of friendship and love that takes you on a bawdy and hilarious journey through the world of ancient Rome.

If you like dramatic and romantic stories about second chances, misunderstandings, and a bit with a dog, then you will love *Sincerity is a Goddess*!

Read this award-winning book today for a theatrical adventure that will have you cringing, laughing, crying, and realizing that there is indeed hope for everyone. Well, almost everyone…

The Etrurian Players are coming! Brace yourselves!

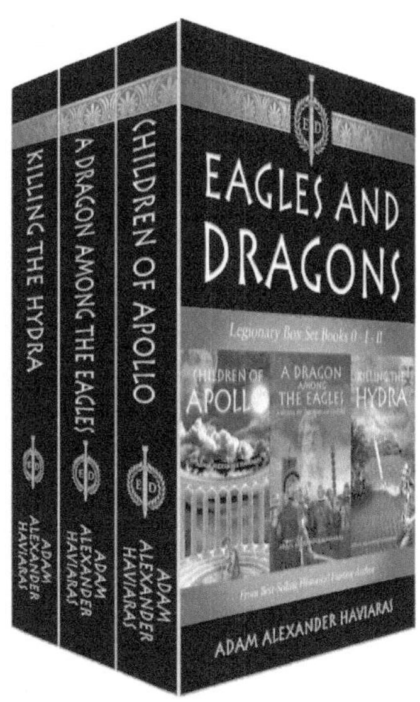

EAGLES AND DRAGONS LEGIONARY BOX SET

BOOKS O - I - II

Begin your adventure in the Roman Empire with a great deal!

Get the Eagles and Dragons series Legionary Box Set today.

This digital box set includes the #1 best-selling and award-winning prequel novel, *A Dragon among the Eagles*, as well as Book I, *Children of Apollo*, and Book II, *Killing the Hydra*.

The Eagles and Dragons Legionary Box Set is available from all major on-line e-book retailers, public libraries, or direct from Eagles and Dragons Publishing.

EAGLES AND DRAGONS TRIBUNE BOX SET

BOOKS III - IV - V

Continue your adventure in the Roman Empire with another great deal!

Get the Eagles and Dragons series Tribune Box Set today.

This digital box set includes the reader-acclaimed novels *Warriors of Epona*, *Isle of the Blessed*, and *The Stolen Throne*.

The Eagles and Dragons Tribune Box Set is available from all major on-line e-book retailers, public libraries, or direct from Eagles and Dragons Publishing at:

www.eaglesanddragonspublishing.com

New books are being added all the time, so you will never run out of adventures!

Begin the *Mythologia* series today and embark on an epic adventure with the Gods and Heroes of ancient Greece!

Available from all major retailers and public libraries in e-book, paperback, and hardcover editions, or direct from Eagles and Dragons Publishing at:

www.eaglesanddragonspublishing.com

HISTORIA

A Gateway to Ancient and Medieval History and Archaeology!

Do you find ancient and medieval history and archaeology fascinating?

If so, then you will love Eagles and Dragons Publishing's *Historia* non-fiction series of books!

In this series, author and historian, Adam Haviaras will take you through such topics as Celtic mythology, medieval knighthood, and the search for the historical King Arthur and Camelot.

If you are interested in ancient and medieval history, and Arthurian studies, then you will want to check out the *Historia* non-fiction series.

Available from all major on-line e-book retailers or direct from Eagles and Dragons Publishing.

Do you love ancient and medieval history and mythology?

Visit 'EDPublishingAgora' on Etsy today to check out our wide array of merchandise for history and mythology-lovers, including books, clothing, housewares, prints, collectibles and more. And all of it is designed in-house by Eagles and Dragons Publishing!

https://www.etsy.com/ca/shop/EDPublishingAgora

See you in the AGORA, the marketplace for history-themed gifts and books!